Just Another Trip

Just Another Trip

A novel

MARTIN WHITTLE

authorHOUSE®

AuthorHouse™ UK
1663 Liberty Drive
Bloomington, IN 47403
www.authorhouse.co.uk
Phone: 0800.197.4150

This is a work of fiction. All of the characters, names, incidents, organizations, and dialogue in this novel are either the products of the author's imagination or are used fictitiously.

Published by AuthorHouse 01/13/2016

ISBN: 978-1-5049-4314-7 (sc)
ISBN: 978-1-5049-4315-4 (e)

Print information available on the last page.

Chapter 1

NUREMBERG

Fifteenth Trip

Pilot Officer Matt White coaxed the heavily laden Lancaster off runway two-zero. It was late August 1943 and if they got back this time they would be halfway through their tour and maybe finished by the end of the year. Four aircraft from 57 Squadron were involved in tonight's raid, a long trip to Nuremberg. One crew was on their first operation and had looked worried and nervous before the take-off. *Poor buggers*, thought Matt; he could remember his first trip. Their anxiety was justified, given the high loss rate amongst fledgling crew, the chances of survival only improving after the first five or six operations.

'Skip, course for rendezvous is one-two-five.'

'Thanks, Navigator, one-two-five.'

Matt turned the aircraft gently onto its new heading. The navigator was Squadron Leader Charles Redman, 26 years old, a regular RAF officer who had passed out of Cranwell in 1937. He had always wanted to be a pilot but had narrowly failed aptitude tests so became a navigator. He was now on his second tour and, rumour had it, likely to be next squadron navigating officer. He had joined M-Mother when their regular navigator was severely wounded on their fifth sortie.

The aircraft was still climbing and had to reach 12,000 feet by the time they joined the bomber stream over Southwold. Timing was everything, and it was vital all four aircraft kept together. Matt checked with each crew member that he was OK, not only a necessary routine but also a way of ensuring that everyone was alert. They all replied, but he asked the tail gunner to report the position of the other aircraft.

'Can you see the other three, Freddie?'

'Yes, Skip—all together so far.' Fred was an 18-year-old Cockney who grew up in the East End of London and who had volunteered to become aircrew from school. His dark hair, brown eyes, and freckles made him look like a naughty schoolboy, which, in effect, he still was. A bit of a lad, he did not take too kindly to authority. However, he was ideal as a gunner since his short stature made it easy for him to fit in the rear turret. He had joined M-Mother straight from gunnery school to replace a gunner killed a few weeks before.

Light was fading fast, and although at their height they could still see the sun, there were now deep shadows on the ground. Matt always thought this a very special time not only because the ground looked so wonderful from this height and at this time of day but also because of the nagging thought that it might be the last time ever that he saw the sun.

'On to oxygen, chaps,' Matt called as the aircraft passed 10,000 feet.

'Five minutes to rendezvous.'

'Thanks, Navigator. OK, everyone, keep your eyes peeled.'

Joining the bomber stream was always stressful. Everyone's timing had to be perfect if collisions were to be avoided, and with rookie crews around, almost anything could happen.

'Don, should have coast coming up any moment.'

'Can see it now, Navigator,' replied Don Grant, the bomb aimer. 'Looks like Southwold at about ten o'clock.' He was 19 years old and had joined the Royal Air Force Volunteer Reserve (RAFVR) from school. Although initially trained as ground crew, he quickly volunteered as aircrew. A Mancunian, he was regarded as rather handsome, being just under six feet tall with blond hair and light-blue eyes. He was an avid supporter of Manchester United, having been taken to Old Trafford by his dad for as long as he could remember.

'OK, Skip, turn on to one-zero-zero—looks like the Met man might be right for once with the winds!'

'Makes a change, eh? Mind, there's plenty of time for things to go wrong!' Matt chuckled.

'Rear Gunner, can you still see the others? It's pretty dark now.'

'Yes, Skip, just about make them out—I think they're all here.'

'OK, we are over the sea now so, Gunners, just check your guns. Please don't shoot any of ours down!'

M-Mother shuddered as the guns were fired. Don climbed into the front turret to test those guns too. Everything seemed to be working.

Some thirty minutes later, Don, lying in his position right in the front of the aircraft, reported he could see the enemy coast. It was a clear but moonless night, and the visibility was very good. *This time, they might even be able to see the target*, Don thought.

'Skip, we are about two miles too far south,' Charles said. 'Maybe the wind isn't quite right after all. Come to zero-nine-five, and, Don, could you keep an eye out for a large expanse of water, which should be coming up way over on the left-hand side in about fifteen minutes?'

'OK, Navigator, will do.'

They were now firmly over enemy territory, and the crew became tense, each man intent on his own task. The flight engineer, Stephen Bamber, adjusted fuel levels and made some small changes to the propeller pitch but otherwise was silent.

'I've got a large chunk of water, Navigator.'

'Thanks, Don. Skip, turn on to one-two-five, about two hours to the target.'

'One-two-five it is. 'Round you come, Mother. Bloody long way Nuremberg, isn't it?'

Searchlights suddenly came on, and flak curled up towards them.

'Rear gunner here, Skip—looks like someone has been caught in the lights. Gawd, he's been hit and is going down.'

The shafts of light from the searchlights were sweeping the sky, probing for other aircraft. One light swept close to M-Mother but kept going. The flak barrage intensified, and every now and then, there was a rattle of shrapnel on the fuselage. Matt tried to ignore what was going on around him by concentrating on the aircraft's instruments, but he called all the crew to make sure they knew he was still there.

As suddenly as the lights had come on, they were off again and there was complete darkness. This was almost as disconcerting as the lights, and it was a dangerous moment— enemy fighters used this time to hunt.

'Keep a careful watch, chaps. You know this is when those bastards are out to get us.'

The aircraft droned on through the night, which seemed blacker than usual. Eventually, Charles Redman called, 'Ten minutes to target, Skip.'

'Thanks, Navigator. I think I can see a glow of something up there ahead.'

As they got closer to the target, they could see fires glowing with the added flashes of bombs going off.

'Five minutes to target.'

'Thanks. OK, Don, go and do your stuff and make sure we don't miss.'

'Will do, Skip.' Don's calm, strong Mancunian accent brought a smile to Matt's lips.

The aircraft edged closer and closer to the target, which was largely hidden by haze and smoke. Matt dreaded this time. Everything seemed to move so slowly and now, once again, they were being heavily attacked with flak. It seemed to be everywhere, but it always seemed particularly thick just at the point they needed to go through to the target. He remembered the first couple of times they did this. It just seemed impossible that they wouldn't be shot down, but somehow they weren't. It was weird.

'Here we go, chaps. Don, are you ready?'

'Yes, Skip, as ready as I'll ever be.'

They had reached the wall of flak, and the aircraft bucked and bounced as it went through. There was a huge bang, which rocked the aircraft, and Matt knew immediately that Mother had been hit. He quickly called round, and everyone answered. The mid-upper gunner reported that a hole had appeared in the fuselage between his position and the rear of the plane.

'Any fire, Townsy?'

'No, Skip, but it's a bloody big hole!'

'OK, let's just concentrate on dropping this lot in the right place. Don, how's it looking?'

'Looks like fires all over the place.'

'Can you see the target area?'

'Not exactly, Skip, but I can see where the others are dumping.'

'Have to do. Let's go for that.'

'OK, Skip, come right a bit, right a bit, steady, steady. Target coming up … steady. Bombs gone … Wait for the photo to show the folks back home.'

The seconds ticked by, and just when Matt's nerves were almost at breaking point, he heard, 'Right. All done, Skip.' It was an important time for the crew. No photo and their trip did not count.

'Good. Let's get the hell out of here.' Matt banked the aircraft to the left and dropped a few thousand feet to clear the bomber stream. This was also a very dangerous time, but as they got farther from the target, the crew could relax slightly.

'Course for home, Navigator.'

'Two-eight-zero should do for now, Skip.'

'Everyone keep their eyes outside—almost certainly fighters around us now.'

Just at that moment, there was a flash off to the right as a Lancaster exploded in a shower of flames and sparks, then, just as suddenly, darkness again.

'Engineer, go back and see what the damage is, will you?'

'Sure, Skip.' Stephen edged his way back past the navigator and wireless operator and beneath the legs of the mid-upper gunner. A few feet further on, he could sense the draft of air coming up from the floor of the fuselage. The light from his torch showed a hole nearly a foot in diameter and another in the roof. Obviously a shell had gone straight up through the aircraft without exploding. It was a miracle that nothing vital had been hit.

'Hi, Skip,' Stephen said on the intercom. 'Well, we have some extra ventilation, but otherwise everything seems OK, but anyone using the Elsan needs to tread very carefully!'

'Thanks, Stephen. So now you know, chaps. If you must use the bog, be careful where you step.' Matt smiled.

The aircraft droned its way through the night, and Matt was thankful that all remained quiet, although it seemed an age before Don called, 'Coast up front, Navigator.'

'Thanks, Don. That should be around Abbeville. Turn on to three-four-zero when we cross the coast, Skip.'

'Will do. Let me know, Don. Mac, call up East Kirkby when you can. We should be all right. It doesn't sound as if the shell did too much damage, and everything seems to still be working up front here.'

Mac was Sergeant Trevor McGuiness, a Canadian who started his basic training in his native home of Winnipeg before transferring to the UK in 1942. He was 22 and a giant of a man who regularly played ice hockey back home. He had met up with the others at the Operational Training Unit, or OTU.

Now was the point Matt liked the best—the East Kirkby beacon was easy to see, and M-Mother had been given permission to enter the circuit to land.

'Downwind.'

'Downwind to land,' the controller repeated. 'You are number three.'

'OK, Stephen, let's see if the bits are still working. Undercarriage down, ten-degree flaps.'

'Looks OK, Skip.'

'Good. Turning finals.'

'Cleared to land, M-Mother.'

'Cleared to land. Hold on, chaps. Down we go,' Matt said.

The landing was perfect, and M-Mother taxied over to her stand. Pilot and flight engineer went through their catechism to shut down the engines and turn off all the systems. 'Well done, chaps. Let's get out, have a stretch, and see what the bastards have done to us this time.'

One by one, they dropped from the rear door of the plane and gathered around the hole in the fuselage.

'Well,' said Matt, 'you've got to get lucky sometimes. A couple of inches one way or another and it could have been a different story. What do you think, Stephen?'

'Well, of course we could have been really lucky and have lost Fred!'

'Sod off,' said Freddie. 'Where would you be without me?'

The others laughed. The strain of the mission fell quickly away from them as they waited for the truck to pick them up. It was nearly always driven by a member of the Women's Auxiliary Air Force, or WAAF, which gave them more opportunity for banter. Then there would be the debrief, a noggin, breakfast, and sleep, heavenly sleep.

The intelligence officer was thankfully brief, confirming the time they had dropped their bombs, discussing the appearances of the target, and asking about any other events.

'We saw two Lancs shot down, sir,' said Townsy. 'One going in and one coming out. We collected our own shell just before we bombed, sir.'

'Thanks, Sergeant. Anything else?'

'No, sir, that's about it.'

'Off you go then and thanks … Oh, and the CO says you have some leave now.'

The crew returned their kit and parachutes and wandered over to the canteen.

'Well, that's a nice surprise. Any ideas, Stephen?' asked Matt.

'I heard there was a bit of a party planned for tonight—not sure what the gen is, but it's down at the Red Lion.'

'Sounds OK for starters. What are you chaps going to do?'

'I am off to see the wife but may look into the pub later on.'

'OK, Charles. It would be good to see you,' said Matt.

The navigator was one of the few married aircrew in the squadron. In fact, wives anywhere near the airfield were generally disapproved of by the senior officers, but they had made an exception for Sq/L Redman partly because he was a regular officer and partly because of his age. He was also on his second tour.

'What about you others?' persisted Matt.

'See you down the pub, Skip,' they chorused. They knew Matt liked them to spend some time together after a raid if at all possible.

'OK, chaps, let's go and get breakfast.'

They made their way to their respective messes.

A couple of the other crews were already in there and well into their bacon and eggs. 'Where's the rookie crew?' Matt asked.

'Think they bought it, Matt,' said one of the pilots.

'Christ, they only arrived a couple of days ago. Don't think I even got to know their names.' Matt slumped down in his seat. 'Ah well, few less for the party then!'

They had finished eating, and many were lighting up either cigarettes or pipes when the adjutant, Sq/L Davies, came in. He wore a permanently worried expression and announced that he had just had confirmation that the squadron had lost one Lancaster on last night's raid, piloted by Flt Sergeant Parry. It was believed there were no survivors. There was a brief silence, and Sq/L Barrow, the senior officer in the room, thanked him before everyone started talking again. *Was it really such a trivial event?* wondered Matt, and then he too took up his conversation where he'd left off.

After breakfast, Matt and Stephen made their way back to the room they shared. Stephen flopped onto his bed, took his boots off, and lay down.

'I'm going to get a shower,' Matthew said. 'I reckon I smell like a farmer's groin!' But Stephen was already asleep.

After his shower, Matt lay naked on his bed, letting the warm breeze through the open window caress him until gradually sleep took over. He woke about three hours later and, for a delicious moment, thought that he was home on his own bed. But as he came to, the dreadful reality of his present situation took over. Usually, he could cope, but in those first few seconds of wakefulness, he felt vulnerable. He shook his head and started to get dressed. Stephen was snoring quietly, and Matthew shook him to wake him up.

'What's the time?' muttered Stephen.

'Lunchtime, shake your arse. Let's go and get a beer first?'

Slowly, Stephen got up, showered, and dressed, and they walked over to the mess. It was hot now in the sun, and it felt particularly good to know that they were out of the firing line for at least a couple of days.

Matt and Stephen had been together a long time. Matt was aged 21 years and had joined the RAFVR in 1941 from Leeds University where he was reading Law. He had been a member of the university squadron and had always wanted to fly. Eventually, he was sent to Alberta for basic training on Tiger Moths and Harvards. He was considered more suitable for bombers than fighters and returned to the UK in early 1943 to an OTU at Wellesbourne near Stratford on Avon, where he met up with Pilot Officer Stephen Bamber. Stephen was 20 years old and like Matt had joined the RAFVR. He was first trained as ground crew, maintaining aircraft at Scampton and Mildenhall. He volunteered for aircrew and after further training, joined Mother's crew at Wellesbourne.

After a gulp of beer, Stephen asked, 'Is that rather delicious nurse still around?'

'Anne, you mean?'

'Yes, that's the one. She's a cracker. Where did you find her?'

Matt had met Anne at a hospital dance in Lincoln about three months before. She was about five feet four inches tall with long auburn hair and hazel-coloured eyes, which were set in a lovely face with high cheekbones and a wide, generous mouth. Matt reckoned it was love at first sight, and they tried to cram in as much time together as possible just in case the unthinkable happened.

After lunch, Matt said he was going to cycle over to the hangar to see how the ground crew were getting along.

'I'll join you,' said Stephen. 'Good to see how the old crate is doing.'

They cycled the mile to the hangars. It was a beautiful afternoon, but the airfield was busy with aircraft being repaired or made ready for the night's raid. They found M-Mother with her ground crew swarming over her.

'What's the damage, Chiefy?' asked Matt.

Warrant Officer Max Bryant looked rather glum. 'Don't know why we let you young chaps go flying. You don't seem to know how to look after a perfectly good aeroplane. Nearly always bring them back with bits missing!'

'Sorry, Chiefy. Problem is they really don't seem too pleased to see us when we go visiting! Anyway, will she do?'

'We'll do our best, sir. In any case, you're off for a couple of days, aren't you? Be patched up by the time you are back.'

'Thanks, Chiefy. And thanks for looking after us so well.'

'Pleasure, sir, I'm sure!' Bryant replied with just a hint of sarcasm.

'What now then, Matt?'

'Well, maybe another beer and then change to go to the pub. I want to try and get a message to Anne to see if she can get a couple of days off too.'

'OK, Matt, see you back in the mess.'

Chapter 2

LEAVE

The Red Lion was pretty crowded when Matt and Stephen arrived even though it was only about five o'clock. They found their crew outside at one of the tables sitting in the afternoon sunshine, and it was pretty obvious that Townsend and Hughes had been there for a while. Sergeant Tom Townsend was 18 years old and had grown up in North London. He was average height but rather rotund and had a bit of squeeze getting into the upper turret. He had brown hair and eyes and had a reputation as a drinker. In fact, Matt could remember one night when he had polished off four pints of beer in a little over five minutes. He had joined the RAFVR and had volunteered for aircrew soon afterwards. Like the others, except Redman and Hughes, he had joined Matt's crew at the Wellesbourne OTU early in 1943. In the typical RAF way, aircrew were self-selected with individuals milling around in a hangar gradually getting themselves together as a crew. Since then, M-Mother had already lost a navigator and tail gunner. It was a dangerous war.

Charles Redman was the only one missing as Matt asked if anyone wanted another beer. He went off to the bar and ordered six pints. He was just paying when he noticed one of the other pilots.

'Hiya, Willie, how's it going?' They had got to know one another at their heavy conversion unit (HCU) and had got on well. Matt reckoned that Willie and his crew had completed about twenty trips. Willie didn't immediately reply, and Matt noticed he looked weary and dejected.

'What's up, old boy?'

'To be honest, Matt, we've had a couple of shaky trips. Three nights ago, we got bounced by a fighter on the way to the target and my rear gunner got killed—shredded by cannon fire. The next night, we were attacked coming over the coast. We were damn nearly home. Flight engineer and navigator both killed—blood and brains all over the kite.'

'What? Gerry and Simon both killed?' Matt asked. He knew them both well too. 'Christ almighty,' he mumbled. 'Are you on your own here then?'

'Yes, the others have all gone on sick leave and the MO told me to take it easy for a few days! Nice of him, eh?'

'Come and join us,' said Matt. He steered Willie over to his crew, who by then were getting impatient for a drink.

'Everyone, this is Flight Lieutenant William Brooke. He's a Scot, but apart from that, he's a good bloke and an old friend. Here, Willie, another pint?'

'Thanks, Matt.'

At that moment, Charles Redman appeared, so Matt went off whilst Charles and Brooke started talking. They, in fact, knew one another quite well and had some catching up to do. When Matt came back with the beer, he noticed Willie seemed more relaxed. He was deep in discussion about the impending cricket match with Scampton.

As he drank his pint, Matt looked around at his crew thinking about them and reckoning he was lucky to have them. Redman could be a bit stuffy, but he was regular RAF and generally they didn't have much time for the RAFVR types. But he was a bloody good navigator and, when on his own, Matt found him a good sort. In fact, he was quite surprised that he had come to the pub at all, but all the better for that.

It was to Tom and Freddie that Matt spoke first.

'How are you two doing?'

'Not bad, Skip,' Freddie replied.

'You going on anywhere after this?' asked Matt. He knew that they both had reputations as boozers and womanisers.

'Nuh! We are saving ourselves for tomorrow night,' added Townsy. 'There's a dance in Lincoln we thought we'd go to. Never know your luck! What about you, Skip?'

'Well, I am hoping to get away with a certain young lady tomorrow if she can get time off.'

'There you are, Fred. I told you the officers get all the bloody fun,' chimed in Townsy.

Matt wandered away and moved up to Stephen, who was in discussion about some mechanical problem with Charles's MG.

'You chaps staying here or going on somewhere?' asked Matt.

'No, old boy. I must get back to the missus and probably best to drive back whilst I can still stand!'

'What about you, Stephen?'

'Oh, I will hang around a bit. Never know, some beautiful, unattached blonde may appear just looking for an engineer to mend her bits and pieces! Are you staying, Matt?'

'No, I'll head off in a while. I am hoping that Anne can get away tomorrow so we can go to the Peak District for the night.'

'Lucky man. I sometimes wish I could find someone I could disappear with and get out of this bloody camp!' Stephen said rather grimly.

***

Matt was up early, planning to pick Anne up from the county hospital in Lincoln when she came off duty at about seven o'clock. He put a clean shirt and pants into his small case, together with toothbrush and razor, and got into his Standard 8 car, his pride and joy. He had bought it when he first went to university and had run up quite a few miles since then. It was a quiet drive in, although the occasional bomber was still arriving back from a raid. They could have been the last to set off, but often they were the ones with damage and death on board.

He pulled up outside the hospital, but there was no sign of Anne. It wasn't unusual for her to have to work beyond the end of her shift so he settled back in the driving seat and pulled out his pipe. He didn't, in fact, smoke but somehow found it comforting—a sort of dummy! It was another beautiful morning, and the forecast for the next few days was good, typical end-of-August weather. It was nearly nine o'clock before Anne appeared, running down the steps. She was wearing a white dress and had her hair bunched up. Matt thought she looked lovely.

'Sorry I am late, darling,' she said. 'We had an urgent case needing to go to theatre.'

'It's fine,' Matt replied. He caught the smell of her scent, and it took him back to when they had first met three months before.

'Let's go,' he said.

'Where to?' Anne replied.

'Well, not too far. I don't have much petrol. Let's see if we can get somewhere in the Peaks.'

'Great,' she said. 'I don't want to spend too much time driving, darling!'

They set off out of Lincoln on to the A57. Progress was slow, but after a while, they turned towards Chesterfield and started the climb up into the Peaks. The countryside looked beautiful in the hot August sunshine, and the fields were full of sheep and cattle. Eventually, they arrived at a small pub in Bakewell. It had rooms, Matt noted, whilst he was getting some drinks.

'Do you have a room free for tonight?' he asked.

'For you and the missus, is it?' the publican replied.

'Yes, that's about right,' said Matt, colouring slightly.

'Of course we have. Pleasure to have you stay with us. Always happy to help the RAF! Incidentally, call me Bob. Would you like to finish your drinks before I show you up?'

'Yes, thanks, Bob,' replied Matt and took the drinks out to Anne.

'Would here be OK to stay?' he asked.

'Certainly would, darling. They have rooms then?'

'Yep, we're in,' he said and drank a large gulp of beer. 'How about something to eat? They have some bread and cheese.'

'Perfect—and then do you know what? I might feel quite tired!' Anne winked at him and pulled him towards her for a kiss.

It was a lovely, warm, peaceful afternoon as they sat, ate, and drank. Matt felt as if he was in heaven, and he wished that time could stand still, just for a while. It seemed almost unbelievable that yesterday he had just got back from the hell of an op and now, here he was.

They were shown up to their room and, as soon as the door was closed, kissed.

'I need to go somewhere first,' said Matt.

'And me after,' Anne replied.

'Well, you go first then, Anne,' Matt suggested, and she left the room and returned a few minutes later.

'Toilet's just down the corridor on the right.'

'Thanks,' said Matt. He made his way quickly down the hall.

When he got back to their room, Anne was already in bed and he undressed quickly and joined her. She had let her hair down and was wearing a blue silk slip, which he gently pulled up to her waist. They made love quickly and passionately and lay together for a few minutes before Anne eased herself from under Matt to lie beside him. She felt him come on again and slipped on top of him, kissing him softly and moving gently on top of him. They came together, and after a while, she looked up at him to see he was asleep. His face, at last, was relaxed; the worry lines, which had made him look years older than his twenty-one years, had disappeared and he looked peaceful.

God, what are they doing to you? she thought as she gently came off him to lie with him, her head on his chest, listening to the sound of his shallow breathing. She suddenly felt tired herself, and they slept together for most of the afternoon.

When Matt woke up, he stroked Anne's hair, listening to the sounds outside, the birds singing and the wind sighing gently through the pine trees that surrounded the inn. It felt a million miles away from the airfield, and they still had a night together to look forward to. Anne gradually surfaced from her sleep, and they held one another for a while, listening to the sounds of the day coming to an end through the open window. The smell of the flowers in the garden below floated up to them, and they could hear the swallows calling, weaving their way through the sky as the daylight softened.

'Need a wee,' said Matt and made his way to the toilet. When he got back, Anne was up and had thrown on her dress. She made her way down the hall, closing the door on her way.

When she came back, they made love again before realising that they were both starving. The bar was now fairly crowded and noisy so after supper they went for a walk through the gathering night. Anne noticed that Matt had become quiet.

'What's on your mind?' she asked, but she knew the answer—the lines were back, and he was obviously thinking about what was going on at the squadron. She put her arms around him and kissed him. She felt him relax again but not like before.

'Shall we go back?' she asked.

'Yes, let's,' he replied, and they walked into the pub. 'Another drink?'

'Yes, please,' Anne replied. 'Could I have a gin?'

'Of course—pint of bitter and a gin and it, please,' Matt asked.

'Everything OK with the room?' asked Bob.

'Very nice, just the ticket,' replied Matt.

They sat and sipped at their drinks, but Matt found it difficult to say anything sensible. They were not like young couples in a world at peace, because the future for him, and therefore them, was so uncertain. He had survived so far, but on average, only about half the crews would have got this far. The odds were stacked against him surviving the rest of the tour. There was hardly any point them discussing where they might live, what sort of house, how many kids. In another world, Anne was the girl he would have married and he loved her dearly.

'Penny for them,' she teased. 'Let's go up.' She took his hand and led him up the stairs. They made love and then went to sleep holding each other and praying the morning would not come too soon.

Matt woke around five o'clock and lay quietly next to Anne, listening to the early morning birds welcoming the dawn. As he had woken, he had first felt a joyful warmth until he suddenly remembered that today he had to go back. It was as if a switch had been thrown and all this peace, tranquillity, and love had to be put aside. Matt lay looking at the ceiling, and the huge injustice of it all weighed in on him. He started crying—silent, deep-felt tears. He shook himself. *This won't do*, he thought, and he leaned over and stroked Anne. She woke up with smiling eyes, and they kissed for a long time and eventually made love. They lay locked together for a while, listening to the birds singing and a wind blowing through the trees around the pub.

Matt went to the bathroom to shave and actually managed to have a bath, a real luxury for him. He felt more cheerful when he returned to the room to find Anne dressed and wondering about breakfast.

'I am sure there will be some,' Matt replied, and reluctantly they left the room and went down the stairs.

'Morning, Bob,' Matt said to the publican. 'Any chance of some breakfast?'

'Well now,' Bob replied, 'we don't have too much, as you will understand, but I can rustle up an egg each and some ham and the missus has just baked some bread.'

'Perfect,' said Anne as they sat down. 'Would a cup of tea be OK?'

'Coming up,' replied Bob, and a pot appeared almost immediately.

'Better than the service we get in the mess,' said Matt and then wished he hadn't. Anne's face tightened as she too began to realise what they were going back to and the simple fact that tomorrow night, when Matt would almost certainly be on operations, may well be his last.

They finished breakfast and went out to the car. It had started to rain, almost as if reflecting Matt's mood, and it was pretty blowy as he started the car and they made their way back to Lincoln. They said very little during the journey, so different to how they had been on the way up. Matt dropped Anne at the hospital, but before she left the car, they kissed and held each other tightly, not wanting to let each other go. Anne started to cry and then bit her lip. This wasn't going to help, but she loved him so much and this might well be the last time they would be together.

'It's OK, Anne; we will be all right. I'll come through this, I know. Maybe when I get some leave, we can go up and meet my parents. They always ask after you.'

'I would love to,' she said as she moved to get out of the car. Matt's look of anguish saddened her further, and she quickly turned away and walked to the hospital entrance. She turned to see Matt wave goodbye. Then he was gone, perhaps forever. She rushed to her room and collapsed in floods of tears. Bloody war, she cried, bloody war.

Matt drove slowly back to the airfield, rebuilding the defensive wall around himself, and eventually got there at four o'clock in the afternoon.

The sergeant in the guardhouse saluted. 'Pardon me, sir, but just to let you know, you are duty officer tonight.'

Matt groaned. 'Thanks, Sergeant. I will come to the guardhouse for a report at 1800 hours.'

'Right, sir.' The sergeant saluted again.

The duty officer's role usually involved sorting out the drunks and the belligerents. It was a complete pain in the arse, he thought. Suddenly, he was back at work!

Matt wandered into the mess to be met by Stephen.

'Good twenty-four hours then?' he asked.

'Wizard,' Matt replied. 'How's it been here?'

'Well, we are currently a gunner down if that helps!'

Matt looked puzzled. 'How's that? No one got killed?'

'Unfortunately not,' replied Stephen. 'But I think you will be meeting him soon. He is on a charge for drunk and disorderly!'

'Terrific,' said Matt. 'Anything else? What did you get up to yesterday?'

'Well, not much but my bar bill has expanded somewhat—and, no, there was no blonde!' said Stephen. 'But you will want to know that Willie has gone missing.'

'But he wasn't on ops, was he?' Matt retorted.

'Well, they had a bit of a show on last night, and one of the pilots reported sick. They wanted to put as many up as possible so the Wingco was scouring the mess looking for a *volunteer* and Willie said he would go. Good job you weren't here. I suspect it would have been hard to say no!'

'Christ,' said Matt. 'Does anyone know what happened?'

'Not really,' replied Stephen. 'It looks like they were attacked by a night fighter on the way to the target. Plane just blew up—no chutes.'

Matt called for a beer and sat down. *You get hardened to chaps dying*, he thought, *but sometimes it really hits home*. He sipped his beer and then turned to Stephen. 'Christ, we were only talking a couple of nights ago!' He drank slowly, swilling his beer around the glass pensively.

'Now once I have had this, I better hop over to the guardroom—which one was it?' he said abruptly.

'Guess,' said Stephen.

'Freddie then,' Matt replied.

'Spot on, old chap.'

He arrived at the guardroom to be met by Sergeant Peter Summers.

'Evening, sir,' he said, saluting.

'Where's the prisoner then?' asked Matt.

'Along here, sir. I think he is feeling pretty sorry for himself just now.'

'Good,' replied Matt. 'What's the story?'

'It looks like he and Sergeant Townsend got drunk and Fred—sorry, Sergeant Hughes—tried to knock an MP's hat off, sir.'

'Anyone injured?' Matt asked.

'No, sir. And no damage either as far as we can make out.'

'Very good. Let me go and see him.'

'Along here, sir,' said Summers.

'Hallo, Sergeant Hughes.'

'Oh, hallo, Skip. Sorry about this.'

'It's *sir*, Sergeant Hughes. What happened?' Matt had a little difficulty not to smile.

'Sorry, sir. Well, like I said, Townsy—sorry *Sergeant Townsend*, and I were going to a dance in Lincoln. It was a good bash, sir, loads of crumpet all ready for it and lots of booze. Townsend and I picked up a couple of girls. His wasn't keen, but mine was a real raver and we went outside to a park. She was all over me, Skip—sorry, sir. When we got back into the hall, we found Townsy and his bird and did some more drinking and we were pretty well Brahms and Liszt when the bloody redcaps burst in pushing and shoving everyone around. Well, I'd had enough of it, Skip, sir, so I just happened to knock one of their caps off and then he kind of fell over. That's when they cuffed me up, and off I went. Wouldn't have minded so much, but I reckon I could have got off with that bird again—cor' she was something else I'm telling you.'

'Thank you, Sergeant. Please spare me the gory details. Well, we better get you tidied up so I can formally charge and punish you, hadn't we?'

'Yes, Skip, sir. Sorry and all. Didn't really mean no harm.'

'OK. As you probably know, I am duty officer tonight, so once I come back from dinner, we will formally hear your case. Townsend, I presume, is coming along as some sort of witness. We have a report from the MPs.'

'Right, sir.'

'Sergeant Summers?'

'Yes, sir,' he replied.

'I want to consider this man's case when I return from dinner. Are there any others we need to see?'

'No, sir. I am pleased to say not. About 2000 hours be OK, sir?'

'Excellent,' replied Matt as he made his way out of the guardhouse towards the mess.

Stephen and Charles were already drinking when Matt entered the mess, and he moved over to them.

'Beer?' asked Charles.

'Thanks, that would help!'

'I hear our rear gunner has been in a scrape again?'

'Yes—to be honest, it doesn't sound that bad, especially if you put it against what's happening all around us. I guess you heard about Willie?'

'Yes,' Charles replied. 'Shouldn't have been allowed to fly, I reckon. He was bloody shaken up by his last two ops. Any case, what are you going do with young Freddie?'

'Dock some leave. Put it on his record,' said Matt.

'Sounds about right. Could be killed tomorrow night, couldn't he?'

'Have you heard anything about tomorrow then?' asked Stephen.

'Nothing much, but I think we're on, and it looks like it's another maximum effort. But where to? No idea!'

'Let's eat,' said Matt. 'I need to get our gunner friend sorted out and back in his billet tonight. What did you manage to do over the last couple of days, Charles?'

'Nothing much, old boy. Popped down to see Clare's parents. They live in Evesham. Nice to see them. Clare's brother Andrew is also in the RAF. Hurricane pilot in North Africa just now so the parents spend a lot of their time worrying about everyone—even me!'

Matt finished his supper and headed for the guardroom. Sergeant Summers had everything ready, and Freddie was marched in. He stood before Matt and saluted smartly. 'Well, Sergeant, you know the charge, I understand? Have you anything else you want to add?'

'No, sir. I am sorry, sir.'

'Sergeant Townsend, have you anything you wish to add?'

'No, sir.'

'OK, Sergeant Hughes. I am docking you two days' leave, and this will be entered on your record. I see, incidentally, that you already have two similar charges on your record?'

'Yes, sir.'

'I would warn you to be more careful in the future because you are heading towards being reduced to LAC.[1] Do you understand?'

'Yes, sir.'

'Thank you sergeant. Dismiss.'

'Prisoner, about turn. Dismiss.'

'Anything else, Sergeant?'

'Not now, sir. Will you be staying in the guardhouse?'

---

[1]   Leading aircraftman.

'Yes, Sergeant, I will and will return at 2300 hours for your report.'

'Thank you, sir.' Summers saluted and marched out, and Matt walked back to the mess for a final drink. It seemed very likely they would be going tomorrow night, and he wanted to turn in fairly early. He hoped the duty night was quiet.

Stephen and Charles were still in the mess when Matt got back.

'Another drink, Matt?' asked Charles.

'Thank you. A beer please.'

'Sort Freddie out then?'

'Yes, until the next time, but at least he will be able to come with us tomorrow if we have a raid. Incidentally, Stephen, have they got the kite back in one piece yet?'

'Yes, they've done a grand job, and Mother should be ready for us tomorrow. Guess you will want to do an air test in the morning?'

'Yes. Can we get the crew together after breakfast tomorrow? Will you speak to Don to set things up, Stephen? Let's meet outside the ops room at 1030 hours. By then, we should know if we are on or not.'

'Will do, Matt.'

'Incidentally, do we know what Don and Mac got up to over the last forty-eight hours?'

'Well, Matt, last time I saw them, they had Mac's car in bits on the front lawn. Everything looked very serious with much head shaking and sucking in of breath!'

'Surprised they didn't ask you for help, Stephen?'

'Well, I did help them for a bit, but it all got pretty complicated with bits of engine everywhere, so I decided that another drink was a safer proposition!'

They laughed, and Matt announced that he was heading for the guardroom and then, he hoped, bed. They said their goodnights, and he walked the short distance, receiving a crisp salute from the duty corporal.

'Evening, sir.'

'Evening, Corp. Everything quiet?'

'Like the grave, sir.'

'Excellent, keep it like that. I am off to get my head down.'

'Right, sir. Goodnight, sir.'

Matt walked into the small room, which contained a single bed and a sink. He took his shoes off and lay down, smiling at the contrast between this night and last night with Anne. He suddenly felt very tired and went quickly to sleep, thankfully not waking until about five o'clock when he heard sounds of aircraft returning from the night's raid. He stretched, put on his shoes, and went outside.

'Morning, chaps. Nice quiet night then?'

'Yes, sir. Might you be flying tonight, sir?'

'Quite possibly.'

'Well, good luck, sir. Give 'em hell!'

'Thanks, Corp. I will be over in the mess if you need me.'

'Right, sir.' He saluted as Matt moved away.

Matt could hear a couple of stragglers in the circuit getting ready for their run in to land, and he felt unease in the pit of his stomach at the thought of how they might be feeling, having realised that although they had made it back, they still had to pull off the landing.

He walked into his room to find Stephen fast asleep and snoring loudly. He picked up his wash kit and went to shower and shave. On returning, he found his friend just beginning to wake up.

'Bloody hell. What's the time?'

'Six thirty,' said Matt. 'Time to stir a leg or preferably two! If you're sharp, we can get down to breakfast before the flying chaps get there.'

Stephen staggered out of bed and disappeared to wash whilst Matt tidied his bed. 'Christ, that was quick,' he remarked as Stephen came back in.

Together, they went off to breakfast. There were a few others there but no one who had been flying, so they finished quickly and then Matt and Stephen went off to see the aircraft.

It was a beautiful late August morning with a slight mist and a clear blue sky above, as the two friends cycled to the hangar.

'Season of mists and mellow fruitfulness,' Stephen quoted. 'Makes you almost happy to be alive,' he added as they got closer to the plane.

Warrant Officer Bryant was outside the hangar and came towards them.

'Morning, sirs,' he said with an exaggerated deference.

'Morning, Chiefy,' replied Matt. 'Have you mended our toy yet?'

'In spite of the odds, we have done our best, and with a bit of luck, it will fly again. Please take more care next time!'

WO Bryant was a regular and had been in the RAF for about thirty years and before the Royal Flying Corps had become the RAF. He didn't think too much of the volunteers, but he was a father figure to many of the young pilots who felt he was someone they could tell their innermost thoughts and fears. He never usually called the officer pilots 'sir' unless loaded with sarcasm or when in front of other ranks.

'You flying tonight, Matt?' he asked.

'Not sure yet, Chiefy. Probably, I would say.'

'You were pretty lucky with this one, Matt. How the bloody shell missed all the important stuff God alone knows. Still, we have strengthened the whole area and it will be fine. You want to have a look?'

Both Matt and Stephen nodded, and they all went into the hangar and walked around Mother. It was almost impossible to see the damaged area.

'Well done, Chiefy. Thank the chaps for us, will you? Incidentally, I want to do an air test this morning. When would be a good time?'

'Sooner the better really, Matt.'

'What about 1100 hours then?'

'Yes, we can manage that.'

'OK, see you around then. We will only go up for about an hour, just check it's all working,' said Matt.

They got back on their bikes and were soon back in the mess, which was now full of crew, many of whom were standing around the notice board in the flight office. Charles was already there, and he waved at Matt and Stephen.

'We are on for tonight, chaps,' he said.

Matt felt the odd sensation of exhilaration and fear he always had at this time.

'OK, good. We will meet as arranged. Thanks, Charles.'

CHAPTER 3

BERLIN

Sixteenth Trip

The crew met up outside the ops room. 'Well, chaps, looks like we are flying tonight—no idea where of course,' Matt said. 'I want us to do an air test this morning, and I want everyone, including the gunners. The kite has been in the hangar for a few days and tired mechanics can leave bits and pieces around. So check your own areas—and, Gunners, make sure the turrets move freely. We don't want any snags at 15,000 feet over Germany. I have had agreement we can take off about 1100 hours, and we'll go up for about an hour, which will give the ground crews time to fuel and bomb her when we get back. Any questions?'

There was silence.

'OK, meet here about 1030 hours, and we will get a truck out to the kite.'

After the others had gone, leaving the three officers, Matt said to Charles, 'Can you get us to Bakewell? Show you where Anne and I spent a night.'

'No problem, old boy. Be good to do a daylight cross country for a change. See you later.'

The air test went without difficulties. Climbing away from the airfield, Matt felt not only the huge pleasure of flying, especially with a responsive, lightly laden Lancaster, but also the strength of the crew's presence. They had been together nearly six months now and had some close calls in that time. Charles shouted up the course to Bakewell. It was a clear day, and the countryside opened up like a map as they gained height. Five thousand feet was the agreed altitude, and as they headed westward, they could clearly make out the Sheffield smoke up to the north and Nottingham down to the south. They were following the A57, the road Matt and Anne had taken, and soon the Peak District showed up dead ahead. Matt checked with each member of crew, asking that everything was working.

'Radios OK, Mac?'

'Sure, Skip.'

'Engineer, engines looking all right?'

'Yes, Skip. Starboard outer is running slightly warmer than usual, but I will get the ground crew to check it when we get back.'

'Gunners, turrets OK and nothing nasty stuck down any grooves or in dark corners? Rear Gunner, you know all about dark corners, don't you?'

'S'pose so, Skipper. It all looks OK here,' Freddie answered, rather more subdued than usual.

'Navigator, all well?'

'Yes, Skip. Bakewell should be just coming up. Bomb-aimer, can you see any tarts?'

'Surely not from this height, navigator,' Matt heard Mac the radio operator say. 'Are they particularly pretty here then?'

'God almighty, you bloody colonials don't have a clue—Bakewell tarts. You bloody eat them!'

Everyone laughed as Matt looked down and identified the pub Anne and he had stayed at. He called Redman up to have a look.

'Nice-looking place, Matt,' said Charles as the plane turned. 'Wouldn't mind a night or two there myself.'

Then it was back to business.

'OK, chaps, it looks like everything is all right so let's get back.'

The airfield came into view, and Matt called for joining instructions. A couple of other aircraft were doing 'touch-and-goes,' but otherwise, it was quiet.

'Finals,' called Matt and a few minutes later flared the plane to a perfect landing, taxied back to their dispersal point, and went through the shutdown drill.

'Well done. Meet you all at the briefing at 1600 hours. Try and get a few hours' sleep after lunch.'

One by one, they jumped down from the rear hatch. Matt went over to speak to the ground crew.

'Well done, chaps. Looks a good job and everything seems fine. Flight engineer felt the starboard outer was running slightly hot.'

'OK, sir, we will have a look at it. Good luck for tonight, sir.'

'Thanks. See you later.' And with that, Matt got on the truck with the others.

'Charles,' Matt said when out of earshot of the others, 'our prebriefing is at 1400 hours. Catch up with you then. I guess you are popping home first?'

'Yes, I'll just go and see Clare; then I will be back.'

***

The preliminary briefing was attended by the pilots, their navigator, and the bomb-aimer. They started to file into the briefing room about 2.00 p.m. Ten aircraft were to be used, and some of the crews hadn't seen one another for a few days and so had some catching up to do. Matt, Charles, and Don sat down together as they waited for the station commander, Wing Commander Jonathon Squires, and his entourage. They arrived at exactly 1400 hours, and the thirty men rose as they came in. The air was fairly thick with cigarette and pipe smoke, and the atmosphere was, as always, tense before the target was revealed.

'Sit down please,' said W/C Squires. He was a big, rather jovial man with a grand handlebar moustache who had managed to survive the first couple of years of the war when inadequate aircraft and generally poor tactics made survival even less likely than it was now. He had won a Distinguished Service Order (DSO) and a Distinguished Flying Cross (DFC) and was considered a good bloke.

'Well, good afternoon, gentlemen. The target for tonight is Berlin. We will be part of a 660 bomber force, and our aim is to destroy the factory area. We are going to pass over the Zeiderzee, aiming for Leipzig, but then turn northeast to approach the target from the southwest to try and catch Jerry napping.'

'Some hope?' someone muttered, but Squires went on to describe the target markers to be laid by the Pathfinder Force (PFF) Mosquitoes and the estimated time of departure, detailed for each plane together with its own estimated time to bomb. The squadron navigator then gave more details of the route in and out from the target together with estimated wind speed and direction, and the squadron bomb-aimer described the bombing run. Both Matt and Charles wrote down the information in detail, thus giving them duplicate notes so that there could be no confusion. Then they spent some time doing the numbers and working out the headings and the turning points on the course.

One of the pilots, Ed Freeman, a Canadian who, with his crew, was coming to the end of his first tour, remarked that they had found some heavy flak around the Hanover area when they were there a few weeks earlier.

'Thanks,' said the wing commander. 'We are aware of that, and we are routing you to the south of Hanover.' After about thirty minutes, Squires drew the discussion to a close and confirmed that the main briefing, attended by all the crews, would be at 1600 hours with take-off planned for 1930 hours. He left with a curt 'Good luck, chaps'.

'What you think, Charles?' asked Matt.

'Well, what can you say—it's Berlin. Another bloody long trip.' And on that happy thought, they headed off to the mess.

There was the usual buzz of excitement that preceded every raid, and as Stephen and Matt sat down with Charles, the mess waitress asked, 'Are you flying tonight, sir?'

'Yes, we are, Maisie, so bacon and eggs as soon as you can, please!' Stephen was not at the briefing, so Matt filled him in with the details as they ate their food.

'Berlin this time,' he said ruefully.

'I reckon this could become a regular trip,' replied Charles. 'What a bloody thought!'

They finished their meal. Matt said he was off for half an hour's rest, and the others dispersed as well. Matt lay on his bed trying to memorise the route that they were to take and mulling over what was in front of them all tonight. As usual, he had written farewell letters, for his parents and Anne, in the event he did not come back. He rested his head back and thought of Anne. He tried to imagine what she would be doing just now. He smiled as he remembered their brief time together a couple of nights ago, and he closed his eyes trying to think of her.

He dozed off and was woken by Stephen shaking his arm.

'Time to go to war, Matt. It's 1545 hours.'

Matt shook himself, rubbed his eyes, got up, and started to collect his kit together. They both made their way back to the briefing room. They picked up the rest of the crew, and they all sat together waiting for W/C Squires, who, with usual promptness, walked into the room at exactly 1600 hours.

'Please sit.' He confirmed the target and then went through the same series of talks as at the preliminary briefing, although in less detail. The important information had already been given.

'Well, that's it, chaps,' Squires was saying. 'Good luck to you all,' and with that, he walked out.

'Blimey, Townsy,' said Freddie. 'We could have been out with those birds tonight.'

'One track mind you've got,' replied Townsy. 'Mind, anything would be better than this lot. Could get serious. Could get killed!'

'Nah, we'll be all right,' said Fred. 'Old Skip's all right, he is—he'll get us there and back—and Navigator seems to know his way 'round a map! Yeah, we'll be OK. Maybe have a crack at those birds tomorrow night, eh?'

'Are you guys always on about dames?' asked Mac as they made their way to the crew room.

'Can't see the problem with that, Mac. You should join us tomorrow night. You'd be a big attraction with that funny accent of yours!' retorted Fred.

'Well, I might just do that. Could do with a good night out!'

'You're on then. All we need to do is get back in one piece,' added Townsy.

By this time, they had put their personal gear in their lockers and were pulling on their flying kit. They wandered over to collect their parachutes. Fred said to the WAAF, 'Nice white one for me, please, and no holes!'

She laughed and gave the old reply, 'Well, here you are. Specially cleaned for you, Sergeant. Bring it back if it doesn't work!'

Outside the crew room, everyone was gathering to wait for the truck to take them to dispersal. It was a tense time, and Matt realised he had already gone to the toilet three times since the preliminary brief. He had a sick feeling and was anxiously rehearsing the flight in his mind.

'You OK, Matt?' asked Stephen. 'You look a bit off.'

'Yes, fine, thanks, old boy. Just hate this bit.' He gently punched his friend's arm. 'OK, chaps, have you got everything before we go out to the kite? Freddie, I hope you are not going to be reading those girly magazines in that turret of yours?'

'Gawd, Skip. It's so dark in there I can't even see to pick my nose!'

They all laughed.

'OK, lads, here comes the bus,' announced Don, and they clambered in together with the crew of F-Freddie and Q-Queenie. Matthew knew the pilot from F-Freddie, a Canadian called Jock Brystone. They had met at OTU, and both had been in operational flying for about the same time.

'What you reckon then, Jock?' Matt asked.

Jock smiled and replied, 'Well, we should be back before breakfast!'

'See you in the pub tomorrow night,' said Matt.

'Yep, beers on you,' Jock replied as they got down from the truck. 'Have a good trip.'

'And you,' replied Matt.

The truck arrived at the dispersal point, and the crew of M-Mother jumped down. Fred and Townsy immediately lit up their cigarettes while Matt went over to the ground crew sergeant.

'Hello, Sarg. Everything OK?'

'Yes, sir, although there is a small oil leak from the port inner. I've shown the problem to Mr Bamber. I think it will be OK, but we will change the seal when you get back.'

Matt and the sergeant started their clockwise walk around the aircraft, checking off the various items from his list. He climbed into the aircraft and moved forward to the pilot's seat on the left-hand side. Stephen had already run his series of checks and reported all well. Matt climbed out again and signed off Form 700, which indicated he was happy that the aeroplane was ready to fly. Charles was in the aircraft checking his charts, numbers, and codes, but Mac, Don, and the two gunners stayed outside smoking a last cigarette.

'OK, chaps. Time to go,' said Matt.

Fred and Townsy had a last pee on the tailwheel and got on board. It was thirty minutes to take-off, but there was a lot that needed doing and no time to think of what lay ahead.

Eventually, all was ready, and at 1915 hours, Matt gave the sign to start up the engines, starboard inner first. The engines all caught without difficulty, and Matt and Stephen worked through their checklists.

'All OK, Stephen?' asked Matt, and Stephen gave a thumbs-up. The first aircraft was moving out on the taxiway, and M-Mother slotted into their place in the queue. This last wait was always stressful, not helped by the anticipated take-off with a Lancaster fully loaded with bombs and high-octane fuel. At last, their turn came and Matt lined up with the runway and rested on the brakes. The green flashlight shone from the control hut, and Matt released the brakes, opening the throttles with Stephen's hand over his. The port throttles were slightly advanced to control the inevitable swing to the left as the four Merlins began to bite. Speed picked up, and the Lancaster lifted off the runway. Another trip had begun!

'Skip, course to Southwold is one-two-five.'

'Thanks, Navigator. I am climbing up to five thousand feet.'

'Roger that, Skip,' replied Charles.

They maintained formality when they were flying as much as possible. Charles was the senior ranking officer on board, but whatever their rank, the pilot was always regarded as in charge.

'We have to be over Southwold at 2010 hours and at 10,000 feet to join the main force.'

'Should do that easily,' replied Matt, and Stephen, sitting next to him, nodded in agreement.

'The others OK, Freddie?' asked Matt.

'Yes, Skip, as far as I can see, everyone is off now.'

At this stage, the aircraft kept their navigation lights on until they reached the coast; manoeuvring in the dark with lots of aircraft around was risky.

There was still some light on the ground, and the lack of cloud made it possible for Don, lying in the nose of the aircraft, to map read. As they passed over the River Waveney, he could see the line of the coast ahead and the River Blythe with Southwold to the southeast and its lighthouse to the east.

'Southwold coming up, Navigator. Looks like we will go right over it.'

'Thanks, Don. Give me a shout as we do, will you?' replied Charles, and as Don called out, he noted that the time he calculated was correct.

'Turn on to zero-nine-zero, Skip,' said Charles. 'Fifty-five minutes to the enemy coast.'

'Thanks, Navigator. OK, everyone, keep your eyes peeled from now on,' said Matt. 'Gunners, test your guns.'

The aircraft shuddered as the guns were fired, and then, apart from the roar of the engines, all was quiet. It was now very dark, although the sheen from the sea about two miles below them was visible.

'Climbing to 15,000 feet. Everyone on to oxygen,' said Matt. 'Engines OK, Stephen?'

'Yes, Skip, all well, and the oil temperature for the starboard outer looks fine just now.'

As forty-five minutes came up, Don reported that there was some broken cloud ahead but that he could just make out the coast. Although it was difficult to say which part of the coast they were over, as if on cue, light flak started to climb up towards them. Flak always fascinated Matt. It would appear to rise languidly at first, but as it got closer, it speeded up and, if you were lucky, shot past. Suddenly, they were in cloud and Matt used the instruments to keep the aircraft steady and on course. 'Thought they said it would be clear tonight?' Matt asked.

'Well, that's the Met men for you,' replied Charles. 'At least they seem to have got the winds right so far! GEE is functioning fine and we are on course,' he said, referring to the navigational tool, which depended on radio beams transmitted by ground stations. 'It's about two hours to the turning point.'

The cloud became more broken again as they moved away from the coast and the flak died down. 'Keep your eyes peeled, Gunners. This is where we find the fighters. Freddie, keep a watch for anything coming below us.'

'Right, Skip. Will do.'

Enemy fighters were proving particularly dangerous at this phase of the war, and more bombers were downed by them than flak. Night fighters were armed with upward firing cannon called *schrage music*, and they would steal up into the blind spot directly under the bomber before firing from almost point-blank range and hitting either fuel tanks or the bombs themselves. There was virtually no chance of survival.

'Forty-five minutes to the turning point, Skip,' Charles said quietly.

'Thanks,' Matt replied. He could see some activity over on their left where Hanover should be, and just at that moment, there was a huge explosion about half a mile to their right.

'Christ,' said Matt. 'Looks like fighters about, chaps. Keep alert. Freddie, nothing to see?'

'No, Skip, black as buggery out there.' Then he caught sight of a faint glow off to port and below their level. 'Skip, corkscrew right!' he shouted and fired a burst from his guns into the area he had seen the glow. The Lancaster fell like a stone for 500 feet before Matt heaved the aircraft into a climb and turned back on to their course.

'See anything now, Freddie?'

'No, Skip. May not have been anything, but I just thought—'

'Just thought is OK,' replied Matt. 'If the bastards nail us, we've had it.'

'Five minutes to the turn.'

'Thanks, Navigator,' Matt replied. 'Can you see anything, Don?'

'Not a bloody thing, Skip.'

They flew on through the darkness for what seemed an age until Charles said, 'OK, Skip, time to turn—new heading zero-four-zero.'

'New heading zero-four-zero,' repeated Matt.

'Time to bombing run, fifteen minutes.'

'Roger,' replied Matt.

As they got nearer to Berlin, Matt could see the glow in the sky from the effects of the first wave of the attack.

'Think I can see the target, Navigator. Looks in the right place! Don, you better get your stuff ready. OK, chaps, we are getting close now, so keep your eyes out there.' Ahead, Matt could see the fingers of searchlights probing the sky and a heavy flak barrage, which they would need to go through to get to the target. What was it Squires had said at the briefing? 'They wouldn't be expecting us to come from the south!'

Matt smiled—always the bloody same. The flak barrage was really close now, and the fires burning below lit up the cockpit. 'Engines OK, Stephen?'

'Yes, all OK,' came the reply.

'Right, chaps. Here we go. Don, you ready down there?'

'Yes, Skip, we are on course.' Matt recalled the first time he had seen a flak barrage and the disbelief that anyone could survive. He was sweating now, even though it was freezing cold, and he concentrated on keeping the aircraft steady. The flak was now all around them, and the closer exploding shells rocked the aircraft, the shrapnel rattling against the side. Matt noticed the usual strong smell of cordite. The bomb run had begun.

'Steady now,' Don called. 'Right, right, steady, steady. Bombs gone.'

The aircraft, relieved of its bomb load, leapt into the air, and Matt had to ease the controls gently to bring it back to a level attitude.

'Hold it there,' said Don as they waited for the photoflash, which would allow the intelligence officers back at base to determine the accuracy of the bombing.

'OK, flash gone,' said Don.

'Thank Christ,' said Matt. 'Let's get the hell out of here.' And he turned the aircraft and lost height.

'Steer about two-four-zero for an hour; then we need to come onto two-seven-zero to aim for the coast,' said Charles.

As they moved away from the flak and searchlights, the sky gradually darkened behind them.

All was quiet as they droned their way back to the coast until Freddie called suddenly, 'Corkscrew right! Fighter behind us.'

The Lancaster shuddered with the recoil of the guns, and then there was a tearing noise. Matt eased the plane back to level flight. He realised they had been hit.

'Everyone OK?' he asked, and all replied except Townsy.

'Mac, go and see what's happened.'

'Sure, Skip, be a minute.'

'Skip, Stephen. I think we have a problem with the starboard inner. Seems to be losing oil pressure. It was all right until that attack.'

'Do you want me to feather that engine or are we OK for a bit?'

'OK for a bit. Let's see how we go,' Stephen replied.

'Skip.' It was Mac.

'Yes.'

'Townsy's been hit. It's his leg, and he's not too bad.'

'OK, get him onto the couch and fix him up, and then you take over as gunner for now.'

'Will do, Skip. He is bleeding quite a bit, but I think I can stop the worst.'

'Good,' replied Matt. 'Navigator, do we know where we are?'

'Yes, we should be over the coast in about ten minutes. Keep a lookout, Don, will you?'

'Sure thing, Navigator.'

'Starboard inner is heating up, Matt. I think we need to feather it after all.'

'Go ahead.'

As the propeller was feathered, Matt steered to the left to counter the swing. Lancasters could fly easily on three engines, especially without the bomb load, although the landing could be interesting.

'Coast ahead!' called Don, and almost immediately, they were surrounded by searchlights and more flak. As Matt manoeuvred the aircraft to weave its way through the searchlights, a shell burst close by, the shrapnel punching small holes in the cockpit canopy.

'You OK, Stephen?'

'Yes, Matt … You?'

'Caught one on my hand but think it's all right.' The fragment felt like a hammer blow on his hand, but he could still use it.

'OK, chaps,' said Matt, 'we are doing all right at the moment and now over the channel. Three engines will be good enough for us to make it back, and the old crate seems OK otherwise.' He tried to sound reassuring, but they still had some way to go to safety. 'Mac, call East Kirkby when you can. Tell them we have one man injured and that we are on three engines. ETA, Navigator?'

'About 0400 hours by my calculation, but I sense the wind has picked up from the west so maybe a bit longer.'

'That will do,' replied Matt. 'Mac, say we should be there at 0400 hours and we will need emergency services.'

'Will do, Skip,' replied Mac.

'I am going to descend to 10,000 feet, and then at least we can come off oxygen,' Matt announced. He eased the aircraft into a gentle dive and was almost down to 10,000 feet when the rear gunner spoke.

'Skip, I think we've got company. Looks like a fighter tracking us. He's a long way off and well out of my range, and I only get the occasional look.'

'Thanks, Freddie. Just keep an eye on him.'

'Mac, we may need to let base know if that bastard stays with us. Other kites could be at risk if he's out hunting.'

'OK, Skip,' replied Mac.

It was a not uncommon problem these days. An enemy fighter followed the bombers home and then shot them up when they were in the landing pattern and at their most vulnerable. Problems were stacking up for Matt, but he reckoned things were still tolerable.

Don called from the front turret, 'Coast coming up. Fairly big town below. Could be Hastings, Navigator.'

'Thanks, Don,' Charles said. 'Looks like the wind has strengthened and has carried us a little north of track. For East Kirkby, we will need to steer three-four-zero—about sixty minutes, Skip.'

'Any sign of that bandit, Freddie?'

'Haven't seen him for a while, but I'm betting he's still out there. The sun will be behind him, and it's difficult to see anything.'

'OK, keep looking,' said Matt.

At last, the beacon for East Kirkby came into view. 'Mac, call them up for joining instructions and tell them we may have a bloody fighter on our tail. They will want to warn the others.'

'OK, Skip.'

Matt heard the base reply and took over the radio.

'Runway two-six in use, right hand circuit, QFE[2] one-zero-one-nine, wind south-westerly about fifteen knots;

---

[2] Atmospheric pressure at aerodrome level.

join crosswind and report downwind. Understand you have wounded and engine out. Possible enemy in tow.'

Matt repeated the instructions and then said, 'Right, chaps, hopefully down in one piece but get ready for a crash landing if the undercarriage has been damaged. Freddie, any sight of our friend?'

'No, Skip, nothing now.'

'Keep looking. Stephen, you are going to have to control the engines. This hand is getting pretty sore.'

'No problem.'

Matt turned the aircraft downwind and settled the height to 1000 feet. He slowed to a speed safe for the undercarriage to be lowered. There was a satisfying clunk as the main wheels locked down and the green warning lights confirmed the undercarriage was down. He was going to extend the downwind run to give himself time to steady the aircraft on its final approach, but eventually, they turned right onto finals.

'Finals,' said Matt to the controller.

Stephen had feathered the port inner propeller and increased the power in the two outer engines so things were better balanced, and Matt started the descent to the runway. He could see some vehicles gathered at the end of the runway, and he eased the aircraft gently down, holding off for a few seconds to lose speed. The wheels touched the runway, and the aircraft gradually lost speed and came to a halt near to the ambulance and fire engine.

'I will taxi to the stand,' said Matt to the controller, and he slowly moved the plane along to their dispersal area.

While he and Stephen went through their shutdown drills, the medical crew were already in the aircraft attending to Townsy.

As silence descended on the aircraft, Matt turned to Stephen.

'Christ, Stephen, I am not sure how many more fucking trips like that I can manage.'

'Well, we are back almost in one piece,' he replied and started tidying up his kit. Charles looked over Matt's shoulder. 'Well done, old chap. Bit dicey at times, eh?'

'Say that again, Charles. Let's get off this bloody aircraft.'

The rest of the crew were outside, and Townsy was just being loaded into the ambulance. Matt walked over to him.

'You OK, old chap?'

Townsy smiled and nodded, but he was obviously in a great deal of pain and had lost a lot of blood.

'Good luck. I'll come and see you tomorrow.' He turned back to the group. 'Well done, Freddie. Glad that last bastard didn't go for us. Maybe he had heard of your fearful reputation!'

Everyone laughed. Gradually, the relief of having finished the trip was taking over. Whilst they waited for their transport, Matt went over to the ground crew. 'Sorry, chaps—some more unofficial ventilation, I am afraid, and probably a buggered engine.'

'We are really going to have to start charging you, Mr White.' The sergeant who had seen them off smiled, and with that, Matt turned away and joined the others, who were just getting aboard the truck. Freddie was not looking his usual self.

'Don't worry,' said Matt. 'They'll fix up Townsy.'

'Looks like I've lost my fucking drinking pal for a week or two, don't it?'

'Well, maybe, but it could have been worse.'

'Bloody right, Skip. Another inch or two higher and he'd have more things to worry about than not drinking with me!' Freddie smiled.

Matt knew how tired everyone was. His left hand was beginning to hurt like hell, and his glove was getting tight.

He hadn't really noticed until now, as the tension of the flight eased. The truck lurched its way back to the briefing room where the intelligence officers were waiting to question them. The padre, as usual, was there, and they were handed a cup of tea liberally laced with rum as they entered. Once they were in the light, Matt took off his glove. His left hand was swollen and had turned a deep purple over the back where the piece of shrapnel had hit him.

Wing Commander Squires came over. 'You OK, Matt? That looks bloody sore.'

'Bit of flak, sir. I don't think anything is broken. I can move my fingers all right.'

'Well, best go and see the MO after the debrief. I hear the kite was shot up a bit?'

''Fraid so, sir. We got jumped by a fighter, but most of the damage was with the flak.'

'Matt, go and get debriefed, then the MO, then bed would seem a good plan. You did bloody well tonight, Matt. Well done.'

'Thank you, sir.' And with that, Matt went over to join his crew at the debrief.

Charles was explaining the events up to the bomb run, and Don described the target and expressed the view that the bombs had dropped in the right spot. They explained about the flak barrages just before the target and the fairly heavy concentration near Brussels as they had returned. Freddie reported the fighter that he thought had tailed them back. And with that, the intelligence team released them.

'Fancy a beer, Matt?' asked Stephen.

'Great idea, Stephen. Set them up, and I'll join you in a few minutes. The old man said I had to see the MO about my hand. Better do that first.'

'OK, old boy, I'll get them in. But don't be too long. I need my shut-eye!'

Matt noticed Freddie was still not his truculent self. 'You all right, Freddie?' he asked.

'Townsy'll be OK, won't he, Skip?'

'I think so, Freddie, but I guess he will be out of action for a few weeks. We'll go over to the sickbay tomorrow. Let's meet about nine o'clock.'

'Thanks, Skip,' and with that, Freddie made his way to the sergeants' mess along with Don and Mac.

Matt walked into the sickbay.

'Is the doc around?' he asked.

The nurse replied that she would get him, and Wing Commander Lawrence Spear wandered into the room. 'P/O White, isn't it?'

'Yes, sir.'

'You had that gunner on board?'

'Yes, that's right, sir. How is he?'

'He'll do. Fortunately just splinters. He lost a bit of gravy, but he's young and fit and we can sew him back together. Couple of weeks should see him right.'

'Good. The CO said I should show you this hand. Got hit by a bit of shrapnel.'

'Let's see,' said Spear. 'It's pretty bruised. You can move your fingers?'

'Yes, sir.'

'Probably nothing broken but quite marked bruising. It will take a while to go down. Nurse, put some ice on this and bandage it up. A sling may help.'

'Right, Doctor,' said the nurse and took Matt through to attend to his hand.

When he emerged, his hand was in a sling with a large bandage and he was instructed to return in the morning. He made his way to the officers' mess where drinking was well underway. He saw Stephen over against the bar and walked towards him.

'Ha, the wounded warrior approaches!' He laughed. 'How's it feeling?'

'Improved by a beer, I should think,' replied Matt. 'What's the gen? Everyone back?'

'No,' replied Stephen. 'Jock's lot has gone missing. No one has heard from them since they took off.'

'God almighty, they were a good crew.'

'There's more,' said Stephen. 'They had a dog, spaniel called Scrap. Somebody needs to look after it, and I said we would!'

'Well, good for you. We could do with a dog around.' Matt grinned and downed his pint.

The next morning, Matt and Freddie went to see Townsy, who was sitting up in bed and looking much improved. He was pleased to see them.

'MO says I may be off ops for a couple of weeks,' said Townsy.

'Yer off boozing as well?' asked Freddie.

'Nah,' he answered, 'I'll be down the pub before you know it—and I think you owe me a beer?'

Once Matt had seen the MO, he went to the station commander, who had asked to see him, and knocked on his door.

'Come in,' his voice boomed, and Matt opened the door to find W/C Squires surrounded by paper.

'Bloody admin,' he muttered. 'Sit down, White. How's the hand—still looks bloody painful. Can you use it?'

'Not just now, sir, but the MO has said nothing is broken and the swelling should go down in a day or two.'

'Good. Well, as I said last night, you did well yesterday. I am going to stand you and your crew down for a couple of days. It's going take a while to fix both the kite and you. We will obviously need to find you another mid-upper; that young man will be out of action for a while. However, White, I don't want any of you to leave the station. Down to the pub is as far as I want you to go. Is that understood?'

'Yes, sir,' Matt replied but realised Squires had something else on his mind. 'We are being asked for a maximum effort sometime over the next few nights, so if one of the other crew are short, then one of your chaps will have to fill in as an odd bod.'

'Right, sir,' replied Matt. 'I'll go and tell them. What's the flap about, sir? Do we know?'

'No, as usual, we will be the last to know … well, you will be.' He chuckled. 'But it's clearly something big so we need to be prepared.'

'Right, sir.' Matt saluted and turned to go.

'Oh, and, White, I am going to recommend you for a gong. You have the right attitude. Well done.'

Matt turned. 'Thank you, sir,' he said and walked out.

Matt made his way back to the mess. It was empty for a change so he went to one of the phones to try to contact Anne. He knew that if he left a message at the porters' lodge at the hospital, they would get it to her somehow and she could then ring him. He found Stephen tidying up their room.

'What's the news then?' asked Stephen briskly.

'Well, the Wingco has effectively grounded us for a couple of days partly so the kite can be fixed, partly so my hand will recover. Only trouble is we can't leave the damn base, and if they need an "odd bod," then they will come looking for us.'

'Shit, I hate that,' said Stephen. 'It's bad enough flying with you, but going with some sprog crew who still need their bums wiped doesn't bear thinking about.'

'Well, maybe that won't happen, and in any case, we can still go to the pub!'

Matt looked at his watch. 'Speaking of which, it's nearly twelve o'clock and time for a small drink, I think.'

At that moment, their batman knocked on the door and came into the room.

'Excuse me, sir,' he said, speaking to Matt, 'Miss Anne is on the blower for you.'

'Thanks, Barker. I'll come just now. Stephen, I'll see you in the mess in a minute.'

He got to the phone.

'Hallo, Anne, just to let you know I am in one piece after last night. We have been grounded for a couple of days so they can patch the kite up, but we can't leave base. Any chance you could come over to the pub for a drink tonight?'

'Not tonight, darling,' she said. 'But probably tomorrow, and I can bring a couple of others as well if you like?'

'Wonderful … Oh, you better ring me tomorrow afternoon just to make sure we will be here. Can't say much more, you understand?'

'Completely, darling. I will ring about two o'clock tomorrow then.'

'Wonderful. Look forward to being with you.' With that, he rang off.

When he got to the mess, Stephen was already well through his first pint.

'Yours is on the bar,' he said to Matt. 'Seems like some of F-Freddie's crew might have been captured.'

'Well, let's hope so,' said Matt. 'Where's this bloody dog?'

'On its way over to us tomorrow afternoon, I hear,' replied Stephen.

Charles came into the mess. 'Is that right, Matt—we are stood down for a couple of days?'

'Well, yes and no,' replied Matt. 'We are confined to base—bit of a flap on it seems. We can go to the pub but no further. We might be needed to make up crews.'

'Bloody hell,' replied Charles. 'Let's hope not—always a bloody shambles.'

They wandered into lunch, and as they sat down, Charles said, 'I was really hoping to take the wife out tonight.'

'Well, Charles, to be honest, once the other poor buggers have taken off, I can't see the problem,' said Matt. 'Your secret's safe with me.' He winked at Stephen.

After lunch, Matt got Barker to contact the crew so he could tell them what was happening, and then he, with his bandaged hand, and Stephen cycled to the hangars to see how the repairs to M-Mother were coming on. It was a dull day with a brisk wind and some heavy showers rushing across the airfield. Even though there was no planned raid for that night, the ground crew were hard at it. M-Mother's starboard inner engine was being replaced, and a new cockpit panel was lying by the side of the aircraft.

'Sergeant,' said Matt, 'how's it going?'

'OK, sir. We will have her ready by tomorrow night. Patched up the holes—everything should be finished.'

'Thanks, Sarg,' replied Matt, and he and Stephen walked around the aircraft. It was looking pretty battered, but she had got them home. They slowly cycled back towards the mess.

'Anne's bringing a friend or two tomorrow night if we aren't needed,' Matt said. 'Never know, you might get lucky.'

'We'll see. I don't feel lucky, although I suppose still being alive is pretty lucky.'

'Well, there you are,' said Matt. 'I am off to see the rest. Are you coming along?'

'Yes,' said Stephen. 'Give you some moral support!'

They went into the crew room to find Don, Mac, and Freddie all there.

'What's the score then, Skip?' Freddie was the first to ask.

'Well, we are stood down, but you can't leave the station, apart from the pub where we can get together tonight if you like? There is a bit of a flap on, and we have to be around in case we are needed as odd bods.'

Freddie groaned. 'I know my bloody luck; it will be me who'll have to go. They're always short of bloody gunners.'

'Well, let's hope not; otherwise, you'll have another night without crumpet,' said Stephen.

'Or booze,' retorted Freddie.

'Let's meet at the pub after supper,' said Matt and turned to go.

'How's the hand, Skip? We hadn't realised you had been hurt.'

'Fine, Don. Thanks. Probably be OK in a day or two— nothing broken.'

'Only,' Don said and smiled. 'We would rather you fly us than some sprog pilot.'

'Thanks, Don. I'll remember that.'

Things were in full swing by the time Matt and Stephen got down to the pub, and they had the usual trouble pushing their way through to the bar. 'Couple of pints, please,' said Matt. 'Busy in here tonight, Joe,' he said to the barman.

'Certainly is, sir. Haven't you lot got anything better to do?' He smiled.

'Well, we have decided to let Jerry off tonight,' replied Matt, picking the glasses up off the bar.

'We're over here,' called Stephen, and Matt struggled his way over to the rest of the crew.

'Cheers, chaps,' said Matt, and then he downed a good half of his beer in one go.

Just then, he noticed Townsend behind Don. 'Hey, Townsy. How did you get here? Did you tunnel out?'

'Nah, sir. They let me out so long as I don't drink too much, don't mix with strange birds, and get back by 10.00 p.m.'

'Oh dear, that doesn't give you much scope,' Stephen said. 'Still, it's good to see you up and about. Any idea when you can get back on ops? We don't particularly want a replacement who can't shoot straight!'

'Doc reckons about a week, I'm afraid, so I think you'll need someone.'

'Know any likely candidates?' asked Matt.

'Nah, sir. Always short of gunners. They keep getting bits knocked off themselves. Speaking of which, how's your hand, Skip?'

'Not too bad, thanks,' replied Matt. 'I can still hold a pint mug, as you can see! Anyway, what are you chaps going to do with yourselves?'

'Bugger all,' said Fred. 'So long as we can't leave base, we are bloody well stuck here, ain't we? Just have to drink beer and dream about women!'

'Well, cheer up, Freddie,' said Matt. 'Usually get a few WAAFs in here once they finish, don't they?'

'S'pose so, Skip. Here's hoping!' And with that, he swilled down his beer.

'Everyone for another?' asked Matt, and he struggled back to the bar.

The singing started about nine o'clock, and it was well past midnight by the time Joe had managed to ease them all out of the pub and on their way. Matt and Stephen walked slowly back to the camp, both friends feeling slightly the worse for wear.

'Lovely night, Stephen,' said Matt.

It seemed very quiet after the noise of the pub, and the stars stood out clearly with the moon just poking above the surrounding trees.

'You know, sometimes it's quite difficult to believe we are at war at all,' said Matt. 'Here we are with this wonderfully peaceful night, and a few hundred miles away, blokes are kicking the shit out of one another. Weird, isn't it?'

The wind made the turning leaves rustle in the trees, and the smell of autumn wafted from the woods around them.

'Actually,' replied Stephen, 'I try not to think about it. This moment in time is just a break from the madness. The longer it goes on, the harder I find it to even recognise the good times.'

'You need a woman, Stephen.' Matt laughed.

'Well, it isn't for want of trying,' he retorted.

'Well, maybe Anne will bring someone suitable tomorrow night. That's if we're here.'

CHAPTER 4

STOOD DOWN

The next morning was cold and bright and the sky a pale blue with small, fluffy clouds being pushed across in a fairly stiff northerly breeze. Matt wandered down to see how the repairs to M-Mother were getting on. He liked to meet with the mechanics looking after his aircraft and was interested, in any case, to see the state of the repairs. One of the sergeants looked up as he approached. 'Morning, sir.' He saluted.

'Morning, Sarg. How are you getting on?'

'Not bad, sir. We have replaced the engine already, and the patching up is going quite well. Chief reckons should be ready to test tomorrow.'

'Bloody good show,' said Matt and walked into the hangar to see for himself.

Six aircraftmen were at work, and he made sure that he didn't get in their way. They had replaced the damaged Perspex panel and had patched the holes made by the bullets that had come so close to killing Townsend.

'Looks pretty good, chaps,' said Matt to no one in particular and then noticed Warrant Officer Bryant coming into the hangar.

'Hallo, Chiefy,' said Matt. 'Your boys are doing a good job—ready for testing tomorrow apparently?'

'Probably, Matt. The engine we've replaced we scavenged from a dud. It should be fine—anyway, better than the one we took out! I was a bit worried about the fuselage around the mid-upper, but we've done a bit of strengthening there and that should be OK too. Your gunner was lucky to get out of there alive.'

'Yes, I know, Chiefy,' said Matt. 'I will be more careful next time.'

They both laughed, and Matt set off back to the mess.

After lunch, Wing Commander Squires asked to see Matt. 'How's the hand, Matt?' he asked as Matt saluted.

'Oh, it's not too bad, sir. I think probably less swollen than yesterday, and the fingers work. Could be a lot worse!'

'Right, we have to field six aircraft for this evening, and I am afraid I need a bomb-aimer and gunner, so I am going to have to use your chaps Grant and Hughes.'

'Which aircraft will they be on, sir?'

'S-Sugar. They are two men down after their last adventure. Sorry, but there we are.'

'How many ops have they done, sir?' Matt asked.

'Well, this will be their fifth, so not absolute rookies.'

'Thank you, sir. Do you want me to tell them?'

'If you would, that would be kind. Their names are already posted on the ops board.'

Matt saluted and walked thoughtfully to the crew room. Almost the first men he met were Don and Freddie, both looking pretty glum.

'Sorry, chaps,' said Matt. 'You have heard already, I take it? S-Sugar's crew are not complete beginners, at least.'

'Yeh, but their last bomb-aimer ended up in hospital and the rear gunner came out of the turret in pieces,' retorted

Freddie. 'My bloody luck to be picked for that lot. I might have been on a promise with a bird tonight. Always bloody happens to me.' With that, he stomped off to the briefing. Matt smiled, but being an odd bod was often a bad experience, and in any case, they all hated not being with their own crews.

***

That evening, Matt made his way down to the pub. It was pretty empty since most of the crews were on operations that night, but Stephen was standing by the bar and next to him was a bundle of brown and white fur, which, Matt assumed, was Scrap. He had a brown head with a line of white running from his nose to between his ears and large, very brown eyes, and he sat up and wagged his tail as Matt moved towards him. Matt was very taken with him and ruffled him under his chin.

'Well, this is Scrap, I presume,' he said to Stephen. 'Oh, and I will have a pint please.'

'Yes, this is him. Cute, isn't he?'

'Yes, he is, but I hope he's not going to bring us bad luck.'

Stephen collected the beers, and they walked over to some chairs, Scrap padding along behind them.

'Well, we are actually his third crew.'

'I am feeling worried already,' replied Matt. 'What happened to his previous owners, or would it be better that I don't know?'

'Well, no, not really. His first crew were Canadians who had finished their tour and were disbanded, and, I think, went back home in one piece. The second crew were, as you know, from F-Freddie, and it now seems that at least some of them got out. So I reckon he's a lucky charm—well, as lucky as you can get in this show.' He smiled and gave Scrap a pat.

'May be you're right, Stephen. I hope he doesn't snore as much as you do at night! I'll go and get some more beer. Incidentally, have we cleared it with Barker? After all, he's going to have to look after him when we're not here?'

'Yes,' Stephen replied, 'he's very happy to oblige. Says he loves dogs. Anyway, old boy, where are these women you promised?'

Matt looked at his watch. It was nearly 7.00 p.m.

'I think they will be along soon. Anne doesn't finish until six, and then she often has to stay on for extra cases. Don't worry, she'll get here hopefully with a backup for you!'

They laughed. Stephen had always had trouble getting to know girls, even though he was good-looking and interesting, if perhaps rather on the reserved side.

They bought some more drinks and walked outside. It was nearly dark now, and as they opened the door, they heard the sound of the aircraft engines being started up. The raid was underway, and they fell to thinking about what was in front of those crews tonight, especially for Don and Freddie. Neither of them knew the target, but the rumour was that it was Berlin. There was an early autumn chill in the air, and as Matt looked up, he could see through small breaks in the cloud the stars twinkling brightly. The air smelt of autumn and the approach of winter, even though it was still only early September. He shivered and turned to go back in. As he did, he heard the first aircraft rev its engines at the start of its take-off run, and he hesitated and waited for the beat of the engines to change as the aircraft lifted off.

'God speed,' he said under his breath and walked back into the warmth of the pub.

'Got the night off then?' asked the barman lightly. He knew only too well the strain these crews were under and also how many were in his pub one night only to have been killed by the next.

'Yes,' said Matt. 'We had a bit of a do a couple of nights ago, which needed the kite to be patched up and us too.' He waved his injured hand.

'Don't know how you do it night after night,' the barman replied. 'Here, have the next two pints on the house.'

'Thanks,' said Matt, and he wandered over to join Stephen and Scrap.

It was about eight o'clock by the time Anne and her friend Jesse arrived, the bus having taken a while from Lincoln.

'Sorry, darling,' said Anne. 'This is Jesse. She is a staff nurse in our unit, and she thought she would like to come and see how the other half live!'

'Nice to meet you, Jesse. This is Stephen. He is my engineer on the plane, so I fly it and he makes sure the propellers keep turning! Oh, and this is our latest recruit. He's called Scrap.'

'Nice to meet you, Stephen—and of course Scrap.'

Anne was already down stroking Scrap. 'He is gorgeous, Stephen. Where did you get him?'

'Well, in effect, he was donated to us,' said Stephen, who was having trouble keeping his eyes off Jesse.

'Donated?' echoed Anne.

'Well, yes, he belonged to a crew which was shot down a couple of nights ago.'

Anne paled. The reality of what could happen to these young men frightened her.

'That's dreadful,' she replied.

'Well, it's not that bad, Anne. We think a few of them might have got out.' With this, he moved towards the bar. 'What would you both like to drink?'

'Gin and orange please,' said Anne.

'Me too,' said Jesse and turned to Matt.

'So you both have the night off then? We heard planes taking off as we got closer.'

'Yes,' said Matt. 'Ours needed a bit of work on it.'

Anne suddenly noticed that Matt's hand was bandaged.

'You never said anything about this,' she said. 'Whatever happened?'

'Scrap bit me.' Matt laughed. 'No, I got hit by a bit of tin the other night. Nothing broken and it's beginning to feel better.'

Anne felt cross that he hadn't told her straight away but then realised that he probably hadn't wanted to worry her. God knows what else he didn't tell her. She shuddered slightly and turned back to Scrap.

'He's lovely. Who looks after him?'

'Well,' said Stephen, 'we do really. Quite a few crews have dogs. Some even have cats, and I heard of one lot, not in our squadron, that had a parrot!'

They all laughed and had a drink. Stephen thought Jesse very attractive. She was short, about five feet two inches, he reckoned, and perhaps a little plump but with red hair and very lovely blue-green eyes. She had a pretty mouth with a ready smile and was wearing a white silk blouse, which certainly showed off some of her assets to good effect, he thought, and a long green-coloured skirt. Their eyes met, and Stephen felt a sudden shiver. He moved over to be next to her.

'It's very quiet in here tonight,' he explained. 'Quite a few crews have gone to work tonight. We have been grounded for a couple of nights while they patch up our kite.'

'Well, I am really glad about that,' Jesse replied. 'Otherwise, we may never have met.'

They laughed again.

Matt and Anne were deeply engrossed with their own world, and Stephen and Jesse seemed to have found a lot to talk about too. Her parents lived in Ipswich, and she had a brother who was in the Royal Navy and currently on escort duty in the Atlantic.

'That must be dreadful, you know,' said Stephen. 'You would be away for months stuck in some small ship pitching about in the cold and wet. At least for us it's all over fairly quickly—well, it depends where we are going of course, but usually eight to nine hours will see it done. Then you can come down to the pub and chat to attractive women.' He blushed slightly. He was not usually so forward, but somehow this felt different. And it seemed that almost as soon as Anne and Jesse had arrived, the barman was calling time.

'We'll take you back,' said Matt. 'I've got the car outside. Scrap can squeeze in with you, Anne, in the front seat.'

Jesse and Stephen got into the back of the car, tipping the front seats forward so they could climb in.

'Hold on a minute, Matt, I need a pee,' said Stephen, and he ran back into the pub. By the time he got back, Jesse was in the back seat, and he climbed in next to her. As he sat down, she snuggled up to him and put her head on his shoulder. Anne and Matt got in the front, and they were off. The lanes were very dark, and Stephen felt that he and Jesse could kiss without Matt or Anne noticing. It was a deep kiss, and he felt Jesse responding. This was new territory for him, but it felt right. Before they knew it, they were back at the hospital.

Jesse leaned closer. 'Maybe next time we could be more adventurous?' She squeezed him gently, and they kissed goodnight.

Matt and Stephen watched the two nurses walk off to the hospital and got back in the car.

'Well, how did that go?' Matt asked.

'Bloody well, old chap. Can't wait to meet her again. Had a hell of a hard in the back of the car, I can tell you.' He laughed. 'What did you think of her? Have you ever met her before?'

'No, I certainly haven't, but I wouldn't mind doing so.' Matt laughed.

'You keep off,' said Stephen. 'You've got one already!'

With that, they drove back to the camp, which now was still and quiet.

'Quick nip in the mess?' asked Stephen. 'I somehow think I owe you one. Or maybe I owe Anne one.'

With that, they went for a drink, after which they went off to bed with Scrap in tow.

***

Matt woke up about five o'clock to the sound of returning aircraft. Stephen and Scrap were fast asleep with Scrap curled up at the foot of Stephen's bed. Matt got dressed and slipped out of the door. He made his way down to the operations room.

'Morning, sir.' One of the sergeants saluted as he went in. Three crews had already returned and were being debriefed. The room was thick with the combination of cigarette and pipe smoke and the low mumbling of crews as they were being debriefed. Matt looked anxiously round, but the ops board showed that S-Sugar was still not back. He wandered over to the desk where a WAAF sergeant was sitting, writing down the details of the retuning flights.

'What was the target?' he asked.

'Berlin,' she replied.

'Anything from S-Sugar?' Matt asked.

'Not yet, sir,' the WAAF replied, 'but they are not overdue —another thirty minutes for that.'

Berlin was a long way and would take the aircraft around eight hours. They were getting close to that, thought Matt.

'Do we know of any losses yet?' he asked.

'One went down just after crossing the coast … It was T-Tommy, we think,' the WAAF replied.

Matt was getting worried but went over to one of the crews who had finished their debrief. They looked tired and glanced nervously towards him. Matt knew the pilot, Tony Parker.

'How was it, Tony?' he asked.

'Bloody awful,' he replied. 'Bloody flak everywhere and fighters pretty well all the way there and back. Saw a lot of aircraft going down. Not even sure we hit the bloody target either. Cloud and shit all over the place. Still we're back.' And with that, he smiled and turned away.

Just as he was leaving, the WAAF said that S-Sugar was on finals, and as he opened the door, he heard the roar of a Lancaster as it touched down nearly a mile away across the airfield. He went back into the ops room and over to the desk.

'Everything OK?' he asked.

'They have some casualties on board,' she replied.

About half an hour later, he heard the ambulance rush past on its way to the medical station, and soon after, S-Sugar's pilot, Sergeant Philips, came in followed by four of his crew, which, Matt was relieved to note, included Don and Freddie. They got their mugs of tea and went over for the debrief whilst Matt waited.

The debrief finished, and the tired crew walked away from the table. As Don and Freddie saw him, they smiled wearily and moved towards him.

'Fuck me, Skipper,' said Freddie. 'Don't let them do that to us again.'

'Bad trip?' asked Matt.

'Bloody awful,' said Freddie. 'Two blokes got the chop. I tell you, Skipper, this is getting bloody dangerous.'

They all laughed, but they all knew how bad it really was.

'Mind you,' said Freddie, 'old Phillips is not a bad jockey. Nearly as good as you!' 'So you won't mind going with him again, then?' teased Matt.

'Bollocks to that,' muttered Freddie, and they wandered out of the ops hut.

'What you reckon, Don?' asked Freddie.

'I reckon I would rather stay with M-Mother. Thanks all the same.'

'Well, you two better get some shut-eye. We could be flying tonight. I am going to take M-Mother up this morning to make sure everything works and the wings are stuck on. Have a look on the ops board when you wake up.'

Matt walked over to the mess. It was 6.30 a.m. already, and he thought that he may as well get his breakfast before the rush. He was nearly at the mess when Squires came up to him. 'Matt. How's the hand?'

'OK, sir, I can move my fingers again, and the swelling's pretty well gone.'

'Good show. I will be needing M-Mother for tonight. How are your chaps from last night? I see that S-Sugar took a bit of a pasting, couple killed unfortunately.'

'Yes, sir. I met my two crew just now. They seem OK, and I warned them they could be on tonight,' Matt replied. 'I am going to take M-Mother up this morning to check it out. We should be ready.'

With that, he saluted and went into the mess. Stephen was already there.

'Morning, Matt. What's the score?'

'Well, our two are back in one piece—Freddie his usual good-natured self.' He smiled. 'Bumped into Squires, and we are on for tonight so we need to take M-Mother up for a flight test this morning. Could you pop over to the ground chaps after breakfast and set that up? I will go to ops and clear it with them.'

'Yes, of course. What sort of time?'

'Well, soon as poss really, so that the kite can be refuelled and bombed up for tonight. Let's see if they can get things together by 0930 hours?'

They tucked into their breakfasts, and Matt noticed Stephen wrapping up some buttered toast.

'For the dog.' He smiled.

'Hey, do you think he would like to come for a fly?' Matt asked.

'Well, he used to go up with Jock, I think. Let's give it a shot.' Stephen smiled and drained his teacup. 'I'll head off now,' he said as he stood up to leave.

'I've finished too,' said Matt, and with that, he set off to the ops room.

***

Matt, Stephen, and Charles climbed up into the rear door to begin their air test with Scrap hidden in Stephen's flight bag, although once inside the aircraft, he ran forward towards the cockpit.

'Hallo,' said Charles. 'Who's this then?'

'We are now responsible for this chappie. New crew member. He belonged to F-Freddie, and since they have gone, he's ours!' said Stephen, somewhat protectively.

'Well, I am not sure what King's regulations have to say about dogs on board the aircraft. Doesn't sound quite right to me. In fact, I think it's best that I don't know he is here,' Charles said rather stiffly.

'Well, that's fine, Charles. We won't tell you then.' Matt smiled. 'Let's get this kite up and see if she is OK.'

The flight went well, and once the engines had been shut down and the final checks made, the three made their way down the aircraft. Scrap was once again smuggled out, and when they were out, Charles seemed to relax.

'We are not planning to take him on a raid, are we?'

Matt and Stephen looked at one another.

'Well, I'm not sure, Charles,' Matt said and smiled. 'I thought we could try and train him to crap out of the bomb doors. Just a little extra for the Hun.'

They all laughed.

'Preliminary briefing is at 1500 hours, chaps, so let's meet in the mess about 2.30 p.m.?'

CHAPTER 5

MANNHEIM

Seventeenth Trip

After Matt had checked the ops board, he spent the rest of the morning resting on his bed and writing letters to Anne and his parents. He found it comforting to think that, should he not return, at least he had had the chance to say goodbye. It was slightly morbid, but many of the others did the same, although few of them admitted to it.

They were carrying another gunner to replace the still invalided Townsend, and Grant and Hughes were listed even though they had been involved in last night's raid. Matt, Stephen, and Charles met for lunch—a fairly dismal piece of chicken, a potato, and carrots, and they all looked forward to the ritual bacon and eggs before they went to war.

'What happens to the dog whilst we are away?' asked Charles suspiciously.

'Don't worry, Barker said he would look after him,' replied Stephen. 'He says he's very good with dogs! Matt, have you spoken to Anne today? I wondered if there was any chance the four of us could meet up tomorrow night?'

'Stephen, you know as well as I do that the CO frowns on anyone making telephone calls within twelve hours of a raid!' Matt said and smiled.

'I know, I know,' replied Stephen. 'Just wanted something to look forward to, that's all!'

'Well, we will give them a call as soon as we get back,' replied Matt. 'Trouble is there seems to be a bit of a flap on just now, and for all I know, we will going again tomorrow night as well. We have been given a couple of nights off already, you know.'

'Well, only because the bloody kite was shot up and you and Townsend were injured,' Stephen retorted. 'Rearrange the following words: horse, flogging, dead, a.' With that, he got up and walked out of the mess.

'It's getting to him, you know,' said Charles. 'It creeps up on you until suddenly you're as scared as hell and in any case can't see the point of it.'

Matt nodded and finished his lunch.

'I am a bit surprised actually. He has been really steady up till now. He met a really lovely girl last night, a friend of Anne's, and then there's the dog as well. Makes you see there is another life, I suppose.'

'You know, Clare and I have become completely fatalistic about the whole thing,' said Charles. 'We both believe I am going to come through this, and when it's all over, we can start planning for the future—kids, house, that sort of thing.'

'Well, that's good,' said Matt. 'Anne and I can't even decide whether it's worth going the first step to get married. Not yet anyway. Doesn't seem any point.'

'The point, Matt, is that at least you have some time as a couple. It's really important. You should think about it.'

'You may be right,' said Matt. 'Come on, let's get down to the ops room and hear what they have in store for us.'

'What do you reckon, Matt?' asked Charles. 'Berlin, do you think?'

Matt nodded, and they joined the others in the ops room.

Don was there already. He looked tired and drawn and was vigorously smoking his cigarette.

'You OK, Don?' Matt asked. 'You look pretty knackered.'

'Feel it,' he said. 'Only got a few hours' sleep, and last night's trip was pretty shitty. It's such a bloody long way to sodding Berlin, and then it's always covered with bloody clouds. Can't see a sodding thing.' Don turned away and sat down.

It was very unlike him to swear. In fact, Matt couldn't recall a time. Maybe the whole thing was beginning to get to them all. After all, the longer they went on, the greater the chance of them not coming back. And the thirty ops target seemed like a bit of a mirage; the closer you got, the further away it seemed. *Enough*, thought Matt. *Won't do. We have got to get through this.*

'Well, chaps,' he said lightly, 'only another thirteen to go after this one,' and with that, he sat down next to Don and Charles.

The room was filling up more slowly than usual, several of the crews having been on the previous night's raid. At 1500 hours precisely, W/C Squires, the squadron navigator, and the bomb-aimer strode into the room, and everyone stood until Squires got to the stage, saluted, and told them to sit down.

'Well, gentlemen, the target for tonight is Mannheim. Some of the main force will be attacking Ludwigshafen.' With that, he drew back the curtain that hid the map. There was muttering throughout the room, especially from those who had been out the night before.

'Christ almighty,' said Don to Matt, 'that looks a long way.'

Squires was talking, and Don refrained from saying anything else.

'Air Chief Marshall Harris wants a maximum effort tonight, so we are sending twelve aircraft from East Kirkby. I know some of you went last night, but I am afraid we have a job to do and bashing the Germans as often as we can is one way to do it!' There was some muted laughter round the room, and the tensions eased slightly.

'The attacking force will arrive at the target from the west, and the markers will be dropped on the eastern side of the town. The total size of the force will be 600 with the usual mix of Lancs and Halifaxes and a few Stirlings. We will now have a briefing from Squadron Navigator S/L Harris and Squadron Bomb-Aimer S/L Chalk. Please pay particular attention.' And with that, he sat down as the navigator stood.

'Well, chaps, here we are again, happy as can be!'

There was a scattering of laughter.

'We are going to send you on a southerly route to Mannheim.' He smiled. 'Hopefully, this will mean that you miss most of the nasty flak and the fighters will be looking elsewhere! In fact, it will keep them guessing about the exact target. Coming out, our route will cross the channel at Hastings and take a south-easterly route towards Rheims before turning east to the target. Altitude en route will be at 15,000 feet and the bombing run will be 18,000 feet. We aim to get you to Mannheim at 0100 hours. Any questions?'

Redman put his hand up. 'There's talk of quite a bit of flak 'round Rheims, and it looks as if we may get quite close to that, sir.'

'Yes, we know that, but the route we have in mind should avoid the worst. Anyone else? Right, next up is the Squadron Bomb-Aimer S/L Chalk.'

'Afternoon, chaps. The specific aiming point for tonight is right across the town. They want us to cause maximum damage to the infrastructure. Pathfinders will drop green flares, and we want you to bomb to those. A full list of target marker colours will be issued at the main briefing. The bomb load will be incendiaries and cookies. Any questions?'

There was silence as the squadron meteorological officer stood up.

'We are forecasting rain tonight for the airfield and moderate westerlies, but at 15,000 feet, the wind will be strong and most likely from the northwest so you will need to keep a careful eye on drift.' There was a ripple of agreement as he went on. 'We are predicting clear skies over the target, although the possibility of mist cannot be ruled out. There may be some icing at 15,000 feet, certainly in cloud. Altitude for the cloud tops is around 20,000 feet, but above that, you may have Jerry to contend with. I will give you a final update on the Met when we have the main briefing.'

Wing Commander Squires stood up. 'Well, chaps, that's about it. Navigators and Bomb-Aimers, please collect your details. We will meet back here at 1700 hours. First take-off time will be 2000 hours. Dismiss.'

Matt left the other two and walked over to his billet. As he entered his room, he saw that Stephen was fast asleep with Scrap on the bed beside him. Scrap wearily lifted his head and gazed at Matt with his dark-brown eyes, his tail wagging. Matt took off his shoes, clambered onto his bed, and soon fell asleep.

He was woken by a generous lick from Scrap. Stephen was already up and dressed. 'Berlin, I suppose?' he asked.

Matt replied, 'No, Mannheim actually, but still quite a way.'

'Christ,' said Stephen.

'Well,' said Matt, 'Squires seems to think this is the start of a campaign, so I guess we better get used to it. Bloody long trip, though!'

They got their kit together and left for the crew room. It was 4:30 p.m., and it was vital to make sure everything was in order so that after the final briefing, they could grab something to eat and get out to the aircraft to meet their take-off times.

'I'll take Scrap for a quick constitutional,' said Stephen, and he set off towards the perimeter fence whilst Matt headed for the crew room. He got his gear out of his locker and started checking everything was there. It was somehow comforting to handle his flying jacket, mask, and gloves—rather like meeting up with old friends. He went to the briefing room and met up with the other members of the crew. Stephen joined them a few minutes later. Freddie was his usual self, complaining about everything but specifically that it just wasn't right for him to go again tonight.

'Bloody hell, Skip,' he said to Matt. 'They nearly got us bloody killed last night, and it was bloody cold, and it lasted a bloody long time.'

'Ah well,' said Matt. 'At least you are coming with us this time!'

'That's something to feel good about, is it?' Freddie mumbled as he drew on his cigarette. 'Oh this 'ere is our mid-upper since Townsy is still swinging the lead. Flight Sergeant Charlie Faith.'

'Good to meet you, Charlie. Welcome aboard. How many trips have you done?'

'Well, this will be my twentieth. My last crew were killed while I was in the sickbay! Next to Townsy in fact. Told me all about you lot!'

At this, W/C Squires came in and the briefing room went quiet. It was crowded now with eighty-four men all listening intently to what was being said. The W/C started off by giving the target, news which raised groans from all over the room. He told them they better get used to it as the C-in-C had indicated this was the start of a number of similar raids deep into Germany. He then said that it was likely they could all have the next night off, and this raised a cheer and some smiles.

Freddie muttered, 'Well, of course we still have to get back from this one,' and got a few laughs from those around him.

The navigator and bomb-aimer each said his piece, but the Met officer said he thought it now quite possible that it might be misty by the time the aircraft returned. There were more groans at this, because for a tired crew, having to land in poor visibility or, worse, divert, just made things more difficult and therefore dangerous.

The briefing finished, and the crews headed off first to get their dinner, the usual bacon and eggs, and then to pick up their parachutes, flasks, and sandwiches and get their kit on.

As they left the fug of the briefing room, Matt noticed that there was a distinct chill in the air. Autumn had come quickly this year, and there had already been some early morning mists hanging over the airfield. He smelt the sharp, chill air with its characteristic scents of dead leaves and moist ground. He always found autumn a sombre time, although the trees this year had looked very lovely with their brown, yellow, and red colours. He suddenly felt a sense of loss that he hadn't been able to share much with Anne and that, yet again, he was conscious how time was slipping away.

He mentally shook himself and joined his crew as they gathered to wait for the trucks to take them out to dispersal. Stephen had turned up with Scrap at his heels, and Matt noticed that he was looking thoughtful. 'Penny for them,' he called across.

Stephen did not answer straight away, and then he too seemed to shake himself out of his thoughts. 'Sorry, Matt, miles away.'

'Anywhere in particular?' Matt asked.

'No, not really. In fact, anywhere other than here would do fine to be honest.'

'Well,' said Matt, 'maybe we will get tomorrow night off and we can go into Lincoln and see the girls?'

'Yep,' replied Stephen. 'Here's hoping,' and with that, he picked Scrap up and gave him a hug.

'Stephen, have you seen Charles anywhere?'

'Haven't seen him since briefing,' Stephen replied.

'Me neither. I know sometimes he sneaks off to say goodbye to his wife after briefing, but he's usually here by now.'

At that moment, Matt saw Redman running towards them carrying his kit, maps, and instruments with him.

'Sorry, Matt. Popped home to see Clare and the bloody car wouldn't start. That's the trouble once it gets colder. Had to give it a push.'

'Still, you're here now,' replied Matt and walked over to where Freddie and Charlie were in deep conversation.

'You OK, chaps?' asked Matt.

'Yes, Skip,' replied Freddie. 'Charlie was telling me about a pub he's found in Lincoln. Lots of birds and the beer's smashin' too. Here, Skipper, his lot got the chop a few nights ago on a bloody milk run!'

'Well,' said Matt, 'shit happens, doesn't it? You OK about tonight, Charlie?'

'Yep, Skip. I am up for another go at those bastards.'

'Good,' said Matt. 'Well done,' and he walked over to Don and Mac.

They were talking about the car Don had just got, an old Morris 8, which, from their conversation, seemed to be in need of some tender loving care.

'Everything all right here?' Matt asked.

'Yes, Skip, but when we get back from tonight, Mac's going to give me a hand to try and get the old jalopy back in shape. We may need to take the engine out sometime soon.'

'You should ask Stephen to help. He's an engineer after all! Although on thinking about it, maybe the ground crew would be your best bet.'

He moved back to Stephen and Charles, and as he did so, the truck came to take them out to M-Mother.

'All aboard!' shouted Freddie, and as they scrambled into the back of the truck, Matt noticed him taking a slightly wistful look around.

It was 1900 hours when they got to M-Mother's dispersal area. The ground crew were just loading the last of the bombs, and Matt and Stephen went over to Warrant Officer Bryant, who was in charge of all the ground crews.

'Evening, Chiefy,' said Matt. 'Everything in order?'

'Best as we can make it, sir. The new engine, starboard inner, you will remember, has been run up and seems fine, and you yourself took her up for a test so we think it's all right. If you want a walk 'round and then sign off her P 700, that would be great. Looks like a long run again tonight, Matt. Hope all goes well. Good luck.'

'Thanks, Chiefy. We will try and bring her back in one piece this time!' Matt replied and then started his walk around the aircraft to make sure all was well. Stephen handed Scrap to one of the ground crew and climbed in through the rear door.

'Look after him until we get back,' he called.

'Will do, sir,' replied the sergeant, and Scrap looked longingly at Stephen, who turned quickly away and walked up to the cockpit where he started to check the instruments were intact. He felt a bit better now that he was busy twiddling knobs and watching dials, but somehow, he felt much less certain about whether he would make it back this time.

Freddie, Charlie, and Don remained outside the aircraft smoking and chatting. The cold air showed their breath, and along with the cigarette smoke, they appeared to be enveloped in a cloud. *Almost surreal*, thought Matt, as he walked past them. 'Better get up in the kite, lads, soon be off,' he said.

All three walked off into the darkness for a final pee, although Freddie, as always, directed his onto the rear wheel.

Both Charles and Mac were busy setting up their instruments, Redman feeding them with track and wind data and McGuiness, radio frequencies. Care at this stage was essential. Mistakes could have disastrous consequences.

As Matt settled himself into his seat, he realised it was one of the few times that he had forgotten to put Anne's letter out. Well, he couldn't do anything about it now, but it gave him an uncomfortable feeling. Still, he had her scarf in his pocket, and there was work to be done. He forced the thoughts from his mind as he and Stephen went through their checklists. It was approaching 1945 hours and time to get the engines started. Mac had already called Control to check his radio set was working and had received the clearance for them to start up, which he passed on to Matt.

All the checks were now completed and the engine ready to start. Matt indicated to the ground staff that they were ready.

'Starboard inner,' called Matt, and Stephen repeated the instruction, switched on the ignition and booster coil, and pressed the starter button.

The propeller slowly turned, and the engine was run up to 1200 rpm and allowed to warm up at this speed. They repeated the procedure for each engine in turn until all four had been started. Once warm, the engines were run up to 1500 rpm and the aircraft shook under the power. Stephen checked temperatures and pressures and gave Matt a thumbs-up. They were ready to go.

'M—Mother ready,' called Matt to Control.

'Line up and take off on your allocated time,' replied the WAAF controller.

Matt taxied the aircraft around the perimeter track and lined up in turn.

'Everyone, OK?' he asked, and each of them replied. 'Right, chaps, here we go again. Good luck.'

The heavily laden aircraft trundled its way down the runway, engines at full boost with Matt countering the swing to port. The speed quickly built up until M-Mother eased away from the runway, and at 800 feet, Matt raised the flaps and commenced their climb away. They were number four in line, and they could see the rear navigation light of the aircraft in front of them as they climbed steadily towards their rendezvous point over Great Yarmouth before setting their course towards Hastings to the south.

'Hi, Matt, Navigator here. My calculations seem to show that the forecast wind is not entirely accurate.'

'Do you mean wrong, Navigator?' Matt smiled. He liked to tease Redman whenever possible.

'Well, yes, I suppose I do. There is more of a northerly component, and we need to adjust our heading a bit.'

'Will do,' called Matt.

They headed down over a darkened England, and after about an hour later, Charles called Matt, 'Should be approaching the coast.'

'Thanks, Navigator. Any sign, Don?'

'Nothing yet, Skip,' Grant replied, and then almost immediately after, 'Yes, I can see the shoreline now ... and the sea in front of us.'

'New course is one-two-five. And we need to climb to 15,000,' called Charles.

'One-two-five and up we go,' said Matt. 'Give me boost, Stephen.'

M-Mother climbed steadily up to 15,000 feet, and as they crossed the French coast, Matt noticed there was, as forecast, a good deal of cumulus, except it seemed to extend well inland. As they passed to the north of Rheims, there was a lot of flak and Matt could see the shadows of other aircraft all around them.

'New course, Skip, is zero-eight-zero, and climb to 18,000 feet. About hour and a half to the target.'

'OK, Navigator, zero-eight-five. Report in, everyone, and, Gunners, keep your eyes peeled.'

Each reported, and Freddie, as usual, had a bonus comment, 'Skip, it's bloody cold down this end of the kite. Any chance of some blankets?'

'Can it, Freddie. It's dangerous around here,' replied Matt. 'Charlie, you OK?'

He realised he had heard nothing from the mid-upper. 'Mac, go back and take a look, will you?'

'On my way, Skip,' he replied and made his way back through the gloom of the fuselage. He found Charlie slumped over his guns, unconscious. With difficulty, he got him out of the turret. He had a thin pulse and looked terrible, even in the glow of Mac's torch. He quickly realised that Charlie was suffering from hypoxia and snatched the oxygen cylinder down from its clip on the fuselage and opened the tap. By the time he reported back to Matt, Charlie was beginning to recover.

'Thirty minutes to the target.'

'Thanks, Navigator. How is our mid-upper?'

'I am back, sir. Sorry about that,' replied Charlie.

'Matt, the starboard inner is heating up a bit—not a problem just now but needs keeping an eye on.'

'Thanks, Stephen, let me know if I need to do anything different, and, Charlie, good to have you back. Keep a careful watch.'

Cloud cover was almost complete, and they had no way of knowing for sure where they were or indeed what was around them.

'Bomb-Aimer, keep a good lookout, could you?' asked Charles.

Matt noticed flashes some distance in front of them.

'See those, Bomb-Aimer?' he asked Don.

'Yes, Skip. There are a few small gaps in these clouds every now and then, but it's difficult to make anything out.'

'There are some marker flares up front,' Matt called. 'Colours of the day, I reckon. Do you agree, Navigator?'

'Confirmed,' said Redman, and he returned to his work.

'Here we go then,' said Matt. 'Get ready, Don. Jesus, look at that flak. Guess they are not very pleased to see us?'

Don looked up to see an approaching, apparently impenetrable, barrier of flak.

'Holy shit,' he muttered under his breath and then more loudly, 'Yes, ready, Skip. I have the target markers lined up now.'

'Bomb doors open,' said Matt.

The line of flak was getting closer, and the noise was almost unbearable. Flak fragments rattled against the fuselage, and a nearby explosion lifted M-Mother a couple of hundred feet before Matt got control again.

Don was giving him directions, 'Left, left, steady, steady, right, steady, steady. Bombs gone.'

These were the words every crew wanted to hear, but now Matt had to fly straight and level until the photoflash went off. 'Flash gone,' called Don.

'Right, let's get the hell out of here,' said Matt and put the aircraft into a diving turn to the right to clear the area as soon as possible.

As they were turning, a searchlight caught them, but they were going fast and the beam could not hold them. Suddenly, they were in complete darkness.

Matt could feel the sweat between his shoulder blades and on his forehead.

'Christ almighty,' he muttered and then as if to keep himself in control asked Stephen about the engine.

'Seems OK, just now, Matt, but we shouldn't flog it to death!'

'Right, Stephen, easing up now. Just wanted to get the hell out of there. Navigator, give me a course for home, will you?'

'Well, three-zero-five would be good for starters, but I think the gyro in the direction indicator may be playing up. This bloody cloud makes it hard to know exactly where we are.'

'Are we lost then, Navigator?' Matt smiled to himself.

'Not lost, Matt, just not entirely certain of our position,' he replied rather stiffly. 'We are trying to get an Oboe[3] signal. Don, keep a good lookout.'

Just at that moment, there was a bright flash off to their right. 'Looks like some poor sod has bought it,' Freddie reported.

'Well, if so, that means there are fighters about so keep watching. Navigator, I am going to start some gentle weaving— we mustn't be caught by those bastards.'

---

[3] Navigational aid that uses radio beams from ground stations.

'Roger,' replied Charles, who was trying to get a radio signal to give him a position fix.

'Screw right!' shouted Charlie, and he began firing as Matt heaved the aircraft down and to the right. They were already at 5,000 feet so there was not a lot of room below them.

'Junkers 88,' called Charlie. 'I think he is still sniffing around.'

'Well done, Charlie. Navigator, I am coming back onto my course now. How much further to the coast?'

Matt was feeling tired; the tension of getting to the target and the bombing run was catching up on him.

'About another ninety minutes, I think,' replied Charles.

Matt felt sick at the thought, and he tried to relax his tight muscles.

Stephen was looking worried. 'We seem to be using quite a bit of fuel,' he said. 'Is the wind strengthening?'

'Could be,' replied Charles. 'No fix, can't tell.'

'What's our fuel endurance, Stephen?'

I would say about another two and a half hours at this rate. Could be a close call.'

'OK,' replied Matt. 'Navigator, let me know as soon as you have a fix—if the wind is greater than estimated, we can drop down on the deck where it will be less. But I can't do that until we know where we are. Everyone all right?'

An hour went by, and they were still enveloped by cloud. The moon had risen, and the clouds surrounding them looked like huge white towers, but there was a sheet of white below them. It was not looking too good, Matt thought. In addition, they would stand out like a sore thumb for any fighters, he mused.

'Navigator, any luck?'

'No, Matt, bloody Oboe's not working. We could risk making a call for a QDM.[4] We must be fairly close to the coast.'

'Stephen, what's the fuel situation?' he asked.

'About hour and a half, consumption seems about the same.'

Matt tried to weigh up things. They were basically lost but probably going in the right direction. Fuel reserve was coming down, and they needed a fix of some sort. Asking base for a QDM could bring the fighters down on them. Most crew tried to avoid calling at this stage.

'OK, let's leave it another thirty minutes and then call for a QDM. Don—no, *everyone*, keep looking out of the aircraft. Don, see if you can't get a glimpse of a coastline. Should be there fairly soon now.'

'Roger, Skip, will do.'

Matt could feel the fear beginning to rise in him, but it was essential that no one else realised. They did not know where they were, fuel was running low, and undoubtedly, there were fighters about. His mouth was dry, and he could feel the sweat again on his back as he scanned the horizon in front of him. The half an hour was up, and they should be at or over the coast.

'OK, Mac, give base a call, but for God's sake, everyone keep looking around.'

A few minutes later, McGuiness had the QDM. They were in fact just over the coast, almost exactly where Redman thought they should have been.

'OK, chaps, I am going to take her down to see if we can beat this wind.' With that, Matt put the aircraft into a gentle dive and turned onto a heading that should take them over

---

4 Magnetic bearing of radio beacon from the aircraft.

Lowestoft about an hour away. It was still going to be a close call, and Matt asked Charles to consider another, closer airfield than their own. There were plenty to choose from in that part of East Anglia.

'There's a Yank airfield, Metfield, about fifteen miles bearing two-four-five from Lowestoft,' Charles said.

Matt came down to 1000 feet, but they were still in cloud and he knew they were not out of the woods yet by any means.

'Fuel?' he asked Stephen.

'About an hour, I would say,' he replied.

'Right, Navigator, let's aim for Metfield. This bloody northerly wind is much stronger than we thought, so basically, we will not make base. But if it's ten-tenths cloud over the coast, we will need help to get there—and let's hope it's not socked in!'

'Mac, call Metfield and see if anyone is home. If not, call base and get them to contact them or anyone around there.'

'Will do, Skip,' replied Mac, and a minute later, he said, 'Metfield can take us, but the viz is only about a mile with a cloud base of 1500 feet.'

'Great!' said Matt. 'It will have to do, won't it? Tell them we are down to running on fresh air … well almost.'

M-Mother crossed the coast over Lowestoft and headed towards the airfield.

Matt used Metfield's call sign and explained their problem.

'Join circuit downwind, M-Mother. The circuit is empty.'

Well, that's something, thought Matt, and he felt relief when right in the distance he could see their beacon.

'Fuel?' he asked to Stephen.

'Almost nothing,' he replied.

'We will have to come straight in,' Matt said to the controller. 'We are very short on fuel. I don't think I can risk a circuit.'

'Understood—we have the crash team out. Report when on finals. Runway three-three.'

'Will do,' Matt replied. 'OK, chaps, this is a one-time go. Suggest you take your crash positions just in case.'

He could just see glimpses of the runway now through the scattered cloud and lined up M-Mother on its final approach. 'Undercarriage down,' he called, and Stephen confirmed.

At last, Matt could clearly see the runway and he reckoned they were going to make it. 'Twenty-five-degree flaps now.' They were a little fast, and he raised the nose slightly to lose speed. 'Full flaps.'

The aircraft settled on its way to the runway, and they crossed the threshold to make a perfect landing, but as they did so, the outer engine coughed and Stephen quickly feathered the propeller.

'Close shave,' muttered Matt and taxied the aircraft to a hard standing before shutting down the engines. 'Well done, chaps, down in one piece.'

Matt sat still for a few minutes. He felt drained and exhausted, and he had trouble stringing thoughts together, but eventually, he forced himself to go through the routine checks with Stephen, who was looking drawn and grey.

'You all right, Stephen?' he asked.

'No, not really—in fact, I think I am going to be sick.' With that, he leaned over to open his side window and vomited onto the ground below.

'Sorry, Matt, I thought we had bought it that time.'

'Me too. But we didn't so we better get things into shape and report to base.'

And with that, he undid his straps and eased himself out of the seat he had been in for six hours.

'Christ, I need a pee.' He moved down the fuselage as quickly as his kit allowed. The others were waiting in the darkness, and he rushed over to the rear of the aircraft.

'Needed that, did you, Skip?' said Freddie. 'Bit of a close one that. Any ideas about what happens now?'

Matt was feeling a bit better as the strain lifted and his bladder emptied.

'Well, we need to let base know we are alive,' he replied. 'And then hopefully we can get ourselves back as soon as possible.'

For the first time since he had left the aircraft, Matt had noticed how sweet the chill morning air smelt, almost tasted. It was quiet too—no one rushing around in trucks or tractors and no ground crew either. He was struck, as always, by the contrast between the smell and noise of the bomber, which, just outside its rear hatch, gave way to an extraordinary peacefulness.

A truck drew up, and they got in, struggling with their kit, but soon, they were in the crew hut being handed steaming cups of coffee.

The duty station officer came in looking a bit flustered. 'You boys OK?' he asked in his American drawl. 'Welcome to Metfield. Sorry not too many folk around, but we were stood down yesterday. Anyone hurt?'

'No,' Matt replied. 'We are tired and hungry but all in one piece, thanks. I need to call base if that's possible?. Oh and we need some fuel'

'Yeh, sure. Come with me.' He led Matt over to the ops room, which was eerily quiet.

'Phone's over there.'

'Thanks,' said Matt, and he quickly got through to their own station commander. 'Wing Commander Squires, this is Pilot Officer White, M-Mother, sir.'

'Yes, White, we hear you are at Metfield. What happened?'

'We reached the target, sir, but had trouble finding our way back with a US compass. There seemed to be a rather stronger headwind than predicted, and we were low on fuel so landed here.'

'OK, White, good show, but you need to get back as soon as possible. I suggest you get some shut-eye, refuel, and get here by midday. Conditions not good here just now with poor viz, which should improve as the day goes on. I am afraid you will have to go again tonight—big show on. See me when you get here.' With that, he put the phone down.

Matt stood with the receiver still in his hand.

'Had he really said we have to go again tonight? We damn nearly got killed tonight, and now they want us to go again?'

Matt replaced the receiver and walked slowly back to the mess where his crew were tucking into some PX ham and eggs, all except Stephen that is, who was not looking well and was hugging another mug of coffee.

They looked up when he came in, and Charles, Mac, and Don noticed his face and stopped eating. Freddie and Charlie were busily discussing the prospects of picking up a couple of girls that night and hadn't seen Matt.

Charles was the first to speak. 'What's the score then?' he asked brusquely.

'Get some sleep and then back to East Kirkby by midday. If they hadn't been socked in just now, I think Squires would have us go back straight away. Yes, and before you even ask, we go again tonight so the promised night off is history!'

Matt thought Stephen was going to be sick again. His friend looked terrible, and he hung his head down.

'Bloody hell,' said Charles and then corrected the insubordination by saying, 'Well, there we are then.' He got up from his partly eaten breakfast to go outside.

'Sorry, chaps. Let's try and grab a few hours. I will ask them to bung some fuel in, and we can leave about eleven-ish. Gives us a few hours.' And with that, he left to go and speak to the duty officer.

***

By the time they were ready to head back to base, Stephen was looking a little better and even managed to smile as he remarked about the quality of food that the Americans seemed to enjoy. Before they started up, Matt asked him about the starboard inner engine that had been playing up.

'No, seemed OK in the end, Matt. Not sure what was going on,' he replied.

The flight back was uneventful, and after touchdown, they had to go through the usual debrief, including their reasons for ending up away from base. They grabbed some lunch, and then Charles, Don, and Matt went off to their preliminary briefing for the coming night. The squadron had lost three aircraft, and there was a feeling of despondency amongst the remaining crews. The briefing followed its usual course, and as they emerged, they were met by Stephen with Scrap at his side. He looked better but tired, and he walked with them to the mess for the traditional bacon and eggs.

'I don't feel I want anything to eat,' Stephen said to Matt.

'No, you must,' replied Matt. 'Even if it's only a couple of slices of bread. I mean, are you feeling well enough to fly tonight?'

'I don't feel well, but I can fly all right. I can't let you lot off on your own. God knows what would happen. I just don't feel well enough to go into the mess. Perhaps you could bring something out for me?'

'Sure,' said Matt, and he went in to join the others. Stephen worried him. He seemed to have suddenly become anxious and to have turned inside himself. It wasn't Stephen; he had been very good at hiding his emotions up until now.

That bloody dog, thought Matt—and maybe that girl he met the other evening. It was the funny thing about war. Everything happened really quickly—you see a girl, you fall in love, you get married. It could happen in a couple of weeks sometimes. Not much point waiting because every evening could be your last. Just then, he thought of Anne and the fact he hadn't been able to ring her and now couldn't. Squires would blow a gasket if he found out he had even tried. He felt trapped and gloomy, and the only thing he could do now was write one of his letters. He finished eating, excused himself, and went back to his room where he found Stephen on his bed with Scrap. 'I've got you a bacon sandwich,' he said, and Scrap sat up, interested in the prospect of food.

'Not for you,' he said, rubbing Scrap's ears. 'Your master's much more in need.' And he passed the food over to Stephen. 'What's up, pal?' he asked gently.

'Thought we were going to die last night, Matt.' With this, he started to cry.

Matt couldn't say anything at first and put his arm on Stephen's shoulders.

'Come on, old chap. We didn't die, did we? And probably after tonight, we will be stood down for a couple of days. We can meet the girls, have a good time.' He wasn't really sure what he should say and felt sorry for his old friend. Eventually, Stephen stopped weeping and looked up at Matt with bloodshot eyes.

'Sorry, Matt, everything suddenly seems so pointless. They bomb our cities; we bomb theirs. What the hell for?'

'Well, partly because they are a mean lot of bastards and we have to stop them—and we bloody well will stop them,' Matt said, trying to raise Stephen's spirits.

Stephen smiled and, as if he had reached some conclusion, sat up and started to eat his sandwich.

'You're right, Matt,' he said. 'They bloody well have to lose. Thanks, Matt. Feel bit better now. We will be fine, won't we?'

'Well, I think we will,' replied Matt. 'Come on, get yourself 'round that sandwich and let's go and get some tea. Final briefing is at 1700 hours. Take-off for us 1915 hours.'

CHAPTER 6

MUNICH

Eighteenth Trip

The briefing confirmed the target to be Munich with a rendezvous over Southwold, tracking to a point close to Mannheim, last night's visit, and then directly to the target. It was long flight, the same distance as Berlin, and Matt looked anxiously at Stephen, but his friend seemed impassive. It appeared as if he had put the last few hours behind him and he was now concentrating on what was before them.

The crews filed out of the briefing, and as soon as they were outside, Freddie was in full cry, 'Blimey, Skip, not another bleeding long trip! Look what happened to us last night!'

Matt looked at him and put both hands on Freddie's shoulders. 'Look, Freddie, just think how lucky the RAF is to have folk like us around to scare the shit out of the Hun. They are probably already crapping themselves at the thought of us coming back to stuff them again tonight.'

'Gawd above, Skip, it just ain't right,' Freddie grumbled as he and Charlie went off to get their kit.

'Poor old Freddie,' Matt said to Stephen. 'I think he has got a reasonable complaint this time. It's his third trip in a row—Don's too, come to that.'

The crew were quiet as they got on to the truck to take them to M-Mother. They were tired from the previous night, and there was a general feeling of anxiety.

The truck drew up at their dispersal, and Matt, Stephen, and Charles got out and climbed through the rear hatch of the aircraft. Matt and Stephen started their routine checks, and Charles sorted out his charts and instruments.

Freddie, Don, Mac, and Charlie, as usual, had a last drag on their cigarettes and then also climbed up into the aircraft with Freddie and Charlie still complaining about how unfair it all was. It was getting dark, and the day itself had been chilly and wet with only an occasional glimpse of sunshine, a fairly typical autumn day, which had left the aircraft feeling cold and damp. They all settled down in their respective positions, and Matt called through on the intercom to check they were all ready.

'OK, chaps, starting up in about ten minutes. Hopefully, we can all have a bit of a rest after this trip!'

'Bloody well should think so,' Freddie replied, and Matt smiled to himself.

Chaps like Freddie did a lot of complaining, but somehow they just kept going. He would be OK so long as he had booze and girls when he got back.

'Start time,' Matt said to Stephen, and they went through their usual start-up sequence. Once everything was checked and running, they joined the line of other Lancasters as they taxied round the perimeter. The aircraft were heavily laden with both fuel and bombs, and they slowly lumbered their way to the take-off point.

As usual, the station commander, Wing Commander Squires, and a number of ground crew and WAAFs were there to see them take off and disappear into the gloom. Matt always felt good to see this small group. It was a bit like the people who used to come along to cheer from the sidelines when he was playing rugby, sort of encouraging.

M-Mother started to move forward, and Stephen juggled the throttles to counter the swing to port. Once they were moving forward, the tail came up and the throttles opened fully. Speed seemed to take a long time to pick up the moment, and the end of the runway began to look very close as they reached take-off speed. Matt eased the heavily loaded plane off the ground and into a steady climb towards Southwold seventy-five miles away to the southeast. They were to climb to 15,000 feet, and Matt set the speed at 170 miles per hour. At 10,000 feet, he warned the crew to go on to oxygen.

They had climbed through the cloud by about this time, and Matt could make out the other aircraft around them, but now the ground was hidden from view.

'Should be at rendezvous now,' called Charles, 'and just about to join the others. Our course is one-two five.'

There were 300 other aircraft somewhere out there, Matt thought, but at least they weren't in cloud and visibility was pretty good.

'See any other aircraft, Freddie?' asked Matt.

'Yeh, Skip. I can see a couple behind us, and there is one on each side—well away from us.'

'Thanks, Freddie. You and Charlie keep your eyes skinned and you can both check your guns now.'

For once, the Oboe equipment seemed to be working and Charles was able to fix their position and, more important, could work out wind strength and drift.

'Looks like the Met man might be right!' he called to Matt. 'About an hour to our turning point.'

Matt was surprised how quiet it was. They were the decoy group this time, trying to convince the Germans that they were heading for Mannheim again. He thought the silence was a bit ominous, and he warned the gunners to keep a careful watch for fighters. They could be walking into a trap, and any carelessness could be fatal.

Matt noticed the cloud below them was beginning to break up, and he could begin to make out some features. 'Don, keep a good lookout below. Clouds seem to be breaking up, and now we are out of Oboe range, we need to do some old-fashioned map reading.'

'Will do, Skip. I have got a chart down here. What's our position, Navigator?'

'We should be north of Stuttgart. Matt, maintain one-two-five. About fifty minutes to the target.'

'Thanks, Navigator,' replied Matt. He was very concerned about the lack of enemy activity; he was sure it wouldn't last long.

Just at that moment, Freddie shouted, 'Fighter! Corkscrew left!' and Matt dived the aircraft sharply to the left. The heavily loaded aircraft was difficult to manoeuvre, but M-Mother responded and Matt heard the clatter of the guns.

'I got him!' Freddie shouted. 'He's on fire and diving away.'

'Well done, Freddie,' Matt said as he eased the aircraft back onto its course and climbed to restore height.

'Don't forget that there will be more of them out there for sure,' and almost before he had finished, Charlie was shouting and Matt heard his guns firing. M-Mother shuddered, and Matt knew immediately that they had been hit and asked the crew to call in. The only one who did not respond was Charlie.

'Mac, go and check on Charlie and see what the damage is.'

'On my way,' said Mac, but very quickly, he was back. 'Charlie's bought it, sir. And I am afraid we've collected some more holes too. No fire and it doesn't look too bad.'

'Thanks, Mac. Stephen, everything all right your end?'

There was no reply, and Matt looked across to him. Stephen was staring straight ahead and seemed in a daze.

'Engineer!' Matt called sharply, and at this, Stephen turned slowly towards him. 'You OK?'

Stephen nodded but did not speak. Matt could see the sheen of sweat on his face, and he could only imagine what was going through his friend's mind.

'Engineer, are the engines all right? Did we take a hit anywhere vital?'

Stephen seemed to stir himself and began checking his gauges. 'No, everything looks all right.'

The aircraft flew on through the blackness of the night, Matt feeling increasingly uneasy.

'Ten minutes to target,' called Charles.

Matt looked up, and he could see the glow of fires through the clouds.

'I can see the target,' he replied, and Don called up that he too could see where they were heading.

Just then, there was a huge explosion over to their left and below them. The aircraft rocked as the shock wave hit them, and Matt had to work hard to keep M-Mother straight.

'Jesus,' he muttered under his breath, 'Some other poor bastards. There are definitely fighters around!' he called. But a few minutes later, the wall of searchlights and flak appeared in front of them.

Matt could feel his hands tighten on the yoke, and he had to force himself to relax. He lowered his seat in case the searchlights found them and he became blinded by their glare. 'Here we go, chaps—about to start our bombing run.'

The flak was getting closer now, and in front of them, another aircraft had obviously been hit. Matt could see it spiralling downwards in flames. Then they were in it too. Nearby flak made them rock backwards and forwards like a bucking horse, but they kept going.

'Two minutes to target,' Charles's clipped voice said.

'Thanks, Navigator,' Matt replied.

'Bomb doors open. Can you see our target area, Don?' Matt asked, trying hard not to reveal how scared he really felt.

'Target markers in sight,' Don replied. 'Left, left, left, steady, steady—bombs gone, waiting for the photoflash. Yes, that's it.'

The aircraft had almost leapt in the air once relieved of the weight of the bombs, and Matt swung to the left and started a shallow dive to take them away from the target and towards home.

'Course for home, Navigator?' Matt asked as the aircraft levelled out at about 10,000 feet.

'Three-zero-five should do for now,' Charles replied, and Matt eased M-Mother onto the new course.

'Everyone, keep a sharp lookout!' Matt called. 'We are still in tiger country.'

This was a dangerous moment in any raid. As crews relaxed, they could drop their guard and get caught out.

'Freddie, anything to report?' Matt asked. He knew he would be looking, but he just wanted to make sure.

'No, Skip, all quiet this end. Is Charlie a goner?'

''Fraid so, Freddie. Mac, we need two gunners. Can you and Pilot Officer Bamber get Charlie out of the turret and you get in? We will do without a radio for now.'

'Will do, Skip,' replied McGuiness. He was a good choice because he had trained as an air gunner and radio operator in the early months of the war and he knew his way around the turret.

Matt glanced across at Stephen, who was just disconnecting his oxygen supply and intercom connections to go back to help McGuiness. He gave a thumbs-up and went back down the fuselage. When he arrived at the mid-upper turret, he saw that McGuiness was already undoing the straps holding Charlie, and he moved forward to help. Faith had been hit by two cannon shells, one in the chest the other in his abdomen. He could smell the blood and shit as they lowered his body onto the fuselage floor and McGuiness climbed up into the turret. He nodded resignedly at Stephen. There were two holes on either side of the fuselage where the shells had come in and gone out, and it was draughty and very cold. Stephen gave him the thumbs-up and then just on his way back fell to his knees, ripping his face mask off before he vomited on the floor near Faith's body. He kept retching for a while until he thought he was going to pass out.

Matt was beginning to calm down after the bomb attack, but he was concerned that things were so quiet. They were flying about 1000 feet below the cloud, and it was just possible to make out some of the ground below. 'How we doing, Navigator?' he asked.

'OK,' replied Charles. 'We are about forty minutes from the coast.'

'Ours or theirs?' Matt replied.

'Theirs, I'm afraid.' Redman laughed back. 'We are on Oboe now, so for once we know where we are.'

'Thank God for that,' Matt replied, and just as he was settling down, the sky all around them was lit up by what appeared to be hundreds of searchlights.

'Holy God!' shouted Matt, and he automatically dived the aircraft to the right. The absence of flak could only mean one thing—they were in a fighter trap. The fighter could see them, but they couldn't see a thing. And then just as suddenly, the lights went out and Matt found himself virtually blind. He could just make out his instruments but nothing else.

'OK, this is it, chaps. There must be fighters around. Freddie and Mac, keep watching if you can still see.'

Freddie had managed to snap down his dark screen almost immediately the searchlights came on and so still had some night-vision left. Mac had been a bit slower but said he still had some vision.

Matt quickly considered that their best option was to get back into the clouds. Just at that moment, he realised that Stephen was not back in the cockpit. He reached over and slammed the throttles through the gate, and the aircraft, now relieved of its bombs and much fuel, climbed rapidly.

Stephen shook himself as he realised what was happening and forced his way back up the steeply angled fuselage and back into the cockpit to switch on the fuel pumps to feed the high-revving engines.

The cloud base was approaching fast, but when they were about 200 feet away, Freddie called, 'Me 110 below us and to the right, Skip.'

Then they were in the cloud and still climbing. 'Oxygen, everyone!' Matt called. 'I am going to take us up through this cloud plus about 1000 feet. We should be able to see any Hun that follows us. Freddie, I'm relying on you.'

'No bloody change there then,' muttered Freddie as he rotated his turret, scanning from one side to the other as they burst out of the cloud into a clear, moonlit sky.

Matt's vision was returning, and with the light from the moon, he was beginning to pick out detail in the cockpit.

Stephen appeared to be slumped on his fold-away seat, but Matt did not want to question how he felt over the intercom.

'We've got company, Skip,' Freddie called. 'It's that 110, and he has just broken through the cloud below us off to the right.'

'Well done, Freddie. Keep an eye on him. Navigator, how far to the coast now?'

'Fifteen minutes, by my reckoning. We are north of Antwerp,' replied Charles.

'OK, I am going to keep above the cloud for now, out of the way of the searchlights and hopefully flak. Mac, keep a good eye up there for anyone coming down on us. We must show up like a fly on toilet paper with this cloud below us.'

'Will do, Skip. It's bloody cold in here with this extra ventilation,' said Mac.

'Mac, sorry, but this looks like the safest place to be just now. I will drop down as soon as poss.'

'Thanks, Skip, appreciate that,' Mac replied. He did not have the electrically heated suits worn by the gunners, so he was feeling the bitter cold of the turret. He tried to keep his hands as warm as possible because fairly soon now he would resume his role as radio operator.

Matt could see a break in the clouds ahead, which he reckoned must mark the coastline. They were almost there, and maybe another hour would see them over England again.

'Everything OK with the engines, Flight Engineer?' he asked. He needed to be formal so the rest of the crew knew he meant business.

'Yes,' replied Stephen. 'Fuel is adequate, and all four engines seem fine.'

'That bastard is getting closer, Skip,' called Freddie. 'He is about 500 yards away, still on the right. Just seems to be shadowing us.'

'Keep an eye on him. May be like that other one we thought was following us home.'

They crossed the coast, and Matt started a steady descent. He needed to cross over Great Yarmouth at about 5,000 feet. The night was clear now, and with the help of the moon, it was possible to see the coast from the white surf against it.

Don reported the coast and River Yare. They were nearly there, and it still looked clear.

'Right, Mac. Come on down and give base a call. Tell them we have a casualty and that we may have company. Any further sight of that Me, Freddie?'

'Not a dicky bird, Skip. Maybe he wants to go home for his bacon and egg or whatever bloody grub they have over there!'

Just then, Mac shouted, 'Fighter, abeam and coming straight for us! Corkscrew right!'

Matt swung the aircraft to a dive to the right, and he heard the rattle of Mac's guns and then the dull thud of M-Mother being hit. The air smelt of cordite.

'Where now?' Matt called out.

'Come left,' Mac replied. 'I think we have scared him off. Might even have got a hit on him.'

'No, here he comes again,' said Freddie. 'Screw left.' And again, the guns rattled. 'I've got him! I've fucking got him!' shouted Freddie, and out of the corner of his eye, Matt could see the fighter apparently going down in flames.

'Well done, chaps. That's worth a beer. Navigator, what course now after all that excitement?'

'Come to three-zero-zero. That should be about right,' Charles's calm voice came back.

Matt felt exhausted, but his job wasn't finished yet. He still had to get them all down in one piece.

'Thanks. Prelanding checks, please. Mac, have you got base?'

Mac had just got back to his radio. 'Yes, Skip. Winding up now.'

'Good, as I said before we were so rudely interrupted, tell them about Charlie.'

Matt eventually was in contact with base. They were third in line to land, and Matt eased M-Mother onto the downwind leg of the circuit and was relieved to turn onto finals. Stephen reduced the throttles and dropped the landing gear and flaps. The landing was perfect, and they taxied round to their dispersal. The ground crew, as always, was there to meet them.

Matt and Stephen went through their shutdown checks whilst the others did the same and clambered out. The blood wagon was there, and the orderlies gathered up Charlie's body and put him in the wagon.

The others were all out when Matt and Stephen jumped down. Stephen dropped to his knees and vomited again. One of the ground crew came over to help him up. He looked a ghastly colour, and Matt asked for one of the orderlies to check him over, but Stephen waved him off. 'I'm all right,' he said and vomited again.

Matt went over to where Freddie, Mac, and Don were standing. 'Well done, you two,' he gestured to Mac and Freddie. 'Could be a gong in it for you.'

'I think I only winged it, sir,' replied Mac. 'Freddie here did for it.'

Freddie did not reply. When Matt looked at him, he noticed that he appeared grey and completely exhausted.

'Lost your tongue, Freddie?' he quipped, but Freddie just gazed at him. This was his third night of operations in a row, and he was completely spent. Matt touched his shoulder gently. 'Come on, Freddie. Let's go and get a cup of tea?'

'Another fucking gunner dead, sir. Hardly got to know him, let alone get him to buy me a bloody drink.'

'I know, Freddie. It's a bugger, but at least we are here now.'

Suddenly, Freddie said quietly, 'Not sure I can go again tonight, Skip, if they ask.'

'Well, hopefully that won't happen. The kite will need repairing. We need repairing too, come to that. Don't we? Maybe they will give us a day or two off,' said Matt unconvincingly.

Sometimes it seemed that the system couldn't really care less about them. Bloody cannon fodder. *Sodding war has always been the same*, he thought, and being a gunner was dangerous; they had more casualties than any other aircrew.

'You OK, Mac?' Matt asked, turning away from Freddie, who was still looking blank with fatigue. 'You did a great job up there tonight. Have you warmed up a bit?'

'Yes, a bit, Skip. Nothing that a shot of rum won't put right,' replied Mac. 'Do you think they will make us go again tonight?'

'Don't know. Hope not. We should know soon,' Matt replied.

He wandered over to the waiting ground crew, and the sergeant came towards him. 'Another dodgy one, sir? You all look done in.'

'Yes, I'm afraid so,' replied Matt. 'Mid-upper's a bit of a mess. Will need a bit of cleaning up, and the fuselage has some non-regulation holes as well.'

'OK, sir, we'll sort it out. Here comes your truck now, sir. Goodnight—sorry—good morning!'

'Thanks, Flight,' he replied and with the others pulled himself up into the back of the truck.

They were dropped at the ops room and made their way through the door to be met by an orderly with a steaming cup of tea complete with a nip.

'Over here, chaps,' called one of the intelligence officers. 'Well, how did it go?' he asked cheerily.

Matt always felt irritated by the IOs. It wasn't their fault, and they had a job to do like the rest of them, but they were in a nice cosy room without people trying to kill them.

'We went to Munich, dropped our bombs on the target, and came home again. But there were only six and a half of us by the time we landed,' he replied curtly.

'Sorry to hear that,' replied the IO. 'Anything else to report?'

'Well, we think we got a fighter on the way in and downed an Me 110 just off the coast. Good shooting by the chaps.'

'Good, very good. Anything else?' asked the IO.

Matt hesitated. He was dog tired, and to raise the issue of the searchlights would mean a lot more quizzing, but it was vital for the system to know.

'Well …' he started slowly. 'There was a problem when we were about three-quarters of an hour from the coast. It was completely black when suddenly there were searchlights everywhere, and then they all went out and my night vision was shot—guess it was for everyone. Then the fighter came in.'

'Do we have an accurate fix on where this occurred?' The IO looked at Charles.

'We were about fifty miles west of Cologne, just north of Maastricht,' he replied.

'Probably part of the Kammhuber Line,' he said, referring to the defensive line stretching from the German-Danish border to Switzerland. 'We know they have placed more searchlight emplacements in some areas. Well done, chaps. That's very helpful. We have had a couple of reports like this. Good to get a picture. Trot along home to bed then,' he said and laughed.

Just at that moment, he saw Stephen's flying suit. It was covered in blood and what looked distinctly like faeces.

'God, I am sorry, chaps,' said the IO hurriedly. 'Off you go now and clean up,' and he quickly tidied his desk, ready for the next crew.

Matt led the way to the crew room where they threw their masks and helmets into their lockers along with flying suits.

'Think you need a new one,' Matt said to Stephen as he was mechanically taking his kit off.

'Leave it on the floor,' said Matt, and he took his friend by the arm and propelled him to the mess, followed by the others.

Just as they were going in, W/C Squires pulled Matt aside. Matt's heart sank. 'Not again,' he prayed quietly.

'You chaps OK?' asked Squires.

'Not too good, to be honest, sir. Our replacement gunner bought it. The chaps are pretty well all in,' Matt replied.

'Sorry to hear that, Matt. Kite's a bit of a mess, I hear?' asked Squires.

How does he know all this stuff? wondered Matt, but he replied, 'Yes, sir. Needs some patching up. Oh, incidentally we think we bagged an Me110 and another fighter. Gunners did really well, sir.'

'Good show, Matt. I think we will stand you down for a few nights. Build your strength up. That mid-upper chap Townsend is reporting fit so you can have him back. What's your rear gunner like … Hughes is his name, isn't it?'

'Yes, sir. He's all in sir. He has done three trips on the trot. I think he needs a bit of a break, sir,' Matt replied, getting ready for a fight.

'OK, Matt, relax.' Squires smiled. 'I was thinking of putting him up for "mentioned in despatches," but maybe now he has shot one of the bastards down, I will recommend a DFM. What do you think?'

'I think he would appreciate that, sir. Can I tell him? It might cheer him up. Never seen him looking so gloomy as he was tonight.'

'Yes, tell him later today. Get yourself something to eat and then off to bed. You and your crew are released for now.' And with that, he walked off, leaving Matt feeling drained but at least a little happier at the prospect of not having to fly for a while and even, possibly, getting to see Anne.

When he got into the mess, he was concerned to see that only Charles was eating the regulation bacon and egg. Stephen looked dreadful and was staring at the cup of tea in front of him.

Charles asked the obvious question. 'Well, do we have to go again tonight?' Although his voice was steady, his eyes appeared to plead the answer they were all hoping for.

'No,' said Matt. 'We can stand down for at least forty-eight hours. Let's make the most of it.'

A hint of a smile went across Charles's mouth, but he said nothing and went on with his breakfast. Stephen just stood up and walked out, without speaking.

Matt went off to tell the news to the other three in their mess. Freddie's face appeared to relax slightly, and as he picked up his cup, he muttered, 'Thank Gawd for that.'

'Oh, and, Freddie, your mate Townsy is apparently fit enough to come back.'

'Bloody hell,' Freddie said and smiled. 'There is life after bleeding death!'

Back in the officers' mess, Matt sat down and drank some tea whilst his own breakfast arrived. He suddenly felt very hungry and looked forward to contacting Anne to tell her he was alive and that, if possible, they could spend at least one night together. It had been a bad trip and losing crew was always upsetting, but he was alive and at the moment that was all that mattered.

After breakfast, he went and showered and then went to the mess to telephone the hospital. As usual, he had to leave a message for Anne at the hospital lodge and then he went back to his room to sleep.

When he got there, he saw that Stephen was in bed with Scrap at his side and as far as he could tell was asleep. But just as he was getting into bed Stephen said, 'Thanks for getting us home, Matt. Sorry I was chucking up all the time. Feel better now.'

'OK, old boy. Get some sleep. You'll feel better then, and we can sink some beer when we surface. Hey, let's see if we can get the girls over tonight. What you say?'

'Sounds like an idea,' muttered Stephen, and before Matt knew it, he was asleep.

Matt pulled his bedclothes up, and in spite of snoring from both Stephen and the dog, he dropped off almost immediately.

CHAPTER 7

LEAVE

Matt woke up about two o'clock in the afternoon, but it seemed to be dark, and then he remembered that the blackout curtains were still closed. He peered through a gap to see that it was cloudy and from the droplets on the window, it had obviously been raining. Not a promising start to their leave, he thought.

Scrap had sat up as soon as Matt moved, and he jumped off the bed to stand with him. Matt leaned down and scratched his ears.

'Better go for a walk, old boy,' he whispered as he got dressed.

Stephen was still asleep, and Matt thought it better to leave him where he was, so Scrap and he quietly left the room.

Barker was in the corridor. 'Ah, Mr White, your young lady rang to ask after you. She says she would be free tonight along with a Miss Jesse Sanders. They could meet you outside the hospital at about eight o'clock.'

'Thank you, Barker. I'll leave a message to say we will be there, that is, if Pilot Officer Bamber ever wakes up!'

'Hear it was a bad do again last night, sir?' asked Barker. 'Four planes missing, I think it was.'

'Four, you say?' asked Matt. 'I better go and check with the ops room. Come on, Scrap.' With that, he hurried out of the building.

The usual WAAF was seated at the desk. 'Hallo, sir,' she chirped. 'Thought you were on leave. Wouldn't hang around here if I were you; the Old Man is on the prowl for crew.'

'Thanks, Betty, but I hear we lost four aircraft last night?'

'Well, certainly three,' she said. 'One crew almost certainly bailed out, and we think the fourth is in the drink, but we have heard nothing more.'

'Which were they?' asked Matt.

'S-Sugar and A-Apple are definite; C-Charlie bailed out; and L-London may have ditched.'

'Christ,' Matt said, and he gathered up Scrap and left the room. They walked along the perimeter road for about thirty minutes, Scrap rushing around and then stopping to smell almost anything that appeared interesting. Matt had picked up Scrap's ball as they left the bedroom, and he threw it for him to run after and fetch. It was about three o'clock by the time they got back to the mess, and Matt was beginning to feel hungry. *Nothing that a beer and a sandwich wouldn't put right*, he thought.

He rang the porters' lodge at the hospital and left a message for Anne to say that he and Stephen would meet them there at 8.00 p.m. and then wandered back to his room, calling in at the kitchen to pick up some lunch for Scrap.

Stephen sat up as they entered the room.

'God, the dead have arisen!' exclaimed Matt. 'How you feeling, old boy? Better for some sleep, I am sure?'

'Yes,' replied Stephen. 'A bit better. How's Scrap? Has he had something to eat?'

'Well, I have picked up some bits from the kitchen. Let me have his bowl, and that will get him started. Good news for tonight. Jess is free as well as Anne. We're to meet them at the front of the hospital eight o'clock tonight. How does that sound?'

'Not sure,' said Stephen hesitatingly. 'To be honest, Matt, I don't feel like meeting anyone just now. Really shaken up after last night. Poor bloody Charlie just blown away like that.'

'I know, Stephen, but it will be good for you—well good for us both really,' replied Matt. 'You know, you really fancied Jess when you first saw her. Be good to get out of this bloody place for a while.'

'Suppose so,' said Stephen slowly. 'But just a drink. No bloody dancing—all that noise and people.'

'It's a deal,' said Matt brightly. 'Come on, get dressed and let's go and have a beer in the mess. I've already left a message for the rest to meet us at the pub at five o'clock so we can have a few beers there and set off. What do you say?'

Stephen grinned. It was always hard to resist Matt, and in any case, he did fancy Jess and a night drinking with the girls would be a happy relief.

'Yes, OK, Matt,' he said as they left for the mess.

A few officers were already drinking beer when they entered, and the first to speak was Flying Officer Tony Judson, who was the pilot for B-Bertie.

'Hallo, chaps,' he called. 'Hear you had a rough run again last night. Four missing, we hear.'

Matt had decided not to tell Stephen, and he looked anxiously at his friend in case the news upset him. But he just shrugged his shoulders and moved over to the bar.

Actually, thought Matt, *that isn't really like Stephen at all*. He was always interested in what was going on, who had returned, and who had bought it. Still maybe it was a prospect of a good evening ahead. He took the glass Stephen gave him and downed a long, satisfying gulp.

'You chaps not flying tonight?' asked Matt.

'No, but three aircraft are off on gardening[5] trips and the Old Man was scratching around for crew. Keep your bloody head down, I say.' And with that, he drained his glass and walked out.

Matt and Stephen had another glass of beer, and then Matt suggested they move to the Red Lion to meet the others. Stephen, by this time, was visibly more relaxed and started to ask about the four missing crew. Matt filled him in as they walked over to their billet to pick up Scrap. They all got into Matt's car and made their way to the pub. They could already hear the din as they got out of the car. There was a chill in the air as they crossed to the pub, but the atmosphere inside was thick with cigarette smoke and felt warm and cosy. M-Mother's crew were up in the corner of the bar, and Matt was pleased to see that Townsend was standing there with them.

'See you've got your drinking mate back?' he said to Freddie.

'Bloody lucky to be here, ain't I?' Freddie muttered. 'I've had enough of this bloody flying. I want out.'

'Not that easy, old chap,' replied Matt. 'In any case, we are still alive and over halfway through the tour. Know what it's all about now, don't we?' Matt was concerned; Freddie was a professional moaner, but his mood could usually be lifted by a pint or two, especially with his pal Townsend back.

'Anyway, I am going to see handlebars tomorrow. Don't care if he makes me LMF.[6] I'll clean out the bloody bogs, but at least I'll be alive, won't I?'

---

[5] Mine-laying operations.
[6] Those refusing to fly were labelled 'Lack of Moral Fibre.'

'I don't think Wing Commander Squires will let you go. In any case, you will probably feel better tomorrow. A night off with Townsy here will set you up a treat.'

'Yeh, come on, Freddie. It will good to be all together again. Anyway, it wouldn't just be cleaning bogs and peeling spuds. They'd bust you down to LAC, and then how would you pay for the bloody women and beer? When do we go next, Skip?' asked Townsend.

'Well, we have got at least forty-eight-hour passes, which are worth forty-three hours now. So you better get drinking and enjoy yourselves. What do you say, Freddie?' Matt replied.

'I don't know. It ain't right sending me three nights running. Bloody Don as well. Not as if it's a bloody cakewalk, is it?' said Freddie.

'No, it's not that for sure, Freddie, but it's got to be done. If it's not us, it will be some other poor bugger,' said Matt.

'Well, let them go and do it.' Then he turned to Townsend. 'And it's your bloody round, mate. You've got a bit of bloody catching up to do. All that time in the bloody hospital ogling those nurses. You should be ashamed.' And with that, he turned to Matt and winked. 'See you in a couple of days then, Skip. Have a good leave.' He and Townsend wandered away to sit down in the one of the pub's corners.

'Well, what are you two going to do?' Matt asked as he turned to Don and Mac.

'Not sure, Skip. We are still trying to get the car going. If we manage, we might pop into Lincoln for a beer and see if we can find a dance.'

'Don, you OK?' asked Matt. 'After all, you had three trips in a row too.'

'Yeh, Skip. Feel better now I've had some sleep. Way I look at it is the more we do, the sooner we can finish the tour.

Couple of shaky dos though. Understand Freddie's point. Feels bloody dangerous sometimes!'

'Well, good luck with the car,' said Matt. 'See you in a couple of days. Let's have another pint before we push off.' And he went to the bar to give the order.

It was about seven o'clock by the time Stephen, Matt, and Scrap left the pub. It was a cold night for mid-September, and the air smelt sharper than usual, largely because they had just come out of the fug in the pub.

'A bit parky, Stephen,' he said as they got into the car. 'Better crank the engine. Not quite sure how good the battery is,' he said, and Stephen went to the front to give the starting handle a good turn. The engine fired eventually, and Stephen got in the front with Scrap on the back seat.

'How you feeling now, Stephen?' he asked.

'Better, thanks,' he replied. 'But if I had the choice, I wouldn't go again. I don't think I have ever felt so frightened. What about you, Matt? Aren't you ever frightened?'

'God, yes,' he replied. 'Maybe flying the bloody aircraft takes my mind off what's going on. You can't really think of much else flying those bloody things.' He laughed. 'But frightened, oh yes, no doubt. I'm sure we all are in our own ways. Probably not normal if you aren't scared some of the time. Best to talk about it, old boy. Get it off your chest.'

Matt steered the car through the narrow lanes, and eventually, they came to the hospital. It was just before eight, and whilst they waited, Stephen looked thoughtfully out of the windscreen, which was steadily steaming up now they had stopped.

'Penny for them,' said Matt.

'Just thinking, Matt. We all get on pretty well together, don't we? I mean, Freddie is always complaining about something, but generally we do all right. I hope we all make it through to the end. It would be a shame if someone gets knocked off on the way.'

'I agree,' said Matt, and he was just about to expand his answer when the hospital front door opened and Anne and Jess walked down the steps towards them.

'Anyway,' said Matt, 'let's make sure we have a good time with the girls. Anne and I are going to head off tomorrow, probably up to Buxton again, so let's see how things pan out.'

Matt and Stephen got out of the car to meet the girls.

Stephen and Jess kissed briefly, and Anne and Matt embraced.

'What are we going to do then?' Jess asked.

'Find somewhere to get a drink?' suggested Stephen rather lamely.

Anne gently pushed Matt away. 'There's a reasonable place about ten minutes from here. You know, Jess, the Dirty Duck.'

'You mean the White Swan, don't you?' Jess laughed.

'Matt and I can park the car in the hospital, and we will join you in a minute,' she said.

'OK, see you there. What do you want to drink?' asked Jess.

'G and T for me,' said Anne. 'And I am guessing a pint of best for him,' she added, pointing at Matt. And with that, Stephen and Jess, with Scrap at their heels, set off down the road.

Anne got in beside Matt. 'How long have we got?' she said, kissing him again.

'Have to be back by Thursday morning about eight o'clock,' he replied, starting the car and driving into the hospital.

'Well, I have that time off too,' Anne replied. 'Over there, park the car there; it will be fine.'

They got out of the car and started to walk. It was much colder now, and it was becoming increasingly misty. Their breath showed as large white clouds. Anne put her arm through Matt's as they walked along and snuggled up close to him.

'How has it been?' she asked.

'Not too good,' Matt replied. 'We had to do two trips back to back, and the first, we had to land away. The second, our mid-upper bought it.'

Matt felt Anne's grip tighten. 'Not Townsy?' she asked.

'No, he was still off sick, although he's back now. No, it was a chap called Charlie Faith. Nice chap. It's a shame. But the person I am really worried about is Stephen,' Matt continued.

'Oh, he seemed all right just now,' Anne replied.

'Well, twenty-four hours ago, I thought he was going to jump ship. I have never seen him like that. We had a talk this afternoon, and I agree he seems better, but he's not in good shape just now.'

'What do you think has happened?' Anne asked.

'Not sure. He said he was scared, but that applies to us all. I think I know what he means though. It sort of edges up on you. I think it's easier for me to cope with because I can't think of much else when I am flying. But it's different for the others. Maybe particularly Stephen—he's just got a load of gauges to look at. Anyway, don't say anything, will you?'

Anne looked at him as if to say, 'Do you really think I would?' and they walked along through the gloom of the blackout and the thickening mist.

'Nearly there now,' said Anne, and they reached an old pub from which could be heard the sound of laughter and loud voices.

'This place OK?' asked Matt.

'First class,' Anne replied. 'And if you haven't eaten, they have some good food too. Jess and I come down here quite often.'

'Oh, you do, do you?' Matt replied. 'With the docs from the hospital, no doubt. We obviously need to keep an eye on you!'

They opened the door, and a wall of sound came out. Jess and Stephen were in the corner, and they had the drinks already on the table. Matt noticed that Stephen and Jess were sitting close together and also what a really very attractive girl Jess was.

'Hallo, you two. Thanks for the drinks. Hey, it's freezing out there,' he said. 'Bloody foggy too.'

Matt and Anne sat down.

'Stephen, you could probably do with something to eat. Apparently, the girls come here with the doctors and get wined and dined! Have you girls eaten already?'

'We have,' replied Anne. 'But don't let us stop you. We will be happy to watch you and carry on drinking. What you reckon, Jess?'

'Sounds OK to me. In fact, I am ready for another already. Matt, I think it's your round.' She laughed.

'Anything for you, Jess. Stephen, I'll go and see what's to eat and report back.' With that, he worked his way to the crush at the bar.

He eventually got back to the table with a tray of drinks. 'Hotpot has been ordered, sir,' and he bowed to Stephen. 'Will there be anything else sir would desire?' Matt asked but sat down before Stephen could reply. 'Do we have any plans for tonight?' he asked. 'After we've eaten, of course. What do you girls fancy doing?'

Jess replied, 'Well, there's a dance on at the Pally, but we would need to drive there and if it's a real pea-souper out there, maybe that's not such a good idea. I was wondering if you wanted to come back to my place. My flatmate is away for a couple of weeks so there is a spare room. We could take a couple bottles of beer and go home. It's an easy walk from here.'

'What do you think, Anne?' Matt asked. 'We wanted to make an early start if poss, didn't we? It would be better to start from here than me drive from the airfield—even if I can.'

'It sounds a lovely idea, darling,' Anne replied, winking as she put her hand on Matt's arm.

'What about you, Stephen? Would that be OK with you?'

'Wizard, old chap!' he replied. 'I say, where's this food? I am famished.'

Just at that moment, two dishes of hotpot arrived, and Scrap's ears pricked up at the prospect of something to eat. The two airmen attacked the food as if they had never seen any before, but about halfway through the meal, Matt noticed that Stephen was beginning to pick at his food. 'You OK, old chap?' he asked.

'Yes, fine, thanks. Maybe not as hungry as I thought I was. Scrap will help me out, won't you, old chap?'

'But you haven't had a proper meal for nearly two days,' Matt remarked.

'Look, I am fine. I just don't feel that hungry anymore, and that's the end of it,' Stephen snapped back.

'OK, old chap, no need to go off the deep end,' Matt replied and glanced over to Anne, who gave an almost indiscernible shake of her head. 'Anyway, I thought it was very nice. Now does anyone want a further drink, or shall I just get some bottles for us?'

'Just some bottles, Matt. That would be lovely,' Jess said gently. 'And then maybe we should go. What do we think?'

Both Anne and Stephen nodded in agreement, and after a short while, Matt returned with a bottle in each hand.

Jess said, 'Anne and I are just going to powder our noses. We will be back in a few minutes,' and with that, they headed off to the toilets to join what looked like a fairly long queue.

'You really all right, Stephen?' Matt asked once they were out of earshot.

'Yes, sorry, Matt. I just feel a bit on edge, that's all. Hey, incidentally, how do you think tonight might work out?'

'What do you mean?' asked Matt.

'Well, you know … sleeping arrangements, that sort of thing.'

'Oh, that.' Matt smiled. 'Well, I will be sleeping with Anne and that leaves you, Jess, and Scrap. Make your choice, old boy.'

'Matt …' Stephen started hesitatingly. 'I actually haven't done this sort of thing before. For instance …' he continued, 'do you have any of those johnny things everyone talks about?'

'Well, as it happens, I do,' replied Matt. 'Would you like a couple?'

'Gosh yes. Thanks ever so much. She's a lovely girl, isn't she?' Stephen continued.

'She certainly is. And she has obviously taken a shine to you, old boy, although can't understand why.'

'No, me neither,' replied Stephen seriously. 'No one ever has, you know. I'm not really very good at this sort of thing.'

'Well, you seem to be doing all right just now, don't you? Plenty of chaps in here would be happy to take your place. Here they come now. Come on, Scrap, look sharp.'

They worked their way through the packed pub to the door, and when they got out, they realised just how cold it had become. Matt and Stephen both had their greatcoats, but the girls' coats were not that heavy, and they wrapped the greatcoats around them to keep warm. The fog was very thick now, and with the blackout, it was really quite difficult to find their way. Matt reckoned visibility was no greater than about fifty yards. The thick air grabbed at their throats, and the fog blanketed sounds around them.

After about fifteen minutes, Jess led them up a small front garden path and opened the door of a terraced house.

'This is it. Not much, but it is home,' she said. 'Let me draw the curtains, and then we can put on the lights.'

The door opened directly into the front room, which seemed very small with them all standing in there. A door opposite led into a room with a dining table and four rather weary-looking chairs. A small alleyway led from this room to the scullery, and stairs went up to the floor above.

It was cold, and Jess said, 'Stephen, there is some wood and paper by the fireplace. Could you make up the fire? It will soon warm up once that's going. Make yourself comfy, everyone. I will put the kettle on for some tea.' And with that, she went through into the diminutive scullery followed by Anne.

'Can I give you a hand, Jess?' Anne asked.

'Yes,' she replied. 'Thanks. Anne, do you and Matt want to sleep together tonight? You are very welcome to my bed. Cathy's is only a single.'

'Yes, we do, and don't worry,' Anne replied. 'We can squeeze in almost anywhere. Anyway, it will help to keep us warm.' She smiled. 'What about you and Stephen then?' Anne winked at Jess, who, she was a bit surprised to see, blushed.

'Well, we will see, won't we?' She laughed. 'Now you get those cups out. There's some milk in the larder.'

Matt, in the meantime, had opened the beer and was intrigued to see how efficiently Stephen set about getting the fire going. 'You've done that before,' he said and smiled.

'Boy Scouts,' replied Stephen. 'Got quite so good at rubbing two sticks together.' He laughed.

The friends started on the beer as the fire began blazing away, and Anne and Jess came in with a tray of cups, a teapot, and some pieces of cake Jess's mum had made a few days ago.

'Very cosy,' said Anne as she sat down next to Matt, who had bagged the sofa.

The room was quickly warming up, and Stephen and Matt took off their jackets. The girls had kept their coats on whilst making the tea, and now they, too, felt warm enough to do without them.

'This is nice,' said Stephen. 'Well, what are you two going to do tomorrow?'

Matt replied, 'It depends very much on the weather really, doesn't it, darling?' he asked Anne. 'We had thought of driving up to the Peaks again, but with this fog, it's really a nonstarter. And in any case, we have to get back day after tomorrow. Maybe we will just look around locally for a pub we can stay in. It's just lovely to have a few hours together, isn't it, Anne?'

'It certainly is, darling. Jess was asking if we would like to stay here tonight. What do you say?'

'I would say that would be a wonderful idea. Thanks very much, Jess. We won't be any trouble, promise.' Matt laughed.

'It might be an idea to light the fire in your room,' Jess said. 'In fact, my room too. Are you up to that, Stephen?' she asked.

'Your word is my command.' Stephen stood up to attention. 'No sooner said than done.' With that, he ran up the stairs, followed by Jess with a bucket of wood.

Anne snuggled into Matt. 'Shall we go to bed soon?' she whispered.

'Yes, I think we should. It's always so good to feel you close up,' Matt said, and they kissed again.

Stephen came back into the room. 'Oh sorry,' he said. 'Didn't mean to interrupt.'

'Don't worry, Stephen,' Anne said. 'We are just on our way upstairs.' With that, Matt and she headed for the staircase, and they stood aside as Jess came back down.

'You two off then?' she asked. 'Toilet is between the rooms, and there is a washbasin in a tiny bathroom next to it. No hot water just yet, but there should be by morning. Sleep tight. Goodnight both.'

'Goodnight, Jess' they said, almost in unison. 'We may slip out fairly early if it looks a bit better in the morning.'

'OK,' Jess replied. 'Close the door quietly.' She smiled.

Matt and Anne went into the back bedroom. It was pretty small, and the fire in the grate made it feel very snug. 'Must just go for a pee unless you want to go first?' asked Matt.

'No, off you go. I'll go after,' and with that, Matt disappeared down the corridor. Anne looked around. It was a very small bed, but she was sure they would manage. She moved closer to the fire and warmed her hands. If only she and Matt could have more time together. *Bloody war*, she thought. In another world, they would be married by now and thinking about kids, and she smiled at the idea.

Matt came back in. 'Your turn,' he said and moved over to the fire, which was now crackling as the wood caught fire.

After Anne had gone out, Matt got undressed and jumped into bed. *Have to be a bit careful here*, he thought. *Not much manoeuvring room.*

Anne came back, and Matt got out of bed again to hold her. 'Best get undressed really quickly and into bed.' He laughed.

Anne took off her dress but left her slip on. She slipped out of her pants and bra and dived into bed.

Matt followed, and they held one another tightly, kissed, and then made love.

***

After Jess had come back downstairs, she sat next to Stephen on the sofa. They finished their tea and then kissed, gently at first but then passionately. Stephen eased away from Jess slightly. 'Gosh, Jess, that was nice.'

'Why don't we go upstairs?' Jess said quietly.

Stephen looked uneasy.

'It will be all right,' Jess said. 'And it's much more comfortable.'

'I would love to, Jess. I'm afraid I haven't done this sort of thing before.'

'Well, now's the time then.' Jess smiled, took him by the hand, and led him to the stairs. 'If you need a wee, it's in there.' She pointed to the toilet door. 'We will be in here.' She indicated the door to the front bedroom.

When he went into the bedroom, Jess was already undressed and wearing a green satin nightdress, which, against her red hair, made her look even more beautiful. He took off his clothes and got into the bed. They kissed deeply for a while, and then Stephen could feel Jess guiding him into to her. It was one of the most delicious things he had ever felt, and he came very quickly. Jess kept stroking him, and after a while, he became hard again. She moved on top of him and eased him into her, and this time, he managed to last a bit longer.

'Christ, Jess,' Stephen whispered. 'I've never felt anything as good as that.'

'Well, we will just have to see, won't we?' she whispered back and then cuddled down onto his chest. In a few minutes,

Stephen could tell she was asleep. He suddenly felt very tired too and dozed off.

Stephen woke, still feeling Jess alongside him. He needed a pee, and he eased himself out from the bed and padded down to the toilet. In many ways, he could not believe what had been happening. He remembered Scrap and went downstairs. The dog was curled up in front of what was left of the fire, but he lifted his head as Stephen came towards him.

'Hallo, old boy,' Stephen said quietly. 'You OK?' He rubbed Scrap's ears.

'Come on, let's see what it's like outside. Maybe you want a pee too.' Stephen took the dog out to the front door. The fog had lifted, but it was now raining and there was quite a wind blowing. It still felt cold, but nothing like last night. Stephen looked at his watch. He could hardly believe it was six o'clock and just beginning to get light through the gloom of the rain.

Scrap did the business and came back indoors, hopeful, Stephen thought, that there might be something to eat.

'Not yet, old boy. Go back to sleep. Be down soon.' Stephen went back upstairs and got back into bed beside Jess, who appeared not to have moved an inch since he got up. Her hair had fallen over her face, and Stephen brushed it gently aside. Jess smiled and pulled him closer to her.

'Morning, tiger. What's it like out there?'

'Not very good, really,' Stephen said. 'In fact, Jess, it is definitely better in here. In fact, a lot better in here.' And he bent over to kiss her. She slipped away. 'Back in a minute,' she said and ran out of the bedroom and to the toilet.

When she came back, she got straight into bed. 'Now where were we?'

'I was just telling you about how it looked out there,' Stephen replied.

'Well, let's not worry ourselves about that, shall we?' Jess smiled and pulled him down to her.

They made love several times in the morning, unknown territory to Stephen. About midday, he suggested they got up and found something to eat.

'Typical bloke,' Jess said and laughed. 'Always thinking of their tummies after they've made love.'

'Don't see the problem myself,' quipped Stephen. 'Let's go out hunting.'

With that, he got out of bed and dressed. As he came down the stairs, Scrap stood up and shook himself. 'OK, Scrap, food is next on the agenda.'

He looked around and realised that Matt's and Anne's coats had gone, but there was no note to say where they had gone or if they would be back. Jess joined him in the front room. Stephen thought she still looked lovely. She had her hair swept back into a ponytail.

'Right then, Pilot Officer Bamber, take me out for something to eat. Scrap's looking pretty hungry too.'

'It's not very nice out there, Jess. Do you have an umbrella?'

'Certainly do. It's just below the staircase. Lead on, Officer Bamber.'

They both laughed. They left the house and turned down the road. 'There's another reasonable pub down here,' Jess said. 'Quite good food, not far.'

The rain was slanting down, driven along by a strong wind. It really was thoroughly unpleasant weather, but as far as Stephen was concerned, it could be blowing a hurricane and he would not have cared less. He hadn't felt so good as this for weeks.

They reached The Bell in about fifteen minutes but in that short time had managed to get absolutely soaked. They burst through the door and into a deliciously warm, slightly smoky bar. It was market day, and several farmers were already lined up along the bar. Jess and Stephen found a table in one corner, and Stephen asked what she would like.

'I will have a pint of beer, Stephen, thank you. Oh, and a sandwich of some sort—anything will do. I'm famished. It's all your fault.' She smiled at him.

Stephen went over to the bar, and a couple of the farmers moved aside.

'You come in here, young man,' one of them said. 'You got a couple of days off?' he asked.

'Yes,' said Stephen. 'Good to have my feet on the ground for a while.'

'You chaps are doing a grand job,' said the farmer, a rosy-faced man of about fifty. 'Here, let me get these for you—least I can do. What will it be?'

'Oh no, it's OK,' replied Stephen. 'I am here with my girlfriend.' He blushed slightly.

'Well, good for you. Let me buy her one too. Be a pleasure.'

'Well, thanks very much,' Stephen replied. 'A couple of pints of beer would be very nice, thank you.'

'Young man, it's us that should be thanking you. You young chaps going off night after bloody night. Bloody Germans.' And much to Stephen's surprise, he spat onto the sawdust on the floor. 'Bloody deserve to get smashed up, so they do.'

There was a murmur of approval from the others as the barman pulled two pints.

'There we are, sir. Two pints of the best,' he said. 'Is there anything else?'

'Well, do you have some bread and cheese or something like that?' Stephen asked.

'We do, sir. Bread was baked this morning by my good wife, and the cheese has been provided by Fred here, one of our local farmers. Would that do, sir?'

'It would,' said Stephen.

'I'll bring it right over, sir. In just a few minutes.'

Stephen walked back to Jess carrying the beer.

'Oh, that looks good,' she said and drank down nearly half the glass.

'Coo,' said Stephen. 'You needed that, didn't you?'

'I certainly did, and I might need another soon,' she replied.

'Well, that nice man at the bar bought these for us. Said he thought the RAF was doing a good job. Wish I agreed.'

'Don't you, Stephen?' Jess asked.

'No, I don't. We fly over there night after night to targets we can't see for reasons we don't know. Lots of chaps get shot down and … Actually, Jess, I don't want to talk about it. Can we talk about one another instead?'

'Of course,' Jess replied, sensing that Stephen had suddenly got tense again. He was looking anxious. 'Well, what about you, Stephen? Where did you spring from?'

Her question made Stephen laugh. He loved the way she put things so directly. No beating about the bush with Jess.

'Well, I left school in Leeds and joined the RAFVR at eighteen, and first of all, I trained as ground crew, maintaining aircraft at Scampton and Mildenhall. I thought that I would like to fly, and so I applied for aircrew after about twelve months and went through the usual training. I was acting pilot officer for a while, then went to a place called Wellesbourne near Stratford on Avon. Nice little place. Matt and I met there, and we have been together ever since.'

'Yes, but what about your mum and dad. Have you got brothers and sisters?' Jess persisted.

'Well, as I said, my parents live just outside Leeds. My dad runs a farm there. Eh, it's not that big,' he said, slipping into his Yorkshire twang. 'But it does for us. Been in the family for a couple o' hundred years. One of my brothers helps Dad out. He's only sixteen but wants to join up too, but Dad needs him there. We'll see.'

'And your mum, what's she like?'

'She's great, my mum. Miss her a lot really. Haven't seen her for nearly six months now. I should be due a decent piece of leave soon. I'll get up to see her then—well, the whole family. Hey, Jess, she would love to see you. She's always saying I need looking after. What you say? Would you come up with me?'

Just at that moment, the barman arrived with the bread and cheese. 'Now anything else?' he asked.

'Another couple of pints would do well, thanks,' replied Stephen.

'Right-oh. Let us know if there is anything else, young man.'

'Well, would you come, Jess? It would mean a lot to us all—me especially.'

Jess looked a bit doubtful. 'Stephen, we've only just started seeing one another. Are you sure want to do this just now? I mean, I would love to go with you. Never seen Yorkshire—heard a lot of bad things about it …' She laughed as she broke up the bread. 'Hey, this looks great, doesn't it?' And with that, she tucked into the bread and cheese along with liberal helpings of pickle.

'I would like to, Jess, really would. Anyway, what about you? How long have you been nursing?'

'Ever since the war started, Stephen, so about four years now, I suppose,' Jess started. 'I left school here in Lincoln when I was seventeen years old. Bummed about a bit, then decided on a nursing career. That's about it really.'

'No one else, then?' asked Stephen.

She hesitated. 'Well, there was a fighter pilot. We got to know one another very well. Well, we loved one another very much, I suppose. He was based Martlesham Green. Flew with Bader, all that sort of stuff, but he got shot down October 1940—his parachute didn't open.'

She paused and looked away from Stephen.

'I'm sorry, Jess. Let's change the subject. What shall we do for the rest of the day?'

'Well, I know what I would like to do.' She smiled at him.

'And that is?' He smiled back. 'Would it be the same as what I would like to do, do you think?'

'I suspect so, Stephen. Let's finish this, walk Scrap, and then go home—to bed.'

***

Matt and Anne had woken up at about seven o'clock. They kissed and made love, and then both got up, dressed, and went downstairs. Matt went first and put the kettle on, and a few minutes later, Anne joined him.

'Any sign of Jess or Stephen?' he asked.

'I think they are busy getting to know one another a little better.' Anne smiled.

'I am really glad,' said Matt. 'Stephen needs someone to take him out of himself. He really was so ropey the other night. I wondered if he was going to be able to carry on, you know?'

'Well, hopefully, he will feel a bit better after tonight. What shall we do, darling?' she asked.

'Let's walk back to the hospital to get the car. We can see what the weather looks like and then decide,' he replied as they got their coats on.

It was still raining, and there was a cold easterly wind blowing. The fog had gone, but it looked very dreary. Nearly all the leaves had gone from the trees, and everything looked rather grey in the early morning light. They hurried back to the hospital and then realised they had had no breakfast.

'Let's pop into the canteen,' Anne said. 'It's only eight thirty, and they serve food until nine.'

Anne led the way through the long hospital corridor, answering to the greetings from other nurses as they went off to work. The canteen was almost empty, and Anne went straight to the counter.

'Hallo, Millie,' she said to the girl who was serving. 'Are we too late for something to eat?'

'Bless you, Sister Anne,' she replied. 'Always got something for you. Is this your young man?'

'It is. What do you think?' She laughed.

'Looks OK to me,' Millie replied and winked. 'Now what can I get you?'

'Well, we wondered about some breakfast. Any bacon to spare and maybe an egg? Couple of cups of tea as well would be perfect.'

'I will see what I can do,' replied Millie. 'I'll bring it over. Don't you worry.' And with this, she went off to the kitchen.

'Looks OK, Matt. I don't think we will starve.' Anne smiled, and she put her hand across the table to take his. 'What do you think it would be best to do today then, Pilot Officer White?'

'Well, Sister Johnson, I think we should find a nice little hotel around here and spend as much time as we can together—close together.' He smiled.

'That sounds very acceptable,' she replied and took her hand away as Millie brought the tea and two plates of bacon and egg and toast.

'Hallo, sir,' Millie said. 'Good to see you.'

Matt stood up. 'Good to meet you too,' he replied. 'Thank you for bringing us the food. It looks great.' And he sat down again.

Matt suddenly felt extremely hungry, and he tucked into his food. Making love to Anne always made him hungry, and in any case, he hadn't eaten much in the last few days. Anne ate more slowly but still with enthusiasm.

'Gosh, this is jolly good,' Matt said, taking a sip of his tea. 'I was famished. Great idea of yours to come in here.'

Anne smiled and finished eating. 'Well, darling, I do get some things right.'

'Oh, you get loads of things right—very right.' Matt smiled.

By the time they had finished, it was nearly ten o'clock and they went out to find Matt's car.

'It would be nice to be a little way outside Lincoln, don't you think?' Matt asked. 'Any ideas?'

'What about Market Rasen? That's a quaint little place and really close. I am sure we could find somewhere there.'

'Done,' said Matt. 'Let's go and have a look.'

Anne got into the car while Matt cranked the starting handle. He was relieved that the car started almost at once, and they set off out of Lincoln and down the A46.

The road was busy, but they got to Market Rasen about one o'clock and found the Gordon Arms overlooking the marketplace. Matt went in to ask if they had a room, and the bartender said he thought they had but he would need to ask the boss. Almost immediately, a jovial-looking man came round the side of the bar.

'RAF? We always have room for you chaps.' He smiled.

'Well, it's for me and my girl, if that's all right,' Matt said, slightly embarrassed.

'Even better, young man,' the publican said. 'Bring her in and let us see her then,' and he patted Matt on the back.

'Well, thank you, that's very good,' said Matt. 'I'll have a pint of your best and a gin and tonic for Anne.' And with that, Matt went out to get Anne.

'It's very nice in there, darling. I think we will be OK. Oh, and I have ordered us a drink.'

'Lovely, darling,' she replied.

Matt picked up their bag, and they went into the inn.

'I've got your drinks, but let me show you to your room. I hope it will be all right for you both.' He led them up the stairs to the back bedroom. Matt and Anne went in, noticing a small room with a double bed and washbasin.

'The toilet and bathroom are down the corridor,' said the publican. 'Will it do?' he asked.

Matt and Anne looked at one another.

'Yes, it's fine. Thank you.' Matt replied.

'Very good,' said the publican. 'No doubt we will see you downstairs shortly. Would you care for some lunch? We don't have much choice, but we have some ham, cheese, and freshly made bread.'

'That will be great. Thank you,' said Matt. 'We will be down in a few minutes.'

The publican left, closing the door quietly behind him.

'Do you really think it is all right?' he asked Anne.

'Matt, any time and any place is all I ask. It will do just fine.' She kissed him gently. 'Well done for finding it. Let's go and eat. Now I'm hungry!'

They went downstairs to find a small bar with some tables scattered around. Some of the locals were already tucking into pieces of cheese and bread and drinking their beer. Matt and Anne found an empty table and sat down with their drinks.

The conversation in the bar had stopped when they came down, and Matt felt a bit self-conscious.

One of the farmers drinking in the bar called across to them, 'What you flying, young man?'

'Lancs, sir,' replied Matt.

'Well, God bless you,' he replied.

With that, the conversation started up again as the farmer walked across to them. Matt stood up as he approached, but the man waved him to sit down. 'It is us who should stand for you, young man,' he said. 'I am called Mike, but what's your name?'

'Pilot Officer Matt White, sir,' Matt replied. 'This is Anne, whom I hope to marry very soon.'

Anne looked up and smiled. 'That's our plan, Mike.'

'Well, let's hope it will be soon. You look a very happy couple.'

'This young couple will be getting married soon,' Mike said to the others in the bar. 'Let's wish them the very best.'

They all cheered and raised their glasses.

'Thank you,' said Matt and sat down, blushing deeply.

The publican came over. 'Well, my congratulations too,' he said. 'Now what would you like to eat?'

'Bread and cheese would be wonderful,' said Anne.

'That's it then. Won't be a minute.'

As he walked away, Anne said, 'Well, when will it be then?'

'Let's make it soon, Anne. Could we go and see your parents on my next bit of leave, do you think?'

'Well, my mum and dad are around most of the time. Dad is a GP so he is pretty busy, but they would love to see you in any case. Worcester shouldn't be too difficult to get to when you next get a break. But in the meantime, Pilot Officer White, I would like to take you upstairs!' Anne laughed.

***

When Jess and Stephen finally woke up, it was late afternoon.

'Better go and see how Scrap is,' said Stephen as he got out of bed.

'Huh,' grunted Jess, 'turned down in favour of a dog. I am obviously losing my touch.' She laughed as she reached up to pull Stephen down to her for a kiss.

Downstairs, Scrap was looking a bit anxious. He rushed to the back door as Stephen opened it. He tore off into the undergrowth, which represented the garden, and returned a short while later, looking rather more comfortable.

Jess had by this time come downstairs in her nightgown. She had put the kettle on for some tea. Stephen moved over towards her and put his arms around her. 'I think I love you,' he whispered in her ear. 'How about a pint and something to eat?'

'God, you really know how to give a woman a good time, don't you?'

They kissed.

Scrap let out a series of growls, and they both laughed. 'I think Scrap could do with something too.' Jess laughed as she made the tea.

'Where shall we go?' asked Stephen. 'At least it's stopped raining.'

'What about where we were last night?' asked Jess. 'The food is pretty good there considering.'

'Done,' replied Stephen. 'Can we walk Scrap anywhere before? He needs a bit of a run.'

'There's the park just off the end of our road, and we should manage to find our way over to the pub even in the dark. It will only take about thirty minutes, but that should be enough, shouldn't it?'

'Jolly well will,' replied Stephen as he drank his tea. 'Wonder where Matt and Anne got to?'

'Out of town, I'll be bound,' replied Jess. 'And probably not back until tomorrow, so we have still some time to ourselves … Well, and Scrap.' She laughed. 'I'll go up and get dressed, and then when you are ready, we can go.' With that, she spun herself round and ran upstairs.

Stephen and Scrap looked at one another, and Scrap wandered over to where Stephen was sitting. 'Hallo, old boy,' Stephen said, rubbing Scrap's ears. 'Soon go out and get some food.' Scrap looked up at him with his dark-brown eyes, and Stephen suddenly felt very sad and very vulnerable. 'It's OK, old boy. You and me will be together for a long time. Don't you worry.' He bent over and hugged the dog, feeling tears come to his eyes.

'Who you talking to?' asked Jess as she came through the door.

Stephen turned away. 'Oh, just the dog.' He got up quickly. 'I'll go and get my things on too,' he said briskly and went upstairs.

As he passed Jess, she noticed that his cheek was wet, and she looked on after him. 'Are you all right, Stephen?' she asked.

She was starting to go back up the stairs when he shouted down, 'Yes, of course I am. Why do you ask?'

'Nothing,' she replied, and she too went over to give Scrap a stroke.

Stephen came down quickly, and after getting on their coats, they went outside. It was less cold than last night, but the sharp easterly wind was still blowing. They crossed the road in the gathering gloom with Scrap at their heels and went into the park. The railings had all been taken away so it was impossible to see where the park started and finished. The trees were virtually bare, and any remaining leaves were being blown off by the wind.

'If we go over this way,' said Jess, 'we can cross the park to the pub.' She linked her arm through Stephen's as they walked along the path. Scrap was being his usual self, racing around in seemingly meaningless circles.

'Well, Scrap is in his element,' said Stephen.

'What about his master?' asked Jess, squeezing his arm.

'Yes, wizard,' said Stephen. 'Never been happier. Looking forward to my beer and grub.' He ducked as Jess swung a playful punch at him with her other arm.

They walked on in silence, dodging round the puddles, which still remained after the night's rain.

'What were you discussing with Scrap?' Jess asked. 'Surely not about the pub?'

Stephen paused. 'No. It's just sometimes when he looks at me with those trusting eyes, I feel very sad. He seems to be asking for reassurance that I will be there for him all the time. And then I think of how I actually got him, and I find that very difficult. Do you understand, Jess?'

'Yes, I do. But it will be all right, you know. You will be there for him, and after the war is over, you and he can settle somewhere and have long walks and as much food as he can eat. It will be OK, I know.' As she turned to kiss him, she saw again that he had tears in his eyes.

They kissed gently, and she could taste the salt from his tears. She felt him trying to fight back his sadness.

'Come on, sweetheart,' she murmured in his ear. 'It will be all right, you know.'

Gradually, she sensed Stephen relaxing, and he moved away from her to dab his eyes. 'Whatever must you think of me?' he asked.

'I think you are a very brave man,' she replied, 'and everything will be fine—even better after you've had something to eat!' She laughed as they carried on walking, Scrap following along behind them.

The pub was already crowded when they went in, but they found a space in the corner and Scrap settled down under the table.

The barman seemed to recognise Stephen. 'Hallo, sir, what's it to be?'

'Couple of pints please,' replied Stephen. 'I suppose you don't have any of that cottage pie, do you? It was very good.'

'Well, it's shepherd's pie tonight.'

'Two of those would do very nicely, thanks,' replied Stephen. 'How much is all that?'

'Two shillings and sixpence, sir. I'll bring it over to you.'

Stephen grabbed the two pints and shimmied his way over to Jess and the ever-hopeful Scrap.

'Grub's on its way,' he said and took a long gulp at his beer.

He sat down and took Jess's hand. 'Thanks for this time. It means a lot, you know?'

'Well, I'm having a good time too, you know. And we can meet up again when you are next off. Do you have to be back tonight, Stephen?'

'Should be really. If I knew Matt was around, I could get a lift. Do you know if there are any buses around early? I mean, I should be back by six by rights, although I can swing it until eight, I am sure. How did you and Anne get out that night when we first met?'

'Yes, we came on a bus that seemed to take forever, and I can't think there will be anything really early.'

'We will go down to the bus garage after this and see what's on. Of course, I would like to stay overnight.' He squeezed her hand. 'What do you reckon, Scrap? Shall we try a bus ride?'

Scrap turned his brown eyes upward, less concerned about going home than if food was on its way.

As if on cue, the pies arrived, and they started eating with Scrap receiving a fairly steady stream of food from both Stephen and Jess.

They had another beer and then set off to the bus station. It was clear that there were no buses out towards East Kirkby until 9.00 a.m. and it arrived about 10.30. There was, however, a bus that evening at 8.30, and Stephen realised he would have to be on it.

They made their way back to Jess's house in silence. Jess had noticed an almost immediate change in Stephen, and she sensed it was best to keep quiet. When they got into the house, she said, 'Cup of tea, Stephen?'

'Yes, thanks, Jess,' he replied. 'Jess, I am really sorry about tonight. I would have loved to have stayed.' He took her in his arms, and they kissed. 'We will do this again, won't we?' he asked.

'Of course, Stephen,' she replied. 'Whenever you are next on leave. Maybe if you have a bit longer, we can go away for a day or two. In the meantime, we still have an hour to waste. What shall we do?'

'I thought we were having a cup of tea.' Stephen smiled, and clutching their steaming cups, they went upstairs.

They made love slowly and gently and lay together, Jess's long red hair lying on Stephen's chest. He stroked her hair and listened to her breathing, trying not to imagine what would be going on twenty-four hours from now.

Jess stirred, opened her eyes, and watched him. 'What you thinking?' she whispered.

'Oh, just about a world very different from this one,' Stephen replied. He leaned down and kissed her. 'I have to be going, sweetheart,' he said, and quite suddenly, his eyes filled with tears. He rolled away from Jess. 'I better get going,' he said and swung his legs over the side of the bed. He leaned back, kissed Jess again, and then abruptly stood up and started to get dressed.

'I'll come down to the bus station with you,' Jess said and also began to get dressed. They both went downstairs, but Stephen stopped as she got her coat. 'Jess, I think I would rather say goodbye here. I'm not sure how well I could take it out in the open. In any case, it's really cold out tonight and you should stay here in the warm. When can I ring you? Is there any way I can get you at the hospital? I could ring tomorrow morning before we have our briefing. After then, as you know, we can't call until we get back.'

'Call me first thing,' Jess said. 'I will be in by seven. Ring the lodge like Matt does. I want to hear your voice.' Jess felt herself getting close to crying.

'Go on then away with you,' she said, trying to keep light-hearted. They kissed at the door, and then Stephen was gone, with Scrap trotting along behind him. Jess noticed he didn't look back, and as he disappeared round the corner, she felt a familiar cold sensation in the pit of her stomach.

***

After Matt and Stephen had left them in the pub, Freddie and Townsy had made their way back to the mess and had managed to sink quite a few beers by the time Freddie remarked that it was really time to get some grub.

'What yer fancy to eat then, me old mate?' asked Freddie.

'Let's go and see what they've rustled up for dinner. Then we may as well go back to the boozer. What yer reckon?' asked Townsy.

'Yep, sounds like a plan,' replied Freddie, and they wandered into the canteen.

Mac and Don were already there, tucking into their bangers and mash.

'Hi ya, guys,' Mac called as they came in, and Freddie and Townsy walked over to their table.

'How's it going, guys? Thought you would be back in the pub by now.'

'Well, we're sort of on our way there,' replied Townsy. 'We thought we should stock up with some grub first. What you two been up to? Looks like the car to me.' He saw their hands still bore evidence of grease and grime.

'Well,' said Don. 'We have got her going at last. Few more bits and pieces and we're there. How about coming out for a spin tomorrow? Should be ready by then.'

Freddie and Townsy looked at one another, and Freddie nodded. 'Thanks! That sounds OK. When d'you reckon? Not too bloody early, mind!'

They laughed, and Don said, 'We should be ready by dinner, we think. That's not too early, is it?'

'No, but we were thinking about going down the old Montana tomorrow night for the dance. Maybe we can all go in your car?' Freddie exclaimed.

'Sounds OK to me,' said Mac, scraping the remains of his mash potato up with his fork. 'What you think, Don?'

'Gets my vote, but you and I can have a drive around in the afternoon,' he said.

Freddie and Townsy were well into their food by this time, and as Don and Mac got up from the table, Freddie said, 'OK, see you about dinnertime tomorrow then?'

'Cor, that's a bit of luck,' he said to Townsy after they had gone. 'I was wondering how we were going get to town tomorrow night. Bloody lift home an' all. That's worked really lovely, Townsy me old mate.' And with that, they both finished eating and lit up. Freddie took a deep drag at his cigarette. 'Bloody wonderful,' he remarked, leaning back on his chair. 'Nothing quite like a few beers, bit of grub, a fag, and then back down the boozer. What d'you think, Townsy?'

'Yer not bad. Few birds would finish it off, wouldn't it?' he replied. 'There was good crumpet in the hospital, you know. Was quite sorry when they told me I was well enough to go. There was a little blonde in there. Gawd, you should have seen her tits; they was something else.' He took a contemplative drag on his cigarette.

'Yer well,' replied Freddie, 'another bloody inch higher with that Kraut bullet and you wouldn't need to worry about crumpet no more, would you?' He laughed so much he started coughing. 'Bloody hell,' he said. 'Don't know what they put in these bloody fags these days. Come on, Townsy, we are wasting good boozing time sitting here. Let's get down the pub.'

They both stood up, picked up their coats, and made their way down to the guardhouse to check out.

'Hallo, Corp,' Townsy said. 'Two for the pub. We'll bring you back a bag of crisps.'

'You bloody say that every time, Sarg, and you never bring us a thing. Not even the smell of the barmaid's apron!' the corporal replied.

'Steady on, old son. You'll get yourself all excited. You're best up here out of harm's way,' replied Freddie. 'See you later,' and they both wandered out into the darkness and down to the Red Lion.

***

The early afternoon was cold and dull with a brisk easterly wind blowing over the airfield as Freddie and Townsy waited outside the NCOs' mess for Don and Mac. They heard the car before they saw it, a black Morris 8, which seemed to be discharging quite a lot of blue smoke from the exhaust.

''Ere we go,' muttered Freddie as the car came round the corner of the mess. 'Blimy, doesn't look too promising to me,' he continued to Townsy.

'Well, it's going,' remarked Townsy, but he too wondered what they were in for.

'Sorry we're a bit late,' called Don through the window. 'Bit of difficulty starting her, but she's fine now. Jump in, and we're on our way.'

Slightly reluctantly, Freddie and Townsy climbed aboard.

'Where to then?' asked Freddie.

'Thought you wanted to go to Lincoln?' asked Mac.

'That'll do very nicely,' replied Freddie as he lit up a cigarette. 'What chance we actually get there?'

'No, car's going well now,' replied Don. 'I think the timing needs a bit of a tweak, but otherwise, she's OK. The car moved slowly forward with Don managing to change gears with some difficulty. 'Gearbox a bit stiff,' he said, 'but I'm gradually getting the hang of it.'

They slowed as they came to the guardhouse. 'Gawd, where are you lot off to this time?' asked the duty sergeant.

'We're off to sample the delights of Lincoln, my man,' replied Freddie, putting on a posh voice. 'Kindly open the gates and let us out.'

'Don't forget to come back, lads,' the sergeant replied. 'And if you come back, make sure you are not completely rat-arsed. Quite likely, you lot will be flying for King and country tomorrow,' he added.

'Up yours,' replied Freddie and then back in his best English, 'Drive on, my man!'

The car staggered its way through the Lincolnshire lanes, and it was beginning to get dark by the time they reached the outskirts of the city.

'Where shall we go?' asked Don.

'Well, the Snakepit should be open by now,' said Freddie. 'What d'you say to a quick pint, just to get things underway?'

'What the hell is the Snakepit?' asked Mac.

'That's the trouble with you bloody colonials,' replied Freddie. 'It's a pub, otherwise known as the Saracen's Head. Usually full of us types, so not too bad. Beer's OK too.'

'Do you know where it is?' asked Don. 'I've never driven in Lincoln before.'

'Yeh, it's down by the cathedral. Can't bloody miss it. Turn left here. I think it's along here. Yeh, there it is. I reckon I should become the bloody navigator; what d'you think?'

Don stopped the car with a squeal from the brakes. 'Need to get those brake linings fixed,' said Mac. 'It's one thing getting the car going but a good idea if you can stop it as well!'

The four men got out of the car and walked into the pub, which was already fairly busy. 'You OK with beer, Mac, or do you want that American muck?'

'Yes, American muck for me, Freddie.' Mac smiled.

Freddie brought the drinks over, and the four looked at one another.

'Well, here's to a good night,' said Townsy and raised his glass.

'Cheers,' and the other three lifted their glasses too.

'It's good to be back,' said Townsy. 'I mean the nurses were great, but I missed drinking with you lot.'

'Are you two really going dancing?' asked Mac.

'That's the plan,' replied Freddie. 'You going to come too?'

'What d'you say, Don? We've got to get these two back in any case. Sure, we'll come along. When does it open?'

'No rush, squire,' replied Freddie. 'Plenty of time for a few more of these,' and with that, he moved back to the bar for another order.

'So where are we going?' asked Don, who had hardly ever been to a dance and felt slightly uneasy about the idea.

'Just dun the road,' replied Freddie. 'Easy walk. No need to take the old jalopy.'

Freddie brought the drinks round to their table, taking care not to spill anything.

'There,' he said. 'Get that wallop down your necks. Yer reckon that bloody car of yours will get us back tonight?' he asked, looking at Don.

'Well … probably,' Don replied slowly. 'Battery's a bit dodgy, but you can always push!' He laughed, and the others joined in.

A few drinks later, Freddie reckoned it was time to head off to the Astoria Ballroom, and he led the others out of the pub and down the road.

The Ballroom looked very busy when they arrived, but Freddie seemed to know the bouncer on the door and they were in without too much trouble. Don was amazed. In fact, the only dancing he had ever done was at school. This place was huge and packed with all sorts of servicemen—brown jobs, RAF and USAAF types, and even a few from the Royal Navy. Women seemed to be all over the place, and as they moved their way up to the bar, Don caught the smell of some rather nice perfume, which seemed to come from a very lovely looking WAAF.

'Hallo,' he said as they both seemed to be pressing forward together to the bar.

'Hallo,' she replied, and Don noticed her deep-brown eyes and long lashes. Her hair was brunette, and she had high cheekbones and a happy, smiling mouth.

Don could not really think of anything to say and blurted out, 'Do you come here often?' Then he realised how corny that would sound and apologised.

'Don't worry,' she said. 'I haven't been here before. Just came along with some friends from Scampton.'

'I'm just getting some drinks for my pals. Can I get you something?' Don asked.

'No, don't worry, thanks. I have got a bit of an order of my own!' She laughed. 'In any case, what's your name?'

'Don,' he replied. 'And yours?'

'Mary. Why don't you join us and then maybe we can have a dance?'

Don got his drinks and made it back to the table where the other three were sitting. 'Hey, just been chatted up by a nice-looking girl. She's a WAAF from Scampton, and I think she must have brought her friends. Shall we go and join them?'

'Nah, not me, old son,' replied Freddie. 'I think I'd rather look for me own bit of skirt, but don't worry about me.'

'Where shall we meet?' asked Don. 'You coming with me, Mac? Might be OK, I reckon.'

'Yep, I'm with you, buddy. Lead the way. Why don't we meet at the entrance, say about ten thirty. Give us long enough to get back to the base.'

'Good idea,' said Freddie. 'Townsy and I will see you then. If we're not there by quarter to eleven, go without us. What d'you say, Townsy?'

'Yeh, that sounds OK. You never know, we may get Brahms and Liszt, eh, Freddie?'

And with that, the two friends wheeled away into a mass of bodies by the bar.

'Well, where are these dames?' Mac asked.

'Over there,' said Don. 'The one in the blue dress is Mary. She was the one I was talking to in the queue.'

They made their way across the dance floor, which was temporarily empty while the band took a break.

'Mary, this is Mac. We fly together,' Don said.

'Glad to meet you, Mac. These are my friends from Scampton—Eve, Shirley, and Joan.'

'Glad to meet you ladies,' Mac replied. 'Can I get anyone a drink?'

Eve lifted her head. 'Well, my gin seems to have gone rather quickly,' she giggled.

'Allow me,' said Mac, and with that, he caught her by the arm and steered her towards the dance floor, just as the band struck up again.

'Mary, would you like a dance as well?' asked Don. 'I have to warn you that you might not be able to walk afterwards.'

'I'll take the risk.'

Together, they walked across to join the many others on the dance floor.

'Hey, Don, you're not so bad. I reckon you are one of those dark horses who say they can't do anything but really can.'

Don blushed a bit. He really wasn't sure what he should do next, but he did realise that he was rather strongly attracted to this young lady. 'No, I only went to school dances, and I bet you can remember what those were like.'

Mary laughed. 'What, where the boys and girls lined up on either side of the room?'

'That's the one!' Don laughed. 'I thought they were purgatory.'

'Me too,' replied Mary.

They had a couple of dances before Don asked whether she would like a break and another drink.

By the time they got back to the table, Joan and Shirley were talking to two USAAF flyers who had come over with them from Scampton. Eve and Mac were still dancing, and the two US men looked up as Don approached. 'Gee, you guys know how to hold a good dance. We're gate-crashing. We had to put down at Scampton and heard there was a gig. It's great!'

'Welcome,' said Don quietly. RAF men were a little wary of the 'Yanks,' as they called them, since they were so popular with the women. Don didn't want any chance of losing Mary. 'We struggle on, you know?'

'Well, you excuse us,' said one who, from his wings, was clearly a pilot. 'We're going to take Joan and Shirley for a dance. Catch you later.' And with that, the two women were whisked away.

Mac and Eve came over from the dance floor. Eve was rather flushed looking, and Mac was gently sweating.

'Mac, be a sweetie and get me that drink, will you?' Eve said as she lit her cigarette.

'Anyone else ready for another?' asked Mac. 'Mary? Don?'

'Beer for me, Mac—that's the brown stuff which has to be pulled, not cold in a bottle. Mary, what would you like?'

'Yes, same for me, Mac, thanks.'

'Busy in here tonight,' said Eve. 'Must be a lot of crews standing down. Maybe the weather's bad. You with Mac, Don?'

'Yes,' Don replied. 'There are four of us here tonight. The other two have gone off for some serious drinking, I think.'

Mac returned with the drinks.

'You're based at East Kirkby Mac was saying?' Eve asked, taking another cigarette.

'We are. Been there since May and looking forward to finishing, aren't we, Mac?' Don replied.

'Sure are,' said Mac. 'I'm looking forward to going home to some proper food and not having to think that some goddam bastard is out to kill me all the time!'

They all laughed, and then Eve asked them what they did in their spare time.

'Well, usually, it's sleep and eat,' replied Don. 'Oh, and Mac and I have been repairing a car. It's going OK now, isn't it, Mac?'

'Well, yes, I reckon it is, but proof will be if it gets us back to base tonight. It's a long walk if not!'

'Maybe you could drive over to Scampton and see us,' interjected Eve.

'Probably wouldn't let us in!' retorted Don.

'Well, you could come over when we have our next station dance. I'm sure they would let you in then,' said Mary. She smiled at Don. 'I would love it if you would come.'

'Well, so would I,' said Don. 'How about it, Mac? We could squeeze a few others in too, if you like! Our skipper has got his own car. He could bring some too.'

'Sounds swell to me,' replied Mac. 'At least it won't finish at ten thirty like this one. In fact, I think they're just tuning up for the last waltz. How about it, Eve?'

'Love to,' she replied, stubbing out her cigarette and taking Mac's arm.

Don stood and gently pulled Mary's arm. 'Come on then, before they finish.' He smiled.

As they danced round, Mary held Don tightly and whispered in his ear, 'I do hope you can make that dance. It would be lovely to spend some more time with you.' And with that, she lifted her face to him and they kissed.

***

Freddie and Townsy eased their way through the crush around the bar. 'Couple of pints of wallop?' asked Freddie. 'Blimy, Townsy, never seen one of these dances so bloody crowded. D'yer think the bloody war's over or something?'

'Nah,' replied Townsy. 'Bloody place is full of Yanks.'

'Here, get this down yer neck.' He handed the glass to Townsy.

'Not much spare crumpet around,' Freddie observed.

'They'll be all around those bloody Yanks with their swanky uniform, silk bloody stockings, and pockets full of lucre,' said Townsy. 'It's just not right them taking over things here.'

''Ere, steady on, old china. Don't get yourself so worked up. It's not so bad, and they are helping us out just now, aren't they? Must admit, I wouldn't like to fly over bloody Germany in the sodding daylight like they do. Good chance of getting your bloody balls blown off, then I'll be bound!' Freddie laughed.

'S'pose you're right,' Townsy replied, looking down into his almost empty glass. 'I'll get some more in, eh?'

'See no reason why not,' replied Freddie. He smiled. 'Going to need a piss pretty soon with all this bloody beer. I'll see you back here in half a mo.' And with that, Freddie headed for the toilets at the back of the hall.

The toilet was full of men in need of relief, and Freddie joined the line to the trough.

'You're Freddie Hughes, ain't you?' said the man behind him.

'Who wants to know?' replied Freddie, and as he turned round, he recognised George Turner, who had been on the gunnery course with him.

'Oh, bloody hell, George!' he replied. 'How's it going? Not shot down then? Where are you now?'

'Swinderby just now. Had a few close shaves, Freddie. Navigator got himself killed, and the mid-upper got it in the legs—the plane didn't look too rosy neither.'

The queue moved forward, and Freddie carried on talking whilst he relieved himself. 'Yeh, it's bloody dangerous, ain't it? Glad when it's over.'

They walked out back to the dance floor. 'Got to be going, Freddie. See you around sometime.'

'Look after yourself, George. See you around,' and Freddie walked towards the bar.

When he got back to where he had left Townsy, he saw that he seemed to have picked up a couple of girls.

'What have we here then?' he asked as he got closer.

'This is Julia and Marg,' replied Townsy brightly. 'They live in Lincoln and popped in for a dance! This is Freddie.'

'Very nice,' said Freddie. 'Have you ladies got something to drink?'

'Oh yes, thanks,' Marg replied.

'What do you do then, Marg? Do you work in Lincoln?' Freddie asked.

'Well, this and that,' she replied, and she winked at Freddie.

'What, a bit of slap and tickle then?' he asked. 'You coming along, Townsy?'

'Nah, I'm OK here, thanks, Freddie, but you go along. I'll meet you back here if you like.'

'OK, my son. Let's go, ladies.' He linked arms with them both and disappeared.

Townsy was feeling pretty drunk by this time but fought his way back to the bar for another pint. Freddie had only gone about half an hour when he came back.

'Blimy, Freddie, that was quick,' he said. 'Did you get a bit of how's your father then?'

'Bloody did, old son. Bloody lovely it was too. You should have come along. Bloody house was full of women!'

'Hope you used a bloody johnny?' asked Townsy. 'Otherwise, you'll be up before the doc with the clap!'

'Better than getting your fucking balls blown off,' Freddie retorted. 'I need another beer.'

The strains of the last waltz drifted across the hall as Freddie and Townsy downed their drink and worked their way back to the exit.

'Real trick now,' said Freddie, 'is finding our chauffeur,' but as they got closer to crush at the doorway, they saw Mac and Don kissing goodnight to their partners.

'Hi, guys,' said Mac as he saw them approaching. 'Good night?'

'Bloody wonderful,' replied Freddie. 'How about you?'

'Yes, we had a swell time, didn't we, Don? Got a date for the next dance at Scampton.'

'Well, if we make it that far!' grumbled Freddie.

They all had their coats now, and Don led the way to the car. The night was very clear and cold, and when they got there, they found the car covered in ice.

'Bloody hell,' said Don. 'Let's scrape the windows so we can see something.'

He opened the door with some difficulty, as it was frozen too, and it was with some scepticism that he put the key in the ignition.

'Someone will have to crank the engine,' he called. 'Mac, maybe best you, as you know how the car works.'

'OK,' said Mac. 'Turn the ignition on, and I'll give it a go.'

The engine didn't start.

'I really think the timing's not quite right,' said Don to the three others gathered around the car.

'Well, what do we do now?' asked Townsy. 'It's a bloody long way to walk, and in any case, we should be back by midnight.'

'We could try pushing the car, and I'll see if the engine will fire,' suggested Don.

They had just started to get the car moving when another car drew up alongside.

'You chaps, OK?'

They were amazed to see Matt in his car. He had just dropped Anne off at the hospital and was driving along the High Street.

'Hallo, Skip,' said Don. 'Bit of trouble, I'm afraid. Bloody car won't start.'

'You got some jumpers, Skip?' asked Freddie, much to everyone's surprise, as they all thought that he had virtually no idea about cars.

'Well, as it happens, Freddie, I have. Let's give them a go.'

The jump leads were duly connected by Mac, and with Matt's car engine racing, Mac tried again, this time with success.

'Everybody in,' called Don. With Matt following along behind, they got to the guardhouse by 11:30 p.m.

Stephen and Scrap were asleep when Matt got into their room. Matt quietly got undressed and dived under the bedclothes. It was a very cold night, and the room temperature seemed very close to that outside.

It had been a good couple of days, and it had been lovely to spend some time with Anne. They had now decided that, when Matt had some leave, they would go and speak to Anne's parents and tell them they were getting married. It could happen quite quickly, Matt reckoned, and in any case, he should get a good chunk of leave in a few weeks' time.

He was pleased that Stephen and Jess seemed to get on because he was worried about his friend and hoped Jess would help him get over what was obviously a difficult patch. With that happy thought, he drifted off to sleep.

CHAPTER 8

HANOVER

Nineteenth Trip

They came back from their forty-eight-hour leave only to be told that all operations would be suspended because of the adverse moon period. However, apart from those due leave, the rest were virtually confined to the base, and they started a series of cross-country night-training sorties, bomb runs, and general flying. Matt always found these times a bit tedious, but no one was trying to kill them and it was a big relief to be out of the firing line for a while longer. The ten days seemed to pass quickly, but it was clear that they were now well into autumn and the weather had become steadily colder. Matt's crew met once more in the Red Lion on their last night of training, and then it was back to war.

***

Matt woke suddenly with Barker shaking his arm.

'Time to wake up, sir,' he said. 'Brought you a nice cuppa.'

Stephen was already awake, and Scrap was standing by the door, wagging his tail expectantly. It felt very cold, and Matt dressed quickly. 'How are you, Stephen?' he asked. 'Ready for the fray again?'

'Yes, thanks. How about you?'

'Yes, feel much better. Anne and I have decided we are going to get married as soon as we can clear it with her old man.'

'That's good news. Well done. I must just pop out with Scrap. Back soon.' With that, Stephen went out.

Matt realised his friend was not, in fact, in that good a shape, in spite of him saying otherwise. Stephen had, until recently, been happy and cheerful. He certainly didn't sound like that just now.

Matt went out. It was very dark and cold, and there had obviously been an unusually heavy frost during the night. In fact, even on the way back from the pub last night, there had been one or two ice patches on the road. Matt went over to the mess where sleepy airmen were trying to get their heads round tea and cigarettes.

'Morning, Matt. Nice change, wasn't it?'

'Yes, Charles. How about you? You managed to steal away for a couple of days, didn't you?'

Charles Redman smiled. 'Yes, Clare and I went down to see her parents on the south coast. Their house is bloody cold. They never seem to have a fire on, and they boil up kettles for hot water. Almost pleased to be back. Warm up the old cockles, you know?'

'Are we on tonight, Charles?' Matt asked, turning serious.

'Reckon so. There's nothing on the board just yet, but the rumour mill seems to be in favour of tonight. Let's go and get some breakfast before it's all gone. These greedy buggers are like gannets.'

Matt and Charles went through to the officer's dining room and sat down with the pilot from G-George, Harry, an old friend of Matt's, and their bomb-aimer.

'Hallo, Matt,' said Harry.

'Hallo, Harry, you old bastard. Back to business then. Incidentally, I am going to get married fairly soon. Anne and I have been talking about it over the last few days.'

'You've kept that very quiet,' replied Harry. 'Is she that rather gorgeous girl who's a nurse?'

'Quite right, Harry. But keep your sticky hands off her; she's mine!'

'Of course, old boy. When's the happy day?'

'Not sure yet. Got to tell her old man when I next get leave! Do you think we'll be going tonight?' Matt added.

'What you think, Pete?' he said, turning to his bomb-aimer.

'Bloody certainty, I would say. Bloody Krauts will think the war's over if we don't pay them a visit soon!'

At that moment, Stephen walked in. 'Is it true?' he asked. 'Are we up tonight?'

'Looks like it, old boy,' replied Harry. ''Bout time you did some work!'

Stephen glared at Harry, turned on his heel, and walked out of the dining room.

'What's got into him then?' asked Harry.

'I think he's feeling the pressure a bit,' replied Matt. 'He's been pretty unhappy lately. Bit of a worry really.'

'Well, he needs to get over it,' replied Harry, who had now done forty-five trips.

'It just gives everyone else the bloody jitters. None of us feel that great blasting off into the sodding night and not sure we are going to be back here eating bacon and egg. Talking of which, where is the bloody breakfast?'

He started to bang the table with his knife and fork and began to sing, 'Why are we waiting?'

Breakfast eventually arrived amid ribald comments and raucous laughter, and after they were finished, the officers made their way to the notice board. M-Mother was listed on the battle orders for that night, and Matt felt his stomach tighten at the thought.

'Looks like a big raid tonight, chaps,' Harry said. 'Ten aircraft from here alone.'

Matt and Charles went out to look for the others. It was getting light, and the sky was very clear with still a few stars visible.

'Looks like a nice day,' said Charles. 'Let's hope it stays that way.'

'Charles, we will need to do an air test this morning. I'll get Stephen to set it up. Probably ten thirty would be best. I'll spread the word?' With that, Matt set off in search of Stephen.

He found him walking with Scrap at his heels, heading towards the officers' mess.

'Stephen!' he called. 'Hold on for a minute, will you?'

Matt saw that Stephen was upset. 'What's the matter, old chap?' he asked.

'It's the flying, Matt. I don't think I can go on. Just the thought of getting back in that bloody plane turns my blood cold, let alone the thought of flying over Germany at night.'

'Listen, Stephen. We are all in this together. We are all afraid. Jesus, it would be bloody unnatural if we weren't. But we have to cope with it, and we are already over halfway through this tour. Sure, we have had a few near scrapes, but we are all here still. You are a really important part of the crew, and we rely on you to keep those bloody engines going so they get us to the target and then back home.'

Matt could feel himself getting angry with Stephen, and he hadn't meant to do that. The alternative for Stephen was not to go and then be labelled LMF, a degrading end to his flying career.

'Look,' he continued. 'Let's do this next trip and then get you along to the doc. He's bound to have some pills to cheer you up or at least help you sleep. Stephen, we need you,' Matt said as he walked away. 'Oh, and incidentally, we will be doing an air test this morning at about ten thirty. Please find the others. I'm going down to see the ground chaps to see what magic they have worked on M-Mother.' With that, he walked briskly off towards the hangars.

Stephen headed off to the perimeter fence, hopeful that, at least there, he could have some privacy. The sun was up by then, and he could feel its warmth on his back. Scrap was tearing around, doing nothing in particular, and Stephen smiled as he watched him. 'Well, you don't care, do you, old boy?' he said aloud to Scrap, who ran up hopeful of getting his ear scratched. Stephen crouched down, and Scrap put his chin on his knee, looking up with his mournful brown eyes. Stephen bent his head and started crying. He had never felt so despondent. Matt was right, of course. To give in now would result in terrible disgrace, but he felt so concerned about carrying on. He was sure they would all be killed before the end of the tour. He was frightened almost beyond reason, but he knew that somehow he had to keep going. He hugged Scrap and let his tears come. After a while, he stood up and wiped his eyes. He felt strangely better, and he straightened his shoulders and walked slowly back to his room.

Barker was there tidying the room when he came in. 'Flying tonight then, sir?' he asked.

'Yes, looks like it, Barker. Can you take care of Scrap for a few hours? We are doing an air test in a couple of hours. Would appreciate it.'

'Of course, sir. I will find him something to eat at lunchtime, don't you worry, sir.'

***

The whole crew of M-Mother clambered aboard the truck to get the air test completed as soon as possible. Matt had considered it essential that everyone take part, and this had started Freddie grumbling to himself and anyone else who was around but mainly Townsend.

'Don't see why we all have to bloody go,' he said. 'I mean the bloody guns are where they always are. It's so bloody cold in them turrets, it's no joke.'

'Well,' replied Townsend. 'It won't last long, and Skip obviously thinks it's best.'

Freddie huffed and puffed and drew rather harder than usual on his cigarette.

The truck dropped them at dispersal, and one by one, they got aboard the aircraft. Matt was struck by the familiar smell of oil and hydraulic fluid, which would forever remind him of this aircraft. They all got into their places, and Matt leaned out of the window to indicate they were ready to go.

Matt and Stephen worked their way through their preflight checks, and then they were ready to start engines. The aircraft shook as the engines were run up, and Stephen carefully checked the oil pressures and temperatures.

'All OK,' he called to Matt, who leaned out of the cockpit window to indicate to the ground crew that the chocks could be removed.

The engine throttles were advanced, and M-Mother moved slowly forward onto the taxiway.

'Cleared for take-off,' came from the control tower.

Matt eased the Lancaster onto the runway, and they were off.

The air test lasted about thirty minutes, and during that time, Matt was keen to check that no one had lost his edge. They went over to the bomb range, and he had Don do a dummy run just to see that his bombsight was working.

Matt took M-Mother up to six thousand feet and did some tight turns and corkscrews just to make sure everything was functioning. The corkscrew manoeuvre was often life-saving when under attack from fighters or if caught in the beam of a searchlight so Matt had to be sure the old aircraft could cope with that.

'OK, chaps. Let's go home for lunch,' and with that, Matt turned the aircraft back to base.

***

As the crew got out of the aircraft, Matt reminded them that the briefing would be at 1500 hours.

'No clues yet as to where we are going,' he said. 'But get some grub and your heads down for an hour or two. Meet you in the briefing room—usual seats.'

Matt, Stephen, and Charles made their way to the officers' mess whilst the others went to their own. Matt was relieved to see that Stephen seemed more relaxed but decided to say nothing, particularly in front of Redman.

They reached the mess, and Charles asked them if they would like a beer.

'Why not?' replied Matt, and he pulled out his old pipe and stuck it into his mouth.

'Didn't know you smoked, old boy,' Charles said as he brought the beers over.

'Don't,' replied Matt. 'Use the bloody thing as a dummy! Well, cheers! Here's to a happy raid if there is such a thing.'

The others raised their glasses and sank their beer.

'God, needed that,' said Charles, 'Well, what's your guess for tonight?' he asked, turning to Matt.

'No idea. I fear that Berlin might well figure. Looks like the powers think that we need to go there fairly often, doesn't it? Bloody long way, bloody cold, bloody awful! Let's go and get something to eat.'

And with that, they made their way to the officers' dining room. There were several officers there already, all of whom were flying on the night's raid. The squadron navigator and bomb-aimer were already tucking into lunch, and they acknowledged the three as they came to sit down.

'Don't bother asking,' muttered Squadron Leader Harris, the navigator. 'I'm not even sure myself yet. Group seem to be fussing around a lot just now, so we will all have to wait until the Old Man comes to tell us.'

'Well,' said Charles, 'it's always better when it comes as a surprise, isn't it, Matt?'

'Absolutely, just upset us sooner if we knew now.' Matt laughed. 'Hallo, Judders,' he continued. 'You flying tonight then?'

Flying Officer Judson had completed twenty operations and was considered quite an old hand.

'Well, I thought I might as well come along and give you chaps a bit of support.' He smiled. 'It looks like a nice day for a change.' And he sat down and started tucking into his boiled beef and carrots.

After they had finished, Matt said he was off to get a nap and Stephen said he would do so too. Stephen had hardly spoken over lunch, and he seemed to eat very little.

'You OK, Stephen?' he asked when they were out of earshot of the others.

'Yes, thanks, Matt. I feel much better but not that hungry, I'm afraid. It will be good to get started.'

They got back to their billet to be met by Barker. 'Scrap's had lunch, sir,' he said. 'I took him for a short walk, and he's now curled up asleep on your bed, I'm afraid, sir.'

'Thanks, Barker. That's good of you. I'll just curl up beside him.'

Matt and Stephen lay down, and Stephen noticed that Matt seemed to go off to sleep almost at once. Scrap was in the middle of his bed, and he grunted as Stephen moved him across so he could lie down. Scrap felt warm in the cold room as Stephen cuddled into him. He lay awake for a while and then dozed off until Scrap having a scratch woke him. When Stephen first woke, he felt almost normal, but it suddenly dawned on him where he was and what he was about to do and he felt a sudden weight on him again such that he knew that any chance of further sleep had gone. He got up, and Scrap peered expectantly as always.

'Come on then, Scrap. Let's go for a walk.' He looked at his watch and realised he had been asleep for only about half an hour. It was nearly two o'clock, an hour to go before briefing.

He opened the door quietly, not wanting to disturb Matt, and with Scrap bounding around, he left the hut and walked towards the perimeter fence. It was a cold, bright day with a few fluffy clouds dotted around. The sun had little warmth in it now, and in spite of his greatcoat, Stephen felt very cold. They walked slowly along the fence, and Scrap found a stick and ran up to Stephen, barking loudly, encouraging him to throw it. The simplicity of what they were doing released Stephen from the thoughts of what was to come, and he felt momentarily at ease. He thought of Jess and hoped that he could see her again soon.

There was a line of beech trees along the outside of the fence, and their dead leaves rustled in the brisk easterly wind. Even this sound was music to Stephen, and it took him back to his childhood when he would walk with his father through some woods close to where they lived. His thoughts were disturbed by the sound of Scrap's barking. 'OK, old boy. Couple of throws and then home. We've got work to do.' The thought of that quickly brought Stephen to earth, and the dread, which had left him for a few minutes, returned. He looked at his watch—2.30 p.m.—half an hour to go before they would know their fate for this evening.

He turned back the way they had come and walked briskly back to the billet. Matt was up and dressed. 'Hallo, Stephen. Good walk. All OK?' he asked.

'Yes, fine, thanks. Guess it's time to go.'

Crews were already gathering outside the briefing room, sharing cigarettes and chatting amongst themselves. At ten to three, they all filed into the room, and M-Mother's crew got into their regular seats in the middle of the room. There was the customary chatter and catcalling, and the room, as usual, was filled with smoke. At three o'clock exactly, Wing Commander Squires walked in, followed by the usual retinue, and the men stood up and became quiet.

'Good afternoon, gentleman,' Squires started. 'Please be seated.' With that, he moved towards the covered map. 'Your target for tonight for a change is not Berlin, but Hanover.'

A groan went round the room, and the sound of muttering became louder.

'Quiet, chaps. We've got to keep taking the war to the Nazis. The Commander in Chief is adamant that we need to put pressure on the enemy in this way. I have decided that I will be joining you tonight.'

There was a cheer from the crews. It was unusual for Squires to come along on operations, but when he did, it raised morale and there was more a feeling that everyone was sharing the risk.

'Excuse me, sir. If you are coming along, could I have permission to have the night off?' asked one of the gunners from B-Bertie. 'Only I was going to a dance with a girl, and she'll be really cross if I don't go.'

The room erupted with laughter, which became louder when Squires said, 'Well, I would like to be able to, but, you know, I don't think we can do without you tonight. Perhaps some other time! Well, gentlemen, now that's settled, here is the intelligence officer to talk to you about the importance of the target.'

After him, there was the Met officer, an unhappy-looking man with small glasses who had an unfortunate tick at the side of his face. 'The weather for tonight is—'

'Uncertain!' everyone in the room shouted out. It was followed by laughter.

'…. likely to be quite good,' he persisted, 'and clear when you get back here tomorrow morning.'

And so it went on through the navigation and bomb leaders to signals and Squires again to finish.

'OK, chaps. This is an important raid, and we are joining a large force. The weather both here and at the target looks good for us, and we anticipate a good result tonight.' He ended with his usual *bon mot*: 'May luck go with you and bring you back safely.' The briefing officers filed out of the room, leaving the crews in their groups with navigators working out the route, wireless operators noting and checking the signals, and the bomb-aimers checking the target indicators to be used.

'Blimey,' said Freddie to Townsend. 'At least it's not Berlin. Did a couple of trips there while you were eyeing up the bloody nurses.'

'It wasn't all sweetness and light nearly getting your balls blown off, you know?' retorted Townsend. 'Not much grub in the bloody hospital neither.'

'Still a bloody pantomime compared with bloody Berlin, you see if it's not. Come on, let's go and get our fodder before it's too late.'

Matt and Charles were discussing the route to be taken with Stephen, who was looking pale and seemed very quiet. 'They are routing us straight there and back,' said Charles. 'Only trouble with that is that they will know where we are going almost before we do!'

Matt nodded in agreement. 'Well, it looks like a pretty big raid with over four hundred Lancasters. We just need to keep in the stream and keep our eyes open for the others. Don, Mac, you happy with everything? If so, let's all go and eat. Take-off is scheduled for 1800 hours, so let's get to the crew room at 1700 hours. Gives us time to collect our things and our thoughts!'

**

The crew room was the usual buzz of activity with the airmen getting into their flying gear and picking up masks, helmets and goggles, parachutes, and the all-important coffee and sandwiches. The gunners were heaving on their electrically heated suits and inner layers of gloves as well as their fur-lined boots. Theirs was a particularly cold trip, the turrets being open to the air, cold enough to freeze the breath in their masks to the point that ice could block their oxygen supply.

They had to leave their personal possessions in their lockers, although many took lucky charms with them and left goodbye letters to sweethearts, wives, or parents—just in case.

The crew of M-Mother gathered outside in the dying light of the day. It was already very cold, and their breath and the smoke from many cigarettes produced a fog, which made it difficult to make out details of the individuals present.

A truck pulled up outside the crew room. 'M-Mother, B-Bertie!' called the WAAF driver.

'Here we go,' muttered Freddie. 'Any more for the skylark?'

The crews clambered in with their parachutes, equipment bags, and refreshments.

'All aboard?' asked the driver, and with that, they were off to war again.

They were dropped off at M-Mother and made their way towards the waiting aircraft and the ground crew.

'Everything OK, Sergeant?' asked Matt.

'Yes, sir, everything is top line.'

Matt walked around the aircraft, making his checks whilst the others got in, and then he went aboard, climbing up the fuselage past Townsy in the mid-turret, over the main spar to where Mac was tuning his radios and Charles was sorting out his charts and instruments. Stephen was checking the engine dials and fuel tank contents and forward of him Matt could just make out Don's feet as he lay down in the nose of the aircraft. He climbed into his seat, turned on the intercom, and checked that the crew were ready and that everything was working. He then ran through his own checklist to satisfy himself that all was well. The ground crew sergeant stood beside him and handed him Form 700 to sign. Everything now became his responsibility.

M-Mother was number three in the take-off sequence, and it was time to start up. Stephen and he went through the checklists as usual, and soon all four engines were running smoothly. The first two aircraft had passed them, and Matt indicated to the ground crew to remove the chocks. They were moving out to join the line of aircraft making for the runway. The two in front roared off down the runway, and M-Mother lined up. Matt held her on the brakes, which he released once he had the green light from the control hut. Several personnel were out in the perishing cold to wave them off. It meant a lot to the crew and more so since they were always there, no matter what the weather.

M-Mother picked up speed, and Stephen advanced the port engine throttles a little to counter the swing to port. The tail came up, and then the throttles were fully opened and Matt lifted the heavy aircraft off and eased her into a gentle climb. They were past 1,000 feet when Matt raised the flaps, and then he put the aircraft into a gentle turning climb to the right, keeping station behind the taillight of the aircraft in front. They climbed steadily to about 5,000 feet over the airfield before setting their course to cross the coast at Southwold, and then Charles gave Matt their course, which would take them almost due east to Hanover. They were now over the North Sea, and Matt asked the gunners to check their guns.

They were part of a 400-strong bomber stream, which, so long as everyone steered the right course at the right speed and height, was a safe place to be. The leg to the target took two and a half hours, and as they crossed into Germany, searchlights came on almost immediately and they came under fire from flak, not heavy but seemingly accurate. An aircraft over to the left of them was hit and started going down with its starboard wing on fire.

Matt looked across to Stephen. He was staring out and seemed to be completely immobile. Matt didn't want to ask him how he was over the intercom when others might hear, so he leaned over and touched his friend, who jumped. Matt gave him a thumbs-up, and Stephen replied.

Then the lights and flak were behind them, and the blackness of the night seemed to swallow them up.

But the fighters still hunted out here, and Matt told everyone again to keep his eyes peeled.

An aircraft in front of them exploded. It was a shocking event. One moment, it was all black in front of them, and the next moment, there was a blinding flash and wreckage was all over the sky. The two aircraft in front of M-mother were silhouetted by the light, and even though the aircraft was probably a mile in front of them, M-Mother was rocked by the turbulence from the explosion.

'Christ, what was that?' Freddie called from the rear turret.

'Kite ahead blew up,' said Matt. 'Almost certainly fighters around, so keep looking out there and under us as I bank. The bastards are out here somewhere.'

The darkness descended again, but just a few minutes later, Freddie cried, 'Corkscrew left. Go.'

Matt dived and turned the aircraft to the left. He heard the stutter of Freddie's guns as he started to heave the heavy plane up and to the right. 'More power, Stephen,' he called and was relieved to see him move towards the throttles but would have rather he had been there without having to be asked.

There was a thudding noise, and almost immediately, Matt heard their guns firing again. This time, there was a shout from Townsy, 'I've got the bastard! Got you!'

Out of the corner of his eye, Matt saw a plane going down with flames pouring out of the cockpit area. It looked like a Me 110.

'Well done, Townsy. Good shot. Keep watching though. Anyone know where we have been hit?'

'It's OK, Skip,' said Freddie. 'Missed me by a whisker and just came in and out of the fuselage. No real damage, I reckon.'

'Thanks, Freddie. Well, chaps, nearly there, but I don't think they will be very pleased to see us!'

'Target ahead, Skip,' said Charles.

'Thanks,' replied Matt. 'I think I can see the object of our desire! Don, everything ready?'

'Yes, Skip. All ready down here.'

The target was already being marked well ahead of their position, but before they got there, they had to run the gauntlet through what looked like, from Matt's position, the usual impenetrable wall of lights and flak.

'Looks like a hot reception for us, chaps,' said Matt.

An aircraft over to the right was caught in a couple of searchlight beams and almost immediately coned. It looked like a fly caught in a web, and in no time, the flak batteries had its range. There was a flash from the aircraft and then a huge explosion and bits of aircraft and debris could be seen falling to earth. The searchlights seemed all over the place, and suddenly, M-Mother was illuminated. The light in the cockpit was vividly bright, and Matt couldn't see the instruments. By instinct, he dived the aircraft and pushed the throttles through the gate for maximum power. M-Mother lurched forward and to the right as Matt struggled to get out of the cone of light. Already, flak had found their level, and the white-hot fragments were coming through the fuselage. A small fire broke out behind Mac, which he quickly doused.

M-Mother was now screaming through the air in a power dive, but the light still followed them. Matt banked the aircraft to the left and levelled out. They were now doing 300 miles per hour, and the airframe was creaking and groaning, but suddenly, they were out of the cone and back into blackness.

Matt felt the sweat under his flying suit and realised he was gripping the controls so tightly that his arms were beginning to ache.

'Throttle back to cruise, Stephen,' he commanded sharply, and he was relieved to see Stephen move quickly. Matt eased the aircraft back onto course for the target. There was still a lot of flak around, and there were sounds of it hitting the aircraft, but they seemed to be out of the worst of it.

'Everyone OK?' called Matt. Everyone replied. 'OK, Don, we are on our way into the target,' Matt said, trying to remain as calm as he could, even though his heart was rattling along and he had trouble stopping his hands shaking.

They were now on their final run to the target.

'Five minutes to target!' called Charles.

Just then, two things happened almost simultaneously. Another aircraft to starboard blew up with a direct hit by flak. Then M-Mother was hit on the starboard wing, and a fire started in the starboard outer engine.

'How bad is that, Stephen?' Matt asked.

Stephen didn't reply.

'How bad, Flight Engineer?' Matt repeated sharply.

There was a further pause, and then Stephen said, 'I'm not sure, but we need to feather the engine and fire the extinguisher.'

'Well, bloody well do it then!' Matt shouted. 'Time to target, Navigator?'

'Two minutes,' his calm voice came back.

'OK, let's press on,' said Matt. 'Engineer, I leave you to sort out the fire.'

'OK.' Stephen's voice was quiet, almost indiscernible above the noise of the aircraft and battle outside.

'One minute,' called Charles.

'Bomb doors open,' called Matt. 'Don, you ready down there?'

'Ready, Skip.' Don's steady voice came back.

'Engineer, how's the fire?'

'Dying down. I've increased power in the right inner. Looks OK.'

'Thirty seconds.'

'Left, left, left,' Don called. 'Steady, steady, right steady, steady. Bombs gone.'

M-Mother leapt upward as the weight of the bombs left her, and Matt had some trouble bringing her back to level flight long enough for the all-important photoflash.

Matt swung the aircraft to the left and started a gentle dive. Further flak looped up towards them, moving slowly at first and then rushing at them as it got closer. Explosions occurred all around the aircraft, which rocked up and down on the shock waves, and flak peppered the fuselage. A piece dropped onto Charles's navigation table and proceeded to burn a hole in one of the charts.

'Jesus, Skip,' he said. 'It's getting a little warm in here.'

Matt completed the turn. 'Just give me a course,' he said quietly.

'Two-seven-zero will do,' replied Charles. 'I'm just putting out a small fire amongst my charts.'

'You OK?' asked Matt.

'Yes, fine. Don't worry about me. Just get us out of here.'

Matt levelled out at about 10,000 feet and aimed for some stratus cloud dead ahead.

'Everyone OK?' he asked, and everyone replied except Stephen. He looked across at him and saw that he was staring out of the cockpit apparently motionless.

'All OK, Engineer?' he asked again.

Stephen's reply was an almost inaudible, 'Yes.'

'Report on the engines and fuel?' Matt asked almost as an order.

Stephen turned towards him and put his thumb up. 'Everything is OK,' he said quietly.

Matt had his own problems with the aircraft. Clearly, they were now facing a headwind, and with only three engines and a damaged wing, it was going to take some time to get back. Also, the aircraft was pulling to the right, partly, Matt reckoned, because there was an engine out and partly because of the wing. It was going to be a tough ride back, and he was having to put a lot of left rudder on to keep the aircraft on course. It was about half an hour before they would start to receive a decent GEE signal, and until then, it was just a question of battling on.

'Navigator, I'm going to drop down to 5,000 feet. There should be less wind there,' he said.

They left the shelter of the cloud to descend to the new height, and Don tried to make out anything below that might help them to know where they were.

'Can't see a bloody thing,' said Don. 'Looks like there is another layer of cloud below us.'

'Keep a good lookout, chaps,' said Matt.

Freddie grinned to himself. 'I wonder how many times he has said that.' Just then, he thought he noticed a dark shape below them and to the left. He turned away and then looked back, and he was sure there was something down there. The slight lightness of the clouds below provided a contrast that helped him pick out the fighter stalking them.

'Skipper, we've got company. I'm sure it's a fighter, and it is gradually closing in just below us.'

'What do you want, Freddie?'

'Dive gently, Skip, and turn slightly to the left. Then I'll have him.'

Matt eased the throttles back and put M-Mother into a shallow dive.

'I need you here now, Stephen,' Matt said sharply, and Stephen moved over to take the throttles.

Suddenly, the aircraft shuddered as Freddie opened up with his guns, and there was a sudden flash behind the aircraft, followed by Freddie shouting, 'Take that, you bastard!'

Matt looked out to the left and saw an aircraft spiralling down. 'Good shooting, Freddie. That's a couple for this trip alone. Well done, chaps.'

Matt brought M-Mother back onto her course and resumed flying at 5,000 feet. About half an hour went by before he asked, 'Any idea where we are, Navigator?'

'Not really, but we should be in GEE range fairly soon,' Charles replied and then almost immediately said he had a fix that put them about fifty miles south of Groningen.

'Christ,' muttered Matt. 'How far to home then?'

'Just under three hundred miles to our coast,' replied Charles. 'Calculate we are making only about 120 miles per hour, so it's a long haul.'

'Can we make it, Stephen?' Again, there was no reply. 'Stephen, have we the fuel?' Matt repeated.

'I'm doing the sums now,' Stephen's quiet voice replied. 'I think it should be all right.'

'Let me know when you are certain,' replied Matt brusquely. 'I need to know as exactly as you can.'

'Got a quick view through some breaks in the cloud,' Don said sometime later. 'Looks like a very large lake down below.'

'That will be the Zeiderzee,' said Charles. 'Let me know when you see the coast.'

'Will do,' replied Don.

'Stephen, those calculations please,' said Matt.

'We'll make it,' Stephen replied almost sulkily.

'Over the coast now,' said Don.

'Right, Matt. Come on to two-six-zero. We are a little north of where we should be, and that should allow for what is a fairly stiff south-westerly and bring us in over Great Yarmouth. We should be there in just over the hour.'

Great Yarmouth appeared as predicted.

'Well done, Navigator. Mac, let them know we have trouble. Stephen, what about fuel?'

Again, Stephen replied only after a further prompt. 'We have an hour's fuel left.'

'Shit. That's going to cut it pretty fine at this speed.' He was feeling exhausted by the problems of keeping the aircraft straight and was irritated by the fact that Stephen hadn't warned him how low they were on fuel.

'Mac, see if Marham can take us.'

After a while, Mac replied, 'It's OK, Skip. Marham said they would be delighted!'

'Right, Navigator, let's go there. Just get ready, everyone, in case the hydraulics have had it or some bits have been damaged with all that bloody flak around.'

'Well, Skip, flak has certainly buggered the coffee flask,' Mac said.

'Could be worse,' Matt replied.

'Come back onto two-seven-zero with this wind,' called Charles. 'Should be there soon.'

Soon, Don called that he had the beacon in sight and Mac said that Marham had said they could come straight in for runway two-four.

'Stephen, I need your help on the throttles. We need to feather the port outer. Please come over here.'

Stephen moved over. 'Port outer feathered,' called Stephen as Matt lined up the aircraft with the runway.

'OK, let's see if the gear goes down, Stephen.'

There was a satisfying clunk as the wheels locked down, but Matt had to increase engine speed to counter the drag from the undercarriage and the two feathered propellers.

'Ten degrees of flap,' Matt said to Stephen.

The runway was opening up in front of them, but Matt judged he was a little low and increased engine speed still more.

'Nearly down, chaps. Hang on,' Matt called as he eased M-Mother back to earth.

They taxied over towards a dispersal point, but as Matt and Stephen were in the process of shutting down the two remaining engines, the engine revs just faded away and both engines came to a sputtering stop.

Matt looked across to Stephen. 'What the hell is going on?' he asked.

'Out of fuel,' Stephen replied. 'Sorry.'

'What do you mean "out of fuel"? We should have had about thirty minutes left?'

'I made a mistake,' Stephen replied.

Matt looked round and saw that the others seemed busy tidying their own possessions whilst Mac was clearing up the coffee, which had sprayed all over the fuselage.

Matt took off his mask and the intercom so no one else could hear.

'What the fuck do you mean you made a mistake? You could have got us all killed.'

He was angry, tired, and still hyped up from the trip, and he knew he shouldn't lose his temper. He rarely did. But this?

'Let's get out,' he said to Stephen, and with that, he was out of his seat and working his way down the fuselage.

One by one, they jumped down from the aircraft to be met by the duty officer and some ground crew.

'You chaps all right?' the officer asked. 'No one hurt or anything?'

'No, thanks,' replied Matt. 'We could do with a drink of something though and somewhere to sleep. We can look at the kite in the morning, but I need to ring base just now. I am afraid we will be leaving it here!'

The duty officer led the weary crew towards the mess, and Matt could hear Freddie and Townsend chatting as they went. The others seemed too tired to be bothered to talk, but Charles came alongside Matt and took him by the arm.

'Bloody good show, Matt,' he said. 'You did bloody well to get us here in one piece, but what about Bamber? What was he up to? I heard a couple of rather curt calls from you.'

'Well, you found the way back, Charles. I'm just the driver. About Stephen—I'm not sure, to be honest. I think he'll be OK, but he's a bit rocky just now to tell you the truth.'

'Let me know if I can do anything to help, Matt. We're all in this together, you know.'

'Thanks, Charles,' Matt replied. 'I will take you up on the offer if I need to.' Matt felt it best not to discuss the fuel issue. Effectively, it was a disciplinary matter if it ever came to light.

They reached the mess, and they almost fell through the door with exhaustion. It was the officers' mess, but no one was counting, and an orderly supplied some coffee.

'I'll go and rustle up some sandwiches,' he said. 'Sorry can't get you anything else.'

'This will be fine. Thank you,' replied Charles.

Matt excused himself to call East Kirkby, and he was surprised that he was put through to the CO, Group Captain Brookes.

'We made it to Marham. Kite's pretty shot up, I am afraid, sir, and we only had three engines to get back. No one hurt and the gunners got a Jerry a piece, sir.'

'Right, White. We will come and get you first thing. I am afraid you will have to go out again tonight. Sorry, nothing

I can do, but you chaps are due a spot of leave, aren't you? Should be OK after tomorrow night. 'Fraid it was a bad night for us. We lost three, and we were nearly putting you down for a fourth FTR.[7] Tell Marham we will send another Lanc for you to arrive at 0700 hours. Goodnight.'

The phone clicked, and Matt was left holding the phone and staring at the wall.

'Out again,' he muttered. 'Surely not after last night?' He could not believe it, and he wasn't quite sure how the rest were going to take it. It could be the end for Stephen, but even the others had been shaken up.

He suddenly felt completely drained and had a sick feeling in the pit of his stomach. There was a chair near the phone, and he slumped down on it and, resting his elbows on the table, buried his face in his hands. For the first time, he felt tears falling on his hands—not tears of sadness but of exhaustion and frustration. How could they do this? Everyone was so tired, frightened too.

He wearily got up and went back to the others.

Don and Mac had dropped off in two of the armchairs still in their flying gear. Even the irrepressible Freddie was slumped dozing in a chair.

Charles came up to Matt as he came into the mess. 'You OK, old boy? You look all in.'

'Felt better, Charles,' he replied. 'Plan is to get a couple of hours' kip here. Lanc will pick us up to take us home at 0700 hours. We can get a bit more sleep at base, but we are on the list to fly again tonight.'

Freddie opened one eye. 'Fucking hell. They really are trying to kill us off.' With that, he turned over and went to sleep.

---

[7] Failed to return.

Matt noticed Stephen sitting on his own by the bar. He was staring into space but seemed not to have heard Matt. He looked grey with beads of sweat on his forehead, and as Matt walked over to him, he noticed his hands were shaking.

'Stephen,' he said quite sharply, 'you'd better get your head down. There's an armchair over by the wall. Go there.'

Almost like an automaton, Stephen stood up and walked slowly to the chair and sat down.

The orderly came in with some more coffee and sandwiches. 'Shall I show you over to the hut, sir?' he said to Matt, who himself was having some trouble getting his thoughts together.

Charles replied, 'Look, old chap. Maybe we could just stay here for a few hours. We will be leaving by seven o'clock.'

'Well, sir. It's just that this is the officers' mess and you are not all officers, sir.'

Charles walked slowly towards the mess orderly. 'I know that, but we are all tired, we've all nearly got killed together, and we would all rather stay together in here. Is that clear?'

'Yes, sir. Sorry, sir, just pointing out. I'll pop in about six o'clock.'

'Good, chap. You do that.' With that, Charles shepherded him out of the door.

'Thanks, Charles,' Matt said. 'I really didn't have the strength. Quick cuppa and let's try and get some sleep.' But even as Matt was trying to settle into a chair, he glanced across to Stephen and saw that he was still just sitting, staring into space. He would have to tackle that particular problem later in the day, but it seemed increasingly likely they would need an odd bod engineer for tonight.

Matt dozed intermittently and woke up about six o'clock. He was cold and felt stiff from the exertions of flying and also the rather cramped position in which he slept.

He noticed that Charles was already awake and looking out of the window, and he walked over to him.

'Morning, Charles,' he said. He suddenly felt a closer bond to his senior officer than ever before. The way he had supported Matt last night had been a big relief.

'Morning, Matt. Get any sleep?' he replied. 'Looks bloody cold out there. Pretty thick frost by the looks.'

Matt peered through the window. The sky was beginning to lighten, and the darkness of the night was beginning to fade to a pale blue on the eastern horizon.

'Bit of a bugger we have to go again tonight, Matt,' Charles said. 'Do you think Stephen is up to it?'

'Frankly, no,' replied Matt. 'I'll get the MO to look at him when we get back. We should probably leave him tonight, get an odd bod.'

'Seems a good idea. Let me know if there is anything I can do. We better get this lot to shift their arses anyway.'

Matt wandered over to Stephen, who seemed not to have moved during the night and was still staring ahead. He looked dreadful and still had a sheen of sweat on his brow.

'Come on, old chap,' said Matt. 'Time to catch our plane.'

'I can't go, Matt,' Stephen said quietly. 'Can't go. It's no good.'

'Let's get you back, and then we can get you along to the MO. You've had enough, old man. It's obvious. We'll get someone else for tonight, don't worry.' Matt put his arm on Stephen's shoulder and helped him up and over to the bar. The orderly had appeared with more coffee, and Matt poured a cup for them both. 'Come on, old chap, drink up; it will make you feel better.'

The others were in various stages of wakefulness, but no one, apart from Charles, seemed to have noticed anything untoward with Stephen.

By 6.45 a.m., they could hear the rumble of the approaching Lancaster and after thanking the orderly for his help and saying goodbye to the duty station commander, they climbed aboard for the short trip back to East Kirkby.

The pilot was Fight Sergeant Tony Calder, a tough Scot who had not been on the previous night's raid. His engineer was on board, and they had taken the opportunity to air test the Lancaster.

'Bad do last night,' he said to Matt as the aircraft lifted off. 'Thought you lot were goners too!'

'Bloody nearly were,' replied Matt. 'Collected loads of flak, had two run-ins with fighters. Bloody awful.'

'Looks like we are all out tonight. You blokes must be pretty knackered.'

'Say that again,' replied Matt. 'Get our heads down for a few hours and then maybe we'll feel better.'

The aircraft arrived in the circuit and landed gently before taxying to the dispersal. The station commander's car was waiting for them along with a truck to take them back to the crew room.

Matt got the crew together once they got down from the aircraft.

'OK, we obviously need to go and get debriefed, and you probably could all do with something to eat. Once that's sorted, I suggest you go and get some sleep. We will meet at the briefing room at the appropriate time. And well done, chaps. You did well last night. Sorry we have to go again, but there is a war on.' He smiled.

As they were walking to the truck, Wing Commander Squires called to Matt. 'Over here, White, I'll give you a lift back. We need to talk.'

Matt hesitated, but Charles said to him, 'Off you go, Matt. I'll go to the debrief with Don and the two sharpshooters and try and sort out something for Bamber. Don't worry about it. Squires obviously has something on his mind.'

'Thanks, Charles. I'll catch up with you later,' Matt replied and made his way over to W/C Squires.

'Hop in, Matt. You look all in. I'm sorry about tonight. Are your chaps up to it?'

'All but P/O Bamber. He seems to be going through a bad patch. He's as brave as a lion, sir, but I think he needs a rest. Could we stand him down for tonight? I think it will help a lot. I was going to get the MO to see him. Probably needs a bloody good sleep.'

'You're friends, aren't you, Matt?'

'Yes, sir,' Matt replied. 'But even if we weren't, I'd say the same. Some seem to last better than others, sir.'

'I know that, Matt, but you know what the RAF thinks. How do the rest of the crew feel about him? Trouble is if you let one off, then everyone else feels they should have a break too.'

'No one else seems to realise, sir. Except Squadron Leader Redman. He's been very helpful, sir. He thinks Bamber could do with a break too.'

'OK, I'm persuaded. Let him off tonight and get him seen by the MO. Now some better news. I will put your two gunners up for a DFM, and I am recommending you for a DFC. I think you have shown exactly the right spirit, and it sounds to me that last night was no exception. Well done. I will see you at briefing. It will be at 1500 hours, so you should manage an hour or two of sleep.'

He dropped Matt at the officers' mess, and Matt went straight to the dining room.

Judson was there tucking into his bacon and egg. 'Blimey, Matt, we thought you had bought it this time!' he shouted across the table.

'Bloody nearly did!' he replied and settled down to his own breakfast. He was feeling a bit better and suddenly realised he was very hungry. He bolted his food down and after a cup of tea, rose to leave.

'You're in a bit of hurry,' said Judson.

'Yes, got a couple of problems to get sorted out, I'm afraid. See you at lunchtime.'

Redman had finished the debrief and sent Freddie and Townsy off for breakfast. When Matt caught up with him, he was guiding Stephen in the direction of the MO.

'Thanks, Charles. Did everything go all right at the debrief?'

'Piece of cake, old man. We are just off to see the MO.'

'You go and get some grub. I'll take him if you like,' Matt said, looking anxiously at Stephen, who seemed completely withdrawn.

'If that's OK with you? Let me know how things go,' replied Charles, who turned around and walked back towards the mess.

'Come on, Stephen,' Matt said. 'Let's see if the MO is around and get you sorted out.'

They were met by one of the nurses in the sickbay, who took one look at Stephen and led him into one of the cubicles.

'Is Wing Commander Spear around?' Matt asked.

'He's just next door. I'll get him straight away,' the nurse said and left them both in the cubicle.

Wing Commander Spear came in a few minutes later. After asking Stephen a few questions with no response, he took Matt outside.

'When did this start?' he asked.

'Well, things seemed to be getting more difficult for him over the last couple of weeks, sir. It was touch and go if he would come with us last night, but he seemed to buck up a bit.

But we had a bloody awful trip. Scared me to death so God knows what effect it's had on Stephen.'

'Yes, I think they nearly posted you missing, didn't they?' Spear replied.

'Well, clearly, he can't fly tonight,' Spear continued. 'Probably needs to be knocked out for a couple of days and then we'll see how he is.'

'No question of LMF, sir, is it?' Matt asked.

'Certainly not. This man has taken himself to the edge but in spite of that has toughed it out. No, we will probably be able to recover him. You chaps are due some leave, I understand?'

'Yes, sir. After tonight's trip, we have some navigation training and then we get a fortnight off, sir.'

'OK, leave him here. I'll give him something that will make him sleep, and then we'll see.' And with that, Spear turned back towards the cubicle.

Matt suddenly felt exhausted but realised he had still not returned his kit to the crew room and in any case needed to get a replacement for Stephen.

About half an hour later, he found himself in front of Squires.

'Sir, I am afraid that Pilot Officer Bamber has reported sick. W/C Spear feels he needs to be rested, which means we need an engineer for tonight.'

'All under control, Matt,' Squires replied. 'Go and get your head down now. You will have Y-Yorker for tonight. Nearly new. Please bring it back in one piece if you can. You chaps are proving rather expensive, you know.' He smiled at Matt.

Matt saluted and made his way back to his room. Scrap was there lying on Stephen's bed and wagging his tail hopefully.

'Not now, old boy,' Matt replied. 'I need to get my head down.'

Barker appeared. 'You OK, sir?' he asked. 'What about Mr Stephen?'

'I'm fine Barker, thanks. P/O Bamber is over with the MO. He needs a bit of attention, but he will be fine. Will you be able to look after Scrap for a day or two?'

'Pleased to, sir. No problem at all. Can I get you a cuppa, sir?'

'No, thanks, Barker. I must try and get some sleep. We are off again tonight. Can you wake me about two o'clock? A cup of tea then would be most welcome.'

'Will do, sir,' said Barker, and with Scrap in tow, he left, shutting the door quietly behind him.

Matt lay awake for a while, thinking through the events of the night. It had been a close-run thing. Then there was Stephen, who seemed to freeze. Just lost it really. Gave them the wrong fuel reserves. Christ, they could all have died if he had tried to get them home. He turned over, and a troubled sleep came gradually. It seemed almost no time at all before Barker was shaking him with a cup of tea.

'Two o'clock, sir,' Barker said. 'Time to get up, I am afraid, sir.'

'Thanks, Barker,' Matt replied sleepily.

'Could you see if you can get me a sandwich? Anything will do. I don't feel quite ready to join the banter in the mess.'

'Understand, sir. Leave it with me,' said Barker.

Matt swung his legs down. His shoulders and legs were aching from last night's flight back, and it required a bit of effort to ease himself off the bed. He took his towel and made his way to the showers, which, for once, provided acceptably hot water.

He wandered back to his room, feeling better, and when he went in he saw that Barker had conjured up some decent-looking sandwiches, which he ate quickly. He needed to get down to the aircraft and check it over before briefing, which was scheduled for three o'clock.

Feeling slightly more human, he called first in the flight office to see who they had been allocated as flight engineer. He was looking at the ops board when Charles Redman came over to see him.

'They've given us a Flight Sergeant Purdy as our engineer. He's only done a couple of trips, so hopefully he will be up to it. How do you feel? You still look a bit knocked up.'

'Not too bad really, Charles. Thank you. Have you met Purdy?'

'No, I haven't. I imagine he is over in the sergeants' mess. Shall we go and see?'

Matt was pleasantly surprised by this apparent change in Redman, who had until now always been a bit standoffish. He really needed some support just now, especially with Stephen going off sick. They walked over to the sergeants' mess and looked in. All the rest of the crew were there, and Freddie and Townsy came over.

'Hallo, Skip,' said Freddie. 'How yer feeling? Come and meet our new member, John Purdy. He's a Scot, but apart from that, he's all right.'

Purdy looked about fourteen years old. He was quite tall but as thin as a rake and had red cheeks and a generous mouth.

'Hallo, sir,' he said to Matt. 'Looks like you'll be lumbered with me tonight!'

Matt shook his hand. The grip was firm, and Purdy's sharp blue eyes looked straight at him.

'Welcome aboard,' said Matt. 'Have you looked over the aircraft?'

'Aye, sir,' replied Purdy. 'It was air tested by the last crew this morning before they were stood down. Looks OK, sir.'

Matt liked that. Purdy clearly had initiative and probably didn't need to be asked twice to do things. 'Oh, sorry,' said Matt. 'This is Squadron Leader Redman. He is our navigator.'

The two shook hands. By this time, the others had all gathered round. 'How is Pilot Officer Bamber, Skip?' asked Don.

'He's not too good just now, Don,' replied Matt. 'He will need some treatment from the MO, but then he should be fine. Should be back with us after our leave, I would say.'

'Good, Skip,' replied Don. 'So it's true we get leave after this trip, is it, Skip?'

'So I am led to believe.' Matt smiled. 'Let's get this one under our belt first, shall we? Briefing is at 1500 hours. Don't be late, chaps.'

CHAPTER 9

LEIPZIG

Twentieth Trip

The briefing followed its usual course, and this time, the target was Leipzig, another very long trip, and there were the usual groans and catcalls. The weather sounded to be good with clear skies over Leipzig, and the route was towards Frankfurt and then splitting up with a diversionary force heading for Stuttgart.

Matt pulled the crew together after the briefing.

'Let's just concentrate on getting this trip done. I know we should get a break afterwards, but don't think about that for now. Let's go and get some grub and meet in the crew room for 1700 hours.'

Matt and Charles made their way over to the officers' mess.

'New chap seems all right,' said Charles.

'Yes, he does,' replied Matt. 'He's looked over the aircraft already. Still, I hope Stephen is going to be able to get back with us soon. Doc's knocked him out for a couple of days—maybe that'll do the trick.'

They downed their bacon and eggs and after a cup of tea made their way to the crew room, which was already busy with men donning their flying gear. It was noisy with shouts across the room and curses as men struggled into their flying suits. It always reminded Matt of his school changing room on sports afternoon. *Smells a bit like it too,* he thought ruefully. The ritual of getting his gear on was somehow important, but he didn't go to the lengths of some, for whom, for example, it was essential to get the correct sock always on the same foot.

He got his parachute and met up with the others. Mac had already picked up the coffee and sandwiches, and with Charles and his navigation bag and maps, they were ready to go. The truck arrived almost immediately, and they clambered aboard, Freddie, as usual, sounding off about how very unfair it was for him to have to go, yet again, on another long trip. He was obviously pleased to have a new face around in the shape of John Purdy, who, Freddie pointed out, had not until now the benefit of his experience and humour.

However, Matt thought even Freddie seemed a bit quieter than usual and his grumbling seemed a little more heartfelt.

They arrived at Y-Yorker, their usual ground crew there to meet them.

'Hallo, Chiefy. Nice to see you,' called Matt. 'Everything OK?'

'Perfect,' replied Warrant Officer Bryant. 'And if possible, sir, we would like to have this one back in one piece!' He smiled. He was fond of Matt and his crew. They had a sense of humour and didn't treat the ground crew like they were another species. He admired them too. They had been through a lot, though they never complained.

'How's Pilot Officer Bamber, sir? Hear he has gone off sick.'

Blimey, thought Matt. *No bloody secrets on this base.*

'I think he is OK, Chiefy, thanks. Just needs a bit of a break. Be back soon, I'm sure.'

They climbed aboard, and Sergeant Purdy and Matt went through their checks. Matt really liked the way the lad did things, but seeing how he coped with the trip was the main thing.

Engines were started, and they taxied down to the runway. Matt called on the intercom to make sure everyone was OK.

They were lined up on the runway with the throttles open to zero boost against the brakes to check the engines were responding. A green light from the control hut and they were off with the usual groups of personnel there to wave to them.

The aircraft eased off the runway and climbed steadily ahead, disappearing into cloud at about 1,500 feet. He put Y-Yorker into a climbing turn to the right, and they gradually gained altitude over the base. The plan was for them to keep climbing once they left the circuit heading down towards Brighton on the south coast where they would join the bomber stream.

'How we doing, Navigator?' Matt asked. 'Toys working today?'

'Well, we are doing OK as far as GEE is concerned, if that helps. We might need to make a wind adjustment fairly soon, but we seem to be going in the right direction,' Charles replied.

'Can't see a bloody thing down here,' Don said from the front. 'Bloody pea-soup.'

'Talking of soup,' called Freddie. 'It's sodding cold back here. You got the heater on, John?'

'Best we can, pal,' replied Purdy in his strong Glasgow accent.

Joining the bomber stream in cloud was just as nerve-racking as climbing over a cloud-covered airfield—more so probably. If someone had got their timings or their height wrong, the chance of collision and usually instant death was high.

There seemed to be no breaks in the cloud as they flew along at 15,000 feet. Matt kept a close watch outside for signs of icing, and just as they reached the French coast, he noticed it beginning to coat the wings.

'Navigator, we are starting to ice up. Can we see if we can climb out of this cloud before it's too late?'

'Bloody good idea,' Freddie retorted. 'I can hardly see out for sodding ice. How about you, Townsy?'

'Yeh, not so good here either, Skip.'

'OK, let's go up and see if we can get clear. Townsy, keep a sharp lookout. We don't want to bump into anyone. And I mean anyone!'

The Lancaster slowly edged higher, and at about 20,000 feet, they were free of the cloud.

Matt looked around him. The stars were beautiful, and the tops of the clouds could be seen in their reflected light. The moon would not rise until the end of the night. Once they were clear of the cloud, Matt noticed other aircraft emerging like so many porpoises from the sea.

'How's the course looking, Navigator?' Matt asked.

'OK,' replied Redman. 'We now have Frankfurt on our right, and we have a new course in about ten minutes. I think we are a few miles south of where we should be; wind's a bit more northerly than forecast.'

Charles had just finished speaking when there was a violent explosion over to their left and pieces of a stricken Lancaster could be seen spiralling downwards. Y-Yorker rolled to the right and was forced upward as the shock wave hit. Matt struggled to get the aircraft level again.

'Christ, what was that?' called Charles.

'Kite blown up,' Matt said quietly. 'Fighters around, chaps. Keep watching.'

'Skip, we've got a bit of a hole in the fuselage back here,' called Mac from his position aft of Redman. 'Can't see any other damage, but there's quite a draft.'

'Mac, take a look down the rest of the kite. We have probably collected some debris from that explosion. Bloody lucky it didn't take us with them. Everyone else OK?'

Everyone answered, but of course, Freddie had to add a complaint. 'Yes, Skip, but still bloody cold back here. I think my sodding hands have dropped off.'

Mac called back that the hole was situated high up on the fuselage on the left-hand side and that nothing vital seemed to have been hit.

The sky seemed very dark after the huge flash from the explosion, and it seemed a long time before Matt could see a faint glow in the distance, which looked to be where Leipzig should be.

'I can see something up front, Navigator. Quite a way off yet but pretty well on the nose.'

'Yes, that will be our target,' replied Charles. 'About twenty minutes to run.'

They were fairly well back in the bomber stream, but the Pathfinder bombers would be just about there and probably attracting quite a bit of interest from the massive defences that surrounded the target. As they got closer, Matt could see the sharp fingers of the searchlights probing the sky, and he felt his guts tighten. A bomber some distance ahead and below them was clearly coned by the lights, and there were flashes of flak all around. *Dive, you idiot*, thought Matt, but the aircraft just carried on as if caught in a web. Suddenly, a shell obviously found its mark, and the aircraft disappeared in a massive explosion. The bomb doors would have been open, and there had probably been a direct hit.

'Five minutes to target,' said Charles.

'Bomb doors open,' replied Matt. 'All yours, Don.'

The noise of the flak bursting was now terrifying, and the rattle of shrapnel on the fuselage seemed continuous to Matt as they crept towards the target.

Bright lights seemed to be everywhere—sky markers and target indicators from the Pathfinders above, searchlights from below, flashes as bombs exploded, and every now and then bright illuminating markers dropped from enemy fighters above.

To Matt, it felt as if he was flying them into hell. He glanced across at Purdy, but the young airman was concentrating on his dials and instruments and seemed almost oblivious of the cacophony around them.

'Right, right, steady,' Don's voice focussed Matt's mind. He altered course slightly, being sure to maintain height.

'Steady, steady.' Don's voice never wavered in its pitch or volume even though the flak was now very intense and rocking the aircraft.

'Left a little, steady, steady.'

This bit seemed like an age, but it was what they were there for. *No point rushing and screwing up now*, thought Matt.

'Bombs gone.' Don's voice as ever was steady. 'Wait for the photoflash.'

The aircraft, as always, leapt into the air. Matt anticipated the change and eased Y-Yorker back onto course and back down to the previous height. He looked out. It was a clear night for a change. Beneath them were the pulsating blazes from exploding bombs with occasionally huge flashes as something ignited.

'Photo done,' called Don.

Matt heaved the aircraft to port and dived down, in a hurry to get out of the target area. It was a particularly dangerous place to spend time with bombs falling from higher aircraft, others blowing up, and, of course, the deadly flak barrage.

Their course home took them over Holland, a much shorter distance than the way in, but there was a bit of a headwind and it was vital that they did not stray south towards the Ruhr. The hope was that the route they had been given would keep them clear of further defensive positions. What it could not do, however, was to keep the fighters away and their route crossed close to many fighter stations.

All remained quiet although Matt kept weaving the aircraft gently round the sky so that the gunners could get a better view of what was going on below. There was still some scepticism amongst the intelligence officers about the effectiveness of attacks from below, but most of the crews had little doubt these sudden explosions were caused by fighters firing up into the belly of the bomber completely unseen by the crew.

'Keep watching,' said Matt. 'How much further to the coast, Navigator?'

'About thirty minutes, Skip. But we are still in tiger territory.'

'Quite so,' replied Matt. 'John, everything OK with fuel and engines?'

'Yes, sir. We will be a bit tight on fuel but should be all right.'

'Thanks,' replied Matt. He liked this lad's approach, he thought. No fuss, just gets the job done.

'Corkscrew right!' shouted Freddie. 'Bastard just creeping up from below.' Freddie had seen the fighter dimly outlined against the sheet of cloud they were now over. There was the clatter of guns, and Freddie called, 'Missed the bastard. He dived off to the left so could still be around.'

'I'll get down into the cloud. It will give us some cover.'

Matt took the aircraft down and into the blanket of cloud, but it was not quite the cover one might think. The fighters had radar, so they could find the bombers in any visibility, although they still needed to see the bomber before they could shoot it down with any certainty.

The cloud folded over them.

'Enemy coast five minutes now, Skip.'

They were nearly there, but even at this late stage, bombers could sometimes be caught napping and shot down into the sea. In winter, that was nearly always a death sentence in any case.

'Mac, get the coffee out, but you gunners keep a lookout.'

Matt suddenly felt very tired. Back-to-back ops had not helped, but after the tension of the attack, he felt drained. He still had to get them home and on the ground in one piece.

They crossed the coast over Lowestoft and were about to head for base when Mac called, 'Everywhere is socked in. Yorkshire's clear, but they are kind of busy. They are suggesting Bourn if we have enough fuel.'

Matt could not believe it. He felt sick at the thought of having yet another problem to deal with when all he really wanted was to get down and go to bed.

'OK. John, how much fuel do we have? Navigator, can we find Bourn?'

Purdy was the first to answer. 'We have sixty-five minutes left, sir.'

'Good. Well, that gives us a bit of scope.'

A few minutes later, he heard, 'Yes, Bourn could take us at the moment. It's a bit misty but not bad. They are giving us runway two-four, but we will need to stack first.'

'We should make it OK if you're right on the fuel, John?'

It took them twenty-five minutes to find Bourn. They were held in the circuit for another twenty minutes, and Matt saw that the fuel gauges indicated the tanks were pretty empty. He glanced at Purdy, but the lad seemed to indicate no concern. Finally, they landed, having been airborne for nearly nine hours. Engines shut down, and the crew jumped down.

'Well done, John,' Matt said. 'We really did have enough. Well, here we are again, everyone. Another airfield we didn't take off from!'

The truck pulled up, and they jumped in. It was bitterly cold, and they were pleased to get into the mess for something warm to drink.

Matt called East Kirkby and spoke to the station commander.

'Sorry, sir. We are in Bourn. Kite's OK, although might need a patch or two. We will come over once the fog clears. Goodnight, sir.'

***

The fog had lifted from East Kirkby by nine o'clock, and Matt and his weary crew arrived back by ten o'clock in the morning. Aircraft seemed to be arriving from all over the place, but it had been a bad night for losses. Fourteen aircraft crashed because the conditions over eastern England had been so bad.

After their debrief, Matt got the crew together.

'Well, chaps, we now have our training fortnight, and then we are off for a couple of weeks, thank God. How about we all meet up in the Red Lion at five o'clock to celebrate? John, you'll come along, won't you?'

'Well, so long as no one wants me for tonight. Aye, I'd like that.'

'Jimmy boy, just tell them you've got another appointment for tonight. Sure they'll understand!' quipped Freddie. 'In any case, Skip, I'm off for some kip.'

'See you later, Freddie,' replied Matt, walking away. 'Charles, I'm going to see how Stephen is. Will you join us all later?'

'Yes, I will,' replied Redman. 'I'll bring Clare. Hope Bamber is better.'

'Thanks, so do I. Incidentally, Purdy seemed an excellent young man. If Stephen is going to be out of it for a while, I wouldn't mind him with us. What do you think?'

'I agree. He seemed just the right sort. Well, let's see how Bamber gets on first. Probably worth mentioning to Squires though. Go and get some sleep yourself, Matt. You looked pretty knackered.'

'Feel it. Just get Stephen sorted first. See you later.' And with this, Matt walked off towards the sickbay.

Wing Commander Spear was just coming out as Matt approached.

'Hallo, Matt. How was last night? There were quite a few lost on this side of the Channel.'

'Yes, sir. Bloody foggy. We paid a visit to Bourn. How's Pilot Officer Bamber, sir?'

'Well, he slept most of the night, but I'm going to keep him in here for a while. You chaps have some training and then you are on leave, aren't you?'

'Yes, sir. Can I pop in to see him, or is he still asleep?'

'No, best leave him to us for now. He's probably asleep by now in any case. I gave him a drop more jungle juice about half an hour ago. Look in later today if you like. Looks like you could do with some shut-eye yourself. Do you need something to help?'

'No, thanks, sir. I think I'll be off as soon as my head hits the pillow.'

Matt set off for his hut and then remembered he had not phoned Anne. He went to the mess and called the hospital. She was, of course, busy, but he left a message with the porters' lodge that he would call her later in the day. Back at his hut, he found Barker tidying up.

'Hallo, sir. Where did you get to?'

'Bourn,' Matt replied. 'And I now need to sleep very much. Where's Scrap? You know that Pilot Officer Bamber is staying in the sickbay just now?'

'Don't you worry about that, sir,' Barker replied. 'Scrap is well taken care of.'

Matt got undressed and collapsed onto his bed. It was cold in the room, and he pulled the bedclothes up over his head and fell deeply asleep.

When he eventually woke, his shower was on the cold side of tepid but refreshing, and he thought how much better he felt. That last raid had been pretty bad with another diversion at the end. He had been beyond tired, but his rest had done him good and he felt ready to face another day. By the time he had got back to his room, Barker had made his tea and had conjured up a sandwich from somewhere.

CHAPTER 10

LEAVE

The two weeks' navigation training went without a hitch. Stephen remained off sick, but the others got on with the work and young Purdy proved his worth. The new navigation equipment being fitted to the Lancasters included an upgraded H2S airborne radar set, which showed ground features beneath the aircraft, and Charles was involved in showing the other navigators the ropes using Y-Yorker whilst M-Mother was being patched up. It involved quite a bit of night flying, but at least no one was trying to shoot them down and they had their two weeks' leave to look forward to afterwards. Matt and Anne managed to meet up occasionally, but they had no chance to get away. The winter seemed to have come quickly, and by the end of the fortnight's training, there were occasional showers of snow and some very chilly nights. Eventually, it was all over, and the crew had arranged to meet, as usual, in the Red Lion before they went their separate ways.

***

Matt woke up about eleven o'clock in the morning. It felt cold, and he could hear the wind whistling around the hut and the rain rattling against the window. He was loath to get up, but he swung his legs off the bed and grabbed his dressing gown. It seemed odd to see Stephen's bed still empty, and he was keen to get down to the sickbay to see how his old friend was getting on. First, he needed to brave the showers, which were always chilly at this time of the year, and he grabbed his towel and opened the door only to see Barker approaching.

'Morning, sir. Would a cuppa help?'

'Thanks, Barker. That would do very nicely. Just off for a shower. Plenty of hot water, I hope?'

'Incidentally, the CO wants to see you sometime this afternoon, sir. Oh, and your nice lady friend rang up. She had got your message and wondered if you could call her about six o'clock this evening at the hospital?'

'Thanks, Barker. Well, that nice young lady I hope is going to be my wife as soon as we can manage it.'

'Very good, sir. Pleased to hear it.' And with that, Barker left, closing the door quietly behind him.

Matt dressed, finished his tea, grabbed his greatcoat, and called at the flight office before heading for the CO's office. He knocked on the door.

'Come,' Matt heard Group Captain Brookes' rather imperious voice say.

'Ah, White. How are you? Hear the training has gone well, and as you know, we are recommending you for a DFC and your two gunners a DFM.'

'Thank you, sir. They will appreciate that, sir. They are both very good, sir. Don't complain too much!'

'Well, I know Hughes is a bit of a rascal, but heart's in the right place, eh?'

'Yes, sir.'

'Now I am going to put you up to Flying Officer with immediate effect. I am very taken with your attitude, White. Well done.'

Matt felt himself flush as he came to terms with the promotion. Anne would be impressed. More important, he hoped her old man would be.

'Thank you, sir.'

'You are off on leave now for a couple of weeks, that's correct?'

'Yes, sir.'

'Good, enjoy. How is Bamber doing? I am a bit worried about him; MO is too.'

'Just off to see him now, sir. I think he needs a bit of a rest. Sure he will be OK after a bit of leave, sir.'

'I hope so, White. We can't have chaps cracking up, you know. Bad for the rest.'

Matt saluted and left the room. He made his way to the sickbay. He wanted to see how Stephen was getting on before he joined the crew in the Red Lion, partly for himself but also because he knew the others would be asking about him. W/C Spear met him at the sickbay door.

'Hallo, Matt,' he said.

'Good afternoon, sir. How's Bamber today? I wondered if now would be a good time to see him?'

'He's not that great, to be honest, Matt. The nurses say he keeps waking and shouting and is clearly having bad nightmares. I suppose he seems a bit better in himself, but it looks a bit like battle fatigue to me and we both know how the RAF view that.'

'Surely we can give him a chance, sir? He hasn't refused to fly, and that must take some guts given his state of mind.'

'I agree, Matt. We can keep him here for another day or two, but we might have some trouble when the station commander does his rounds tomorrow. However, go in and see him. See what you think yourself.'

Matt walked into the ward and found Stephen in a bed over in one corner. He thought that he was asleep, but Stephen opened his eyes as Matt approached.

'Good to see you, Matt.' He smiled. 'How did the training stuff go?'

'Pretty good, thanks,' he replied. 'How are you feeling anyway?'

'Not too bad,' Stephen replied. 'Get a lot of nightmares, but I feel a bit better with some sleep. I hope I can get out tomorrow. I would really like to spend some time with Jess if possible. It's good to think we have a couple of weeks off, isn't it? Are you seeing Anne tonight?'

'No, I doubt it. I haven't even managed to speak to her yet. And I suspect she may not be too pleased to see me after tonight's session in the Lion. You know what the lads are like. Anyway, we are hoping we can get married fairly soon. Stephen, would you consider being the best man?'

'Gosh. I would jump at it, old man. Terrific idea.' His face lit up as he shook Matt by the hand. Matt had not seen him look so animated for several weeks. If only it would last.

'Well, I better trot along,' said Matt. 'I will give the lads a good report on your progress. If you get out tomorrow, it sounds a good idea to try and meet Jess. You've got the hospital number. It should be possible to get her there. Anne and I will probably head off to her parents. Have to ask permission of her old man, of course!'

'Well, good luck to you both,' called Stephen. 'If you come back into Lincoln, let's try and meet up?'

Matt walked briskly out of the ward. Stephen seemed much more like his old self, but clearly the MO was still quite worried. Anyway, it looked as if some progress was being made and feeling less tired would help. Matt was in a happier state of mind as he headed off to the Red Lion.

***

Although it was bitterly cold outside and some earlier snow was still lying on the ground, the log fire made the pub warm, and there was already quite a fug. A cry went up as Matt came through the door, and he had no trouble in locating his crew. Clearly, Freddie and Townsy had been at the beer for a while, and Mac and Don looked pretty cheery too. Charles had a half-finished pint in his hand and was the first to offer Matt a beer. Matt was pleased to see that John Purdy was there joining in with the others.

'Glad you could make it, John,' he called across the crowd.

'Yes, W/C Squires has given me a couple of nights off. Incidentally, sir, my friends call me Jimmy.'

'Very good, Jimmy,' Matt replied. 'We have been pleased to have you on board,' he continued. 'Where's home?' he asked.

'Glasgow, sir. The family live in Hillhead near to the university. My pa works there as the head porter. I was hoping to go to university mysel'. Got my Matric and all, but then along came the war so I decided to join up. After a while, I fancied aircrew so here I am.'

'Were you going to do engineering in any case?' asked Matt.

'Och aye,' Purdy replied. 'I'll get there eventually, I reckon.'

'Well, good luck to you,' replied Matt, reaching out for the pint of beer Redman had got him.

'How's Pilot Officer Bamber, Skip?' asked Freddie.

'Not too bad, Freddie. I think he will be OK by the time we all get back. He asked to be remembered to you all. How about a toast?'

The beer flowed, and the relief of not having to fly again for a couple of weeks released a lot chiding and humour. Freddie was in great form, and he and Townsend were clearly elated not just from the fact they were still alive but that they were both to receive DFMs for their roles in shooting down a couple of enemy aircraft.

'Everyone's in good spirits, Matt,' said Redman. 'They have a lot of time for you, you know?'

Matt smiled. 'Well, they and you are not a bad lot really. Gosh, is that the time? I must just go and call Anne. I missed her call when I was asleep.'

Matt went out to the telephone and managed to get through to the nurses' home almost straight away.

'Sister Jones here,' came the rather severe voice.

'Could I speak to Sister Johnson please?'

'Who is asking? It's not usual for nurses to receive phone calls here, you know?'

'Yes, it's Flying Officer White,' Matt replied and almost without thinking added, 'DFC. Oh, and she is my fiancée.'

There was brief silence at the other end of the phone, presumably as Sister Jones took all this on board.

'Right, I will go and see if she is in her room. Hold the line, will you?' she said imperiously.

Matt smiled as he conjured up the image of Sister Jones bustling down the corridor.

It was a couple of minutes before Anne got to the phone, and Matt had had to feed some more money into the phone box.

'Darling, I was getting so worried. What's been happening? Are you all right?'

'Yes, OK now, thanks. Listen, I am with the crew just now, but as you know, we start our leave today. Shall I come and get you early tomorrow morning? We need to go and speak to your parents and start getting things sorted out.'

'Matt, I would love to see you tomorrow. I have managed to get nearly two weeks off too. How lucky is that? What time can you get here? Sooner the better.'

'OK, how about eight o'clock? I'm running out of coins. See you outside the hospital then. I love you, darling. See you tomorrow.'

Matt put the receiver down. He felt very good, probably from a combination of the thoughts of seeing Anne, a few beers, and the fact they had survived twenty trips and were well on their way to completing their tour.

When he got back in the bar, Freddie, Townsy, and Jimmy were already in full song. It looked like it might be a long night, but Matt was determined not to get completely legless.

'What are you two going to do for the fortnight?' Matt asked Don and Mac.

'Probably head down to London for a few days,' Mac replied. 'Then Don's family have asked me to go to join them in Manchester. It will be nice to be with other folk for a while. Plus, Don says he has a sister. Mind you, if she looks like him, there's no hope!' He laughed.

'What about you, Skip?'

'Well, Anne and I are going to her parents' in Worcester. Like you, it will be nice to be in someone's house rather than a billet!'

Charles Redman was looking a little bleary-eyed as he worked his way across to the group. 'I'm going to head off, Matt. Nearly closing time in any case, and I am definitely not going back to the mess.' He smiled. 'Have a good fortnight, and I will see you when you get back.'

'Yes, you enjoy your leave too, Charles. I am just about to go myself.'

Matt said his goodbyes to the rest of the crew. Freddie, Townsy, and Jimmy seemed well away, and they all cheered loudly as he left them. It was cold outside, and the night was very still and quiet with the occasional owl hooting from the trees. He hoped that all would go well when he and Anne went down to see her parents. It seemed so important to get on with it now that they had decided on marrying.

***

The next morning was cloudy and cold, and as Matt put his luggage in the car, he noticed some frozen snow on the windscreen and was slightly surprised when the engine started the first time he tried it. Even with his greatcoat, scarf, and gloves, it felt cold as he set off. The sky was gradually brightening, and the almost luminous clouds helped to light the way. The roads were completely empty, and the covering of snow made things quite slippery, but after about forty minutes, he was getting into the outskirts of Lincoln and eventually arrived at the hospital just before eight o'clock. Anne was waiting for him in the porters' lodge, and she threw her arms around him.

'Darling, I was so worried about you when you didn't ring.' She sighed. 'Now we have some time together.'

They kissed as Matt led her off to where the car was parked.

'I thought you nurses weren't allowed to do any kissing in hospital grounds?' He laughed.

'Only with the man you are going to marry. Incidentally, I didn't know we were engaged or …' she added and smiled, 'that you were now a Flying Officer no less.'

'Ah well,' Matt replied, 'I had to say something to the old witch who answered the phone. She wasn't keen to get you! Oh, and it's "sir" to you!'

'Well, I'm very happy with the idea,' Anne said. 'Mummy and Daddy are expecting us tomorrow.'

'I thought we were going today,' Matt replied.

'Well, the problem is, Matt, that we will be sleeping in separate rooms, and I thought it might be quite nice to spend tonight together.'

'Well, I agree with that,' Matt said. 'We can stop off on the way somewhere. Any case, let's get started. This weather doesn't look too good, does it?'

The low clouds seemed to promise some more snow, and the easterly wind had strengthened since Matt had left the base. They clambered into the car, which, with their cases, looked rather overloaded. The roads were still quiet as they made their way south down the A46 towards Anne's parents' home, and it was a while before they spoke.

'How's Stephen?' Anne asked.

'Not good,' Matt replied. 'The MO took him off flying so we had to do the last op with an odd bod, who, I have to say, turned out to be jolly good. I popped in to see Stephen before I left. The doc had given him some knockout pills so at least he had had some sleep, and he seemed a bit better. But God knows if he will be back flying. He's really only got this fortnight to get himself straightened out. It's not long. He was hoping to see Jess sometime. I'm sure she will help.'

'Matt, what happens if he can't fly again?' Anne asked. 'Is it really as bad as everyone says?'

'Pretty well. He would be labelled LMF and reduced in rank and could end up cleaning the latrines. It's often that bad. Meant to make the rest of us think twice before running off.'

'But he's not running off really, is he?' Anne replied. 'I mean, he's ill.'

'Not the way they see it, I'm afraid,' Matt replied, and they fell silent again.

The weather was really awful with further flurries of snow as they got towards Leicester, and Matt was feeling distinctly hungry and in need of a cup of tea.

'Let's see if we can find somewhere to stop. I need a break for a while,' he said, and as they went into Leicester, they saw a small café set back from the road. Matt turned in and parked the car. It was not very salubrious-looking, but it would have to do. They went in to a fug of cigarette smoke and fried food and found a table by the window, which was steamy and none too clean. Matt looked at Anne, but she seemed unconcerned, and as the waitress came over, she asked for a cup of tea.

'Do you want anything to eat, Anne?' Matt asked. 'What do you have?' He turned to the waitress.

'We can do bacon and eggs, sir, with some toast.'

'Perfect,' replied Matt. 'That OK for you, Anne?'

Anne nodded and leaned across the table to take Matt's hand.

'It's so good to feel we now have some time together,' she said. 'And I am sure Mummy and Daddy will be thrilled to see you. When can we get married, do you think?'

'Soon as poss, old girl,' he replied. 'I will have another two weeks' leave at the end of January. Do you think your parents would be OK with that? I thought I would ask Stephen to be my best man. And if he's home, your brother could be an usher.'

'My, you have been busy thinking about things, haven't you?' She smiled. 'Let's see if we can work something out. Late January sounds good to me.'

Their food arrived. The bacon was pretty greasy but tasted good, and Matt had finished his in no time and then started on Anne's. It seemed a long time since he had really felt like eating, and this was perfect for now.

They paid and got back in the car. There was more traffic on the roads now, and their progress towards Anne's home in Worcester was slower. It was lunchtime before they arrived in Warwick, and Matt found a pub that he knew from his time in Wellesbourne.

It was in the old town, and there was a welcoming fug as he and Anne went in. There was a huge log fire burning, and Anne settled down at a table close to the fire.

'What you having, sir?' asked the barman.

'Well, a pint of best bitter and a gin and orange would be good for starters,' said Matt. 'Do you have anything for lunch?'

'A nice cottage pie, sir. Would you like two of those?'

'Yes, thanks,' Matt replied. 'That will help to keep out the cold. It's really freezing out there now. Incidentally, do you have a room for tonight?'

'We certainly do, sir. If you give me an hour, I will get a fire lit up there and make sure the bed is aired. It would be a pleasure to have you and your wife stay with us.'

Matt made his way back to Anne.

'Food is on the way. Bed for the night fixed. And he definitely thinks we're married!' he said, smiling as he sat down.

'Well, I must say I am pleased to get a break from the car, darling. And …' she said, lowering her voice, 'I am very much looking forward to you know what?' She laughed.

They finished their lunch in silence, Anne watching Matt rush his food as if it was his last meal. But then she shuddered at the idea that that might be how he felt sometimes. He looked very tired, and the worry lines around his mouth seemed deeper than she remembered. They had another drink, and then Anne got up and went over to the barman.

'Is the room ready, do you think?' she asked. 'My husband is rather tired, been on ops for two nights running, you know?'

'It should be ready by now, ma'am. We put a hot water bottle in the bed so that should be warm. It's room number four just up the stairs.'

'Thank you very much,' Anne said, and she went over to Matt. 'Come on, sleepy. The room is ready now. Time for a bit of shut-eye.' She winked.

Matt got the bags out of the car, and they went upstairs. The room was still quite cold, but the fire burning in the grate made things seem warm. Matt shut the door, and almost before he had turned back to Anne, she was undressing.

'Come on, Flying Officer White!' She laughed. 'You'll catch your death out there.'

Anne had left her black silk slip on, and as Matt got into the bed, he felt it brush against him. She lifted it up to her waist, and he rolled on top of her. They made love, and, as usual to begin with, they both came quickly. They lay together for a while, and then Anne started to stroke Matt gently as he kissed her. They made love again, but this time, more slowly and feelingly.

Matt fell into a deep sleep as Anne watched him, and again she was struck by how his face changed as he relaxed, more like the old Matt she had met those months ago.

They both slept for some hours, and when Matt eventually awoke, it was dark outside.

As Matt surfaced from his sleep, he had an extraordinary feeling of well-being—the joy of being with Anne, the fact they had got some time together, and the love he felt for her. It was delicious, but then other thoughts came crowding in—the war, the flying, and Stephen.

He looked over at Anne, and she opened her eyes and smiled at him.

'Welcome back,' she said.

She snuggled up to him, and he could feel her fingers gently stroking him before she came on top of him.

They eventually got up and went downstairs. The bar was full of locals, some of whom stopped talking as they walked up to the bar. They ordered drinks and a meal, and then Matt noticed a couple of RAF aircrew and he went over to them.

'Hallo, chaps. Where are you from?'

'We're having a night away from Wellesbourne, sir,' the wireless operator replied.

'I was there a couple of years ago. How much longer have you got?'

'Only just arrived, sir. Sir, what's it like flying over Germany? It must be exciting!'

'Well, it certainly can be.' Matt smiled. 'Anyway, good luck to you both,' and he walked back to Anne.

'Poor buggers have just started,' he said. 'Wellesbourne. Same place as me. What have we got to eat then?'

Anne smiled. 'You and your stomach. I better warn Mummy to get in more supplies.'

***

The next day was bright but cold, and Matt felt much better after a night's sleep and for being with Anne. They arrived at Anne's home on the outskirts of Worcester in the early afternoon. The Edwardian house was large and set in its own grounds surrounded by a wood. Its entrance was below the level of the road, and Matt drove the car down a short drive to the front door. Matt noticed the doctor's plate next to the front door, which opened as they got out of the car.

Anne's mother was a short, slim, attractive woman, like Anne. She had deep-brown eyes, which seemed to sparkle as she spoke. She hugged Anne and took Matt's hand.

'Hallo, Matt?' she said and smiled. 'Do come in. It's such a cold day. Dr Johnson is out on his rounds just now. He should be back by about five o'clock. Come into the kitchen where it's nice and warm.'

Matt and Anne followed her into the large kitchen. An Aga was giving out a glorious amount of heat and had a steaming kettle on top of it.

'You both must be freezing. Was your journey not too bad? Let me make you some tea.'

'No, Mummy. We had a good trip down, but it was jolly cold in Matt's car, wasn't it, darling?' Anne said, turning to Matt. 'Shall I show him up to his room, Mummy?'

'Yes, do. You know where. I'm afraid the heating isn't up to much, but there are plenty of blankets.'

Matt and Anne took their cases up the stairs. Matt looked around. The house was vast compared with the farmhouse he had grown up in, but it had the same homely feel. His room was at the back of the house, and there was still enough light to see the garden below and the forest beyond. He unpacked, and Anne came back to collect him so that they could go downstairs together. They had just finished their tea when Dr Johnson came home. He was about Matt's size with a face that smiled easily and grey, kindly eyes. He had a shock of grey hair, and Matt reckoned he was a good ten years older than Anne's mother.

'Hallo, Matt,' he said. 'We have so much been looking forward to meeting you. Has Florence been looking after you? Maybe something a little stronger than tea?'

'Thank you, sir. It's good to meet you both at last. Anne has spoken fondly of you both.'

Dr Johnson poured a couple of large whiskeys and shepherded the couple into the sitting room.

'Anne, dear, what would you like to drink? I know it's not scotch. Your mother has a sherry about now, don't you, dear?'

They all sat down in the living room. There was a hearty log fire blazing away, and Matt felt very much at home although he was anxious about how the next half an hour might go, once the subject of the wedding was raised.

'Well, Matt, how are things going with the RAF? You fly Lancasters we hear from Anne.'

'Yes, sir. We are well over halfway through the tour—another ten ops to do.'

'And what then?' Dr Johnson asked. 'Do you get a rest?'

'Yes, we do, sir, and then we will usually be sent off as instructors. Some choose to go back for a second tour. Not sure I would want to do that.'

'Mother says you and Anne are thinking of getting married? When had you in mind?'

'Well, as soon as possible, sir, if you had no objections. We were thinking about the end of January next year, sir. I will be due some leave, and it would fit nicely.'

The doctor looked at Matt over his glasses.

'When do you think you will finish this present tour, Matt?'

'Difficult to say, sir. It's taken us six months to get this far, so I suppose another three months or so should see it done.'

'Why not wait till then? Wouldn't it be better to marry when all the strain of flying these missions is behind you?'

'Daddy,' Anne started, 'we want some time together as soon as we can. I think we both feel that it would give us some hope for the future.'

Dr Johnson's brow became furrowed. He loved his daughter, and he could see how tragedy could so easily intervene in this young couple's lives. He looked across at his wife. 'What do you think, dear?' he asked.

She looked sadly at Anne. 'Maybe it would be a good idea to get on with it, dear. It's difficult to know what's in front for any of us at the moment, isn't it? Maybe Richard could get home then. It would be a lovely family occasion.'

'OK, I'm persuaded. Matt, you will realise that once there are two women against you, you don't stand much chance! The very best of luck to you both.'

Matt and Anne looked at one another. They had worried in case Anne's parents had said no, but now that they hadn't, they could look forward to January with real hope.

After dinner, Matt and Anne took a walk outside around the house. It was very cold, and the snow that had fallen earlier crunched under their feet. The snow-covered trees showed up easily even in the dark, and for the first time, Matt realised how quiet it was. On the base, there was continual noise, but here in the country, there was not a sound.

They got back into the house just as Dr Johnson was leaving.

'Mrs Bain's just about to have her third.' He smiled. 'See you in the morning.'

And with that, he rushed off to his car, bag in hand.

***

They said goodnight, and Matt went into his room, undressed, and got into bed. Again, the extraordinary quiet of the place struck him and he rolled over to go to sleep. A floorboard creaked, and he heard the rustle of silk as Anne took off her dressing gown and got into bed beside him. They made love quietly and gently and then lay together for a while before Anne kissed him, got out of bed, and walked quietly out of the room.

Matt turned over and looked out of the window. He could see the stars glowing against the blackness of the night, and whilst he was thinking how beautiful it looked and how wonderful the day had been, he fell asleep.

It was light when Anne came into his room with a cup of tea.

'Morning,' she said. 'Here's a cuppa. It's nine thirty before you ask.'

They kissed.

'I wish Barker was as good-looking as you.' Matt smiled

'Breakfast is downstairs when you are ready. Mummy said there is plenty of water if you would like a bath.'

A bath. It was a while since he had had one of those—in fact, when he and Anne were in Bakewell. What luxury. He got his dressing gown and padded down to the bathroom. The bath was delicious, and he felt much refreshed after soaking for half an hour.

He finished breakfast as Anne came into the room. Their plan had been to go into Worcester and see the shops. Matt really wanted to buy an engagement ring, if at all possible. Then they could have an engagement party whilst they were still here with Anne's parents. They would stay for a while and then planned to spend a couple of nights on their own before going back to Lincoln.

Once in Worcester, they went into a rather fancy-looking jeweller's and found the ring they wanted and one, even more importantly, that fitted Anne's slender finger. At that moment, Matt could not remember feeling so happy, and they hugged one another there and then in the shop. Once outside the shop, Anne found a phone box and gave the news to her mother, who immediately started to organise a party with their friends and neighbours so they could celebrate before Matt and Anne headed back.

***

The time passed quickly, and almost before they realised it, they were loading up the car. Matt had felt at home with Anne's parents, and they had made him very welcome. The wedding had been set for Saturday, 29 January, and Matt had managed to contact his parents in Yorkshire to let them know. But now, as he was getting ready to go back to the squadron, the warm feelings that he had were beginning to wane and to be replaced by the dread of what he had to go through before the end of January. And the problems with Stephen, which he had managed to put to one side, started to come back into focus, together with the very real fear that his friend, whom he had been with from the start, would be kicked out of flying.

Anyway, they still had a few days and he was determined that nothing would get in the way of the rest of their time together. Stephen and the squadron could wait for now.

***

They left Anne's parents' after ten days. It had been a lovely interlude, and Matt was relieved that the subject of their wedding had passed without difficulty. He felt refreshed from his uninterrupted sleeps, apart from when Anne came into his bed, and some decent home cooking. Anne looked better too, and they set off with an intention to stay somewhere well away from the airfields that smothered East Anglia and Lincolnshire. Shrewsbury seemed a good choice, and they were certain that they would find somewhere to stay there and equally certain they would not meet anyone from the squadron. Although early November, there had been several more falls of snow, especially over on the Welsh mountains, making them look very picturesque.

Once in Shrewsbury, they found a hotel that had some rooms free, and it was good to close the door of their room and to be alone. Although their time at Anne's parents' had been enjoyable, they were never able to have some time just on their own. They got undressed and into bed where they could make love without fear of interruption. They had dinner and then went back to their room. To Matt, this seemed like heaven, but the thoughts of going back were gradually becoming more intrusive.

***

As they made their way back to Lincoln, Matt drove in almost complete silence. He felt sick at the thought of having to leave Anne at the hospital and even worse at the prospect of returning to the squadron. He was due back at midnight, and it was 6.00 p.m. when he drove into the hospital grounds. It seemed impossible to think that they had left only a couple of weeks before. Anne was crying even before she got out of the car.

Matt came round to help her with her bag. 'Thanks for such a lovely time,' he said. 'Won't be long before we are together again. At least we now have something to aim for in January.'

He wrapped his arms around Anne and held her. He could feel her crying and felt her tears on his cheek. 'Come on, old thing,' he said. 'I will let you know what the score is once I get back to base. See what Stephen is up to.'

The most difficult thing was now—saying goodbye and trying not to feel that it might be forever. Matt turned to get back in the car. Anne was already on the steps of the hospital, and she turned and waved and then went inside. Matt had a heavy heart as he got back into the car and started up. He drove slowly back, trying to adjust his mind to what was ahead, but he kept thinking of Anne and all that she meant to him.

***

After Matt and Charles had left the Red Lion on the night they had finished their navigation training, Freddie got into his stride, talking about officers in general and some in particular.

'Gawd above!' He started waving an empty glass about to emphasise his points. 'It makes you wonder how some of them ever got to be officers. Some seem just stupid. Don't know nuffin'.'

'Another pint then, Freddie?' asked Don, who could see they were in for a rather long night of it.

'Don't mind if I do, squire,' Freddie replied. 'Mind you, our lot seem OK really. I mean Skip's a pretty good driver, and Redman don't get us lost. Not so sure about Bamber, but he's probably OK too!'

Don returned with the pints. 'Well, I reckon White is bloody good. He doesn't take risks like some of them do. He's not a bad bloke either. Anyway, what are we going to do once the pub shuts?'

'Well, nothing bloody doing on a Sunday in Lincoln,' said Townsy. 'May as well go back to the mess and get lathered with cheap NAAFI beer.'

'Good idea,' said Don. 'Let's drink up and head back. Anyway, Mac and I have got an early start in the morning. He needs to catch a train to London, and I need to get up to Manchester to see my folk.'

They drank up and headed out of the pub and onto the road up the airfield. It was very cold, and the contrast with the fug and warmth of the pub was striking. There was still some snow in the air, and what was on the ground was crisp and crunched under their boots.

'Bit bloody parky out here,' said Mac.

'Parky?' replied Freddie. 'If you want bloody parky, mate, you should come and sit in my bleeding turret for eight fucking hours.'

'I wouldn't go anywhere near any bloody turret you'd been in, that's for sure,' replied Mac, and with that, he bent down and made a snowball, which he threw with some accuracy, hitting Freddie full in the face.

This was a sign for a full-scale snowball fight, which continued until the airfield gate. Freddie managed to throw one at one of the sentries.

'Bloody hell,' said Townsy. 'It's a bloody shame you can't shoot as well as you can throw a sodding snowball. Bloody Luftwaffe would give in straightaway.'

As the sentry was clearing the snow out of his eyes, he said, 'I should put you on a bloody charge, Sergeant!'

'Just an accident,' said Freddie. 'Was aiming at one of these bastards and they moved, didn't they?'

With that, the five walked off to the mess for a further round of drinks. Mac, Don, and Purdy finished their drinks and left Freddie and Townsy together, sipping yet another pint. It was obviously going to be a very long night for the two friends.

***

Stephen eventually left the sickbay over two weeks after the Leipzig operation. He was feeling much more rested, and he was looking forward to almost two weeks of leave. The doc had given him a few pills to help him sleep at night and had said that he thought Stephen would be fine with a few days of rest. He turned into the billet and had just got into his room when Barker came in, followed closely by Scrap, who proceeded to jump on the bed and reach up to lick Stephen's face.

'That's the sort of welcome you like, sir,' said Barker. 'Are you feeling better, sir?'

'Yes, thank you, Barker. Is there any chance of a cup of tea?'

'Coming up, sir,' replied Barker. 'Are you going to get away this leave, sir?'

'I don't think so. There really isn't time now to get up to Yorkshire and see the parents. I will probably potter around Lincoln.'

'Tea coming up, sir,' said Barker. 'Good to have you back, sir. Mr White has gone off with his lady friend. I don't think he will be back until he has to!'

'Absolutely, Barker. Good for them, eh?'

In reality, Stephen did not really know what he was going to do. There was always the mess here full of folk, but he would have rather got away. Jess should be around sometime. He would love to see her again, maybe spend a night with her. He resolved to ring the hospital and leave a message for her to see if she was free.

Barker brought in the tea and quietly shut the door behind him. Scrap was spread-eagled on the bed, looking at Stephen with his large brown eyes.

'OK, old boy. Have my tea and then we will go for a nice long walk.'

Scrap's ears pricked up at the magic word, and his tail wagged furiously.

Stephen drank his tea and pulled on his greatcoat. He picked up Scrap's lead and made for the door. It was cold outside but bright, and Stephen felt better than he had done for a long time. They were into November now, and another couple of months should see their tour completed. And now there was Matt and Anne's wedding to look forward to at the end of January. It was almost good to be alive. The only blot on the horizon was that they still had ten ops to do. That was a lot.

Out of the front gate, Stephen set off down the lane towards the Red Lion. *Should be open by the time we come back*, he thought. Scrap was way ahead, sniffing just about every foot of the banks along the side of the road. This was his country, Stephen thought. *A dog free as a bird.* He smiled to himself at the thought. They turned into a wood, and Stephen was struck by the sound of the wind sighing through the leafless branches. It was a little warmer in the wood out of the wind, and the sun was just strong enough to dapple the snow-covered ground with light.

After about an hour, Stephen turned back towards the road. The sun had gone, and it had started to sleet, a reminder that winter was there already. He turned onto the road and after a short distance got to the pub just as it was opening.

The publican recognised Stephen as he approached. 'Hallo, sir,' he said. 'Not flying then?'

'No, Joe. We've got a few days' grace. I thought a pint of your best would be just what I would be looking for.'

'Come on in, sir. I'll get it right away for you. And you, young man,' he said, looking at Scrap, 'let's see what we can find for you an' all.'

There were a couple of locals already in their usual places when Stephen went in, and they nodded at him as he sat down.

'Joe, where's the telephone in here. I need to make a call into Lincoln.'

'You come around here, sir, and use our phone. It would be a pleasure.'

'Thanks, Joe. That's very good of you. I won't be a couple of minutes.'

He got out a bit of paper with the hospital number on it that Matt had given him a couple of weeks ago and rang it. One of the porters answered, and he left a message for Jess. 'Joe, can I give this number for now? It's so my girlfriend can ring me,' he asked.

'Course, sir. You do that,' Joe replied.

Stephen also gave the station number, although he had a funny feeling that they would know that already.

'Don't you fret, sir,' said the porter. 'I'll be sure she gets it as soon as she is free.'

Stephen put the receiver down and went back into the bar, which was quickly filling up. It seemed that there was no flying scheduled for the night, and crews were taking the opportunity to get out of the station and have a drink or two.

Soon enough, Freddie and Townsy drifted in.

'Hallo, sir,' called Freddie. 'How's it going? We missed you last time.'

'I'm OK. Thanks, Freddie. What will you both have to drink?'

'Oh, couple of jugs of wallop will do just fine, sir. Thanks.'

Stephen brought them over. 'I thought you chaps would be out and about rather than here.' He smiled.

'Ah well, sir. It's like this. Neither Townsy or I have any relatives hereabouts so we thought we would just come here and get stoned! Also, sir, also …' Freddie said with a conspiratorial wink, 'there's a dance in town tonight at the old Astoria that Townsy here and me thought we might chance our luck at!'

'Well, I hope you do *get lucky* then.' Stephen winked back.

Just then, Toby Judson and his crew from B-Bertie came in, and he immediately made his way over to Stephen.

'Hallo, old boy. You feeling better? Heard the doc had got hold of you!'

'Yes, thanks,' Stephen said. 'Much better. How are you lot getting on? The last trip that Matt was on sounded bloody awful?'

'Christ, it was that,' replied Judson. 'Our bloody rear turret got shot right off. Poor rear gunner just disappeared. Bloody awful business. Where's that Matt anyway? Off with his young lady, no doubt? Lucky blighter!'

'Yes, I think that's where he is,' replied Stephen. 'Lucky indeed.'

'Here, old man, what's your plan for tonight? We were going to have a few here and then stooge into Lincoln. You're very welcome to join us if you are at a loose end?'

'Thanks, Toby,' he replied. 'I was trying to meet up with someone in Lincoln, but I'm not sure she will be free. She may phone soon if I can leave it until then?'

'Of course, old boy. Just let us know,' Judson replied and smiled. 'Pretty, is she?'

'I'd say so,' replied Stephen. He smiled. 'Bit of a cracker actually.'

'Well, good luck then. Come on over and meet the chaps. You know George, our engineer, don't you?'

'Yes, we were at the OTU together. Hallo, George. All well?'

Stephen gradually fitted into their chatter and was surprised when the publican came over to give him a nudge. 'Someone on the phone for you, sir,' he said, winking. 'A lady.'

Stephen walked over to the phone and felt his pulse rise as he lifted the receiver.

'Hallo?' he said, feeling quite nervous.

'Stephen, it's me, Jess. How have you been? It seems ages since I heard from you.'

'It's rather a long story, Jess, to tell you the truth. And not one I want to talk about here in the pub. Are you free sometime so we can meet up? I am on leave until a week on Saturday.'

'Ah, that's a bit of a problem, Stephen. I have just started two weeks of nights so ten until six in the morning. In fact, I am due on fairly soon now but just wanted to speak to you first. How about tomorrow for a spot of lunch? I could get a few hours' sleep, and we could meet about twelve o'clock. What do you think?'

'Can't you call in sick or something?' Stephen replied. 'I really need to see you.'

'No, sorry,' Jess said. 'In any case, they know I am here now. Let's make it midday tomorrow.'

'OK,' said Stephen. 'Where shall we meet?'

'Why not at Lyons? They do a good lunch. And then we can take a walk with Scrap.'

'OK, see you there then.' Stephen put the phone down and waited for a moment before joining the others. He was disappointed not to see Jess, and it looked like they weren't going to be able to spend much time together. Still, even a short while would be good. He took a deep breath and went back to the bar. The noise was building up almost as fast as the fug from pipes and cigarettes, and he worked his way back to Toby and his crew.

'Any luck, old chap?' Toby asked, giving Stephen a wink.

'No, she's bloody working tonight. She's a nurse from the county hospital. Still, hopefully we can meet up tomorrow. So if it's OK, can I join you for this evening?'

'Good to have you along.' Toby smiled. 'Let's have one for the road and we are on our way. Apparently, there's a dance on, so some clever chappie has arranged for us to be picked up by bus!'

Stephen drank his way through another beer and then piled into the bus with everyone else. He found himself near his friend George, but before they could strike up a conversation, the singing started and they could hardly hear themselves think, let alone talk.

The bus dropped everyone off at the Astoria, and Stephen and most of Toby's crew went in search of a pub. The centre of Lincoln was heaving with servicemen, mostly RAF and USAAF, and the pubs were all pretty busy, although they emptied a bit once the dance hall had opened. Toby had fought his way through to the bar and returned with three tankards in each hand.

'Christ, it's a bit of a scrum in there,' he muttered between slurps of beer. 'Maybe we should look around and see if we can find somewhere quieter.'

Stephen remembered the pub he, Jess, and Matt had drunk in close by the hospital, and after their first round, they all trooped off to find it.

The pub was certainly quieter, and the time raced by whilst they were all trying to catch up with each other's news. It seemed no time at all before they were calling last orders.

'Well, back to the mess then!' shouted Toby above the din, and they staggered out into the cold night air. Stephen felt slightly light-headed, and then he realised he had hardly eaten all day. He was also conscious of the odd mix of cold, fresh air and the warm, smoky atmosphere of the pub. It had started snowing again, and the pavements were beginning to show up as white ribbons on either side of the road.

'Well, we need some transport,' said Toby, looking around for something suitable. An RAF truck was driving past at that moment, and he stepped out into the road to stop it.

The corporal driving wound down his window. 'What's the matter?' he said.

'Where are you going, Corporal?' Toby said in his most commanding voice.

'Coningsby, sir,' he replied, 'and then Scampton. I've got some important supplies on board, sir.'

'Good,' replied Toby. 'You can call into East Kirkby on the way. We need a lift home. Thank you very much.'

And before the man could reply, everyone was piling into the back with Toby getting in beside the driver.

By the time they got to base, it was almost midnight, and they headed off for a small snifter in the mess.

Stephen was decidedly woozy and very hungry by this time, but he felt better after he had devoured a plate of sandwiches he found on the mess bar. By this time, the crowd had broken up, and Toby and his crew, who were on ops the following day, wandered off to their billets.

Stephen found Scrap fast asleep on his bed, and he eased him over so that he could get in. The bed was warm where Scrap had lain, and Stephen found no difficulty in dropping off to sleep.

His sleep was deep and, for once, untroubled by the recurrent nightmare in which the aircraft had been attacked and was breaking up in midair. It always left him waking drenched in sweat, feeling drained and shaking with fear.

Scrap woke up as soon as Stephen moved and was off the bed and wagging his tail expectantly.

'OK, old boy. Let's go and see what we can find for you to eat.'

Stephen looked at his watch and realised he had slept a long time. It was nearly ten o'clock, and he needed to be setting out for Lincoln fairly soon. There was usually some transport going from the airfield, but he better look sharp.

Barker was outside in the corridor as Stephen opened the door.

'Morning, sir. I didn't wake you. Hope that was all right? I've got something for Scrap if you want to go off and get something for yourself.'

'Thanks, Barker. I will just go and grab a piece of toast if you could sort out the hound. I'll be back in about half an hour. Got a date for lunch in town.' He winked at Barker.

'No problem, sir. See you back here shortly then.'

Scrap looked initially torn between following Stephen and the prospect of food, but it didn't take long for the food to win and he followed Barker off to the kitchen.

Whilst Stephen was downing some toast and marmalade with a cup of tea, he thought about his meeting with Jess. Actually, it would be easier to leave Scrap here, especially if they were planning lunch at Lyons. He didn't think that they would allow dogs in. He was sure that Scrap would understand, and when he got back, Scrap was laid out again on his bed. There was just time to whisk him round the airfield and then head to town, especially as one of the navigators was driving into town himself and said that he would give Stephen a lift in his car.

Scrap had his walk, and Stephen got back to his room to tidy himself up and then set off to see Jess. He was excited at the prospect of seeing her again, and he was hopeful that somehow or other, they would be able to spend some time and even, he hoped, go to bed.

***

It was very cold, and the roads were icy in one or two places. It required some care. However, they got into Lincoln in one piece, and Stephen was pleased to see that Jess had yet to arrive. He went into the restaurant and got a table near the window. About ten minutes later, she came through the door and saw him immediately. Stephen stood up, and they kissed before

Jess asked him how he was. She, of course, had no idea that he had been taken off flying duties or that he had spent some time in the sickbay, and it took a while for Stephen to explain what had been going on. Jess put her hand across the table and took Stephen's.

'Are you feeling better now?' she asked.

'Yes, much, thanks,' Stephen replied, but he skirted around the real issue about whether he could continue to fly or not and what that might mean.

They had lunch, and then Jess suggested that they went for a walk. 'What have you done with Scrap?' she asked.

'Well, I thought it might be easier to leave him at home on this occasion,' he replied rather lamely. 'I didn't reckon that Lyons would fancy having a dog in.'

'Oh, but they do!' exclaimed Jess. 'I've seen them in there. Never mind. Let's amble through the park.'

They set off hand in hand into the park. The wind had got up again, and it felt bitterly cold. Stephen talked about Matt and Anne's impending marriage and told her that he had been asked to be best man.

'I can imagine Matt as Farmer Giles when this is all over.' She smiled.

'Yes,' replied Stephen. 'With a piece of straw hanging out of his mouth!'

They wandered on for a bit further, and then Stephen turned to Jess. 'Jess, could we go back to your place for a few hours? It's getting bloody cold out here, isn't it?'

'Why not?' she replied. 'No fun and games though, I'm afraid. Out of commission just now!' She laughed. She hugged him, and they set off for her house.

It was cold when they got back, and Jess asked Stephen to sort out the fire whilst she got the kettle on. Stephen quickly got the kindling together and soon had the logs in the hearth blazing away. They pulled the settee closer to the fire and drank their tea.

'How are you feeling, Stephen? Really, I mean?' asked Jess.

'Not too bad,' he replied. 'I am sleeping better and feel I can cope with things just now. Not sure how I will feel when I need to go back to the squadron though. We'll see.'

They finished their tea, and Stephen put his cup down and wrapped his arms around Jess. It was dark outside now, and he could hear the wind rumbling in the chimney. The fire was the centre of a circle, which was bounded by the settee and Stephen and Jess. It felt very cosy, and they kissed gently. They sat for a while watching the flames in the hearth, kissing every now and then and chatting about the war, Jess's job, and how they saw things ending up. Stephen leaned forward and put a couple more logs on the fire

They kissed again, more passionately this time. Jess could feel him hard against her.

'Remember what I said,' she whispered gently. 'But maybe we can do something to help.' And she loosened his belt and his fly, leaned over, and took him tenderly in her mouth. He came quickly, and they lay on the settee for a while before either moved. Jess lifted her head, and when they kissed, he could taste the saltiness of her lips.

'Thank you,' he said and stroked her hair. 'Jess, could I stay tonight whilst you go to work? I really don't want to go back to the base, and it would be lovely to see you in the morning.'

'Of course you can. We had better go to the pub just now and get something to eat though. I am afraid there isn't much in the house.'

They kissed again. Stephen got himself sorted out, and they went down the road to the pub. It was crowded as usual, but they found a table and ordered. At seven o'clock, Jess said she needed to get going because although she didn't start until ten o'clock, she had to be in by eight. They kissed, and she left. After another pint, Stephen made his way back to the house.

He slept well and didn't hear Jess coming in at seven o'clock. She had made some tea and brought the two cups up to the room. She was in bed before Stephen stirred.

'Hallo. Good sleep?' she said, and they kissed as Jess snuggled down.

'Well, at least it's warm in here. Bloody freezing out again this morning. I could get used to coming home to a human hot water bottle!' She laughed.

They drank their tea and lay together for a while before Jess drifted off to sleep. For Stephen, it was an untold joy just to be lying there listening to her breathing, feeling warm with the wind rattling the windows in the gusts. He could see flakes of snow passing the window through the crack in the curtains and suddenly felt a pleasure and security he had thought had disappeared forever. They slept until lunchtime, and after dressing, Stephen said that he would treat Jess to lunch—her choice.

After they had eaten, they went for another walk and then walked back towards the house.

'When do you have to be back, Stephen?' Jess asked as she was filling the kettle for tea.

'Well, by rights, next week,' he replied.

'So why don't you stay for a while then?' she said. 'Everything might be working again in a few days.' She smiled at him. 'I like having someone to come home to in the mornings! But what about poor Scrap? Won't he miss you?'

'Scrap will be fine!' Stephen laughed. 'In fact, he will be better looked after than if I was there. Barker spoils him rotten. The only thing he will miss will be long walks, but I suspect some of the chaps give him those in any case. No, he'll be fine.'

'Well, if you are staying,' said Jess, 'we will have to go and get some things to eat. Luckily I have got some food coupons on me so we can go and get some bits and pieces.'

They went into the grocer's just up the road from the house.

'Afternoon, miss. What can I get you?'

They picked up some corned beef, cheese, a couple of eggs, some milk, and some more tea.

'I think that will do,' Jess said.

She was about to pay when Stephen said, 'Hey, no, let me get these. Is there anything else you need? I mean, after this week? Let's get them now.'

'OK, Stephen, if you're sure.' She set about getting the odds and ends she really could not afford on her nurse's pay.

'Thanks, Stephen. That's very kind,' she said and squeezed his arm.

They were fairly loaded up as they made their way back to the house, but Stephen felt so content and he realised, almost without thinking, that he had pretty well forgotten about the war and flying. In any case, this was his first real experience of domesticity, and he realised he really liked it.

They tidied away their purchases, and Jess said that she would make them an omelette before she went off to work. After Jess had gone, Stephen went down to the pub for a pint and was back and in bed by about ten o'clock.

The days passed, and almost before he realised, it was nearly time to go back. This was his last night away from the base, and he felt the old fears beginning to surface again. He lay in bed for a while, tossing and turning, before eventually sleep overtook him, but again, there were a few times when he awoke with a start and found himself covered in sweat. In the morning, he heard Jess coming in and grabbed his greatcoat to go down to meet her.

'You OK, Stephen?' she asked, seeing him come down the stair. 'Not sleep too well, eh?'

'Not too bad, nurse.' He smiled. 'Few funny do's. How was your night?'

'Long and hard.' She smiled. 'Which reminds me!'

They kissed, went back to bed, and made love several times before Jess fell asleep.

The settled feelings of the days before had deserted him, and he lay listening to Jess breathing but thinking what he was to face tomorrow. *God*, he thought, *we might even be flying tomorrow night*. He felt sweat break out on his hands, and the feelings of vulnerability started to return. He had to get up and do something to take his mind off what faced him. He eased out of the bed and kissed Jess. She groaned slightly as he left her. He made some tea, turned on the radio, and prepared himself some toast—anything to occupy his mind.

Jess joined him about lunchtime, and they went out for something to eat. It was suddenly awkward between them, and Jess decided it better to say nothing and let Stephen talk if he wanted to. He didn't, and they sat in silence.

After lunch, they went for a walk again. It was still very cold with a biting wind.

'I'm sorry, Jess,' Stephen said eventually. 'It was all so lovely the last few days, and now that I have to go back, everything seems horrid. It's not you, just this bloody war.'

'I know,' she said gently. 'I do understand, you know. But we will have some other lovely times together, you see.' She held him very tight so he could not see the tears in her eyes. 'It will be fine.'

They parted about six o'clock so that Stephen could catch the bus to East Kirkby. He had not been able to say anything much during the afternoon, locked, as he was, in his own thoughts about what lay ahead. He felt the dread rising in him as the bus neared its destination, but he knew that somehow he would have to cope and that was the end to it.

***

When Stephen got to the base, he went first to his billet to look for Scrap.

'Welcome back, sir,' Barker said as he got through the door. 'Everything OK? Scrap has been fine, but I think he misses you. He's sleeping on your bed.'

Sure enough, Scrap lifted his head as Stephen went into the room and wagged his tail.

'Hallo, old chap,' Stephen said, rubbing Scrap's ears. 'Shall we go and have a look in the mess and maybe a little walk around?'

Scrap tumbled off the bed and was at the door almost immediately. Stephen led the way, just, and after taking a turn round the billets, they headed off to the mess.

As Stephen went in, he sensed that something was wrong, and as he went up to the bar Adjutant Squadron Leader Davies came across.

'Hallo, Stephen. How you feeling after a few days off?'

'Not too bad, sir. Thank you. Where is everyone? Place is like a tomb.'

'Tomb's not a bad analogy to be honest, old boy. You obviously haven't heard. We lost four Lancs last night going off to Berlin. Overall losses were damn near 10 per cent. Bloody fiasco.'

'Christ, sir. Who's gone?'

'Well, Mike Frost, Toby Judson, Harry Humphries, and Nobby Clarke are all posted missing. Bloody shame.'

It was like a body blow to Stephen, bringing back to him the reality of what he was coming back to.

'Want a drink, old man?' Davies was asking him.

It took a while for Stephen to register he was being talked to. 'Yes, yes, thanks very much,' he mumbled in reply.

Davies came back with a couple of pints and handed one to Stephen.

'Went out with Toby and his crew last week.' Stephen spoke as if in a dream. 'Can't believe it. Gone, just like that.'

'Yes, bloody shame,' the adjutant replied and quickly finished his beer. 'Oh, by the way, mine's a pint.' With that, he wandered over to talk to a couple of pilots Stephen didn't recognise. He assumed they had just joined the squadron.

Stephen finished his drink and wandered outside. He felt cold, deep inside, which was really nothing to do with the freezing wind blowing across the airfield. Of course, it wasn't a new experience for friends not to come back, but it happening so soon after he had been with them was a real shock for Stephen. They were such a jolly lot with the NCOs off to the dance and the others just settling down for a few pints and a laugh. And now they were all gone.

Stephen stood still for a while, trying to take in what had happened. Scrap looked up expectantly. Eventually, Stephen had to almost physically shake himself, and he started walking back to the billet, Scrap, as always, by his side. It was nearly eleven o'clock, and the only thing Stephen could think of was trying to get some sleep. He didn't want to think any further than tonight. Matt would be back early tomorrow, and at least he would have some company and perhaps they could talk about something other than this bloody war.

The room was cold, and Stephen did not have the energy to take off his clothes, so he lay on the bed covered by his greatcoat with Scrap snuggled up next to him. The station was unusually quiet, which only served to remind him of the terrible loss the squadron had suffered the previous night—probably twenty-eight lives just blown away. He lay there a long time before sleep overtook him, holding Scrap as the only symbol of what might be described as normality.

Matt eventually got in about seven o'clock and found Stephen still asleep on his bed. Scrap looked up, and with that, Stephen stirred and woke up.

'Hallo, old chap,' said Matt cheerfully. 'How you feeling?'

'Hallo, Matt,' Stephen replied. 'Well, not too bad until I got back last night and spoke to the adj. We lost four Lancs night before last. They were off to Berlin. One of them was Toby Judson. They were nearly finished, you know?'

Matt sat on his bed. Even he was shocked by that order of loss.

'Bloody hell,' he muttered. 'That's not too sharp, is it? Do we know if there were any survivors?'

'Doesn't seem so,' replied Stephen. 'Matt, we're not going to make it, are we?'

'Come on, Stephen, don't start that again. We have as much chance as anyone else. We're a good crew, and we have come through more than our fair share already. But if we get negative, we'll be in trouble. Now come on, let's go and get some breakfast and then see what we have for tonight. Let's just get this bloody thing over and done with.'

He threw his bag on his bed and headed for the door. Scrap was always one for a walk or food and was waiting by the door when Matt opened it. On the way to the mess, Matt called in to the flight office to check the battle order on the board. It was clear that there was going to be some action in spite of the dreadful losses. He went back to his room where Stephen was slowly getting himself together.

'We're on for tonight, Stephen,' Matt said. 'Let's get everyone together and we can do an air test this morning.'

'God, surely they can't expect us to go out after the last shambles. The guys must be exhausted as it is, apart from the carnage!' Stephen almost shouted at Matt.

'Look, Stephen, I don't make the bloody rules. We're on the list, and we have to fucking go. Now let's get ourselves together.' Matt felt angry partly because he privately agreed with Stephen but also because he was tired of Stephen complaining. He always felt bad about losing his temper, but he realised the strain was beginning to tell on him as well.

'The more we do, the quicker it's over,' he said brusquely and had to try very hard not to slam the door on his way out, adding over his shoulder, 'In any case, we must do an air test this morning, Stephen.' And with that, he headed for the mess.

CHAPTER 11

BERLIN

Twenty-First Trip

After breakfast, they made their way back to the flight office, which was now filled with crew checking if they were in the battle orders. Matt's crew were waiting. Don and Mac were looking pretty pleased with themselves.

'Good leave, chaps?' Matt asked as they came over to meet him.

'Very nice,' replied Mac. 'Don's family were a delight. Great time. Some good pubs in Manchester as well.'

'And now it looks like we can make the dance over at Scampton on Saturday night,' Don added. 'Once we've got tonight out of the way.'

'Mind you, them squadron dances can be bloody stuffy,' Freddie added. 'Now them ones down the old Montana, they're something else.' He nudged Don in the ribs. 'Birds you get there are up for anything,' he said, winking at Townsy.

'You two not coming with us then?' Don asked.

'Now, hold yer horses. We didn't say we weren't coming. We'd be happy to keep you company, wouldn't we, Townsy?'

'Well, before all that,' Matt said, 'we've got some work to do. We need to run an air test this morning so we can be ready for tonight, so you chaps stick around whilst we work out when.'

'I'll go and speak to the ground crew. See when we can do it this morning,' said Stephen, and he headed off with Scrap close behind.

After he'd gone, the others moved away, leaving Charles and Matt together.

'Bloody mess a couple of nights ago,' Redman said. 'That young chap Purdy, who was with us last op, is on the missing list. And Judson's crew too. Bad show,' he muttered.

'Yes, couldn't happen at a worse time as far as Stephen's concerned. Apparently, he was pretty chipper until he heard the news. Hope he can cope; that's all. Can't have him falling apart like he did a couple of ops ago. Shame about Purdy, he seemed a really nice chap.'

They wandered back to the mess and drank some coffee. Stephen joined them about half an hour later with the news that they could do the test around midday. He said that he had told the others to meet in the crew room at eleven o'clock, and then he went off to take Scrap back to the ever-patient Barker.

The crew met up as arranged and collected their flying gear and parachutes as usual. Then they clambered into the truck waiting to take them out to their old faithful, patched-up M-Mother. She had been flown by another crew for the last disastrous Berlin raid but had come home without a scratch on her.

Matt jumped down from the truck and walked over to Warrant Officer Bryant.

'Hallo, Chiefy. All in order?' he asked.

'Well, for once, sir, it is. Perhaps you could talk to the last crew and get some tips on avoiding trouble?' He smiled.

'It's not our fault, Chiefy, if the bloody Hun singles us out every time, is it?' Matt joked back.

He set off to do his check round the aircraft whilst the others climbed aboard. Everyone was in place as he walked through the fuselage to the front and settled into his seat.

Matt and Stephen went through their checks and eventually got to the point of engine start. The starboard inner propeller slowly turned, and with a couple of coughs and smoke out of the exhausts, the engine caught with Stephen checking to see that the oil pressure was rising. They then moved on to the next engine and repeated the procedure until all four were running smoothly.

'Right, everyone,' Matt said over the intercom. 'We are going to head east over Skegness and climb to 10,000 feet. You can check your guns over the sea when I say. We will do a bombing run over the range, head back over Sheffield and then home. Let's make sure everything is working. We can do GEE and H2S checks as we go, Navigator. OK, everyone ready? Let's go.'

Matt taxied the bomber carefully around the perimeter. It had snowed heavily overnight, and the track was quite icy. The runway had been largely swept clear, and as Matt turned the aircraft, its greyness showed up starkly against the snow. He got a green light from the control tower and opened the throttles. The Lancaster gradually picked up speed until she lifted off and climbed steadily out to the east.

It was a gin-clear day, and the land opened out as they gained altitude. It was quite a sight for them all since usually they took off either as dusk was falling or at night and the snow-covered land almost shone at them in the sun. The roads, rivers, and dykes showed up clearly against the whiteness of the snow.

'Looks lovely out there today,' Matt said into the intercom. Redman came forward from his position and looked out of the cockpit.

'Don't think you need me today, Matt. Navigate yourself, I reckon,' he said.

In no time at all, they were over and past Skegness and reached their planned altitude. Matt turned the aircraft to port. 'Starting my bombing run, Bomb-Aimer.'

'OK,' Don replied. 'I can see the range clear as day. Ready when you are.'

'Navigator, can you test H2S as we close the range?'

'Will do,' Charles replied. 'I can see the coastal outline very clearly. Seems to work better in the daytime!'

Matt smiled. The upgraded H2S sets were a big improvement, but they still had a tendency to unreliability, usually when they were most needed. They worked best when there was a clear demarcation between land and water so their current path down the coast was perfect. Matt could see the target ahead and lined up the aircraft.

After the bombing run, they set off towards Sheffield. It was a short run, about sixty miles, but from their height, Matt could see the dark smudge of the city very clearly. He could also count off the airfields on either side of them as they flew along. *It is truly beautiful up here*, thought Matt. Usually they couldn't see a bloody thing, but this was what flying was really about.

'Cor, bloody Scampton. Down there on the left!' shouted Freddie from the rear turret. 'Bet we meet some great crumpet there tomorrow night. What yer reckon, Townsy?'

'Well, so you say,' replied Townsy. 'I'm not sure that mine and your idea of crumpet match up, you know, Freddie. In any case, we've got to get back from tonight yet, haven't we?'

Matt interrupted. 'Sorry to break in, but if it's OK with you two, are you happy the bloody guns are working?'

He smiled as he imagined Freddie casting his eyes to heaven.

'Mine OK, Skip,' Freddie replied with just a hint of sarcasm.

'Mine too,' Townsy added.

'Good,' said Matt. 'Fine day for flying, isn't it?'

'Lovely,' came back Freddie. 'But it's bloody freezing back here … sir!'

Matt could now clearly see the Pennines beyond Sheffield, and the road snaking below them was the A1.

'I am going to turn back to base now, Navigator,' Matt said.

'OK, Matt, steering about one-zero-zero should get us there,' Charles said as the aircraft turned steeply to port to take up the new heading. They flew back on the other side of Scampton, but the many airfields about were easy to identify against the glistening white of the snow.

'All your toys working OK, Navigator?'

'Yes, Matt, even H2S seems to be doing its best today. Of course, it would on a day like today when a blind man could find his way home.'

Matt was almost amazed how clear it was today. He could see the line of the Wash as soon as he turned for home, and after about twenty minutes, he could pick out the East Kirkby beacon.

'Mac, let them know we are on our way back in please. In this easterly breeze, they may let us come straight in from this side.'

After a while, Matt spoke to Stephen to set things up for the approach, and he was relieved to hear Stephen reply quickly and clearly, going through the checklist of actions.

'They have given us a straight in for zero-eight-zero, sir,' Mac said. 'Wind is zero-four-five, fifteen knots.'

'Thanks, Mac,' replied Matt. 'OK, Stephen, let's take her down to 1,500 feet.'

The Lancaster's engines were throttled back, and with a gentle dive, they got down to the approach height. Matt could clearly see the runway now, and he eased the speed down to 110 miles per hour and checked the undercarriage was down and that the warning lights were green.

'Let's have the flaps down, Stephen.'

The aircraft slowed and lifted her head, but Matt eased the nose down and trickled on some more power to keep up the speed. The wind from the left was pushing them to the right, requiring some left rudder until Stephen had applied more power from the right-side engines. Straight now, the aircraft steadily drifted downwards, and Matt flared the aircraft to make a perfect three-point landing.

Matt taxied to the dispersal, and he and Stephen went through the shutdown procedures.

'Good,' said Matt. 'Looks like the last lot didn't do her any damage. Let's get back to crew room, chaps. Don't forget briefing at 1600 hours.'

Everyone tidied up his station and one by one dropped out of the rear door. They were met by Warrant Officer Bryant. 'Well, sir,' he said to Matt, 'no bullet holes to patch up then?' He smiled.

'No, Chiefy. All back in one piece, and everything seems to be working. Even H2S!'

He smiled.

The truck came to pick them up to take them all back to the crew room. Freddie and Townsy were already in deep conversation about the prospects for Saturday's dance as they got into the truck.

'You going too, Don?' asked Matt.

Don blushed a bit. 'Well, yes, I was, Skip. I met a rather nice WAAF at a dance a few weeks ago. They invited us over to Scampton for Saturday night. Her name's Mary.'

'Well, good for you. You all going over in the car?'

'Ah no, Skip. They are organising some transport for us,' Mac replied.

'Hmm,' replied Matt, 'probably safer, but don't get too rat-arsed, you lot.'

They arrived at the crew room where they took off and stored their kit and then returned their parachutes.

'OK, everyone,' said Matt. 'Let's meet in the flight office at 1530 hours so we can check what's going on.'

The officers wandered their way over to the mess whilst the others headed for something to eat.

When they were on their own, Matt asked Stephen how he had felt.

'Not bad, Matt. Better than I thought I would. I'm hoping I will feel OK tonight. That's the real test. Matt, I will meet you in the mess. I am going to get Scrap.' And he turned and walked briskly away.

Matt got into the mess to find Charles already at the bar.

'All OK?' he asked. 'Saw you speaking to Bamber.'

'I think so,' replied Matt hesitatingly. 'As he said, the test is when he's flying and people are trying to kill us. What will you have, Charles?'

'Pint please. We will need to keep an eye on him, Matt. He's a bit of a risk to us all, you know?'

'I do, and you're right. Let's see how he shapes up under fire. Cheers.' And Matt downed his pint. 'Bloody lovely up there today, wasn't it?' he said.

'Well, better for you than me, old boy,' replied Charles. 'Don't see too much from where I sit. Mind you, I'm usually rather pleased not to be able to see out most times! Another pint, Matt? Incidentally, I hear you are going to tie the knot. When's the happy day?'

'Well, end of January. Anne's old man has to check a few things before we get the date set. He wasn't too keen on the idea, I have to say. Should wait until the war's over was his view.'

'Bloody rubbish,' said Charles. 'Need to get on with these things. Never know what's round the corner. Anyway, well done.' He passed Matt another beer and raised his glass.

One of the orderlies came over to Matt just as he was downing his pint. 'Excuse me, sir,' he said. 'The station commander was looking for you about half an hour ago. He wanted you to report to him as soon as you came back from flying, sir. Sorry but I didn't notice you until now.'

'Thanks, Parks,' Matt replied, and grabbing his cap, he set off for Squires's office. The adjutant was not around when he got there so he went in and knocked on W/C Squires's door. He went in, in reply to the brisk, 'Come in'.

'Ah, Matt. Thanks for coming over. Take a seat. Matt, you know about our losses a couple of nights ago, which, of course, included B Flight's commander. I want you to take over. I am raising you to acting Flight Lieutenant, and I will set about getting a permanent appointment as soon as possible. What do you say?'

'Well. thank you, sir. I feel honoured,' he stuttered his reply.

'Well deserved, in my opinion. You have had a hard run, but you set a fine example to the others, believe me.' With that, he stood up and shook Matt's hand. 'Well done. We will announce it at this afternoon's briefing. I am afraid it's another tough one. Sorry to spring it on you, just as you come back from leave.'

'It's OK, sir. Has to be done. See you at the briefing.'

Matt saluted and turned to go out as Squires said, 'Good luck tonight.'

Matt had been in the flight office since his meeting with Squires and promotion to B Flight commander a few hours before his crew came to meet him. There were things needing to be arranged and dealt with, including writing letters to the relatives of those crews who had failed to return. The others were surprised to find him there, but Charles guessed what the meeting with Squires had been about and that Matt was now in charge of the flight.

Matt came out of the flight commander's office to meet them. 'Right, chaps,' he said. 'Let's go down to the briefing, and then we can have a chat.'

Stephen looked quizzically at his friend but said nothing. He was already beginning to feel anxious about the evening and did not really feel like talking to anyone, including Matt.

They went into the briefing room to find most of the thirty-five men involved in the raid already there.

At exactly 1600 hours, the CO and the other senior officers came in and everyone stood to attention. Brookes motioned to everyone to sit, and the men shuffled about to find chairs whilst others lit up a cigarette or their pipes.

'Right, chaps,' the CO began. 'I am sorry you have to go again tonight after the recent experience, but tonight's target has been judged to be of crucial importance and we are coming to the end of the period in which the moon is favourable for an attack. In fact, this will be the last show for a while.' Then he drew back the curtain to reveal the map showing the night's target, and there was both a gasp and a groan as it was obvious that they were off to the Big City again.

'We have to keep the pressure up on the Germans,' Brookes carried on. 'And several nights of bombing their capital is one way of doing it. You will see that the route is the same as last time, which we hope will come as a surprise. There will be Pathfinder markers for you, but I leave further detail to others. However, before that, I want to let you know that Acting Flight Lieutenant White will be leading B Flight from now on.'

Those close to Matt leaned across to pat his back, and Charles turned round and pumped his hand. 'Well done, old boy,' he said.

Even Stephen looked delighted with the news.

Details followed from the squadron's intelligence officer, navigator, bomb leader, signals, and finally the station commander, W/C Squires, who added his congratulations to Matt.

The briefing finished, and the crews filed out to get their bacon and eggs. Several gathered round Matt, especially his crew, all genuinely pleased with his promotion, and the officers wandered over to their mess for a congratulatory drink—just one—before their meal.

Later that afternoon, as the crews picked up their equipment in the crew room, Matt noticed Stephen on his own and moved over to talk to him.

'All right?' he asked.

'Not too bad,' Stephen replied. 'Matt, I am really pleased for you. It's great news.'

'Well, luck of the draw, I reckon,' Matt replied, and his voice hardened. 'Are you going to cope with tonight, Stephen? I need to be sure.'

'Yes. I will manage, Matt. Don't worry,' he said quietly and walked away, collecting his things as he did so.

The truck came for the crew, and as usual, Freddie was chatting to Townsy about Saturday's dance.

'For God's sake, Freddie, can't you talk about anything else!' Matt snapped at him. 'Let's get tonight out of the way first, shall we? Concentrating on that may give us all a chance to see tomorrow.'

Freddie hesitated. It was not like Matt, and he quickly realised that the best answer was to say, 'Yes, Skip,' and leave it at that.

They were dropped at M-Mother to be met by the ground staff. It was a bitterly cold night, and the clouds of vapour from the men enveloped them as they chatted.

'Everything in order, Sergeant?' Matt asked.

'Yes, sir.' He saluted.

Matt replied cursorily before saying, 'Come along, everyone. Let's get checked out and underway.'

Freddie and Townsy shrugged their shoulders and simultaneously opened their flies and peed on the rear wheel before climbing aboard.

Matt went through his own checks and then spoke to each crew member to be sure all was well. He signed Form 700 and handed it to the sergeant. Their take-off time was fast approaching, and he and Stephen went through their checklists and finally started the engines.

'All OK, Flight Engineer?' Matt asked.

'Yes, all fine here, Skip,' Stephen replied. He sensed something had troubled Matt, who was usually very relaxed at this point, and he was sure it was nothing to do with the promotion.

The engines fired up satisfactorily, but before he released the brakes to taxi, Matt checked again with everyone that all was well.

They taxied out to the end of the runway. *Christ*, thought Matt, *only five aircraft*. The squadron had been decimated.

The green light showed, and Matt opened the throttles to start yet another trip. M-Mother was heavily laden with fuel and bombs, and she was slow to lift off. Even Freddie muttered, 'Bloody hell,' as they just cleared the perimeter fence.

Matt kept the aircraft low for a few minutes to gain speed until he eased M-Mother into a gentle climbing turn to the right. They could see nothing in the pitch-black as they turned to cross Great Yarmouth at 10,000 feet to join the bomber stream.

'Freddie, can you see anyone else behind us?' Matt asked.

'I've got K-King, Skip. She took off after us and has kept pretty close.'

'OK, keep an eye on them. They are a rookie crew and might feel safer keeping us in sight!'

'Will do,' Freddie replied.

'All on to oxygen,' Matt said. 'Gunners, test your guns please.'

'Enemy coast should be coming up any minute now,' Charles said about three-quarters of an hour later.

'Keep your eyes peeled, everyone,' Matt said. 'They will probably be expecting us tonight. Everything still working, Navigator?'

'Miraculously, yes,' replied Charles. 'Not unexpectedly, the wind strength and direction is not exactly as predicted, but I have made a correction for that. About another hour or so before we get near to Hanover. Usually a bit of flak there.'

'Thanks, Navigator. Everyone else OK?'

'Apart from being bloody freezing, yes … Skip,' Freddie added.

As predicted, the flak picked up as they flew to the north of Hanover. The sky was very clear, and as the searchlights lit up, Matt could see the aircraft all around them. It looked quite impressive until one aircraft over to their left was hit and exploded in a violent flash of bright orange and red.

Matt heard Stephen mutter, 'Christ almighty.'

'Engines OK, Flight Engineer?' Matt quickly asked.

'Yes, Skip,' Stephen haltingly replied. 'Yes, everything is all right.'

They droned on over the dark land below them.

'We're about an hour from our turning point,' Charles said. 'Don, please keep a sharp lookout. We should be following the Mittelland Canal, and we are looking for where it crosses the Elbe. I've got quite good images on H2S for once, but a visual would be good!'

After a while, Don reported that he could make out the canal and shortly after the clear outline of the Elbe.

'Turning point coming up, Matt,' Charles said. 'New heading is zero-eight-five. Turn now.'

Matt banked the aircraft to the left to take up the new heading, conscious that there were several hundred others around supposedly doing the same thing. Just as they settled on their new course, there were searchlights everywhere, but for once, they didn't seem to be interested in M-Mother and her crew. They were approaching Berlin just as the Mosquitoes were dropping their markers.

'Looks like we are right on time, Skipper!' called Don from the front of the aircraft. 'I can see the target markers very clearly, and they are slightly over to the left.'

'I've got them, Don,' Matt replied and edged the aircraft towards them. Just at this moment, a wall of flak came up in front of them and an aircraft over to the right was hit, flames jetting from the port wing. The aircraft started to lose height, but they kept on towards the target, which was only a couple of miles from them.

'Jump out, you guys,' Matt muttered under his breath. 'Jump for Christ's sake!'

But the aircraft carried on, the fire spreading towards the fuselage. The aircraft was now in a shallow dive, heading straight for the target markers. Matt saw a couple of parachutes followed soon by the bombs. *A little short, but they will still do some damage*, Matt thought. Just after the bombs, the aircraft suddenly blew up and the shock wave rocked M-Mother.

'Steady,' said Don. 'Right a bit, right a bit, right. Steady, steady, steady. Bombs gone.'

M-Mother leapt in the air as her load was released, and Matt held the course until Don said that the photoflash had been taken. He banked the aircraft away to the right to set them back on a course for home.

'Seen anything of the sprogs, Freddie?' Matt asked.

'I saw them in the light from the bombing, Skip, but nothing since.'

'OK, we're on our way home. It's going to take us at least three hours to get to the coast. We haven't seen many fighters, but don't be fooled. They'll be out there.'

Not long after, Freddie called, 'I think we are being followed, Skip. Difficult to make out, but I think there is something out there on the port quarter.'

'Not the sprogs?' Matt replied.

'Could be. Can't see clearly enough.'

'I'm turning left. See what happens,' Matt said, easing the aircraft round.

'Whatever it is, is turning with us,' Freddie said.

'I can see him now,' said Townsy. 'I think it's a Me 110. Definitely got two engines.'

'I'm turning back on course,' said Matt. 'How far away is the bastard?'

'About 500 yards, I reckon,' said Townsy. 'He's just sitting out there.'

'Townsy, you watch him, but, Freddie, you keep looking around. Could be a decoy,'

Matt said, and at that moment, another fighter ripped into them from the right.

'Corkscrew right!' shouted Freddie. 'You bastard, try some of this!'

Matt could feel the shuddering as the Brownings fired.

There was a strong smell of cordite, and Matt realised that, once again, they had been hit and quickly checked to see if there had been any major damage.

'Everyone all right?' he asked. There were replies from all except Townsy, and Matt asked Mac to go back and check if everything was still in one piece.

As Mac climbed over the main spar, he could see flames in the fuselage near the flare chute, and he grabbed an extinguisher and ran through the clouds of smoke towards the back of the aircraft. The flames died away quickly, but the fuselage had been peppered by the fighter.

Mac got on the intercom. 'Skip, the fire's out, but there's an awful lot of fresh air back here, and Townsy's been hurt—looks pretty bad, sir.'

'Stephen, go back and see what's going on, will you?'

Stephen disconnected his oxygen and taking his reserve tank crawled back, climbing over the main spar. Mac was waiting for him, and as his eyes adjusted to the pitch-black of the fuselage, he could see that there had been a lot of damage. Townsy's legs were hanging down from his turret, and Mac was trying to manhandle him down. Stephen moved forward to help and was immediately aware that there was a lot of blood around and that Townsy was not moving. Together, they managed to lower him to the floor, and Stephen's flashlight showed that he'd been hit in the chest by fire from the attacking fighter and that he was clearly dead.

He looked up at Mac and shook his head before checking around the damaged fuselage. He saw that nothing vital appeared to have been hit, but the fuselage was peppered with holes.

He connected himself to the intercom. 'Matt, I'm afraid Townsy's bought it. There's quite a bit of damage, but we should be OK for now. Nothing vital.'

'What d'you mean Townsy's dead?' asked Freddie before Matt had time to answer. 'Jesus Christ, I don't believe it.'

'You better believe it,' Matt snapped. 'And keep your bloody eyes skinned; otherwise, you'll be next. Mac, can you man the turret for now? Stephen, get back here. The starboard inner's looking a bit flaky.'

As Stephen got back into the cockpit, Matt noticed his pale, sweaty face. 'You OK?' he asked.

Stephen nodded and turned his attention to the problems with the engine.

'Freddie, any sign of those bastards?'

'No, Skip. All clear for now. Is Townsy really a goner, Skip?'

'I'm afraid so,' Matt replied quietly. 'Sorry. Stephen, what's the score with the bloody engine?'

'I'm going to feather the prop. I think it must have been hit by something—oil pressure is really low,' Stephen replied. 'Otherwise, everything seems all right.'

'Skip, that bastard is out there again. I just caught sight of him a long way off, just like before.'

'OK, well, both of you keep your eyes wide open. They are probably going to try and catch us out again.'

Matt suddenly felt very frightened. This hunting in pairs was not something he had come across before. He felt very vulnerable and uneasy. The aircraft droned on for another half an hour, but still nothing happened.

'Where are we, Navigator?' Matt asked. 'How long to the coast?'

'Matt, I think we are north of Arnhem. Probably about half an hour to the coast. That last attack seems to have knocked the H2S off, and GEE isn't looking good either. So it's down to some DR, I'm afraid. If you wanted to climb above this cloud, I could take a star sight.'

'Thanks. I feel better with us just under this cloud with those two fighters around.'

Can you still see that one behind us, Freddie?'

'Not now, Skip. I think he's got bored or hopefully run out of fuel.'

They were heading almost due west, but about fifteen minutes later, searchlights suddenly lit them up, the glare from the cloud just above being almost blinding. The searchlights were followed almost immediately by some heavy flak, which was so close that it rocked the aircraft around. Fragments could be heard pinging against the fuselage, and there was a strong smell of cordite.

'Christ,' muttered Matt as he heaved the aircraft up into the protecting clouds. 'Don, did you get any idea where we were when that lot started up?'

'Not really, Skip, but I thought I could see a large river away over to the left. Could have been the Rhine.'

'If you could see the Rhine, Don, we are further south than I thought,' replied Charles.

'Maybe we are around Rotterdam. Might explain the reception.'

'Everyone OK?' Matt asked. With all that flak, it was a miracle if no one got hit. They were now in cloud, and Matt determined to descend only when they were sure that they were over the sea.

After another half an hour, Matt indicated to Stephen to throttle back so they could start their descent, and as they broke out of the cloud, Don called out that he could see a coastline.

'Mac, get back to the radio and give them a call. We should be coming back over Harwich.'

'No reply, sir,' Mac said. 'I think the radio is U/S.'

'God almighty,' Matt said. 'Can anything else go wrong? OK, get ready with the colours of the day as we get to the coast. All we need now is to be clobbered by our own side.'

Don shouted that it definitely looked like Harwich as they came over the coast, and Charles gave a course to take them back to East Kirkby.

'Everything OK, Stephen?' Matt asked, but there was no reply. Matt could see Stephen's ashen face and noticed that he was slumped against the right side of the cockpit.

'Engineer, I need to know now if we have a problem in case we need to divert.'

Stephen seemed to stir himself and replied, 'Yes, Skip. All well. Fuel OK.'

Half an hour later, Don called to say that the airfield was in sight, and a few minutes after, Matt guided the aircraft over the field and signalled that they had radio failure.

They got a red light from control, indicating they were not clear to land. 'Bloody hell,' Matt said as he swung the aircraft round into an orbit. For once, he felt that he really wanted to get down on the ground. It was an odd feeling—not vertigo exactly but just a need to get down there on terra firma.

'Fuel, Stephen?' he asked as he shot a glance across the cockpit.

'We have about an hour left.'

'Everyone,' Matt said into the intercom, 'we've arrived, but it looks like they are busy just now so we need to hold. It looks like someone on finals is in worse shape than us.'

From high above the airfield, Matt could see the approaching Lancaster crabbing its way towards the runway. They also had only three engines, but as the aircraft flew below M-Mother, Matt could just see in the early light that the outer part of the starboard wing was missing and the rear turret appeared to have gone.

'Christ, poor buggers,' Matt mumbled to himself. 'At least the undercarriage's down.'

The pilot managed to straighten the aircraft over the runway, but as the wheels touched down, it veered off to the left, the undercarriage collapsing some way from the runway.

The crash crews were nearby, but the right wing suddenly caught fire, which spread quickly to the fuselage.'

'Get out! Get out!' Matt called, involuntarily gripping the control column. The fire was gradually brought under control, and the crash crew opened the rear hatch and were pulling the crew out. Matt counted three before Stephen called to say that they had a green to land.

Matt turned the aircraft downwind and set the controls for landing. He got Stephen to feather the port inner to balance things up and then turned on to finals, and once sure they were going to make it, he dropped the flaps and then the undercarriage. He was relieved as always to see the green indicators showing the wheels were down. Matt eased the aircraft to a gentle landing.

As Matt taxied past the other aircraft, he could see three of her crew standing with the ambulance, and there were three covered bodies on the ground. As he taxied M-Mother to their stand and the waiting ground crew, dawn was just breaking. It had been a long night, and Matt suddenly felt exhausted. Stephen and he went through the checklists to shut down the engines, and at last, all was quiet. Matt immediately thought of Townsend and quickly undid the straps to go aft. When the ground crew realised what had happened, they had called an ambulance, which had arrived by the time Matt reached the body. Townsend had clearly died instantly. Mac was by his side.

'Well done, Mac,' Matt said quietly. 'You obviously couldn't have done anything to save him. Was the turret damaged much?'

'Few extra holes, sir. Otherwise, it worked. Shame about Townsy, eh? Old Freddie will be gutted.'

'Where is Freddie?' Matt asked, expecting to see him there with his friend.

'Outside, Skip, having a fag.'

Matt found Freddy leaning against the fuselage.

'You OK, Freddy?' Matt asked.

'Fucking war, Skip,' Freddie replied. 'Fucking shame. Good bloke.'

Freddie walked away before Matt could answer, but he turned as the stretcher with Townsend was lowered from the aircraft and muttered, 'Fucking shame.'

The truck had arrived to take them back for the debriefing, but Matt wanted to talk to the ground crew and they left without him.

As usual, Warrant Officer Bryant was there waiting for him. 'Blimey, Matt. They really don't like you, do they?'

'Bloody fighters again, Chiefy,' Matt replied. 'They ganged up on us. Old Townsend is a goner, I'm afraid.'

'Heard that, Matt. Sorry,' Bryant replied. 'We'll patch her up as usual. Sorry we can't do more for your crew.'

Matt smiled and thanked him, and one of the ground crew borrowed a truck to take him back. The debriefing was well underway by the time he got there and picked up his mug of tea. They described how they thought they had been ambushed by the fighters and how the raid had gone. Apparently, everyone was back, but there were several casualties. The station commander came over when the debriefing was done. 'Well done, Matt. Another shaky show for you, I am afraid. Sorry about your mid-upper. Definitely no flying now for a while so you can get yourselves together. When you have had some shut-eye, come and see me this afternoon, will you? Two o'clock in my office.'

'Thank you, sir. See you this afternoon,' Matt replied and joined his crew as they left for breakfast.

***

There was a bitter wind blowing as Stephen, Matt, and Charles Redman went into the officers' mess.

'Bad business about Townsend,' Charles said as they sat down to eat.

'Yes,' Matt replied. 'Could have been any of us with those bloody fighters. I'll need to write to his parents. He was a good chap, good gunner too. Due to get his bloody medal in a couple of weeks.'

'Breakfast, sir?' the orderly asked Matt.

'No, no, thanks,' he replied. 'Just a cup of tea, please.'

Stephen said the same and then stood up and walked away.

'You OK, Matt?' Charles asked. 'You look all in, old chap. Better get some shut-eye.'

'Charles, you know something? I felt really frightened up there last night. Couldn't wait to get down—never felt like it before.'

'Well, Matt,' Charles replied. 'It doesn't get any easier, does it? You know, it's amazing really. Some chaps go through and hardly see a searchlight let alone a fighter. We just seem to catch it every time. May be we've been lucky not to have come unstuck so far. Number was up for poor old Townsend last night. Like it was for the chaps on K-King. They were attacked on the way in, and only the bomb-aimer, engineer, and pilot survived. Flak blew the bloody rear turret straight off, and fighters did the rest.

'In a way, it's easier for me. I don't see what's going on. Bloody glad.' He smiled. 'Take yourself off to bed, Matt. Don't worry. You're a bloody good pilot. Wouldn't fly with anyone else, I'll tell you that. Get some sleep. Let's have a drink before lunch. What d'you say?'

'Thanks, Charles. See you about one o'clock. Mine's a beer.' He smiled and left for his room, bed, and sleep.

CHAPTER 12

TRAINING

Matt got into his room. He thought that Stephen was already asleep, but when he looked closer, he realised he was lying on his back just staring at the ceiling.

'Stephen?' he said, but there was no reply and Scrap lifted his head as Matt moved closer to the bed. 'Stephen?' he repeated and gave his friend's arm a shake.

'God, that was terrible,' Stephen said almost in a whisper.

'Yes, shame about poor old Townsend,' Matt replied.

'No, I don't mean that,' continued Stephen. 'The whole bloody trip. Everyone shooting at us, trying to kill us.'

'But you did all right, Stephen. In spite of everything, you did OK. That's the important thing, don't you see?'

'I don't!' he replied, shouting this time. 'No, I bloody don't. They'll kill us one by one! You see if they don't!'

'Stephen, I'm going to get the doc. You're tired, and it's been a bloody awful night. You need to get some sleep. We won't be on ops again for quite a few days, so you can recover.'

'I don't want the bloody doc's pills. I just want to stop going up in the bloody plane.'

With that, he got off the bed and put his greatcoat on, and with Scrap at his heels, he walked out, slamming the door behind him.

For Matt, it was the end of a dreadful night. He felt exhausted and certainly too tired to chase after Stephen. He would try and sort something out later on. Maybe Stephen would have gone to the sickbay by then. He fell onto his bed, and almost before he knew it, Barker was shaking him awake with a cup of tea.

'Understand the station commander wants to see you at two o'clock, sir. Cup of tea to get you going. It's one o'clock just now.'

'Thanks, Barker. Any sign of Mr Bamber?'

'No, sir. Not seen him since this morning. Nor the dog neither, sir.'

'Thanks, Barker. I am just off to lunch and then W/C Squires. We are off ops for a few days, just so you know.'

'Thanks, sir. I'll look out for Mr Bamber.'

Matt dressed quickly and found Charles already in the mess.

'Looks like a quick sandwich and a pint,' Matt said. 'Have to see Squires at two.'

'I went down to see the kite,' Charles said. 'Bit of a mess really. Bloody fuselage has been peppered. Bloody lucky no one else was hurt. We must have charmed lives.'

'Yes, bad show really, wasn't it?' Matt replied. 'Incidentally, you haven't seen Stephen around, have you? Found him staring at the ceiling when I got back this morning, and then he just took off with the dog, saying he couldn't stand it anymore. Looked like he meant it this time. Looks like he needs some more of doc's magic pills.'

'You know, old boy,' Redman replied, 'I think you have enough on your mind without having to wet-nurse Bamber.

Take some advice, leave it to the doc. I know he's your friend, but there comes a limit, you know?'

'You're probably right, Charles,' Matt replied. 'Got B-Flight to worry about as well now!' He smiled. 'Anyway, must shoot off. Maybe a drink later on?'

'I'll be here, old boy. Wife's gone off to visit relatives so I'm on my own for a couple of days!'

Matt walked briskly to Squires's and got there at five to two to find A-Flight's commander, Flight Lieutenant Francis Bird, waiting outside the door.

'Hallo, Dicky,' Matt said. 'What's the score? Do you know?'

'Not a clue, old boy. Maybe it's to remind us there are not too many of us left!'

'Bloody awful really. The last few days,' Matt replied, and at that moment, Squires came to the door and asked them into his office.

'Sit down please,' he said. 'To be brief,' he started, 'the squadron has been severely mauled over recent weeks, although I know you both realise that. Group has said that we can stand down from ops for a week. As you know, things are quieter at this phase of the moon in any case, but it will give us a chance to pick ourselves up. You don't need me to tell you that morale is pretty low just now. We have some new Lancs arriving tomorrow and new crews on Sunday evening. I want you as flight commanders to see to it that those sprogs are well received. Get them into the air as soon as possible, and get them trained up by the end of the week. So although there are no ops, there's no leave either. Please make that very clear to your crews. Any questions? No? Well, off you go then. I understand there's a dance at Scampton this weekend. Encourage your men to get along to that. And, White, please wait behind.'

After the door had shut, Squires said, 'Matt you are now Flight Lieutenant, congratulations, and officially B-Flight commander. Things happen quickly just now.' He smiled. 'Your investiture is in two weeks, isn't it? Take a couple of days off and go along with your fiancée and perhaps your parents.'

'Thank you, sir. I'll take Anne if she can get the time off, but it's a bit far for my parents. We'll take some photos.'

'Good. Well, off you go. I want you around all next week, but why don't you have the weekend off and come back Sunday night?'

'Thank you, sir. I'll see if Anne's around.' He hesitated not being sure whether to mention Stephen or not and finally decided not to. It would probably only cause more trouble, but as his now flight commander, he would have to eventually come clean, of that he was sure.

He saluted, left the room, and walked back to the mess where he found Redman and a few other officers, including Bird.

'Dicky's filled us in,' said Redman. 'Bit of a break, but then we need to knock these sprogs into shape.'

'Matt,' said Dicky, 'I think you and I should sit down tomorrow and have a look at these new crews. We could do it after lunch, if you like?'

'Fine,' said Matt, seeing the possibility of a few hours with Anne rapidly diminishing. 'Yes, just fine,' and beer in hand, he went away to try to phone her.

Matt got through to the porters' lodge at the hospital and asked where Anne might be.

'She's working nights just now, sir,' the porter said. 'I can ring her corridor to see if someone can get her to the phone?'

'Yes, please do that,' replied Matt. He realised he was not feeling himself after last night's raid. It had shaken him up badly, and he knew it.

Anne came on the phone after a couple of minutes, and he almost immediately felt more relaxed.

'Anne, are you all right?' he asked before she could ask the same question. 'We had a bad night, lost Townsend I'm afraid.'

'But you weren't hurt?' Anne asked quickly. 'And everyone else all right too?'

'Yes, fine really, considering,' Matt replied. 'Look, Anne, we are off ops for a few days. Any chance we could meet up. I really need to see you. Trouble is we have quite a bit of work next week, so I can't take leave, but perhaps we could meet one evening. I realise you are working at night.'

'Well, darling, why don't we meet for an early dinner? As you know, I start at ten o'clock, so if you could get down here by sixish, we could at least have some time together.'

'Sounds perfect, darling,' Matt replied. 'We might have to make it up as we go along because I have no idea when I will be able to get away. Let's aim for Monday and see how we go?'

'What are you doing tonight, darling?' Anne asked.

'Well, working,' Matt replied. 'Two bits of good news are that I am now Flight Lieutenant White and I have been appointed flight commander.'

'Darling, what wonderful news! Well, we will have plenty to celebrate then on Monday! Will you call me tomorrow? It's lovely to hear your voice. I was rather worried when you didn't ring, but I guessed you were off flying. I miss you so much, darling. Hear from you tomorrow?'

'Yes, will call you as soon as poss,' Matt replied and rang off. He returned to the bar. 'Let me get you a pint, Dicky,' he said.

'Ah, Matt, I'll have one too, if you are buying,' said Charles. 'Everything OK on the home front?'

'Yes, fine, thanks. Anne's working nights this week, but we should manage to squeeze in a meal sometime.'

'Of course you must, old boy,' said Dicky. 'I'll cover for you. In any case, once we've got the new chaps sorted, it should be fairly straightforward. It's just that so many are coming at once. In any case, just let me know and we'll fix something.' He smiled.

'Thanks, Dicky. We thought Monday if that was all right.'

'Good choice, old boy. The new boys will all be wetting themselves that night, and it will be a complete waste of time talking to them then. Consider it sorted!'

'Incidentally,' asked Matt, 'has anyone seen Stephen? Batman hasn't seen hide nor hair of him or the bloody dog. It's a bit awkward if he doesn't show up soon, as he will be officially AWOL. And I'm his bloody flight commander!'

'Have you checked with the sickbay, Matt?' Charles asked. 'I mean, he went there a few weeks ago, didn't he?'

'God, I should have thought of that. Good idea, Charles. I'll go there now.'

Matt knocked on the sickbay door, and one of the nurses opened it.

'Sorry to trouble you,' Matt said. 'Have you seen Pilot Officer Bamber? He was in here a little while ago. We had a bad do last night, and he seems to have disappeared. I just wondered if he was here?'

'No, sir. I remember him, but he hasn't been here today. In fact, we have no one in just now.'

'Thanks,' replied Matt. 'Is the doc around anywhere?'

'I think he is in his office just along the corridor,' she said. 'You going to the dance at Scampton, sir?'

'No, I'm afraid not.' Matt smiled. 'But you should go. It will be a good time.'

He knocked on the doctor's door and received a gruff, 'Come in'.

'Sorry to trouble you, sir. It's Pilot Officer Bamber. He seems to have gone missing after last night's raid. I am just a bit worried about him, and of course, soon he will be officially AWOL. I had suggested to him to see you for some pills to help him sleep. They seemed to help him last time.'

'Sorry to hear that, Matt,' he replied. 'He was always a bit high risk, you know, but he certainly seemed much better after his short stay. I'll keep an eye out for him and let you know if we capture him!' The doctor smiled. 'I hear you have been promoted. Well done, much deserved.'

Matt blushed.

'Matt, can you think of anyone he might have gone to? Girlfriend perhaps?'

'Of course, he might have done, stupid of me. Thanks, Doc. I'll see if I can track him down.'

He went back and rang the hospital to speak to Anne again.

'Coo, two calls in a day!' She laughed down the phone.

'No, rather serious actually, darling,' Matt replied. 'What I didn't tell you was that Stephen was badly affected by last night's raid and has disappeared. Is Jess around, do you know? I was talking with the doc, and he wondered whether Stephen could be with someone, and I suddenly thought of Jess.'

'Well, I think Jess is off this week. I haven't seen her, but I'll see if anyone else has. Do you really think Stephen has run away?'

'I don't want to think that, but it looks distinctly possible. I might not be able to save him if he has.'

'I'll ask around and give you a call. Where will you be?' Anne asked. 'The bar, I suppose!' She giggled.

'Outside chance.' Matt laughed. 'I mean, it is the centre of everything, you know!'

He wandered back to the mess both checking his room and with Barker, but there was still no sign of Stephen or the dog.

***

Freddie walked into the sergeants' mess to find it crowded and full of smoke and noise.

'How you doing, Freddie?' Don asked as he made his way across to him and Mac.

'Fucking awful. I'll have a pint,' he said. 'What's all the bloody fuss about here then?'

'It's a pre-dance drink.' Mac smiled.

'Forgot all about the bloody dance,' Freddie said glumly. 'What with poor old Townsy and all. Poor old bugger.' He drank his pint almost in one go and shrugged his shoulders. 'Another of them will set me up fine, thanks very much. No bloody point in pining, is there? When do we leave?'

Don, Mac, and Freddie clambered into the bus for the Scampton dance, along with the others, many of whom had already sunk a few beers in the mess. It was bitterly cold outside, but the bus was warm with a great fug from the many cigarettes being smoked. The three men found seats together, and once everyone was on board, they set off, the singing getting underway almost immediately. It took a good hour with the bus winding its way through Horncastle, Wragby, and Lincoln before arriving at the gates of Scampton. Once through the gates, the bus pulled up outside one of the hangars, and everyone piled out into the cold air. The three friends wandered over to the hangar entrance with Don wondering how he was going to find Mary in the crush inside. They managed to fight their way to the bar, and Mac ordered the drinks by shouting louder than those around him. Once they had their beers, they moved back from the bar to check out what was going on. Each crew tended to stick together, but they occasionally bumped into others they knew, and gradually, the melee seemed to sort itself out.

Almost by chance, Don saw Mary in a large group of people and he waved and moved off towards her. She was with the same two girls who were with her when they had first met up in Lincoln. Mac stayed with his friend, but Freddie clearly had other plans and moved off towards a large group of sergeants who seemed intent on getting legless rather than dancing. Don and Mary kissed, and Mac got into conversation with Eve.

'Fancy a dance?' Mary asked.

'Still a glutton for punishment then?' Don laughed as they set off to dance to one of Glen Miller's tunes. They danced off and on for an hour before Mary asked Don if he would like to go outside for a breath of air.

They grabbed their coats and went outside. It was bitterly cold, and their breath showed in great clouds of vapour. The sky was full of stars, and the new moon was close to the horizon.

'Come with me,' Mary said, and holding Don's hand, led him along to one of the Nissen huts.

'Hear you boys had a bad time last night?' Mary asked as they walked along.

'Yes,' Don replied. 'One of our crew got killed. And we got pretty shot up as well. It wasn't good, Mary.'

She looked at him and thought for a moment that he was going to break down. She stopped walking and put her arms around him.

'Come on, in here,' she whispered as she opened the door. It was almost as cold inside as out, and the room seemed empty at first until Don noticed all the beds had been pushed up to one end. The room smelt of paint and was obviously in the process of being decorated. Mary led him up to the beds, and they sat down on one of the mattresses.

'I thought it would be nice to have a moment together,' she said. 'It's always so noisy at those dances. I knew this place would be empty,' she added and then leaned over to kiss Don. Their kissing gradually became more passionate, and Mary loosened her coat and put Don's hand on her leg.

'I would very much like to have you,' she whispered. 'We could manage here. No one will come in.'

They carried on kissing, and Don moved his hand up her leg and realised that she had no knickers. He rolled her onto the bed, undid his coat, and lay on top of her. She loosened his trousers, and they made love quickly. It was a delicious feeling, and they lay there for some moments before Mary said, 'That was lovely, Don, but I am getting bloody cold.'

He laughed, got up, and then helped Mary to her feet.

They walked slowly back to the hangar. Couples were dotted all over the place in various stages of engagement. It was a bit like that in wartime. You had to do what you had to do and not worry too much about tomorrow. Mary and Don went back into the fug and noise of the hangar to find that the band was playing the last waltz. They put their coats down and shuffled around the floor, this time holding one another closely.

'Don,' Mary said, 'can we meet up again soon? It's been a lovely evening, and it would be good to spend more time together.'

'Well, that certainly gets my vote,' Don replied, giving her a little squeeze. 'When are you next off?' he continued.

'I am working nights next week, but then I have a few days off. What about you?'

'Well, as you know, that's classified information.' He smiled. 'We have just finished some leave, so it will be another six weeks before we are off again. But we don't fly all the time, you know. I am sure we will get together sometime soon.'

The music stopped, and they kissed again and then went to get their coats. Everyone was moving out of the hangar now, and Don saw Mac standing by the bus saying goodbye to Eve. As they got closer to the bus, Eve and Mac looked up.

'Nice night?' Mac asked, smiling at Mary.

'It certainly was,' she replied and turned to Don to kiss him goodbye. She said, 'See you soon.'

The girls walked away, and Don and Mac turned to get on the bus, which was already filling up with rather bleary-eyed men.

'You seen, Freddie?' Mac asked.

'Not me,' Don replied. 'I have been rather occupied this evening!'

Just at that moment, one of the sergeants came running over to the bus.

'Anyone seen Freddie?' he asked to no one in particular, and several of the men shook their heads and started to get back in the bus. Don and Mac hung back and were just getting on the bus when there was a cry from one of the huts and Freddie could be seen simultaneously pulling up his trousers and getting on his coat. He scampered towards the bus and entered to loud applause to which he bowed deeply.

'Bloody lovely,' were his only words as the bus pulled away and the singing commenced.

***

Matt woke up about six o'clock on the Sunday morning. The room was dark, and he glanced anxiously over to Stephen's bed, willing him to be there but knowing that he was not. By then, Stephen was officially AWOL, and Matt, as his flight commander, would need to report to Squires. He got dressed quickly and went to the telephone in the mess to ring Anne to see if she had found anything out from Jess. The gate porter at the hospital answered.

'Hallo, sir. Bit early this morning, isn't it?' he said brightly. 'Sister Anne who you want, sir?'

'Yes, please,' replied Matt. 'It's rather urgent, actually.'

'She should have finished by now, sir. I'll ring her corridor and see if she is up there.'

Matt waited and could hear the porter talking to one of the other nurses.

'Hallo, sir. It looks like she is still in theatre with a late case. I'll leave a message for her to ring you as soon as she can?'

'Yes, thank you,' replied Matt. 'Ask her to call me here in the mess. I'll hang on here.'

'Righty oh,' the porter replied and rang off.

Matt went to get some breakfast, although he did not feel that hungry.

It was about ten o'clock before Anne rang.

'Good morning, Matt. I haven't managed to find out where Jess is just now, I'm afraid. I am pretty sure she has been off this weekend. I could run 'round there and see if she knows anything if you like. We've had a bit of a weekend here as well, darling. Hardly stopped since Friday and I still have tonight to do, but I will go straight away and call you back as soon as I can.'

'Thanks, Anne. Sorry to do this, but I think this could be the crunch for Stephen. It's serious now. He hasn't shown up. I haven't told Squires yet, but I will have to by the end of today if he doesn't come back. And I really think he will boot him out. You usually get one chance, and he's had that already! Hear from you soon.' He rang off.

The papers had arrived in the mess, but it was hard for Matt to concentrate on what was in them. Flt/L Bird came into the room.

'Ah, Matt, been looking for you. Can we meet at two o'clock to go over these new crew lists? Incidentally, you need another mid-upper, don't you? There's a chap just out of the sickbay who might do. His crew got the chop while he was sick so he's a bit of an orphan. Shall I send him to the flight office before lunch and you can meet up?'

'Thanks, Dicky, that would be good,' Matt replied. 'Dicky, I've got a bit of a problem. Can we talk?'

'Let's take a walk, Matt,' Dicky replied, looking around the mess. 'Probably best between us, do you think?'

They stepped out of the mess. The sky was grey, and there were a few flurries of snow pushed along in the brisk easterly wind.

'It's Bamber, my engineer. He's gone missing.'

'Well, I heard he was having some trouble. He ended up under the doc for a few days, didn't he? Where's he gone? Any ideas?'

'Not really, although I suspect he's gone to his new girlfriend. She works at the hospital in town, and I've asked Anne to go and check. Thing is I will need to tell Squires sooner or later, and I don't think he will be too sympathetic this time.'

'Well, he might be, you know. You chaps seem to have had a pretty rough ride, and now there's someone killed as well. He's quite an understanding old bugger, but I can see you might not want to risk it. He's been cut up by our recent losses, you know. Lost some damn fine crews. Why don't you see what Anne finds? If he's there, do you want to try and fish him out?'

'Yes, Dicky. I do. Do you think it would be possible to go after our meeting this afternoon? If he won't come back, I think that's it frankly. He's not doing that well on the job either to be honest, and soon the crew will start to get twitchy as well, me included.'

'No problem, old boy. I'm going to be around anyway, and I can fend off Squires if he starts poking around. Must say, old chap, it's bloody cold out here; let's get back in the mess. Oh, and don't worry, we will sort something out. And I'll get the new boy to see us before lunch.'

'Thanks, Dicky. That's really helpful. Very grateful.' Matt turned off into the flight room to post a notice that he wanted to meet his crew after lunch so he could brief them about the coming week and arrange to meet up at the Red Lion later in the day.

He went back to the mess and got there just as the phone was ringing. One of the mess orderlies answered it. 'For you, sir,' he said as Matt ran in.

It was Anne. 'Hallo, darling. I went 'round and yes, Stephen is with Jess. He's told her that he is on leave!'

'Oh God,' Matt muttered. 'Thanks, darling. I'll go down this afternoon and see if I can talk any sense into him. We are probably off ops for a few nights so maybe he can see the doc and get some rest. Anyway, thanks again, and I love you. Are you free Tuesday? I can't make Monday now, I'm afraid. We have some new crews to sort out.'

'That's OK. Tuesday it is then.'

'I'll phone when I can. You get some sleep now.' Matt rang off and sat down heavily on a nearby chair.

CHAPTER 13

NEW BOYS

Matt met his crew just after lunch and briefed them about the next few days. Their new mid-upper gunner, William Price, was there too, and Matt wondered what to make of him. He was a short, thin man with intelligent brown eyes and a rather academic air. In fact, he had been a language teacher before joining up and had soon decided that he would volunteer to become aircrew. He seemed quiet and slightly withdrawn, and Matt was uncertain how he would fit in with the others, but after the introductions, it was clear that he would be all right. In spite of the fact he appeared to be the complete opposite of Freddie, they seemed to get on.

'Well,' said Matt, 'I thought it would be good for us all to meet down the Red Lion this evening. About time we got together outside the aircraft. Shall we say seven o'clock? Freddie, no doubt you will be there first in which case mine's a pint!'

'You bloody officers are all the same.' Freddie smiled. 'But if it's an order, we'll be there, eh, Billy?'

They all moved out except Charles. 'Any sign of Bamber?' he asked.

'No, Charles, but I know where he is now, thanks to Anne. I am going to try and bring him back this afternoon.'

'Need a hand, old boy? We can take my car if you like?'

'Thanks, Charles, but it might be best with just me, although I can't handcuff him. If he won't come, then that's it, in which case I reckon it's LMF.'

'I think you're right, Matt. The real worry for the rest of us is to know whether he's really up to it. Bloody important job his, you know?'

'I know, Charles. If I can get him back, we will need to make sure he can do the stuff. Otherwise, he is out in any case.'

'Good luck. Hopefully, we'll all meet in the Red Lion!'

It did not take too long for Matt and Flt/L Bird to devise a plan for the next few days. The six new crews were arriving Sunday evening, and they divided them three each. There was not much to tell between them. They had been together since their OTU days and had all been through the HCUs, but none had been over enemy territory so they were completely green. It didn't look too good, and they certainly were not going to have time to bed in gently. The good thing was that they had all done quite a few hours on Lancasters, so on Monday morning, Matt and Bird would take up three crews each and see how they got on. It did not look like it was going to be possible to give the new pilots a chance to fly on a raid as a second dicky before they went off on their own, but that was just the way it was or, at least, how it had become.

Once they had finished, Matt told Bird that he had found out where Stephen was and he was going to go to try to bring him back. Bird wished him luck, but Matt had a bad feeling that this was not going to be his most successful mission. It was snowing quite hard as he got into the little Standard, and it took a while to get the engine started. It was four o'clock and already getting dark, and the snow swirling in front of the windscreen made it quite difficult to see the road, although the tracks of some previous vehicle made things easier. He turned left outside the gates and made steady progress into Lincoln where, at least, the main roads were more easily passable. He eventually drew up outside Jess's house and, having pushed the gate open against a bank of snow, went up to the door. Jess came to answer his knock and seemed surprised to see Matt.

'You'd better come in, Matt,' she said. 'What's the matter?'

'Well, I wondered if you have seen Stephen,' he replied. 'He's in a lot of trouble, you know, although we can still sort something out at this stage.'

Concern showed on her face as she replied, 'Well, he's here. He said he had some leave and asked if he could stay.'

'Well, that's not quite the case, Jess,' Matt said gravely. This was looking worse and worse.

'He should be back at the station. No one has leave,' Matt continued. 'Where is he?'

At this point, Stephen came into the room, followed closely by Scrap.

'I'm not coming back,' he said. 'We are all going to get killed. You know that, don't you, Matt? We will all be dead soon, just like Townsend.'

'Well, you know what this would mean, Stephen. Cleaning out latrines for the rest of the war and then trouble getting a job afterwards. It's a terrible indictment. It was bad luck with Townsend, and of course it's bloody dangerous, but we are a good crew and we have been through some bad times. We are over two-thirds through. We could be finished in a couple of months. It's crazy to leave now.'

Jess paled as she realised what the two airmen were talking about.

'I thought you were on leave, Stephen. That wasn't true, was it?' she cried.

'Jess, I just couldn't bring myself to tell you. I'm finished. I can't go back,' Stephen said his shoulders hunched over.

'You must, Stephen. As Matt says, you can't just give in. It must be terrible for you, for you all, but if others gave up too, then where would we be?'

'I just can't bring myself to go back in the aircraft. I feel useless, and one day, I will make a mistake and everyone will get killed anyway.'

Jess looked at Matt. 'Will he really be disgraced, Matt?'

'Probably. Squires is pretty fair really, and he realises that we have been getting a real bashing lately, but if you don't come back with me, Stephen, I think it won't go well. Maybe we can get the doc to help you again. We've got a bit of a breather just now. Some new crews to train for a couple of days, so maybe he can get you into shape.'

'Surely it's worth a try, Stephen,' Jess said, taking him by the arm. 'And then we can have some more time together when you next get a break. Can be only a few weeks,' Jess continued, looking at Matt for some confirmation.

'Jess is right, old man. Come back with me now, and we can see the doc. And then a couple of ops, and we will be on leave again,' he added encouragingly.

Stephen slumped into a chair and buried his head in his hands, his shoulders shaking as the tears came. Scrap came up and rested his chin on Stephen's knee. Jess sat on the arm of the chair and put her arm around Stephen's shoulders. She looked close to tears herself, and Matt thought it best to leave them alone.

'I'll be in the car,' he said. 'I'll wait fifteen minutes, and then I have to get back. If you are not with me, I'll have to speak to the CO. I'm sorry,' he added as he walked out.

It was still snowing as he made his way back to the car. The wind had picked up, and it was bitterly cold. The sky appeared darkly luminescent, heralding more snow to come. The car was like a fridge, and Matt pulled his greatcoat around himself in an attempt to keep warm. He looked at his watch and determined that he was going to drive away at precisely six thirty. The minutes passed, and Matt was just getting ready to drive away when he saw the front door open and Jess came running out.

She tapped on the window, and Matt opened the door to get out.

'Matt, can you come back in for a minute? Stephen is so muddled in his head, but I think he will come back with you. I really think that's what he wants to do.'

Matt got out of the car and followed Jess back indoors. Stephen was standing, and Matt noticed that his pale face had a crumpled look.

'I'll come back, Matt,' he said. 'But I will have to go sick. I can't sleep, and I am so tired and can hardly think. Maybe a few days off will help?'

'Good, Stephen. Very good. I am sure the doc will fix you up. And, Jess, a million thanks. We must all go out again when this is over. Come on, old chap, let's get back before anyone realises we've gone. Oh yes and you too, Scrap, in the car.'

Stephen climbed into the passenger's side with Scrap in the back. Matt got the car started and gingerly drove out of Jess's street onto the main road. The snow was lying quite thickly now, and the car slipped and slid along the road. Once they had turned off to towards the airfield, the minor roads were even more difficult although the old wheel tracks helped. It was eight o'clock before they were back, and Matt drove round to the side of their hut. They had hardly spoken on the way back, and at one point, Matt was sure that Stephen had fallen into an uneasy sleep.

Once the engine had stopped, Matt looked at Stephen.

'Well, what do you want to do?' he asked. 'Straight to the sickbay or down the pub? We are all meeting there this evening.'

'Matt, I am going to report sick. Thanks for coming to get me. I'm not sure it's the right thing, but Jess was pretty straight. I came back with you, or she and I were history.'

'Not much choice then, have you?' Matt replied sharply 'Well, you can find your own way to the sickbay, or would it help if I saw the doc with you, do you think?'

'No, thanks, Matt. I will be OK, I think. Need some sleep.' And with that, he got out of the car.

'I'll come over and see you in the morning,' Matt called as Stephen shut the door and made his way to see the MO.

Matt parked the car by their hut, and Scrap jumped out and walked along beside him.

'Fancy a drink, Scrap?' Matt said as he started walking towards the camp gates. He needed a breath of fresh air to clear his head. In many ways, the last few hours had been almost as stressful as flak on a raid, and a nagging doubt remained in Matt's mind about whether, in fact, Stephen was still up to the task in any case. It was still snowing as he walked out of the camp, and he hardly noticed the guard's salute but did manage a curt, 'Goodnight'.

Scrap scampered along beside him, his paws picking up big balls of snow, which was still falling steadily. He turned left down the road towards the Red Lion and picked his way along the road. It was quite windy, but the sound in the bare trees was muffled by the snow.

The pub looked closed because of the blackout, but as he opened the door, the noise, light, and thick air caught him by surprise. A cheer went up from his crew, who had bagged a place close to the fire, which burnt brightly.

'You're a bit behind, Skipper!' Freddie laughed. 'But Mr Redman has been getting them in for you, haven't you, sir?'

'Yes, Freddie.' Redman smiled. 'We'll look after him, won't we?' Redman turned to Matt. 'Everything OK?' he asked quietly. 'You look all in, old chap.'

'Not too bad,' Matt replied. 'He's back at least. In the sickbay, hopefully asleep by now. See how he is in the morning.'

They all sat drinking and yarning for a couple of hours before Matt declared he had had enough and turned to leave. Redman caught him by his elbow and steered him towards the door.

'Matt,' he said, 'if you need any help, just let me know, won't you? It's bad enough having to drive us lot around with Jerry trying to kill us, without the worry of someone like Stephen. You know yourself there may come a point when we have to let him go, for our sakes as much as for his.'

'Thanks, Charles,' Matt replied. 'I'll bear that in mind. Let's see how he does this time. I'll see you in the morning. I'll probably feel a bit more positive once I've got my head down for a few hours. Goodnight. And thanks again.'

The biting cold was a sharp contrast to the fug in the Red Lion, and the wind made Matt's eyes water as he trudged his way back to the base, his shoes crunching through the crisp, frozen snow. The sky was clear now, and the stars shone out against the black of the sky. Orion was clearly visible, and Matt realised how comforting he had always found that constellation, a huge man in the sky with his starry belt, looking out for them. It only took a short while for him to get back to the base, and the sentry saluted as he went past the guardroom. He got back to his room and rubbed Scrap down with one of Stephen's towels. The room was cold, and

Matt quickly got into bed with Scrap next to him. They were soon fast asleep.

***

The next morning dawned bright but bitterly cold, and Matt quickly drank the cup of tea Barker had brought him, dressed, and went out with Scrap.

'Come on, old fella,' Matt said. 'Quick pee and dump and then we will find you something to eat.' They trudged around the perimeter for about thirty minutes whilst Scrap did the necessary and then went to the canteen in search of food. That fixed, Matt left Scrap with Barker and went off to the flight office.

The six new crews were already there, and Matt arrived just as Bird was about to talk to them. He introduced Matt and then divided the six, Matt taking his three off to the far corner of the office. As he and Bird had thought, they were all about at the same stage but at least seemed to know how to find their way around a Lancaster.

'OK, chaps,' Matt said. 'I will go up with each crew in turn, and then we can see where we are. It rather looks like there will not be time for any of the pilots to come along as second dicky, so you will have to cope with the raids on your own. Flight Lieutenant Bird and myself will do our best to brief you when the time comes. None of you have been over Germany, is that correct?'

The young men in front of Matt looked anxiously at one another before one of the pilots replied, 'No, sir. We were geared up to go a few weeks ago, but the op was scrubbed at the last moment.'

'Well, at least you will have had a taste of preop nerves; that's something.' Matt smiled.

Poor bastards, he thought, *they have no idea what to expect.*

'Right, Pilot Officer Simmons, you get your crew ready first. You will be using A-Apple. Not the youngest kite in the squadron but she is sound. Come and let me know when you are ready. You need to clear take-off with your ground crew and ops. Don't forget to collect your parachutes and make sure you dress properly. It's bloody cold down here, so it is even colder up there. I want you to plan a cross country to Sheffield and back.'

'Right, sir,' Simmons replied, but he looked as if the Devil himself had spoken to him.

'Christ,' Matt said to himself, 'he looks about sixteen and as if he's about to crap himself!'

'The rest of you, I suggest, go and check out your own kites and be ready to fly when I get back with A-Apple. I would like to try and get these check flights sorted by lunchtime, and then we can spend the afternoon talking through some of the problems flying an op.'

They all saluted and wandered out of the flight room, Bird's group finishing about the same time.

'Blimey,' muttered Bird. 'What was your lot like? To be frank, I would be surprised if any of them last very long. Where are you taking them?'

'Over towards Sheffield,' Matt replied. 'I thought we should be able to get things tied up by lunch and then spend the afternoon with them telling them how it is. Any of your group seen action?'

'Nope. Nor will they if they don't sharpen up quickly. I mean, Matt, were we really that green when we joined our squadrons or is my memory failing?'

'Well, they are having to shove them through pretty quickly just now because we are all getting knocked off so quickly!' Matt smiled. 'I am off to see how Bamber is getting on.'

'Ah, you managed to snatch him back then?' Bird asked.

'Yes, Dicky. But not a good experience, I can tell you. God knows if he will be all right in the end.'

Matt walked out of the office and over towards the sickbay where he bumped into one of the nurses.

'Excuse me,' he said. 'How is Pilot Officer Bamber this morning? Is it possible for me to see him?'

'He's still asleep, sir. The doctor gave him something last night, and he just crashed out. Doctor is around if you want to have a word.'

'Yes, thank you, that would be very helpful.'

The nurse led him through to Wing Commander Spear's office.

'Morning, sir,' Matt began. 'Just wonder how Bamber was.'

'Well, still asleep and may be for some time. I thought we would just knock him out for a day or two and see what happens. No ops planned at least until Wednesday?'

'No, sir. We have a new bunch of crews to try and get ready in the next two days,' Matt replied. 'When do you think he will be able to talk?'

'Probably tomorrow, Matt. Why don't you look in then? And after you've seen him, we can have another chat.'

'Thanks, sir. I'll do that,' Matt said and walked back to the dispersal area to see how Simmons and his crew were getting on.

**

Matt found them gathered around A-Apple, some of them smoking nervously and all of them looking anxious.

'OK, Simmons,' Matt said, 'have you got your route sorted out and all your gear? Has everyone got their parachute, and has someone got one for me?'

Their navigator, Baines, spoke up. 'Sir, I have plotted the route. Do you want to see it?'

'No, thank you, Baines. I am assuming that plotting routes is second nature by now so we shall just see where you take us, won't we?' Matt smiled to try to release the tension, but none of them smiled back.

'And my parachute?' he asked again.

There was silence until Simmons sheepishly said, 'We thought you would like to get your own, sir.'

'Quite right, Pilot Officer Simmons. Each of us is responsible for signing for our parachute. It's no good when the moment comes to start asking whether another member of crew managed to pick up your chute on the way, is it? I will go and get my gear on, oh, and my parachute.' He smiled again. 'And then we will be on our way. Simmons, I suggest you get everyone aboard, do your checks, and be ready, so when I get back, we can push the starter and go. Gunners, check your guns are loaded. Know why?'

The two gunners stared back blankly.

'Because,' Matt continued, 'although we are over home territory, it is not unknown for the Luftwaffe to pay us a visit even during the daytime, just to see what they can find. Then we would look very silly if all we could do was wave, wouldn't we?'

Matt picked up his flying suit and signed for his parachute. He chatted to the ground crew before climbing in through the rear door and closing it. He tapped the rear gunner's back and moved forward past the mid-upper, the radio operator, and the navigator and alongside the flight engineer. The bomb-aimer was down in the front of the aircraft.

'We ready, pilot?' he asked.

'Yes, sir. All checks are complete, and I have signed off Form 700. I think we are ready to go once we have clearance.'

'OK! Well, call control and go through your engine-start procedure. Let me see how you and your engineer work. You're called Stark, aren't you?' he said, turning to the engineer.

'Yes, sir,' Stark replied, and then he and Simmons went through their checklists before starting the engines. Eventually, all four engines were running and Simmons asked for clearance to taxi and line up with the runway. He called everyone to make sure they were OK, lined up, and took off. The lightly loaded Lancaster almost leapt into the air, and Matt made a mental note to warn Simmons how different it would be on a raid. They headed east, climbed to 5,000 feet, and began turning south. Matt waited to see what would transpire, and they were over the Wash before he asked where they were going.

'Are we on a sightseeing tour, Baines?' he asked.

'No, sir, but I thought we should keep clear of the other airfields. We have been told about the dangers of collisions with other aircraft around airfields, sir.'

'You know something, Baines? It's almost impossible to fly across this part of the planet without going over another airfield. So let's go directly to Sheffield, shall we? And let's make sure everyone is looking outside the aircraft. You must keep a sharp lookout both now and when on ops; otherwise, you're all dead meat. Is that clear?'

They were about ten miles from Sheffield when Matt told Simmons to turn around and head back to East Kirkby. He moved up alongside Stark and surreptitiously closed the throttle of engine number 4. The aircraft immediately swung to the right, and Matt waited to see what, if any, action pilot and engineer would take. He was impressed that Simmons responded quickly, asking Stark to feather the prop and increase revs in the starboard inner, and by applying left rudder, he brought the aircraft straight again.

'Well done,' he said. 'Let's see if we can restart the engine.'

Again, he noticed that they performed well. With time, he thought, they could probably be OK. Unfortunately, they did not have much time.

'OK, let's go home,' he said. 'But don't drop your guard,' he warned. 'That's when accidents happen. Baines, give us a course for Kirkby.'

There was a momentary silence before Baines said, 'Just trying to work that out now, sir.'

'It should be pretty easy, Baines. Just draw a straight line from here to there.'

'Yes, sir. I'm just not quite sure where here is, sir.'

'Well, either get your bomb-aimer to look or get off your arse and come up here to look outside yourself.' Matt felt more exasperated than angry, but if this lot could get lost on a short cross-country trip to Sheffield and back in daylight, then God help them.

Baines came forward and was clearly struggling to recognise significant features. They had done most of their training in Yorkshire, so this was a new area for them, but nevertheless, it was concerning. And this was a crystal-clear day.

'Well, Baines, see anything you recognise?' Matt asked sharply.

'Not just yet, sir,' he replied.

'Anyone else help?' Matt called down the intercom.

'I think it looks like Lincoln Cathedral up ahead,' said Johnson, the bomb-aimer.

'Oh yes,' replied Baines, 'I see it now.'

'So where are we then?' asked Matt, now beginning to get irritated. 'And don't say on our way to Lincoln. Show me on the chart.'

'Well, I'm not entirely sure,' Baines hesitated. 'It looks like we are over a biggish road, and there seems to be an airfield below us. That could be Gameston. So I think we are here.' He pointed to the chart.

'About bloody time too. I will ask Squadron Leader Redman to spend a bit of time with you this afternoon and set you a cross country for tomorrow. Not impressed. You must all work together when you are flying. Let's get down.'

Simmons lined the aircraft up and performed a perfect touchdown, and as they taxied over to their stand, Matt patted him on the shoulder.

'Well done. Some nice flying, but we need to get the nav sorted, don't we?'

Simmons nodded as he and Stark went through the shutdown procedures.

Matt jumped down from the aircraft first, having arranged to meet Simmons and his crew after lunch. It felt as if it was going to be a rather trying day after all, and as he made his way over to the next rookie crew, he began to share Bird's feeling of despair. However, the second and third crews seemed much sharper, and they performed well together as teams, so when he landed for the third time that morning, he began to feel rather more confident about their prospects for survival.

Bird was already in the mess when Matt walked in. 'Fancy a pint, old boy? Looks like you could use one.' Bird smiled. 'How bad was it?'

'Well, two out of three OK,' Matt replied, 'but the Simmons lot look very shaky. Their navigator managed to get lost between here and Sheffield!'

'Well, my three crews look OK, I reckon, and I am happy for them to go operational, I think. Looks like we may have another day before we have to pop over to visit the Third Reich again. What are you doing about A-Apple then?'

'Going to get Charles Redman to try and gee them up and then take them out again tomorrow. I'm hoping to get to see Anne for lunch tomorrow, but we should be able to fit everything in.'

'How about Bamber? What does old sawbones say?' Bird asked.

'Well, this morning, he was still asleep. I'll pop in later this afternoon, but I can't see him being fit if we go again on Wednesday. Probably have to blag another engineer from Squires. He may get away with it this time, but I think that will be that.'

'You're right, old man. There's been a bit of grumbling around already. Once these things get out, the Old Man has to put his foot down. Bamber will be made an example of if he's not careful.'

'I know, and I've told him it's the end of the line. He's a good chap, though, you know, and actually, it takes guts to keep going when you feel like he must do. Any case, do we have a gash engineer around, do you know? The one on A-Apple seems bloody good. Wouldn't mind snaffling him!'

'There is a chap coming back from leave tomorrow, I think,' said Bird, downing his pint. His lot got shot down in the recent carnage whilst he was home on compassionate leave. Name's Clarke. Don't know anything else about him, I'm afraid.'

'Thanks, Dick. Want another?' Matt replied.

'Don't mind if I do, old boy, then let's go and get some grub.'

***

Matt went over to see A-Apple's crew after their session with Charles. They were in the crew room gathered together like a group of naughty schoolboys.

'How did you get on?' Matt asked.

Simmons was the first to answer. 'Not too good really, sir. I don't think Squadron Leader Redman was too impressed with us either, but he did give us some helpful tips.'

'Good,' replied Matt. 'Well, tomorrow morning, we will do another cross country and I will ask S/L Redman to come along as well. Let's see if we can straighten things out. It will probably be our last chance before the action starts again, and we definitely don't want you getting yourselves lost over Germany. Meet me in the flight office at 0800 tomorrow. Any questions? … All right, go and join the other crews who are being briefed by our regulars. And listen very carefully to what they have to say.'

They shook their heads and ambled out.

Poor bastards, thought Matt. *Probably haven't a hope in hell.*

He walked slowly over to the sickbay, wondering how he would find Stephen and hoping against hope that he was getting better. The first person he saw was the doctor.

'Bit better, Matt,' he said. 'But won't be fit for a day or two, I would say. If we can steer him through the next forty-eight hours, then who knows? You will need someone new in the meantime. I'll go and speak to W/C Squires for you and explain. But you know, Matt, this could be it for him, I think.'

'Thanks, sir. Yes, I think we all know this is the end of the line, but thanks for trying to get him fixed.' Matt smiled and went into the sickbay.

Stephen was sitting up by the side of his bed reading.

'Hallo, old chap,' said Matt cheerfully. 'How are you feeling?'

'Better thanks, Matt. Actually being able to sleep seems to help enormously. Whatever the doc gives me knocks me for six—no dreams, just wake up ten hours later. How are things out there?' He nodded towards the door.

'Not bad. We have had six crews as replacements. Bit of a mixed bag, so we are trying to knock them into shape.' He smiled. 'First lot I took up got lost between here and Sheffield. Not bad, eh?'

Stephen laughed, and Matt realised he had not heard him do so for a long time.

'Matt, I have written a letter to Jess. Do you think you could put it in the post for me?'

'Better than that,' Matt replied, 'I'm hoping to see Anne tomorrow for lunch. I can give it to her for Jess.'

'Thanks, Matt. At least no one else will see it then, will they?'

Matt nodded and started to get up.

'Matt,' Stephen said, 'I am going to get back flying, you know. This has been a bad spell, but I will stick it out. Just need a bit of a breather; that's all.'

'Good to hear it, Stephen. Incidentally, Scrap is doing fine too. In fact, I am just off to walk him now, and Barker seems to be feeding him God knows what! I'll tell the boys you will be back soon. Bye for now.'

And with that, Matt turned and walked out. It was getting dark, and the easterly wind had picked up. The bitter cold made him wonder if his offer to walk the dog was such a great idea. It was good to see Stephen looking better, and he would be able to give a fairly positive report when he met up with the crew in the Red Lion later on.

He found Scrap outside Barker's door, which he pushed open to find Barker fast asleep. He quietly shut the door and with Scrap scampering along went to his room to get his greatcoat. It was completely dark when the two went outside, and it had started snowing yet again. The wind blew the flakes almost horizontally, and Matt leaned into the wind as he made his way to the perimeter fence. They walked along for a while, but the snow was falling more thickly now, and the wind was wailing through the bare trees outside the station. Matt tried to remember what it had all been like in the summer with the same trees heavy with leaf and he and Anne walking hand in hand through the woods. It seemed almost impossible to think that it was only a few months ago. The snow was quite thick now, and Scrap was getting little balls of snow on his pads. He tried frantically to lick them off. Even he did not seem to be too keen on walking further, and Matt turned around to make his way back to his billet. The wind came from behind him now, and it felt less biting. It was good to know that no one would be flying tonight. They got into Matt's room, and Scrap immediately jumped on Stephen's bed, snow balls and all. Matt had not the heart to get him off, and he lay on his bed and closed his eyes. It had been a rather difficult day all in all, and the new crews were clearly going to be in for quite a shock when they went on their first trip, especially, he thought, Simmons's lot. He still needed to get a flight engineer, because Stephen clearly was not going to be up to flying for a day or two. He would ask around tomorrow, and with that thought, he closed his eyes and fell deeply asleep. It was nine o'clock when he surfaced, and realising he still had to go down to the Red Lion, he grabbed his greatcoat again and went out, leaving Scrap snoring on Stephen's bed.

The pub was full when he got there and filled with the usual noise, laughter, and cigarette smoke. He found his crew up in one corner, looking decidedly the worse for wear.

'Hallo, Skip!' Freddie shouted above the din. 'We thought you was off with some other crew. Thought you'd gone off us, like.'

Matt smiled. 'As if I could, Freddie. Whatever would I do without you all? Oh, and mine's a pint whilst you're there, Freddie.'

'Blimey,' said Freddie. 'Typical bloody officer. Can't even get their own beer. Anyway, how's Pilot Officer Bamber, Skip?'

'Oh, much better, thank you. I think he will be back with us very soon. We might have to do one or two trips without him.' He looked over to where Redman was sitting and winked.

'Gawd,' said Freddie. 'Not another odd bod for us?'

'Well, I think we have been very lucky with our odd bods,' Mac replied. 'They don't seem so lucky once they leave us though, do they? Look at poor old Purdy; he got the chop the next trip.'

'Well, that's their problem,' grumbled Freddie. 'It feels good when we're all together. What d'you think, Skip?'

'Well, yes, I agree, but sometimes it just doesn't work out that we can always fly together. Look at today. Didn't see any of you volunteering to go up with the new crews.' He smiled and turned to the bar. 'Six pints, Joe, please.'

When Matt came back, Freddie and the new mid-upper were deep in conversation, and it was Don who asked about the new crews.

'What they like, Skip? Any good?'

'Well, I think they will all be fine after their first trip. I'm sure we can all remember what that was like and how we felt before it?'

'Yeh,' replied Don. 'It was bad. First two or three weren't that shiny, to tell the truth,' he continued. 'Still, after a while, you get used to folk trying to kill you all the time.'

They stuck around until closing time, and Matt and Redman went out into the cold together.

'Is Stephen really so much better?' Charles asked.

'Well, better, yes. But I would say still a long way to go, although he seems more positive. We'll see. We will need someone for certainly one and maybe two trips. To be honest, Charles, if he doesn't make it by then, I think he's out and I am sure it will mean being labelled LMF in the end.'

Redman cut off to the married quarters, leaving Matt to make his own way back. He felt tired and was missing Anne very much. He hoped all would go well tomorrow, and he would manage to get off in time to meet her for lunch. It seemed ages since they had met although, in fact, it was only a few days and so much had happened in the meantime. Scrap popped up as he went into the room and seemed keen to go outside for a pee. They came back in, and Matt undressed and got into the cold bed. After a few minutes, he was off to sleep with Scrap beside him for some warmth.

***

Barker brought Matt's tea in at six the next morning and announced that it was very cold outside. Scrap jumped down from the bed and trotted out, leaving Matt to relish his tea and to think about the day ahead. He hoped he could dust off Simmons and the cross country fairly quickly, come back, shower, and change in time to meet up with Anne. Bird had kindly agreed to cover for him so they could have a slow lunch and a bit of time after, as well. He missed her very much, and once this short break was over, it was hard to see when they might get a chance to meet again in the near future. Everyone realised that things were not going exactly to plan in the air war and the so-called Battle of Berlin was proving very costly in aircraft and crew. The crews were under a lot of pressure to keep going, and the losses meant there was virtually no slack in the system to allow time for a break and much-needed leave.

He swung his legs over the side of the bed, pulled on his tunic and flying boots, and made his way to the mess for breakfast. Bird and several other officers, including Simmons, were already there, and Matt felt quite hungry. He then realised he had not eaten a proper meal for a couple of days.

'You ready, Simmons?' he called across the table. 'Looks like a nice clear day if a touch cold,' he added, trying to keep things fairly light-hearted. He had realised that Simmons was nervous, and he did not want this to destroy his self-confidence.

'Squadron Leader Redman is joining us this morning so we can make sure you chaps will be ready to fly on your own. See you down by the kite at about 0800 hours?'

'Right, sir. We will be ready by then. I think there is quite a bit of ice on the wings just now, but the ground crew are working on that.' With that, Simmons got up and left.

Bird looked over. 'Nervous as a bloody kitten, isn't he?'

'Yes. That doesn't help, although he seems a good pilot for all that. They don't work too well as a crew, I would say. Maybe that's Simmons's fault. Who knows?'

Matt finished his breakfast and got up. 'Still cover me this afternoon?' he asked Bird.

'Of course, old chap. Have a nice lunch and take your time. I think we'll be on tomorrow night,' he said quietly. 'The Old Man hasn't said anything as such, but there seems to be quite a bit of activity. How's your engineer?'

'Just off to see him now,' replied Matt. 'We will need a spare if it's tomorrow for sure. Anyone around?'

'Not sure, old boy. There was a rumour that the squadron flight engineer was looking for a ride. You'll have to be sure to bring him back in one piece!'

Matt walked briskly over to the sickbay. It was freezing cold, and the sky was the colour of matt grey paint. In contrast, it felt very warm in the sickbay and Matt walked through to where Stephen had been the day before to find his bed empty. One of the nurses came over, and he asked her where he had gone.

'Wing Commander Spear wanted someone in Lincoln to have a look at him,' she said. 'Should be back later this afternoon,' she continued. 'The MO is in his office, if you want to see him, sir.'

'Thanks,' replied Matt, and he made his way down the corridor and tapped on the door.

'Come,' he heard from within and opened the door to find the doctor studying some papers on his desk.

'Ah, Matt,' he said. 'Sit you down. I have asked a colleague to have a look at our friend in case I am missing something. He seems much brighter, and I have a feeling that a large part of the problem is sleep deprivation, which if that is the case, we can do something about it. In any case, he is out of action for a couple of days, I'm afraid.'

'Thanks, sir,' Matt replied. 'It's good to know there may be a chance for him in any case. I will pop in tomorrow. I am just taking one of the new crews for a jaunt, then off to see the future Mrs White.'

'Well, have a nice time,' the doctor replied. 'See you tomorrow then.'

The check flight with Simmons and his crew went quite well, and at least they didn't get lost this time. Matt noticed that, in fact, they seemed to be working better together as a crew, and after about half an hour, he told Simmons to take them back to East Kirkby.

Matt went back to his room and washed and shaved and then headed off to his car. Scrap looked up hopefully, but Matt made it clear this was not a trip for dogs.

The car was covered in snow, and the ice overnight had produced a hard crust, which was quite difficult to scrape off. He realised that he was running late, but fortunately, the engine fired first time, and he roared down to the front gate to receive a salute from the guard as he sped through. The roads were slippery, and he needed to follow the ruts in the snow. It took him nearly an hour to get to the hospital to pick up Anne. She was waiting outside, and once Matt had parked the car, they walked to the restaurant that Matt had booked.

'I was getting worried,' Anne said as Matt joined her. 'How did the new ones do?'

'Oh, not too bad,' Matt replied. 'Let's talk about us, not them.'

The tone of his voice made Anne look sharply at him. He looked tired, and the worry lines round his mouth and eyes seemed deeper than ever. She tucked her arm through his. 'How are you, darling? You look very tired.'

He turned to her and smiled. 'Not bad. Quite a lot going on just now. Went to see Stephen before I came down, but he was seeing a specialist here in Lincoln. Doc thinks he's not too bad. Let's grab some lunch.'

'Matt, how long have we got today?' Anne asked.

'Well, I think so long as I am back this evening, we should be all right. But I thought you were still working today?'

'I managed to get the rest of the day off too. But if you don't have to rush back, I have arranged something for us.' She smiled naughtily, and Matt thought she blushed a little too.

'Well, what might that be?' he asked. 'Not sitting in the park all afternoon, I hope?'

'Why, wouldn't you want to do that then?' She pouted.

'We would freeze to death.' He put his arms around her and kissed her. 'I do love you,' he said. 'Let's go and eat, and then we can discuss what to do after.'

'Oh, there's no discussion,' Anne replied, laughing. 'None at all!'

They found the restaurant and ordered lunch and some wine. They chatted about Anne's parents and the approaching wedding, but she noticed that Matt was picking at his food rather than bolting it down as usual.

'Matt, would you like to order something else? You've hardly eaten anything.'

'No, this is fine, darling. Appetite not so good during the day just now,' Matt replied, pushing his plate away. 'Maybe some pud?'

Anne could not believe that they had been down to her parents' only about a month ago. Matt seemed to be changing in front of her eyes. Before, he had been outgoing, enthusiastically eating everything, but now he seemed entirely different, a changed man. They finished their meal, and Matt ordered another bottle of wine. That was another thing, Anne thought; he seemed to be drinking more as well. Maybe her plan of an afternoon making love in one of the local hotels was not such a good one after all.

'Well, what's your plan then?' Matt asked.

Anne hesitated. 'Well, I wondered if you would like to go somewhere where we can be alone and, well, very close? I have booked us a room, but if you'd rather not, then that's fine too.'

She watched him anxiously and noticed that he, too, hesitated before he replied, 'Anne, sweetheart, if I lie down, I will go to sleep. That's not very romantic, is it?'

'No, but it's very human,' she replied. 'Let's go and cuddle up, and you can go to sleep.'

They settled their bill, and she took his hand as they walked out of the restaurant. 'I have booked us in just down here,' Anne continued.

The room was small but cosy, and there was a fire burning in the grate. Anne took off her coat and dress but left her silk slip on and climbed into bed. 'Come on, slow coach,' she called to Matt. 'I need warming up.'

Matt stripped off to his pants and got into bed, and they held one another very tightly.

She held Matt so that his head was resting on her breasts and kissed his head. She thought he was trembling but then realised that he was crying, and she held him tighter.

'Matt, Matt,' she whispered. 'My dearest, what is it?' Then she felt him relax as he went to sleep snuggling into her like a child to his mother.

They lay like that for what seemed hours. Anne looked at the firelight reflecting from the walls and listened to the wind, which seemed to have picked up, whistling past the window. It was completely dark when Matt started to stir.

'I'm sorry, Anne,' he said. 'It was a lovely idea, but I was afraid that would happen. Not much of a bloke, eh?'

'You're my bloke,' she replied. 'That's all that counts. Do you feel better?' She did not mention the crying, and neither did Matt.

'A bit. Thank you, Anne. Let's try and get away on my next leave. It's only a couple of weeks now. It's all so much better when we have time together. I'd better be getting back. Anne, we may be going tomorrow night, but I will ring when I get back.' He smiled weakly.

They dressed in silence and made their way out to the street. It was snowing yet again, and the wind was bitterly cold. They walked quickly back to the hospital and kissed outside the door. Matt realised Anne was crying silently, and he held her.

'I will be OK, Anne. Let you know when we are back.'

And with that, he turned and got into his car and drove away.

CHAPTER 14

ESSEN

Matt returned the salute of the guard as he went through the gate back into the camp. It was snowing slightly again, and the wind had picked up, so it felt bitterly cold as he got out of the car and walked over to his hut. To his surprise, he found Stephen and Scrap on the bed and both got up as he went into the room.

'Hi, Matt,' Stephen said and shook his hand.

'Stephen,' Matt replied, 'what are you doing here?'

'Well, I felt so much better after a couple of good nights' sleep, I thought I should get my arse in gear and come back!'

'Christ, Stephen. That's a bit of a turnaround, isn't it? Does the MO approve?'

'Not really, but I feel better about it to be honest. And in any case, Scrap needs someone to look after him!'

'Hmm. Seemed to be doing pretty well to me.' Matt smiled. 'In any case, great to have you back. Be a bit of a disappointment for the Squadron Flight Engineer. Dicky said he thought that he was looking for a trip—rather fancied us, I think!'

'Sorry to disappoint.' Stephen smiled. 'I am sure there will be plenty of opportunities in the future!'

'Fancy a beer?' Matt asked. 'I just want to see what the buzz is about tomorrow.'

'No, I won't, thanks,' Stephen replied. 'Incidentally, I did hear a rumour that we will definitely be going tomorrow, although no one had any idea about where to and the weather looks completely crap.'

'OK,' replied Matt. 'I'll go and see what's around.' And with that, he walked out into the freezing cold.

The mess was crowded as usual and thick with cigarette and pipe smoke. Dicky was at the bar and waved to Matt as he came in the door.

'Pint of wallop?' he asked. 'How's Anne?'

'Yes and fine, in that order,' said Matt. 'Hey, Stephen seems to be back in the land of the living. Keen as mustard. Seems very odd, doesn't it?'

'Maybe the doc's put him on some magic potion. Perhaps we could all get some.' Dicky laughed. 'Incidentally, the rumour mill has us on for tomorrow. Big show apparently, but no one knows where.'

'Well, we knew it couldn't stay quiet for long,' Matt replied. 'In any case, everyone starts getting the creeps if we don't do anything.'

Matt bought another round before making his excuses and leaving. He felt very tired, and the time with Anne had, in fact, been anything but fine. He was feeling desperately tired, and he needed to sleep, especially if they had an op tomorrow night. He staggered through the snow to the hut and went straight to his room. Stephen was fast asleep, and although Scrap sat up as he went in, he too lay down and curled up almost immediately.

Matt climbed into his cold bed and then remembered he hadn't rung Anne, but he felt just too weary. He would get through first thing in the morning, and with that thought, he got under the bedclothes and went straight to sleep.

***

Barker came in to wake up Matt and Stephen at six o'clock in the morning with the customary cup of tea.

'Morning, gentlemen. It's stopped snowing, but it's bloody cold!'

Matt felt that he had never been asleep but swung his legs over the side of the bed and grasped his steaming mug of tea. Stephen showed little response, and Scrap had already jumped down to follow Barker out for a certain breakfast.

'Come on, Stephen, show a leg!' Matt shouted. He was relieved to see signs of life as Stephen emerged from the covers.

'Is it really time?' he asked, reaching out for his tea.

'Certainly is,' Matt replied as he started to get dressed. 'Can you slip down to the kite after breakfast and just see what the state of play is? I have got to meet Dicky and probably the Old Man first thing.'

Stephen mumbled that he would as Matt went out of the door into freezing cold wind. In fact, there was a beautiful clear sky and the stars were fading as the eastern horizon was getting lighter. Matt walked into the flight office, and Dicky arrived a couple of minutes later.

Already on the notice board were the words 'Operation tonight. Flight commanders to station commander at 0700 hours'.

'Oh well,' said Matt. 'That seems straightforward!'

'Yes, let's go and grab some breakfast,' Dicky said as he turned to go back out of the door. 'How's Bamber?'

'Sleepy but probably OK,' said Matt. 'I've got him to go and check with the ground crew. See how that goes. Dicky, I'll join you in a minute. I must ring Anne. If I don't do it now, I know that I won't manage later on. And as it is, I forgot to ring her last night!'

'Right. See you in the mess.'

Matt went to the phone and after an age managed to get through to the hospital and eventually Anne.

'Morning, darling. Sorry about last night. Stephen seems to have made a miraculous recovery. Says he is happy to fly tonight. Great news, isn't it?'

'A weight off your mind, darling. Will you be able to ring again today, or shall you ring tomorrow when you are back?'

'Yes, that would be best,' replied Matt. 'Might be a bit busy today with one thing and another. Hopefully, all will go well.'

'Yes, take care, darling. I know you will and we can speak tomorrow. I love you.'

Matt always felt lost as soon as he rang off, and it brought to mind what might happen to him and the crew over the next twenty-four hours and how much he wanted to be with Anne and away from all this. He found Dicky tucking into his bacon and egg.

'Everything fine?' he asked. 'Must say I feel a bit peckish. Bloody cold weather, I reckon.'

Matt, in contrast, did not feel that hungry but forced down some toast and a cup of sweet tea.

'Better go and see Squires then,' Dicky said, getting up from the table once Matt had finished. Together, they walked round to the office.

'Come,' the voice of Wing Commander Squires boomed through the glass panel in the door.

'Morning, chaps. Please sit down,' Squires said. 'We have a bonus trip for you tonight, which should be a milk run for the old lags and a nice entrée for the new boys. We are going to pay another visit to Essen. The powers that be seem to feel they need to keep the pressure on there. There will be Mosquitoes to do the marking and a force of about 200 Lancs. Obviously hush-hush until briefing this afternoon. Now, how are the new boys? Up to scratch, do you think?'

Matt and Dicky both nodded and after the usual pleasantries made their way back to the flight office.

'Well,' said Dicky, 'he may think it's a milk run, but the last time we went to the Ruhr, we got a bloody pasting. Short sodding memory these guys have.'

Matt could only agree. He could not think that any trip over Germany could be described as a 'milk run'. True, it was a relatively short trip compared with Berlin, but easy, it was not. He thought of the new crews and how they might work out.

Stephen was in the flight office when they came back.

'Everything OK, Stephen. How's the kite look?'

'Yes, fine, Matt. The ground crew have done a good job. They have even cleaned up Townsend's blood. Like nothing happened. I suppose that's what we should expect, eh?' he said grimly.

'Don't start, Stephen,' Matt snapped back, almost immediately regretting it. 'And can you let the ground crew know we will do an air test at 1100 hours.'

Stephen turned away and headed out of the door without speaking, Scrap following along at his heel.

'You OK, old boy?' Dicky asked.

'Not really,' Matt replied. 'Stephen is beginning to get on my nerves, I think. It's difficult when he is so negative. On the other hand, he is, at least, here. I'll be all right. Just feel I am beginning to feel a bit ragged myself.'

'We all do, old boy. Only a bloody psychopath could go through this lot and not be affected.'

Matt smiled. Dicky was a good sort and the type you needed around when things went sour. His thoughts were disturbed by the number of new pilots coming in to look to see if they were on the board for tonight. There was a sense of excitement, which, Matt reflected, was how he had felt, really until quite recently. Now it was more dread and having to steel himself for what he knew to expect—the searchlights, flak, and fighters night after night.

Matt tidied up some papers before going out to meet his crew at M-Mother for the air test. They climbed into the aircraft and when everyone was ready roared down the runway. Matt was particularly keen to see how Stephen performed, and he was pleased, and relieved, to note that everything was done correctly. However, Stephen seemed very quiet and didn't speak to Matt other than for the checklists or something technical. All seemed well, and they landed without incident. Warrant Officer Bryant met them as they got out of the aircraft and went over to Matt.

'Everything OK, Matt?' he asked.

'Yes, your boys have done their usual good job patching her up. Everything seems to work, doesn't it, Stephen?'

'Yes, it's fine,' Stephen replied curtly and then walked away to find Scrap.

'Thanks, Max,' Matt said and then to his crew, 'Briefing at 1600 hours. Don't forget, or we'll leave you behind.'

'That's fine, Skip,' replied Freddie. 'I'm sure you could find someone else to take my place.'

Everyone laughed. The old jokes were always the best.

After lunch, Matt sat around in the mess talking to Charles.

'I was a bit surprised to see Stephen back with us so soon,' Charles said. 'Thought he would be out of it for a week at least.'

'Yes,' Matt replied. 'Does seem a bit soon, but apparently, he feels OK and wants to get on with it.'

'He's going to be all right on the night though, is he? I mean, we don't want him cracking up just as we are dealing with our regular appointment with the fighters?'

'Well, we can only hope he will manage, can't we?' Matt said irritably. 'To be honest, I can't spend any more time worrying about him. He wants to go, so that's it.'

'OK, old boy, keep your hair on. Just asking, but you get my point. It's our bloody lives on the line.'

'I know, Charles. Sorry,' said Matt. 'I'm sure he will be fine. Let's leave it, shall we? Looks like time to get some grub.' With that, Matt stood up and walked through to the dining room.

After lunch, Matt found he had quite a bit of paperwork to sort out, one of the dubious pleasures of being a flight commander. Bird was at the other desk and after a while lifted his head. 'Who the hell writes all these bloody requisition forms? Wouldn't mind if the bloody stuff ever arrived, but we never seem to have the right things when we need them.'

'What, like aircraft and men?' asked Matt.

'Well, you know, Matt. If we ran out of toilet rolls, it would probably take a month to get them. Let's go and have a drink. I've had enough of this crap.'

They wandered over to the mess. The wind was blowing quite strongly, and the clouds seemed very low and almost certainly loaded with snow.

'Sky looks bloody awful,' muttered Bird. 'Can only hope it will be even worse over there.' He pointed to the east.

They had a beer and then realised that the briefing was only in ten minutes.

'Better go and round the boys up,' Bird said, and they went their different ways.

As usual, the briefing room was already full of smoke as Matt and Stephen pushed their way in. They and the crew stayed at the back of the room, and Matt noticed the new crews to be right at the front, ready to take down every small detail.

Poor buggers, Matt thought as he recalled his own first trip.

The briefing followed its usual course with the station commander entering the hall dead on time and followed by his squadron team.

He turned and indicated that all should sit down. 'The target for tonight, gentlemen, will be Essen.'

There was the usual quip. 'Happy bloody valley.'

'Thought we had flattened that last month, sir? It's amazing how quickly them Jerries can build, sir.'

'Well, if you want to know, Parker ...' Squires smiled. 'It's the bits you missed we would like you to hit this time. And in any case, Mr Krupp seems to have amazing regenerative powers!'

Laughter rang nervously around the room as the navigation officer stood up and moved to the wall map.

As usual, the details for navigation, bombing sequence, met. situation, and radio details were presented and discussed. When all had finished, Squires stood up.

'This is an important trip, chaps. At least it's much shorter than the Big City and should be a nice opener for you new chaps. Remember, stay with your formation, and you won't come to much harm. OK, see you at 1900 hours.'

Everyone stood up as the entourage walked out. They were followed by one of the new boys almost running out. Matt saw that his face was almost green, and once they got outside the hall, Matt noticed a figure huddled over by one of huts clearly vomiting.

Matt drew his crew around him. 'Well, not exactly a milk run but could be worse,' he said. 'Let's meet up at 1730 hours so we can get everything ready. Charles, do we need to go over anything or are we all OK?'

'All OK, I think, Matt. The H2S was working well this morning, and we know there will be target markers. In range for GEE as well. I should say we are clear to go.'

They made their ways to the relevant messes, but Stephen walked off to their hut. Matt followed him.

'Stephen,' he said, 'might be good idea to get some grub.'

'I'm OK, Matt. Thanks,' he replied shortly. 'I'm not hungry and want to get an hour's sleep. I'll be fine, honest.'

Matt followed him into the hut. Scrap got up when they came in, and Stephen got on the bed next to him. Matt wanted to write his usual letter for Anne, but somehow, he found it hard to get the words right. After an hour, he gave up and put what he had written into an envelope and sealed it up. He lay on the bed and shut his eyes, but sleep would not come and eventually he got up and dressed to go down to the crew room. He realised he hadn't eaten either and first went into the mess and grabbed a couple of sandwiches. It had started to snow slightly again as he got to the crew room. Everyone was there except Stephen, and just as Matt was hoping that his worst fears were not going to be realised, Stephen came in and started to get kitted out. They collected their parachutes and rations and went outside to await the truck to take them out to M-Mother.

'Just like bloody home,' quipped Freddie. 'Never a bleeding bus when you want one!'

Just at that moment, the truck appeared, driven by one of the usual WAAFs.

'Hallo, luv,' said Freddie. 'This one going to Piccadilly?'

'No, that's the one behind,' the WAAF shouted back. 'All aboard.'

They arrived at M-Mother. The snow was a little heavier now, and the cold ensured that they all quickly got aboard.

Matt and Stephen went through the usual checks, and just as they were ready to start the engines, there was a red light from the control tower.

'Bloody hell,' muttered Matt, and then in his headset, he heard, 'Operation aborted.'

'It's scrubbed, chaps,' he said quickly on the intercom. 'Let's do the close down checks and get back in the warm before our nuts freeze off!' Matt had the peculiar split feeling of elation at the thought he would live another day and the misery knowing that he was not going to be closer to the magic thirty operations by the end of the night.

Stephen left the cockpit straight away and was the first out of the aircraft. Matt was stopped by Redman as he was clearing up his charts and bits and pieces.

'Bit of a hurry, isn't he?' he muttered to Matt.

'May be needs to see a man about a dog.'

'Or a dog about a man. Come on, let's get out of here.'

The others were all gathered by the door, but there was no sign of Stephen.

'Anyone see which way Pilot Officer Bamber went?' Matt asked.

'Caught a passing bus, Skip,' said Freddie. 'Looked in a bit of a hurry to me.'

'Well, Billy, sorry we couldn't provide you with some entertainment tonight,' Matt said to their new gunner. 'Let's go back and see what this is all about.'

A truck drew up beside them, and they piled into the back. It trundled off back to the crew room where the others were already stripping off. To everyone's surprise, the CO himself came in, causing many to straighten up and stand, as best they could, to attention.

'Stand easy, chaps,' Brookes said. 'Sorry to call things off, but the weather is appalling over Essen and not that great here. Go and get a beer.'

There was a loud cheer as the CO left, and there was renewed enthusiasm to get stripped off and into the mess. Matt had suggested that they all meet in the Red Lion, and after he had left a message for Anne, he walked through the thickening snow to the pub.

'Any further news, Skip?' Freddie called from the bar.

'No, and mine's a pint!' Matt shouted back.

The six men gathered together and drank a few pints before Matt said, 'You know, maybe they won't send us off over the next few days unless they really have to. There's a lot of moon over the next week.'

'Well, I'm up for that,' said Freddie, who seemed to be a pint or two ahead of the others. ''Ear there's a dance on this Saturday down at the Montana. Let's hope the bloody moon keeps shining. What you say, young Billy?'

'Sounds good to me, but I don't dance really.'

'Bloody detail that, in'it, Don?' Freddie winked.

The crew seemed to be enjoying themselves, and Matt and Charles made their excuses and headed for the door.

'You going to find out where Stephen took himself to?' Charles asked.

'Probably propped up with his bloody dog,' Matt replied. 'I'm not sure how much more any of us can take of this.' And with that, he headed off to the camp, calling into the mess to try to speak to Anne.

Back in his room, he found Stephen still in his flying gear, as he anticipated on his bed with Scrap.

'You OK?' he asked curtly.

'Yes, thanks. Just a bit difficult when they pull the rug like that.'

'Well, better that than risking everything only not to be able to find the target.'

Matt undressed, got into bed, and went to sleep almost at once. He felt exhausted, and that and a few beers did the trick.

CHAPTER 15

STOOD DOWN

The next morning, Matt met Bird in the flight office. He had left Stephen where he was still dressed in his gear. At least he was asleep.

'What's the news, Dicky? Are they sending us home for a couple of months?'

'Well, not exactly, but we are stood down for a few days. If we can find the runway under the snow at least, that gives us some time to try and lick the new chaps into shape. They could do with a couple of fighter affiliation exercises as well. And I suspect we can get an occasional twenty-four hours off ourselves sometime as well.'

'Well, the kites are still fuelled up from last night and the ground crews will have removed the bombs so we are set to go. Shall we get the new boys together? Maybe some formation flying would be a good start?'

They arranged to meet both flights in the briefing room at 1100 hours, and then Matt went off to phone Anne. She had finished her night shift so it was relatively easy to run her down.

'Anne, we are off ops for another few days' he said excitedly. 'When can we meet? Are you still on nights?'

'Matt, how wonderful. No, nights are done with for a while. Can you get off tonight, do you think?'

'I'm sure I can. How about dinner somewhere, so long as the roads aren't blocked? This snow looks pretty heavy. I will ring you about seven o'clock. Let's see how it looks.'

His next task was to sort out Stephen, who was just getting up as Matt went into the room.

'Bit of a lie-in then?' Matt said, trying not to show his irritation.

'Yes. Thanks,' Stephen replied. 'What's the form? Do we have another go tonight?'

'No. We are off ops for now. It's the moon rest period! But we are still flying, Stephen. We meet in the briefing room at eleven. Perhaps you should shower and shave and get something to eat. You look dreadful.'

'May as well keep this lot on if we're flying again. I'll do the other stuff when we finish.'

'Well, I'm not ordering you, but you look a bloody shambles. Not good enough, I reckon. We all have standards, you know?'

'That's the flight commander talking, is it?' Stephen sneered.

'If you like. Christ, Stephen, I could have had you out of here a couple of days ago. Don't bloody forget it.' Matt was shouting now, and he realised how close to the edge he was himself. 'Sorry, Stephen. I think we are all pretty wound up, but it is important we at least appear as if we care about how we look. I'll see you at eleven.' And with that, he walked out and went down to the mess.

The briefing room was full when Matt and Bird walked in. To Matt's surprise, everyone stood up as the two of them walked to the front, and Bird turned and indicated for them all to sit.

'Morning, chaps. Well, after last night's damp squib and after discussion with Wing Commander Squires, we have decided that since we have a few days' grace, we could usefully get in some practice, which, as you all know, will make us absolutely perfect.' Bird smiled.

There was a ripple of laughter round the room, which added to the relaxed atmosphere, a marked contrast to how they usually felt in this room.

'So,' Bird continued, 'both A and B Flights will be involved, and we intend to do some formation flying and also whistle up some Hurricanes to do some fighter experience for you all, but especially you new chaps. Now the runways are being cleared at this moment, and we will take off at 1400 hours. Our route will take us north along the coast, inland towards Sheffield, south towards Nottingham, and then back here. It should be dark by the time we get back here, so that will allow you to do some circuits in the dark. Please don't bump into one another, but if you feel you must, then make sure it isn't Flight Lieutenant White or me or you will most definitely be on a charge!'

A chuckle went round the room, and Matt heard Freddie saying to no one in particular, 'I knew our Skip would come in useful eventually.'

They broke up, and Matt joined his crew. He was pleased to notice that Stephen had tidied himself, and he nodded at him.

'OK, chaps. Let's meet down at the kite at one o'clock. Stephen, could you check everything? They will have left the fuel but better check. Gunners, your guns should still be loaded and you can test them once we are up. Let's make this an air test for us at least. We will need to keep a close lookout for the rookies, but at least they can practise their formation flying now, when we have half a chance of getting out of their way! Anything else, Navigator?'

'No, that sounds OK to me, Skip. Should be a simple box course, although presumably we will do a bit of twisting and turning to keep the chaps on their toes?'

Matt nodded, and then they broke up to go to their messes for lunch before meeting by M-Mother.

***

The snow had stopped, and the sky was pale blue and cloudless. The wind had dropped as well and was blowing from the northeast so pretty well straight down the runway. It looked like a rather nice day to go flying, and once again, Matt had that feeling that the job would be great if others stopped trying to kill him.

Matt lined up M-Mother and opened the throttles. Without the bomb load, M-Mother was airborne after a short run, and Freddie called that the rest of the flight were also off the ground soon after. Matt followed A Flight in a climbing turn to the left, and as they came round, he could see the airfield below him. They levelled off at 5,000 feet, and Matt heard Bird call for them to take up their course along the coast, a heading of almost due north once they were overhead Skegness.

'How are the children doing, Freddie? Have they formed up on us yet?'

'Well, Skip, I can see two of them, A-Apple and P-Peter, but the third seems to be a long way off and quite a bit lower.'

'U-Uncle,' Matt said over the R/T. 'What are you doing? Do you have a problem?'

'We don't seem to able to climb very well, sir.'

'OK,' Matt said. 'Go back to base and check it out. We'll speak when I get down. A-Apple and P-Peter, close up on me and try and keep station. The air is quite still, so you shouldn't have any trouble. I am turning due north now.'

The three aircraft banked into a turn so that they were flying along the coast nearly two miles below them.

'Blimey, Skip, that was a bit close when we turned there. Thought he was going take me bloody tail off!' Freddie exclaimed.

'OK, let me know if he does it again, Freddie,' Matt said, trying to keep calm. 'A-Flight are doing a bit of weaving, so let's watch out. You two follow me into these turns.'

Matt banked the aircraft quite steeply to the right, keeping it in balance with the rudders. and he levelled out as they were flying out to sea.

'Still with us, Freddie?'

'Well, P-Peter is, but the other one looks all over the place.'

'Keep up, A-Apple,' Matt said. 'I am turning left and descending now.'

Matt turned the aircraft left and dived to about 8,000 feet before levelling out and returning to his northerly course.

'Now?' asked Matt.

'All over the place, Skip.'

'Right,' he said to the other aircraft. 'You two form up again, and we will do the same again.'

And so the afternoon went on, and eventually, it seemed that P-Peter was getting the hang of things. It was, however, very easy to lose A-Apple, although even they seemed to improve. They were down towards Nottingham when Matt asked Charles to give them a course for home. It was beginning to get dark, and Matt could see the stars beginning to appear. He turned on the rear, red, following light so the two behind could see the aircraft, and after about half an hour, he could see East Kirkby's beacon flashing.

'Chaps, nearly home. Everyone happy their own stations working? Gunners, everything OK? Don, bomb sights working?'

Everyone replied in the affirmative, and as Matt prepared to join the circuit, there was a huge flash about five miles away in front of them.

'Jesus, what was that?' Don asked from the front of the aircraft.

'I don't want to think,' replied Matt. 'Mac, give base a call and see what's up.'

After a few minutes, Mac replied, 'Two aircraft, Skip. They collided just west of the field. They want us to divert to Coningsby.'

'Christ,' muttered Matt and then over the R/T said, 'P-Peter, A-Apple, we need to divert to Coningsby. Follow me into the circuit, but keep well back. We don't want any more foul-ups. P-Peter, you will be number 2, Apple 3. All understood?'

Everyone replied, and Matt returned to concentrate on flying the aircraft.

'Navigator, can you give me a course to Coningsby? They should let us in on runway zero-eight.'

'Skip, just stay on this heading. You should be able to see their beacon, I would think.'

'I can see it, Skip,' said Don from the bomb-aimer's position. 'It's just off to the left.'

'Yes, got it, thanks,' replied Matt.

'Skip, they are giving us permission to come straight in,' Mac said.

'Stephen, let's get set up for the landing. Brake pressure OK, flaps twenty degrees, undercarriage down, fuel boosters on.'

'All OK, Skip,' Stephen confirmed.

'Down we go.'

Matt picked up the landing lights, and they drifted down to a perfect landing.

'Can you see P-Peter, Freddie?'

'Yes, Skip, they are on our tail. Look like they want to get down in a hurry.'

'Not too close?'

'No, Skip, they look OK from here. See the other lot too.'

They were met by a van, which they had to follow to their dispersal point. It was always a bit odd landing at a strange airfield, but there seemed to be quite a few ground crew milling about. They stopped and went through the shutdown checks, and then Matt said, 'Hang on around by the aircraft, chaps. I'll go and see what the hell is going on.' He moved past Stephen, who seemed to be staring out of the cockpit.

'All right, Stephen?' Matt said as he passed.

Stephen just nodded and kept staring so Matt moved on to the rear door. Price was just prising himself out of the turret.

'OK, Billy?' Matt asked as he went by.

'Yes, sir. Thanks,' he replied. 'What happens now, sir?'

'Just going to find out. We will probably be out of here in no time. They won't want us drinking their beer, will they?' Matt smiled.

As he jumped out of the aircraft, a jeep drew up.

'Evening, sir,' the sergeant driver said, saluting. 'I've come to take you to the control tower. The station commander says your crews should stay where they are for now. The NAAFI van is on its way to give you a cuppa, sir.'

'Thanks, Sergeant,' Matt replied, and they drove away across the field to the tower.

When Matt got there, he found a very serious-looking station commander. He explained that two of the A-Flight aircraft had collided, and one had crashed in flames and exploded just outside Coningsby's airfield boundary. The other aircraft had reached East Kirkby and had managed to land safely. Matt's immediate thought was of his friend Bird, hoping that he had not been involved, and he asked if he could telephone his airfield.

'Go ahead,' said the station commander. 'They should be able to let you know when you can go over there.'

Matt got through to Wing Commander Squires only to find that, thankfully, Bird had not been involved and that the collision had been between two of the new crews. All seven had died in the crashed aircraft. The others were OK, but the aircraft was badly damaged.

'They did well to get down in one piece,' he continued. 'Your chaps can come along now. We better have a debrief as soon as possible.'

Matt got back to M-Mother. The others were inside, sheltering from the cold wind.

'Let's go, chaps,' he said. 'Kirkby's open for business, and I need a drink.'

The three aircraft taxied out to runway zero-eight and took off in turn almost immediately preparing to land again at East Kirkby.

They all went for the debrief, and Matt was pleased to see for himself that Bird had been unhurt. Squires went through the collision in as much detail as they had. It appeared that the aircraft, which was number three in the landing sequence, had run into the back of the number two, probably killing the pilot because the aircraft had gone into a spiral dive before hitting the ground. The number two aircraft had sustained some serious damage to the tail fins, and certainly the rear gunner had had a narrow escape. It was probably fortunate that they had the runway almost in front of them and could land without having to make any turns.

After the briefing, Matt moved over to where Bird was standing. 'Bloody mess, eh? Let's go and get a drink. Stephen, Charles, you coming over?'

Stephen shook his head, but Charles said he needed something as a matter of some urgency and they headed off.

'How are the chaps in the damaged aircraft, Dicky?' Charles asked as he sank his first pint.

'Pretty shaken, actually,' Bird replied. 'Might be a challenge getting them back up tomorrow, but that's what we have to do. I have booked a couple of fighters for tomorrow in any case. How did your lot get on?'

'Well, one of them seemed to have a problem. In fact, I need to sort out what that was all about just now. The other two improved as we went along, which is encouraging. But they are all pretty shaky one way or another. God help them when it comes to the real thing in a few days. Another quick one, and then I must dash and run down U-Uncle's lot. Incidentally, Dicky, do you think it would be OK for me to speak to Squires about getting an evening off? I was wondering about pushing off tomorrow after we finish flying. We probably won't get much more time off once the moon begins to shrink!'

'OK with me, old boy,' Bird replied. 'I suspect Squires will give us all some time after tomorrow. Maybe even a twenty-four-hour job. Who knows?'

'That would be good. We can all probably do with a bit of a rest. I'm going to find that crew and then try and call Anne. Maybe a miracle will occur and we will both have the same day off! Perhaps meet you down at the Red Lion later?'

Matt finished his beer and went over to the flight office. He posted a notice asking the crew of U-Uncle to meet him there at 2000 hours and then went to phone Anne.

He got through quickly, and he was relieved to find that she was back on a day shift so that she should be free in the evenings.

Anne had heard about the crash and was thankful that he was OK.

'Do you think you can get off tomorrow night?' Matt asked. 'I should be off by about seven o'clock, and I could be down by eight. Let's go somewhere for dinner and stay for the night?'

'That would be wonderful,' Anne answered. 'Do you want me to book something? It's probably easier for me.' Secretly, she hoped the night would not turn out like their last one, but time with Matt was all she really wanted. They rang off, and Matt went back to find Sergeant Towers and his crew. They were waiting in the flight office and looked rather crestfallen.

'Well, what happened to you lot?' Matt asked irritably.

'Plane wouldn't climb, sir,' Towers answered in his singsong Welsh voice. 'We checked everything we could think of but couldn't find anything wrong, sir. So we just turned back and landed.'

'Ground crew checked the kite?'

'Yes, sir. They couldn't find anything either.'

'Not impressed,' Matt said shortly. 'If this happens again and we can't find anything to explain it, you'll all be on a bloody charge. Make myself clear?'

'Yes, sir. Do we have to go out tomorrow as well, sir?' their navigator Burgess asked.

Matt nearly exploded. 'Of course you bloody do! Do you think that this is some kind of sodding holiday camp? In fact, you will be up there nearly all bloody day. You still have to do today's detail, in case you'd forgotten. Now get out of my bloody sight or I'll put you on a charge in any case.'

The crew saluted and sheepishly left the office.

Matt was furious, and he could feel his heart pounding away. Seven men just wiped out, and these snotty-nosed kids wondered if they had to do more flying. He rushed out of the office, slamming the door as a way of releasing some of his pent-up anger. As he walked back to his hut, he realised how infrequently he lost his temper in the past and that recently it was occurring more and more. He knew that he was getting increasingly tired and the 'Stephen' issue never seemed to go away.

Stephen was asleep in his bed when Matt got back to their hut. Scrap, as usual, was snuggled up beside him. He let them both sleep, although he wanted to understand how Stephen was feeling after the flight. He grabbed his greatcoat and headed out, walking out of the gate and down the road to the Red Lion. There was a gentle south-westerly breeze, and the biting cold had gone. The lying snow was beginning to melt. The trees, however, were still etched white with snow, with water dripping off the icicles that hung from the branches, glistening in the moonlight.

Matt pushed open the door of the pub to be met by the usual combination of smoke, the smells of sweat and stale beer, and noise. His crew were over in the corner of the pub. Matt thought about the close bond that had formed between them all and noticed that even Charles had come down from the mess to join them.

Surprisingly, Price was the first one to speak. His face was red and sweaty, and he had obviously been plied with quite a few beers. 'Is it true, sir? Might we get a twenty-four-hour pass?'

'Billy, you don't need to call me, sir. "Skip" will do nicely. And no, I am not sure about the pass yet, but I think it is possible. Oh, and mine's a pint.'

'Thank you, sir—sorry, Skip. Does anyone else want one?'

'Well, since it's you, me old china, don't mind if I do,' said Freddie. 'Oh, and pints for me mates too.' He smiled.

They stayed in the pub until closing time and made their way noisily back to the base.

'I want to get off sharply tomorrow, chaps,' Matt said as they said their goodnights. 'Let's meet in the flight office at eight o'clock. We can look at the weather and make a plan.' And with that, he made his way back to the hut and sleep.

***

Matt was still asleep when Barker shook his arm. 'Morning, sir. Cuppa?'

Matt looked over and saw that Stephen's bed was empty.

'Pilot Officer Bamber went out about six o'clock, sir. With the dog.'

'Did he say where he was going?'

'No, sir. He didn't say anything, in fact, sir.'

'Great,' Matt muttered as he swung his legs over the side of the bed. He looked out of the window and noticed that it was raining and that the snow had been largely washed away. He shaved and dressed and made his way to the mess for breakfast only to bump into Stephen, hurrying back to the hut.

'You OK, Stephen?' Matt asked only to receive a nod. 'We meet at eight. Flight office.'

Bird was finishing his breakfast, and Matt joined him.

'God, you're early, or maybe I'm late. Slept like I was dead last night. Feel much better,' he said to Bird.

'Good. It could be another trying day, I fear.' Bird smiled. 'Weather looks shitty too and not much chance of an improvement in the next couple of days. To be honest, given the crappy lot we have got, I wonder if Squires would contemplate giving us our leave now. Especially after yesterday's fiasco in clear weather. Tell you what, I'll go and speak to him and see what he says before the troops form up.'

Matt went straight to the office from breakfast and Bird arrived soon after him.

'Not keen on that idea, Matt. Says they will have to get used to flying when it's rubbish so we need to get on with it. However, he warmed to the idea of a twenty-four-hour one for each of us. Says we deserve it! So when do you want to go?'

'Well, after we finish today would be very good. Would that be all right for you too?'

'Perfect. Oh, and I think he is hinting that our next op is likely to be next week when there is less moon around. So the chaps can probably plan to get to the dance in Lincoln on Saturday.'

Men were milling around the flight office, and Bird told them to meet at 0900 hours in the briefing room while Matt posted a note to that effect on the notice board. They were going to do some more formation flying, and Matt felt the skin on the back of his neck prickle at the thought of these aircraft flying close together in cloud. Still, it had to be done, and better now than when the bloody Luftwaffe was firing at them.

The briefing went well, and everyone seemed pleased at the prospect of a few days without ops and even more pleased at the thought of being free to go to the dance on Saturday night. The older crews could take a twenty-four-hour pass after today, but the rookies would be held at the base so they could get more flying time in.

Predictably, the crew of U-Uncle were the first to complain to Matt. He managed to contain his temper but made it very clear that probably of all the crews, they needed to get themselves straightened out, but they looked unhappy and disgruntled as they walked out with Sergeant Towers.

Against the odds, the day went well in spite of the weather, which, in any case, started to brighten up in the afternoon. Even Towers and his lot seemed to do better, and Matt felt tired but content that they had achieved what they wanted. His spirits were also raised by the thought he was seeing Anne in a few hours, so when Stephen came up to him and asked if he could have an extra couple of days off, he was probably not as irritated as he should have been.

'I need to go home and see my parents,' he explained. 'This seems like a good time.'

'Stephen, I understand, but all we have been given is twenty-four hours, you know that. If we say yes to you, then it will be difficult to say no to anyone else. Is there a problem at home?'

'No, I just want to go. Haven't seen them for several months, and I might not get to see them again for a while; that's all.'

'OK, I will go and speak to Squires, but I don't hold out much hope. And I am trying to get away myself just now, but don't you worry about me,' he added sarcastically before heading off.

Stephen was in their room when Matt got back from seeing Wing Commander Squires.

'Best available is thirty-six hours. Take it or leave it. You can go tomorrow,' Matt said whilst getting a few things together for his evening with Anne.

'Thanks, Matt,' Stephen replied quietly. 'Really appreciate that. I'll be back in time, promise. Have a nice evening.'

Matt just nodded and walked out of the door to his car, which, for once, was not covered with snow. It was still raining, and a gusty wind was whining through the surrounding trees. He still felt angry about Stephen, but the thought of the warmth and love awaiting him in about an hour's time helped him to calm down, and he slipped the car into gear and sped away.

***

Anne was waiting for him at the hospital, sheltering from the rain under the entrance. He stopped the car and got out, and she smiled as he approached. She put her arms up to hold him. They kissed, but when she looked at him more closely, she realised how tired he looked. It had been noticeable last time, but now it was even more obvious. There were deep lines round his mouth, and his eyes looked sunken.

'Matt, darling. You look exhausted. Are you sure you don't just want to get some sleep?'

'No, Anne, I'm fine. We have had a few days with some new chaps, and then there was the crash yesterday, of course. And the scrubbed trip; that's always bad. At least Stephen doesn't seem too bad at the moment. Let's get going, and then we can talk about us.'

They got into the car and made their way to a small inn just on the outskirts of Lincoln. It was crowded, but once they had got through the scrum, the landlord showed them to their room and said that they had a table booked for them at eight o'clock. Matt and Anne held each other after the landlord had left.

'Are you hungry?' Anne asked.

'You know,' Matt replied, 'I think I am. That's not very romantic, is it?'

'It's just fine,' she replied. 'Let's go and eat.'

'Maybe a beer first?' Matt smiled.

They went downstairs and into the dining room, which was full mainly of servicemen and their partners. They sat down and ordered their food and some wine.

'Well, Matt,' Anne started, 'what's wrong really?'

Matt looked at her, smiled, and reached across the table for her hand.

'Maybe it's as you get closer to the end,' Matt said. 'That scrubbed trip really got to me. Then Stephen walking off like a spoilt child as if he's the only one with feelings. And these young chaps, bloody cannon fodder. Sorry,' Matt hardly ever swore with Anne present.

'It's all right, darling,' she said softly. 'It all sounds terrible for you. And looking at you, you're not sleeping either?'

'Well, I thought I was actually. Maybe wrong type of sleep?' He laughed, and his eyes creased up just as she had remembered.

'When is your next leave, Matt? We are just going to go away from all this and get some peace and quiet. Do you think the old car would get us as far as Scotland?'

'Of course she would,' he replied, pretending to be hurt. 'But shouldn't we go and see your parents about the wedding arrangements?'

'Don't worry about that,' she replied and smiled. 'Just worry about you for once.'

He leaned across the table and kissed her, and they got on with their dinner, Anne just filling in the conversation about Jess and how she was getting on.

'Oh, thanks for reminding me, Anne,' Matt said, suddenly taking Stephen's letter from his pocket. 'I nearly forgot about it. Give it to Jess when you next see her, can you?'

'What's in it do you think?' Anne asked conspiratorially.

'No idea, old thing,' Matt answered. 'Maybe a statement of his undying love!'

When they had finished their meal, Matt asked for a brandy, and they went over and sat down by the wood fire, which was crackling and sparking in the hearth. Matt felt more relaxed than he had for days. It was always so easy being with Anne, listening to the warmth of her voice. Eventually, they went off to bed and made love quickly and silently, before Matt fell into a deep sleep beside her. Anne leaned up on her elbow to look at him. As he drifted off to sleep, the lines around his mouth softened and his face took on an almost child-like appearance. She turned away and tried to sleep but was too concerned about Matt. How much more could he take? Let alone Stephen. It sounded like Flight Lieutenant Bird, Dicky, was a great support for him and old Redman sounded as if he had come good too. He was fond of the crew, and they all got on well. Townsy's death was a blow for Matt, and she thought that he had changed from that time. She felt angry herself as she thought how unfair it was to get these very young men to fly night after night until they got killed.[8] They ate their breakfast in silence the next morning. Anne noticed that in spite of what appeared to be a good sleep, Matt still looked tired with dark patches under his eyes and his hands shook slightly as he ate.

'Sleep, Matt?' she asked quietly.

'Yes, fine,' Matt replied. 'It was a lovely night. Thank you.'

'Will you be busy when you get back?'

'Well, we still have some flying to do with these new boys. But maybe not much else.' He smiled weakly. 'Could you come

---

[8] Less than one in five aircrew would get through to the end of a thirty-op tour.

over on Saturday? I'm sure the boys would love to see you. Maybe Jess too?'

'Yes, I'm sure,' Anne replied. 'It will be nice to see everyone. Will Dicky be there? I would like to meet him. I like the sound of him. He sounds like he is looking after you.'

'I'm sure he will be. In fact, I'll tell him you want to check him out! That will get him worried.'

'Matt, I hate to say this, but I have to be getting along. Shall we go?'

'Yes, of course. I'll get the things.'

The drive back was easy. The skies were clear, and the night's rain had left the roads sparkling and clean. Matt dropped Anne at the hospital, and she tried not to show how anxious she was.

'I'll see you Saturday,' she said as lightly as she could and turned quickly so not to show her face.

Matt drove back to the base, and as he got nearer, he had the now familiar sinking feeling in the pit of his stomach that all might not be well. He parked the car and went straight to the flight office. Bird was there as usual and was looking anxious.

'What's up, Dicky?'

'Your chap, I'm afraid. Rang in and said he wouldn't be back for another day. Good night yourself, I hope?'

'Bloody hell, Dicky. Does Squires know?'

'I'm afraid so. He's none too happy! Probably a good idea to go and see him yourself. Head him off at the pass, so to speak.'

Matt went over to Squires's office to find him busily signing letters. He looked up as Matt walked into the room.

'Hallo, Matt. This is really not good enough, you know. You gave him the pass I agreed, I understand?'

'Yes, sir. For thirty-six hours, but now he's said he's not coming back for another day.'

'Do you think he's fit to fly? I mean, we've had all this trouble with him over the last few weeks. I tell you this, Matt, if he's not back twenty-four hours from now, I am going to make him LMF. If you have any way of contacting him, I suggest you tell him that and that I want to see him as soon as he gets back.'

'I will, sir. I think he said he wanted to see his parents, but they are not ill or anything. Just wanted to see them.'

'OK, Matt. I understand you got to see Anne last night. I trust she is well? When are you two getting hitched? January, I think, wasn't it? And I have just received notice that you get your gong this coming Monday. Hope you can take her with you. And stay the night in London if you can—and that's an order!'

Matt smiled and saluted. 'Thank you, sir. Hopefully she can get off.'

Matt found Dicky still in the flight office when he got back.

'How'd it go?' he asked.

'Not bad. He's as mad as a bear with a sore head about Bamber going off like that. God help him if he doesn't get back tomorrow. Must see if I can get a telegram to him. On a brighter note, I get my gong next Monday. Squires has ordered me to go.' Matt raised his eyebrows.

'Well, good for you, old boy. You should take Anne as well.'

'So he said—that was an order too!' Matt smiled.

'Oh, you are in favour. Use it while you can!' Bird laughed. 'Now, this Saturday, are the rumours true that for those not going to the dance in Lincoln, there will be a booze-up at the Lion? And that you're buying?'

'Well, I'm not sure about the last bit. But Anne is coming over so you can meet her. She will bring a couple of nurses with her, just to keep you interested.'

'That sounds OK to me. I don't think there is much more we can do with this lot, and it would probably not be a bad idea to give the ground crew a chance to get the aircraft up to scratch. Sure we will be at it again next week. Can't let Hitler rest for too long!' He smiled.

CHAPTER 16

BERLIN

Twenty-Second Trip

Stephen came back on the Saturday as promised, and Squires had him confined to the base, but apart from that, he seemed to have got away with his absence without leave. Although quite a large contingent was heading for the dance, the Red Lion was still pretty busy by the time Matt and Bird got there. Anne, Jess, and another nurse called Elizabeth were already there and surrounded by a lot of blue uniforms. Anne waved as Matt came in, and he worked his way over to where she and the others were standing with Bird in tow.

'Sorry, we are a bit late. Has everyone got a drink? Dicky, usual pint? Let me introduce you—Anne, Jess, and I am sorry, I don't know your name,' he said to Elizabeth.

Dicky and Anne got on well and spent quite a bit of time talking about Matt. Matt spoke to Jess about Stephen and explained why he was not there with them. She seemed to know already, and Matt guessed that Anne had told her all about it. As the evening wore on, Dicky and Elizabeth seemed to become deeply engaged in conversation to the exclusion of everyone else. Matt smiled. Maybe a budding romance there—these things happened quickly in war.

Matt discovered that Anne could get away on the Monday for the investiture, and they made plans above the din in the pub to meet early on Monday to catch the train to London, but she needed to get back that evening and so the more extended plans were on hold.

Dicky and Matt walked to the bus with the three women, and Anne gave Matt a hug as she got on the bus. Dicky promised to see Elizabeth when he was next free.

'Well, that went all right,' Matt said as they walked back to the base.

'Yes.' Dicky smiled. 'That Elizabeth is rather a peach. She's a nurse with Anne and Jess, you know?'

'Well, I didn't, but I guessed as much,' replied Matt. 'Why don't we try and get out as a foursome?'

'Yes. I'd like that,' Bird replied as they parted to go to their billets. 'Like that a lot.'

***

The base was very quiet on Sunday with a good proportion of the crews recovering from the dance the night before. Matt had arranged to meet the crew in the Red Lion that evening, and he and Dicky spent most of the day getting paperwork sorted out.

Once again, the pub was busy soon after it opened, and Matt found his crew perched up in one corner.

'Evening, Matt!' called Redman. 'How's the paperwork?'

'Bloody awful,' Matt replied. 'Who's ready for a drink?'

'Well, Skip, since you ask, mine's a pint,' said Freddie. 'And I think the others are ready too.'

'How was the dance, Willie?' Matt asked as he worked his way to the bar.

'Good fun, sir, Skip, thanks. Freddie and the others took care of me.' He smiled.

'That may not be such good news,' Matt said. 'Don, did you come across that lovely girl you found at Scampton?'

'I did, Skip. And she was just as lovely. Mac and I are going to drive over to Scampton when we next can, to see her.'

'And she's got a very nice friend too,' added Mac. 'She's at Scampton too.'

They carried on in this vein for a couple of hours before Matt and Charles made their excuses to leave.

'I'm off to London early tomorrow, chaps,' Matt said. 'So need to get some shut-eye. Don't mess up the place while I've gone. Let's meet here tomorrow night. I will have something to celebrate. I'm getting my gong tomorrow.'

There was a loud cheer, and Freddie insisted that they have another round before Matt left.

The day in London went well, and Matt was pleased that Anne had managed to get the time off to come. It was a bit of a dash to get Anne back in the hospital by eight o'clock as promised. Matt made his way to the Red Lion where, true to form, he found the crew of M-Mother. He was pleased to see Stephen there with Scrap, deep in conversation with Willie. They apparently shared a common interest in birdwatching and were comparing notes about some of the recent migratory species they had seen around the airfield.

Amazing what you find out about folk, Matt thought to himself as he bought a round of drinks. He sensed they were coming to the end of their rest and that the next week would have them back in the air, trying to blow Hitler's cities to kingdom come. He looked around at his crew. Freddie, as usual, was ready with a joke; Willie seemed to be fitting in well; Mac and Don, as ever, were the stalwarts of the team; and Redman, who was a good sort, would probably leave them soon to become the squadron navigator. He was bloody good, Matt thought. Never once had he got them lost. And then there was Stephen. He looked happier than he had for weeks, so maybe his leave had done him some good after all. They drank until they were asked to leave and walked back to the base in the cold, clear night air to bed and then another day.

***

The morning dawned bright and appeared remarkably good for early December. Matt had been surprised when he woke up to see that Stephen had already left their hut, but as usual, he went straight to the flight office and was not surprised to see a huddle of crew looking at the battle orders posted on the notice board. Briefing was set for 1300 hours. Mac and Don were already there, and Matt asked them to gather up the others with a view to get in an air test as soon as possible. Some of the other pilots thought the test was a waste of time, but Matt felt it was useful not only to check the aircraft but the crew as well.

After lunch, the crews gathered for the briefing. He and his crew sat towards the back of the hall, which quickly filled with airmen. The new crews tended to sit in the front rows, anxious that they should not miss anything from the briefing. Matt had a bad feeling about this trip. He reckoned it would almost certainly be Berlin again, and they had yet to go to the Big City without running into trouble.

The CO and his entourage strode into the room and up to the front as everyone got to their feet. The CO waved to them to sit, and he then moved across the stage towards the wall.

'Your target tonight, gentlemen, is Berlin.'

As usual, there were gasps and groans around the hall, and the general feeling became increasingly concerned as the

Met officer indicated the possibility of fog both at the start and when the aircraft returned. There was still quite a lot of moon, but it seemed that Harris wanted them to undertake the raid as a matter of urgency. As they walked out of the briefing, Freddie, as usual, was the first to speak.

'Bloody hell, Skip. What have we done to deserve this? It looks a bit bloody misty already.'

'Don't ask me, Freddie,' Matt replied. 'Let's just get cracking and worry about the whys later!'

After a meal, they got into their flying kit and collected parachutes, coffee, and chocolate bars. Then, as usual, they waited for the truck. The typical banter followed the truck's arrival, but Matt noticed it was not quite as light-hearted as usual, and even Freddie's endless wit seemed blunted.

'You OK, Freddie?' Matt asked as they got off the truck at their dispersal.

'Yeah,' he replied. 'But not looking forward to eight bleeding hours in me turret. It's bloody cold back there, you know. No bloody heating like you lot have up front.' He smiled, and Matt realised it was probably the usual old Freddie after all.

'Everyone else all right?' he asked as they walked up to the rear hatch of M-Mother. There was a general murmur of agreement, and Freddie and Price walked past the back of the aircraft for a final smoke and a pee against the rear wheel.

Matt and Stephen settled into their seats and started going through the routine checks before engine start. Charles spent the time sorting out his charts and warming up his instruments, and Mac did the same for the wirelesses. Don went forward into the nose of the aircraft and checked his bomb sight.

Matt and Stephen finished all their checks and were ready to start when Mac called that they were to wait for five minutes before starting.

'Christ,' said Stephen, 'they're not going to scrub us again, are they?'

'Doubt it, Stephen, unless they think the fog is going to get worse later on for when we get back.'

The silence in the aircraft was palpable, and it was difficult for Matt to see what was going on around the other aircraft. Certainly, no one else had started up, and apart from the odd staff car racing around, nothing seemed to be happening. Then just as Matt was beginning to believe they might be scrubbed, Mac told him they had permission to start up.

The Merlins roared into life, and M-Mother was eased out on to the taxiway and down to the end of the runway. They came to a halt, and Matt and Stephen went through the pre-takeoff checklist.

'Navigator, are you happy with things?'

'Yes, Skip. All OK back here.'

The lamp by the control tower showed green. Matt released the brakes, and they sped off down the runway. As usual, the heavily loaded aircraft seemed to take an age to lift off, but eventually, Matt felt the controls beginning to come alive and the huge aircraft took to the skies and up into the darkness and low cloud. They flew east until close to the coast, and then Charles gave them a course, one-three-zero, towards Lowestoft, where they were to join the bomber stream and, on this occasion, to head almost due east to Berlin some 650 miles away.

'Are we being followed, Freddie?' Matt asked just to check the rest of the flight were following on.

'Well, I can see what I think is A-Apple but nothing else. It's pretty shitty up here, Skip.'

'Yes, I know, but hopefully that lot are behind us and not somewhere where we can bump into them. You and Billy can test your guns now.'

They made their way south-easterly towards Lowestoft. It was impossible to see anything because of the cloud, but Redman got a good fix using GEE, and for once, the H2S appeared to be working well. They needed to be at 18,000 feet by the time they got to Lowestoft, and Matt coaxed M-Mother up to the altitude.

'We're about there now, Skip,' Redman said. 'You can turn onto zero-nine-zero, and we should be there in a bit over four hours.'

'Thanks, Navigator. Well, here we go. Everyone keep your eyes open. We might expect some company tonight. Don't forget, they've had a few days off too. Only good thing is that the fog the Met forecast for here might keep them on the ground.'

It was too much to hope for, and soon after crossing the Dutch coast, Matt noticed an aircraft burst into flames over to their right.

'They're out here with us, everyone. Watch out,' Matt called into the intercom.

The aircraft droned on. There were further aircraft going down in flames, and one ahead of them just blew up, the burning debris falling before being engulfed in the clouds below.

'We are just north of Hanover,' Charles reported. 'About eighty minutes to the target.'

'Thanks. Everything OK, Engineer?' Matt asked.

'Yes, Skip. All fine here,' Stephen replied quietly but firmly. 'I am going to switch over the tanks in about thirty minutes.'

Just at that moment, Don called from the nose.

'Climb, Skip. Bomber right below us and climbing.'

Matt pulled on the control stick and pushed the throttles through their gates to full power. Stephen leaned over to help as Matt banked the aircraft to the right just as the other aircraft appeared under their left wing.

'Jesus Christ,' Matt muttered. 'Anyone get a look at who it was?'

'It looked like D-Dog,' said Don. 'Only caught a glimpse.'

'But they should be ahead of us,' said Matt. 'What the hell are they doing here?'

'Lost,' Charles said quietly. 'Shall we get back on course?'

Matt eased the aircraft back towards Berlin, and after a while, he could see a glow through the clouds ahead together with flak coming up through them. Almost simultaneously, Redman called that they were getting close to the target and that their timed run would be commencing in about ten minutes.

Matt saw the sky-markers, which had been dropped by the Pathfinders, and could see that they were on course.

The timed run started, and Don picked out one of the target indicators whilst Redman confirmed that they were nearly there. There was quite a bit of flak, but it all appeared rather random because the searchlights couldn't penetrate the cloud. Don led them in, and just as the bombs dropped, there was a blinding flash just to the right of the aircraft, which was thrown upwards and to the left with the aircraft itself banked to the right.

Matt tried to bring M-Mother under control, but the aircraft seemed to be diving to the right. The bright flash had left Matt unable to see his instruments clearly, and he instinctively tried to correct the turn with the rudders and to stop the dive with the control stick, but it was too heavy. He gradually grasped what was going on and realised that there was a howling gale on his right side and that Stephen was lying on the cockpit floor.

He could hear Freddie shouting into the intercom, 'Skip, what the fuck is happening? There's sparks and smoke pouring past me on the right side.'

'Yeh,' said Price from the upper turret. 'Looks like the starboard outer is on fire or something.'

Matt suddenly realised why the aircraft was turning to the right, and as he eased the throttles to the port engines and feathered the outer starboard, M-Mother gradually started to straighten up and he got control.

'How is everyone?' he asked quickly. Everyone replied except Stephen.

'Mac, come up here and see what has happened to Stephen, will you? There seems to be a large hole on the right side of the cockpit. Just be careful.'

Apart from the noise, the hole in the side of the cockpit was effectively sucking air out of the aircraft. Charles's charts and notes were flying around, and everywhere seemed to be in chaos.

Mac came crouching into the cockpit and saw Stephen's body on the floor. What Matt could not see was that his right side was covered in Stephen's blood, and as Mac looked closer, he saw that Stephen had been hit by a large fragment of shrapnel, which had almost torn him in half. Death would have been instantaneous. He stood up and walked over to Matt. He shook his head and put his thumb down.

Thoughts crowded in to Matt's mind, but in spite of knowing his friend was dead, he still had to fly the aircraft or they would all join him. Firstly, he had to get that fire out, and he leaned across to push the button that would set off the engine fire extinguisher, praying that it would work first time. The fire went out, but the aircraft was difficult to control because of the damage not only to the fuselage, Matt guessed, but probably the wing and some of the controls as well. It looked pretty grim from where he was sitting, and they still had a long trip home.

'Listen, chaps, looks like Stephen has had it,' Matt said, trying to sound positive. 'We are turning for home. Mac's up here now and will check what else has been hit. Mac, let Don know if you need some help. Navigator, is everything OK with you? Can you give us a course home?'

'Bloody charts are everywhere, Skip. Give me a few minutes to sort things out. Head three-five-zero for now,' Charles's voice was quiet and calm.

At least everything seemed to be working, Matt thought as he turned the aircraft towards the north.

Mac came on the intercom. 'The engineer's panel is pretty badly damaged, Skip, but the fuel gauges still seem to be working. The starboard wing tanks seem to have much less in them than the others, so maybe they've been hit? I can move the selector cocks to shift the fuel around though.'

'Skip, there is a stream of something going past the turret. Might be fuel?' said Freddie. 'Good job I haven't got a fag on!'

Charles came back on to say he had sorted things out, and as far as he was concerned, they could get back and now needed to turn due west, he hoped, still in the bomber stream.

'OK,' Matt said to the crew. 'We can get back, I think, but if we get attacked again, we may need to jump. I am not sure how much damage there is to the right wing, so everyone make sure they know where their parachutes are. How long till we get out of Germany?'

'Well, we are managing about 120 miles per hour, so we should be well over the coast in about four hours or so.'

'OK, everyone, keep a sharp lookout. We don't want to become easy meat for a fighter. Freddie, if there's still fuel spilling out, firing the guns may not be a terrific idea.'

'No, Skip. Seems to have stopped now.'

**

M-Mother clawed her way west towards home, which was still a long way off. Mac had been switching over tanks and reported that the right inner wing tanks seemed empty but that he could still shift fuel from the other tanks.

There was still thick cloud cover, and although this hid them from the ground, they were almost certainly all alone and would stand out a mile for the fighters.

'Should be just crossing Dutch coast now, Skip,' Charles's calm voice reported after what seemed an age.

'It's bloody cold back here, Skip. How are you up front?'

Matt had almost forgotten about being cold. He was struggling to keep the aircraft going in the right direction, and he figured that there must have been some other damage to make the aircraft handle so badly. *If we ever get to England, the landing will be nothing if not exciting and maybe we will need to bail out in any case*, he thought.

Gradually, they got closer to England, but the cold was intense and the endless roar of the air past the damaged aircraft began to eat into Matt's concentration. He thought about Stephen. They had been together so long it did not seem possible that he was dead. Maybe Mac had it wrong. Certainly he could not go and check.

After what seemed like an eternity, Charles said that they were just coming up to the coast somewhere near Lowestoft.

'Fuel OK, Mac?' Matt asked anxiously.

'I think so, Skip. Unfortunately, I can only tell if there is something in the tank, not how long it can last.'

'OK, go back and see if you can raise anyone. Don, you come up and take over from Mac. We will need to see if the bloody legs come down sometime soon.'

'Skip, I've been on to base,' Mac called. 'It sounds pretty bad. Low cloud and some fog. The boys further north are landing anywhere they can. Kirkby can take us if we want.'

'Tell them we've been shot up and have injured. And say we are going to check our landing gear.'

'OK, Skip. Come on to three-zero-five,' Charles said. 'Amazingly, H2S is still working so I should get a good view of the Wash.'

'Right, let's try the undercart,' Matt said. 'Don, try and see if it comes down.'

Don operated the switches, but the red warning light remained on, and Matt certainly could not feel any difference in how the aircraft was flying.

'Recycle the switch, Don,' Matt said.

This time, there was some movement, but the undercarriage was not fully down and the hydraulic pressure was low.

'Try the compressed air,' Matt said, and this time, the green undercarriage down lights came on.

'OK, everyone!' Matt called. 'Undercart is down, but we have no hydraulics for the flaps and brakes so we need to divert to Woodbridge. Mac, check the fuel. Do you think we can make it? Navigator, how far to Woodbridge from here?'

'We're about forty miles away, say about twenty minutes. We are a bit slower with the undercarriage down.'

'Mac, once you have checked the fuel, tell base what we are doing and call Woodbridge to see if they can take us.'

'OK, Skip,' replied Mac as he checked the fuel. A few minutes later, he called Matt to say he thought that there was enough fuel to get them there and that Woodbridge was busy but they could take them.

'Thanks, Mac,' Matt replied. He could feel the sweat breaking out down his back, even though it was freezing cold in the cockpit. He felt close to exhaustion, and he was having trouble concentrating on the instruments that his eyes had now been glued to for over eight hours.

They were held for nearly a quarter of an hour once they got to Woodbridge, and Matt had real concerns about the fuel running short as he turned onto the crosswind leg.

The cloud was still very thick, and it was impossible to see the runway even though they were only at 1,500 feet. The aircraft was difficult to manoeuvre, and Matt was careful not to fly too slowly as he eased M-Mother onto the downwind leg, which he extended for several minutes to give him space to turn onto base and line up on the final approach.

'Don, you help me with the throttles, and, everyone else, get to your crash positions. I am not sure what will happen with the undercart once we land.'

Matt was peering out into what was a white fog with no runway in sight.

'Don, call the height will you.'

'M-Mother cleared to land,' Matt heard in his headset.

Lower and lower they went with Don calling 'Five hundred, four hundred, three hundred …'

Just at that point, Matt made out the runway flares right in front of them.

'OK, Don, ease off the throttles. Slowly, slowly. Nearly there. Hold tight, everyone.'

M-Mother touched down and ran along Woodbridge's two-mile-long runway with Matt waiting for the undercarriage to collapse, but they eventually came to rest on the grass at the end of the runway, closely followed by a fire engine and ambulance.

Matt went through the shutdown sequence, indicating to Don when things needed to be done, and at last there was silence, apart from the wind blowing in through the shattered cockpit. Matt leaned down to see his old friend. Of course he was dead; there had never been any real hope, and Matt suddenly felt both sad and completely exhausted.

Charles came into the cockpit. He put his hand on Matt's shoulder and helped him to his feet.

'Come on, old chap,' he said quietly. 'Let's get out of here.'

Matt turned and looked at Stephen's body once more before making his way down the fuselage and out of the rear hatch to be met by the rest of the crew. As usual, Freddie was the first to speak.

'Well, we got down in one fucking piece. Well done, Skip.'

Matt could only raise an arm in acknowledgement. He was too tired and upset to say anything. A truck had come to collect them, and as Matt got in, he looked back to where the ambulance team were taking Stephen's body out of the aircraft. He stared out, feeling tears in his eyes as they drove back to the operations room.

Once they got down from the truck, they were met by the duty officer, who directed them to the debriefing hut.

Charles almost had to push Matt through the door, and he steered him to a nearby chair.

'Matt, I'll go and call East Kirkby and let them know what's happened. You just take it easy for a minute.'

Matt didn't reply but continued just to stare ahead. He realised he was shaking, partly with the cold and partly as a reaction to what had happened. He could not believe his friend had gone. He did not notice the padre come and sit next to him.

'I am sorry to hear that one of your crew died tonight,' he said quietly. 'I understand he was a friend of yours?'

Matt nodded. He felt numb and unable to reply. He wanted to go away, get out of this place, and go to be with Anne.

Charles came back. 'They are sorry to hear about things,' he said. 'They will fly a Lanc down and pick us up. The MO is going to come and have a look at us, and they have a billet for us for a few hours. Oh, and some breakfast.'

Matt nodded again and lifted his hand in thanks. He really could not care a less what happened to them, and he certainly did not want to eat. He was shown over to the billet and threw himself on a bed, curled up still in his flying suit, and went to sleep.

***

The crew gathered together when it was light. They all looked dishevelled and tired with their young, unshaven faces appearing grey in the early morning light. They agreed that they wanted to go and have a last look at M-Mother before they were flown back to East Kirkby, and Charles had managed to organise a truck to take them down. It was a relief to Matt that Charles had taken charge because he, himself, was beyond thinking of anything. But he needed to see the kite and where Stephen had died.

They dropped down from the truck and wandered over to the aircraft. Matt was horrified by what he saw in the cold light of day. There was a huge, jagged hole in the right-hand side of the cockpit where the chunk of flak had gone through, killing Stephen. The starboard outer engine covers had been blown off in the explosion, and it was a wonder that the engine had not followed. The leading edge of the wing had been shredded by shrapnel, and it was no surprise that the fuel tank had been punctured. They had had another lucky escape.

Matt broke away from the rest and climbed in. There was a smell of death, which got stronger as he walked forward. The cockpit was covered in Stephen's blood, and he noticed, for the first time, that his flying suit was also splashed with blood. He sat on the pilot's seat, looking over to the hole and running through the events of the last night. Almost before he realised it, he was crying, quietly but deeply, and he buried his head in his hands. They had left him alone, but after a while, Charles came up to the cockpit.

'Time to go, Matt,' he said gently. 'Transport is just arriving.' And in the background, Matt could hear the familiar roar of the Lancaster that was coming to pick them up. He stood up and followed Redman out, quietly saying a goodbye to M-Mother and to Stephen.

It was a subdued group who climbed into the aircraft for the short trip home. Matt was relieved to see that Bird was the pilot, and he shook Matt by the hand as he came into the cockpit.

'Sorry to hear about, Stephen,' he said. 'Let's talk when we get back.' And with that, he opened the throttles and flew them back to the base.

**

Matt's feeling of utter exhaustion was beginning to ease by the time they got back to East Kirkby. The others were clearly not quite sure how to talk to him, and it was Charles who broke the ice by suggesting they met down in the Red Lion that evening.

'Good idea,' Matt said. 'Sorry, chaps, about last night. As you know, Bamber was a good friend, like Townsy, eh, Freddie?'

'Yeh, Skip, like Townsy. Skip, just wanted to say it was bloody good how you got us down in one piece. Thought we were fucking goners at one point.'

'Thanks, Freddie,' Matt said putting his arm on Freddie's shoulder. 'Thought occurred to me too.' He smiled. 'OK then, Red Lion 1800 hours sharp.'

Bird joined them from the aircraft and gently pushed Matt away from the rest.

'Bloody carnage last night, Matt,' he said quietly. 'Worse for one group up north, mainly because of the weather when they got back. Crashes all over the bloody place. We lost two of our sprog crews, one from A, one from B flight. Your Sergeant Towers in U-Uncle turned back just after crossing the coast with supposed "engine trouble" except no one can find anything wrong. Think we've got trouble there. Against your better judgement, Simmons got there and back without a bloody scratch! Oh, the Old Man told me to send you over as soon as.'

'Dicky, thanks for coming to get us. Really appreciate that. Meant a lot, believe me.'

'Away with you,' he replied. 'I reckoned you wouldn't want Towers at the controls!'

Matt made his way to Brookes' office.

'Hallo, White. Come in and sit down. Christ, you look all in. How about some coffee?'

'No, thanks, sir. I'll be fine once I have got cleaned up and had a sleep.'

'Sorry to hear about Bamber,' the CO continued. 'Bad show. You were quite close, weren't you?'

'Well, we had been together right through training, sir. So yes, we were. Still, it would seem his end was quick at least.'

'White, you did bloody well last night getting the kite back. Sounds it was pretty shot up. Had Woodbridge on the phone already; they think she can be put back together, but it will take a good few months. So we need to get you another, but before that, you and your crew will get stood down for forty-eight hours. Should have got you an aircraft by then. And although I know you have only just got your DFC, I am going to recommend a DSO as well for last night. Bloody good show.'

'Thank you, sir. I am sure we could all do with a breather. If possible, sir, I would like to attend Bamber's funeral. I would think it will be held up in Yorkshire.'

'Of course. Let's find out and talk later. Why don't you go and get your head down? Maybe the doc can give you one of his magic pills.'

Matt made his way to the mess to try to get a message to Anne. He needed to speak to her so badly, just so he could share some of his grief, and he was frustrated to find she was busy and could not come to the phone. *Sleep first, then call*, he thought. At least she would know he was OK. He went to his billet to find Scrap sitting on Stephen's bed. The dog looked at him and wagged his tail, but he obviously felt something was wrong. Just looking at the dog's faithful brown eyes brought tears to Matt's, and he slumped down next to Scrap and held him tight for a while until he was feeling better. Matt undressed and quickly got into bed, but Scrap stayed where he was and was still there when Matt woke up in the middle of the afternoon.

Barker materialised as if by magic to bring a cup of tea.

'Sorry about Mr Bamber,' he said. 'They will be along later, sir, to pick up his belongings to send them on to the Central Depository. Was there anything of Mr Bamber's that you wanted, sir?'

'No, thanks,' Matt replied, but then he noticed Stephen's birdwatching book beside his bed. 'Well, maybe this.'

He had felt quite good when he first woke up, but now the fact that Stephen was dead swam back into his consciousness, along with the dreadfulness of last night.

'I need to speak to his parents,' he said almost as if Barker was not there.

'What about the dog, sir?' Barker asked. 'I'm sure some of the boys would take him if you'd rather.'

'No, leave him here. He'll be company, but he has an ominous track record, doesn't he?' Matt smiled ruefully. 'I must go and make a phone call.'

At last, he managed to get in touch with Anne. When he told her about Stephen, there was a long pause before she answered.

'I'm so sorry, Matt. Are you all right?' she asked. 'I mean really all right?'

'Not bad, Anne,' he replied. 'I have forty-eight hours of leave. Any chance we could meet tomorrow? Could you get off, do you think?'

'Oh, don't worry; I'll just walk out,' she said quickly. 'Can you pick me up tomorrow morning? We'll just go somewhere. Will you be all right tonight?'

'Sort of. We are all going to get leathered at the Red Lion. It won't be a pretty sight.'

'Good, you need that, my love,' Anne replied. 'I must dash, darling, and will see you tomorrow.'

The evening went much as expected, with Freddie getting back into form again. It was good that they all had some time together, but Matt found it difficult to believe that just a night ago, they had all been together at 18,000 feet on their way to Berlin—and Stephen had still been alive. They staggered their way back to the base after closing time, and Matt found he suddenly felt completely exhausted and excused himself. He made his way back to the billet. As he opened the door, he was met by a cloud of pipe smoke and found Stephen's bed occupied by a lanky-looking lad with a thatch of fair hair and sharp blue eyes who got up as Matt walked in.

'Who are you?' Matt asked.

'Pilot Officer Tom Fellows, sir. I arrived this evening. Barker explained things. I am sorry, sir.'

Matt walked over to the window and opened it. 'It's a bit thick in here, old boy,' he said. 'What do you do? Which flight are you in?'

'Pilot, sir. B-Flight, yours, sir. All my crew came with me, sir.'

'Well, welcome, Tom. We are stood down for possibly a couple of nights, and I am not here tomorrow, although get your chaps cracking in the morning and I'll meet you about eight o'clock.'

'Right, sir. Thank you.' But when he looked over, Matt was already asleep and snoring quietly.

Matt woke up at six thirty with Barker at his elbow with the usual cup of tea. The bed next to him was empty, and for a moment Matt thought he must have dreamt that Tom was there, although he could smell the pipe smoke.

'Gone out with the dog,' Barker said, reading his thoughts. 'Don't seem right, really, sir. I mean the bed is hardly cold, and someone else is in it.'

'Ah well, Barker. It's the way life is just now. I shall be staying out tonight but back first thing tomorrow morning. I suspect we will see some more action soon.'

Matt ran into Bird in the office and explained what he was going to do.

'No problem, Matt. We don't have any aircraft for the replacement crews, and you don't have one either, so not much to do just now. Go and have a nice time, and give Anne my love.'

'Thanks, Dicky. I am going to meet Fellows and his lot who came in yesterday, and I am also going to read the riot act to Towers and U-Uncle.'

When he saw Towers, he and his crew were full of excuses, but none of them stuck. In the end, Matt told them that if they turned back again without a good reason, they were for it.

***

He drove through the frosty lanes to meet up with Anne. He felt a little better about things now and tried to put Stephen into the background. He had managed to speak to Stephen's parents, but they had already heard and were obviously very upset. Matt managed to give them some details about how and when he had died and could also say that he died instantaneously and without pain. Mrs Bamber was crying by the time he finished, but she said she hoped that Matt would be able to come to the funeral, which was probably going to be in about a week's time. Stephen had spoken so much about Matt, especially when he saw them recently, and she would be pleased if they could meet.

Anne was waiting outside the hospital, and once she was in the car, Matt drove away in silence to the pub they had so often gone to for lunch. They sat in the car for a few minutes, and once they got to the pub, Matt turned and gave her a kiss.

'Thanks for coming,' he said. 'Means a lot.'

Anne was shocked at how gaunt and grey Matt looked. If anything, the circles under his eyes had got darker and the lines on his face around the mouth and eyes even deeper, and it looked like he had lost some weight.

'Of course I would come, darling. You look so worn out. It must have been dreadful last night. Was anyone else hurt?'

'No, just Stephen. He wouldn't have known a thing. Let's go inside.'

They sat down at their table and ordered lunch.

'I've booked a night in our usual hotel,' Anne said, trying to get Matt to talk.

'Good, that will be nice,' he replied. 'Oh, Dicky sent his love.'

She noticed Matt's hands were shaking, and she reached across to Matt. He looked up at her and smiled.

'I'm sorry, Anne. You know, I am not sure how much more I can take.' He dropped his eyes away from hers, and his shoulders slumped. His lunch had been virtually untouched, and Anne felt they had to get out of there as soon as possible. As she asked for the bill, she said, 'Matt, why don't you go outside and I will join you in a minute.'

Matt stood up and walked, almost as if in a trance, and waited for Anne on the pavement outside. She joined him, and they walked over to a park with Anne's hand firmly on his arm.

It was a bright, cold afternoon with the cloudless sky of pastel blue, so typical of winter. There was a light wind, but it felt quite warm in the low winter sun.

'Matt, what can I do to help?' Anne asked. 'Can't you go off sick or something? You look awful, and you need a break.'

'Not a bloody chance,' Matt replied sharply. 'If I could, I would. But then everyone else needs a break too, don't they? Don't you understand we are in the middle of a bloody war?' He was almost shouting by this time, and Anne was pleased no one was around to hear.

'I do understand. I see the remains of young men every day, you will remember.' She turned away. She felt like crying because she was so upset by Matt's appearance and how obviously angry he was. It was not Matt anymore. Just as Stephen was not Stephen either in the end. She turned back to Matt only to see him with his hands up at his face, clearly crying. She put her arms around him tenderly, and they walked over to a bench and sat down.

'Come on, Matt, darling. Let it all out. You will feel better,' she whispered to him, holding his head against her. They sat for a while, and then Anne began to feel the cold and suggested they went back to the car and head off to their hotel.

Matt walked along with her, almost in a daze, but when they got back to the car he said, 'Sorry about that, Anne. Let's head off unless you would rather go back to the hospital. Probably more fun than being with me!'

'That would be saying something.' She smiled. 'I think I would rather stick with you, if that's OK?'

They got to the hotel, and the owner, who knew them now quite well, showed them up to their room. It was cold in the room in spite of the fire crackling in the hearth. They took their coats off and kissed gently.

'Matt, let's go down and have a drink. And maybe you will feel like something to eat now. You had nothing at lunch.'

'You know, I am feeling a bit peckish,' Matt said, and Anne noticed that he was smiling his old smile. 'We need to think about another best man, old thing.'

'That's better, Matt. Let's look ahead. I am so excited about our wedding. Maybe Dicky would oblige?'

'Well, that's an idea. I'll ask him when I get back. Old Man might baulk at two flight commanders being away at once, but we can always ask.'

This time, Matt tucked into his food, and Anne was pleased that he was chatting more freely now. It was eight o'clock when they had finished dinner, and they had another drink before Anne suggested they went up to their room. It was still quite cold, but some more logs had been put on the fire and the curtains were drawn, making it feel cosier. Anne went and washed. She let her dark hair down so that it fell over her shoulders. Matt loved it when she did that. He also went to wash, and when he came back, Anne was already in bed with the covers up to her chin. He climbed in beside her, and they snuggled down together. Anne pulled his head down onto her breasts. They lay for a while, and then Anne noticed that Matt had gone to sleep. He looked so peaceful, the lines of stress and tiredness on his face having faded. She stroked his head and held him close to her until she herself slipped off to sleep. The nightmares started about two in the morning with Matt twitching, crying out, and eventually sitting bolt upright. She held him until he calmed down and finally went back to sleep herself. She woke at about six o'clock to find Matt out of bed and staring out of the window into the dark. The moon cast its silvery light into the bedroom and outlined him. She knew almost instinctively that he was crying again, and she got out of bed to stand next to him. He was freezing cold, and she led him back to the bed where they lay close together. After a while, she felt his hand resting between her legs. His hand was like ice, and she shuddered and was about to say something when he rolled onto her and she felt him inside her. He said nothing, but in two or three thrusts, he came and almost immediately rolled back off her. She went to shake him but realised he was fast asleep, so she put her arm around him and held him until she herself drifted off into a troubled slumber.

They woke at about eight o'clock, and Matt said nothing about what had happened earlier. He was quiet again and had to be coaxed to eat the breakfast. Anne was at a loss about what to say, but when Matt dropped her at the hospital, she just told him to be careful and keep in touch. She kept her tears for later. He nodded tiredly, let the clutch of the car in fiercely, and roared off back towards the base without a backward glance.

CHAPTER 17

FRANKFURT

Twenty-Third Trip

The previous day had seen the arrival of some new aircraft and replacement crew as well. The ground crew had already named Matt's aircraft M-Mother, and when he looked at the battle order on the notice board, he saw that his crew were there. Matt organised an air test for that morning with Don acting as flight engineer. The rumour was that the squadron flight engineer, Squadron Leader Timothy Buckley, was keen to get a flight in, but he was not going to be around for just an air test.

Warrant Officer Bryant came over as Matt got down from the truck.

'Hallo, Chiefy. How's the new arrival?' Matt asked.

'She'll do,' he replied. 'They obviously put this one together carefully. You'd never guess what we find sometimes with the ones straight from the factory. All sorts of things wrong and bits and pieces left lying around.'

Matt climbed into the new aircraft. It smelt so different to the old girl, but the essence of oil and hydraulic fluid were still there. Not much was different from M-Mother, and Don and he worked well together through the different checklists. Once they were airborne, both Freddie and Willie were happy that their turrets and guns were working, and Charles seemed content with his navigation gear. They landed about midday. The briefing was at three o'clock. Matt picked up Scrap and headed out of the front gate and across to the woods. He felt he had to get out. Being on the base was beginning to give him the creeps.

Matt and his crew took up their usual place at the back of the briefing room and stood up along with everyone else as the CO came in with his entourage.

'The target for tonight, gentlemen, is Frankfurt.'

There was a sigh of relief around the hall. At least it wasn't Berlin. The forecast was good, and Pathfinders would mark as usual. They were due to get away at 1900 hours, and Matt was to lead his flight. He went up to Dicky after the briefing for a chat and to wish him luck. It was Dicky's twenty-eighth trip, and the crew were excited by the possibility they would finish their tour by the end of the year. Dicky asked about Matt's night out with Anne, but Matt only gave a noncommittal grunt. They shook hands and agreed to meet the next evening in the Red Lion.

'Beer's on you,' Dicky called back as they went their separate ways.

Matt repeated his warning to Towers in U-Uncle that returning early would result in them being put on a charge unless there was obviously something wrong with the aircraft and wished luck to his new room-mate, Tom Fellows.

S/L Buckley had, as promised, joined them and jumped into the back of the truck along with the rest. It was always a bit awkward for the crew when someone new was on board, but he was a jovial sort who put everyone at ease.

The crew went through their usual routine with Freddie and Willie peeing against the rear wheel.

The new Lancaster seemed to take-off more readily than the old Mother, and Matt climbed away into the night.

'Everything OK with the engines, sir?' Matt asked.

'Fine, Matt. Please call me Tim at least for now.' And he smiled across to Matt and gave him a thumbs-up.

They circled and climbed up to 10,000 feet before heading off to overhead Lowestoft to join the mainstream. The total force was to be 650 aircraft, some 390 being Lancasters. Once over Lowestoft, they turned towards the target and climbed to 20,000 feet. It was bitterly cold, and Freddie reported that there was ice inside his turret, which made it difficult to see out. Every now and again, Matt could see other aircraft going down, and he warned that there were fighters about, just as Freddie shouted, 'Corkscrew left!' and let fly with his guns. The heavily loaded aircraft swung down and to the left, and then Matt heaved it back up into a turning climb to the right and back onto their course. Now there seem to be aircraft getting hit all around, but they were nearly at Frankfurt and Matt could see the target markers. There appeared to be thick cloud almost everywhere below them and a bright fire glowed up through the clouds over to the south of the markers. They were now on a timed run, and Don said he was convinced that the glow was a decoy fire seemingly confirmed by Charles's navigation plot.

'Have got the TI's, Skip. Look on track to cross them.'

'OK, Don.'

'Right a bit, right a bit, steady. Bombs gone. Hold for the flash—what good that will do,' said Don's quiet, calm voice. 'Flash gone.'

'We're out of here,' Matt said as he turned and dived the aircraft to port. It was a remarkably quiet flight home, and as they entered the East Kirkby circuit, Matt was already thinking of his bed and sleep and wishing that all the trips had been like that one. If they didn't make them go again tonight, he would have his beer with Dicky in the evening—well lunchtime as well. Why not?

He steadied the aircraft onto their final approach, and Buckley helped with the throttles.

'Flaps down,' he said. 'Gear down. Three greens.'

Matt made a faultless touchdown, and they taxied over to their dispersal and went through the shutdown checks.

Matt looked over to Buckley and smiled. 'Thanks, sir. Wish all the trips were like that.'

'Well, you chaps usually seem to attract some trouble, don't you?' He smiled back. 'Glad to have been of help.'

They climbed out and were met by Warrant Officer Bryant.

'What you doing up at this time, Chiefy?'

'Just wanted to make sure you got back OK. You've been running a bit close to the wind recently. There's been quite a few losses again tonight. I hoped you weren't amongst them.'

'Thanks, Chiefy. Appreciate that. We had a remarkably quiet run. Just a short skirmish but no damage, I think. That's what happens when you've got the squadron engineer on board.'

Bryant smiled and walked with Matt to the waiting truck. 'My boys will be pleased they don't have to rebuild the bloody kite for a change.'

When the truck dropped them off for debriefing, it was clear that things were not looking too good. A sure sign was that the both the CO and Squires were present. Matt glanced quickly at the ops board and noticed that Dicky was not yet back, although he had taken off sometime before M-Mother. They went over to the intelligence officer doing their debrief and went back over the raid with him. It seemed that the thick cloud over the target had taken everyone by surprise, but it sounded as if the raid had been successful, although it looked like losses would be high. After the debrief, Charles asked Matt if he was coming to the mess, but he declined and went over to speak to Squires.

'Anything from Dicky, sir?'

'No, Matt. Nothing heard since he took off, in fact. He may have diverted somewhere, but he's close to endurance just now. Your two chaps, Towers and Fellows, haven't been heard of either. Why don't you get your head down for a few hours and then we'll see who's back?'

'Right, sir,' Matt replied and made his way back to the billet. He had a bad feeling in his gut. The exhilaration he had experienced as they got back to the airfield had left him, and he felt sick and weary. He opened the door of his room to find Scrap curled up on what had been Stephen's bed only a few days ago and then Tom's. Surely he could not have gone too. He had only just arrived.

Matt undressed and fell onto his bed. Scrap came over and snuggled up next to him, and Matt fell asleep with the dog nestling in his arms. The door opened at about six o'clock, and Matt woke to find Barker looking at him.

'Cuppa, sir?' he said. 'No Mr Fowler then?'

'Thanks,' Matt replied sleepily, and he sat up as Scrap jumped to the floor and followed Barker off to the kitchen. Matt was dressed by the time Barker brought in the tea. He felt dreadful, and although the sweet tea was welcome, he certainly did not feel like anything to eat. He finished his tea and went over to the ops room. Squires was still there, and he looked pale and exhausted.

'No news, Matt, I am afraid. Looks like Dicky's bought it somewhere. Trouble is that it was such a thick night that no one saw very much of anything. Looks like we've lost three others as well. Your two and another from A Flight. Twenty-eight chaps blown away. Christ, Matt, if we go on like this, there will be no one left by the end of the year.'

Matt had never heard a senior officer talk like that before, and he supposed that it was brought on by tiredness rather than the feeling of desperation that he himself felt. The endless trips to Berlin and the huge losses amongst the crews had sapped the energy out of everyone.

Matt walked out of the ops room into the cold morning air. It was getting light, and there was a cold easterly wind blowing. The clouds were low and racing across the grey sky. He could not believe that Dicky might have gone for good. He was such a great person, always willing to help those around him, and a bloody good pilot, two ops off a completed tour. He had agreed to be best man as well. And then Tom Fellows—bet he had never even managed a drink in the mess. One moment here, next one bloody gone.

Matt walked over to his billet and picked up Scrap. He needed a serious walk. He had to get out of there even if it was only for a couple of hours. They headed out past the gates, and Matt could not be bothered to return the guard's salute. They walked into the woods, and Scrap ran off in search of rabbits. Matt realised he should have called Anne, but he felt so completely disconnected from his life that he just couldn't be bothered anymore. The last few days had been the worst he could remember. He had lost good friends, felt exhausted, and for the first time, thought that he probably could not go on for much longer himself.

Scrap came running back to him with a stick, which he dropped at his feet, and started barking, urging Matt to throw it. He did, and Scrap brought it back again and again. Matt realised that the dog was gradually dragging him back to Earth, to reality. As they walked, the sun began to break through the clouds, and Matt could see small patches of blue sky. The wind had dropped, and the sunshine felt quite warm on Matt's back as they walked along. He tried to rationalize what was good in his life and figured that maybe it was not so bad after all. Anne and he were happy, and he and the crew were well into their tour—only another seven trips to do. Another few weeks and it would be done and Anne and he would be married. Then, at least, there would be some semblance of a normal life.

He arrived back at the camp, and this time returned the salute and dropped off Scrap at his billet before he went to the flight office. His crew was not on the battle order. In fact, there was no battle order, which meant they all had the night off. Thank God for that. He went to the mess and found Charles still at the bar and looking fairly drunk. Matt excused himself and went over to call Anne. He got through to her almost at once and realised she was very upset.

'God, Matt, I thought I had lost you. Where have you been?'

'Sorry, Anne. It's been very bad here this morning.'

'But are you all right?' she cried down into the phone. 'Oh, this bloody war! I can't take much more.'

Matt could hear her weeping at the end of the phone. He had almost never heard her cry or swear, come to that.

'Anne, it's OK. I am all right. But there is some bad news, I'm afraid. Dicky is missing.'

There was silence, and then a dreadful scream of anguish before the phone was put down and there were sounds of footsteps running away. Matt did not know what to do. It was so unlike her. *Christ, this bloody war is tearing us all apart*, he thought. He tried redialling, but there was no reply. He got through to the head porter and explained what had happened. He asked him to get Anne to ring him in the mess when she could. He was stuck in the base and couldn't go and see if she was all right, but he decided he would if she didn't ring. He'd just walk out, and they could do what they bloody liked about it. Just now, he couldn't care less.

He went back to join Charles at the bar. 'What you having?' he slurred.

'Pint please, Charles,' Matt replied. 'Shouldn't you be at home?'

'No. Bloody wife has gone off to her mother's for the week. Off the leash, eh?'

Matt was still too upset by his phone call to make any comment. He nodded and downed his beer in one. Maybe getting smashed was the only way to cope with the shit that was happening around them just now, and he got another round.

CHAPTER 18

BERLIN

Twenty-Fourth Trip

The next morning, Matt awoke with a fairly thick head and could not really remember what had happened the night before. When he got down to the flight office, he almost expected to see Dicky standing there telling him what was going on. Instead, there was Acting Flight Lieutenant Brough, asking Matt *his* advice about what was going on! Dicky, it would seem, was already history. When Matt went to see what was on the notice board, instead of the usual battle order, there was a notice announcing that there was to be a party that night in hangar 2. The notice read, 'Pre-Christmas Dance tonight. All welcome, including girlfriends, mistresses, and wives'.

Some bright spark had added, 'But not all of them together!'

Matt smiled at the note. Could he get Anne along at such short notice? That would be the thing. He would give her another call later on, but today was going to be busy getting the new boys up to scratch. He and Brough had to see the CO at ten o'clock, and Matt could only think it was going to be bad news.

'Hallo, you two,' Brookes said as they entered his office. 'Sit down. You will see I have decided that we won't be flying tonight. And Squires had the good idea about the dance. I think you chaps need a short break. Now, Brough, I am expecting some crew replacements for you. Should be here by this afternoon. Suggest you brief them and get them up in the air as soon as possible. They have to expect to be on operations by Friday. White, I have two crew for you as well, and the same applies to you. Any questions?'

'No, sir,' they said together.

'Right. Now, White, stay behind for a minute, will you?'

Matt sat down again.

'White, you have had a tough time recently. I have been discussing things with Group, and I am making you acting Squadron Leader. For your information, I need to let you know that you will be losing Redman as a navigator early in the New Year.'

'Right, sir. Thank you, sir,' Matt stammered.

'Good. White, you can go now. Can you look by at five ish and let me know how things are going. You're the senior man now.'

'Yes, sir,' Matt turned and saluted.

Matt bumped into Charles, who was talking to the station commander.

'Well done, Matt,' he said. 'Absolutely deserved. Looks like another drink or two this evening at the party.'

'Congrats to you too, Charles. Hear you will be leaving us in a couple of weeks?'

'Sounds like it,' he replied. 'I will miss getting my arse shot at every time I go flying with you.'

'Well, congratulations to you both,' Squires said. 'I do hope you will be coming to the dance tonight. And, Matt, bring that lovely girl with you.'

'I am not sure she is talking to me just now,' Matt said. 'She has been pretty upset about what's been happening over the last few weeks, and now there's Dicky too.'

'Get her along, Matt. She'll pick up. 'Fraid war is a bloody awful thing. But life goes on, eh?'

***

Matt went back to the flight office and began sorting out things for when his new crews arrived. Both were sergeant crews, which was sometimes easier. At lunchtime, he tried to ring Anne and eventually got through to her. She was calmer, but Dicky's death had shaken her badly.

'Anne, there's a dance here tonight. Please say you will come. I don't see another chance for a while.'

'I'll try, darling. Maybe Jess would like to come as well, although she was very upset about Stephen. There are a few others who I can try and round up. I'll see what I can do.'

She rang off, and Matt realised he had forgotten to tell her about his promotion. He suddenly felt very alone. She was his rock, and he desperately needed to see her. He couldn't leave the base, so tonight would be his only chance, probably for a while.

The afternoon went quite well, and the new crews seemed to fit in, although there were a few grumbles when they realised they were going to have to fly straight away. Matt went up with both crews, and they flew around the local area so they could get to recognise some of the landmarks. They all brightened up at the thought of the dance, and Matt was able to report to Squires that both his and Brough's new boys were probably

OK. He hoped there would be another day for them to practise. Matt had organised some cross-countries. But that was going to be about it until they faced their first operation.

Matt met M-Mother's crew in the Red Lion that evening before the party. Freddie was in full flow and regaling Willie with stories of his many conquests at dances.

Don offered Matt a pint as he came in. 'Hear congratulations are in order, Skip?'

'Yes, thanks, Don.' Matt smiled. 'Promotion seems to happen rather quickly just now. Are you going to the dance?'

'Yes, and Mary is coming too. There is a bus coming over from Scampton later on.'

'Should be good fun. Take our minds off things for a while at least,' Matt said ruefully. His 'Who wants another drink?' was met by a raucous chorus.

As he brought the drinks back, he noticed that they had been joined by a sergeant who looked about fifteen years old.

'This is Tommy Pain, Skip,' Freddie said, being careful not to use Matt's first name. 'He's our new flight engineer.'

'Welcome, Tommy. Would you like a drink as well?'

'Yes, sir. Thank you. Just some orange juice would be fine. I am sorry not to have come to meet you sooner, but I've only just arrived and the guardroom told me that I would find you here, sir.'

'Right,' Matt said slowly. 'Oh, call me "Skip." Everyone else does.'

Once Pain had a drink in his hand, Matt asked him where he had come from.

'Just from the training school at St Athan, sir—Skip, sorry. I was ground crew and then decided I wanted to fly. So here I am. Sir, once I have had this, I need to go to get my kit unpacked. Hope you don't mind.'

'No, off you go, Tommy. You coming to the party tonight, I hope? If not, we will all meet at 0800 hours tomorrow in the flight office. We will go along with the two new crews on their nav. exercise and do our own air test at the same time.'

Pain saluted and quickly left the pub.

'God Almighty,' muttered Freddie. 'They'll be sending them in short trousers soon. Orange juice an' all.'

'Well, not everyone has a personal mission to drink the bar dry, you know, Freddie,' Don said and smiled. 'Still, did look pretty young, didn't he?'

'Well, so long as he knows which bloody knobs to turn, I don't mind,' Charles exclaimed. 'And talking of knobs, do we know who of the fairer sex is likely to be coming tonight?'

That started Freddie off on another rundown of the likely female contribution to the dance, and Matt realised he needed to speak to Anne. He excused himself and went back to the base to telephone.

***

Anne and the other nurses from the hospital arrived at about seven o'clock. By that time, the crew of M-Mother were well ensconced at the bar in the hangar, which had been decked out with Christmas streamers and lights. It was already crowded, but Matt saw Anne as she came in and pushed his way across the floor to meet her.

'Hallo, darling. You can't imagine how pleased I am that you managed to get here. How many of you?'

'Just half a dozen, I'm afraid,' she answered. 'It's really difficult to get time off. And the bus was really slow coming here. Still, we're here now. Let's just get our coats out of the way.'

Once they were ready, Matt led them back across the floor to his waiting crew. Freddie had already picked out one of the WAAFs from the station, and it looked as if this was not the first time they had met. Don and Mary returned from the dance floor, looking flushed and very happy. Matt introduced the girls to his crew and noticed that Charles focussed on a rather lovely nurse with long, fair hair and the most incredible light-blue eyes Matt had ever seen. Mac seemed to be chatting up one of the WAAFs who had come over from Scampton with Mary. The party seemed to be going well, and they all seemed to be enjoying themselves, but suddenly, Matt realised that Tom Pain was not around.

'Anyone seen Tommy?' he asked. He was worried that he was sitting in his billet and not coming here because he did not drink alcohol.

Then Mac nodded his head towards the dance floor, and through the gloom and the smoke, Matt saw Tom dancing with an absolutely gorgeous redhead. Matt could feel his jaw drop, and he was brought to by Anne asking him what he was looking at.

'Well, we have a new engineer. Looks like he is just out of school and very quiet. Hope he knows his stuff. And I wondered if he was here, and Mac has just shown me who he's dancing with. Got to watch the quiet ones, you know.' He smiled and thought that for all that had happened in the last forty-eight hours, he felt remarkably happy. It was so good when Anne was around. She made all the difference, and he had even managed to sleep fairly well. His crew was a good lot, and the two new boys were good too.

Anne looked very lovely. She had her hair tied up, which showed her long white neck. And she was wearing a dark-blue velvet dress, which Matt always thought she looked so good in. She had the string of pearls that Matt had bought for her birthday last June around her neck.

'Fancy a dance?' he said, bowing in front of her.

'Might do,' she replied. 'Who's asking?'

Matt smiled. 'Acting Squadron Leader White. At your service.'

'What? Have you got another promotion?' she asked, and they both laughed and headed onto the floor. They danced for a while to the Glen Miller tunes the band was playing.

'This is nice,' Anne said. 'Almost feels like the things normal people do!'

'Should get a few days off after Christmas. Shall we try and get up to Scotland? It's rather a long way, and we may get stuck up there if the weather changes.'

'Oh good,' replied Anne, holding Matt very tight and kissing him. 'Matt, can we get away from here for a while? I want just to be with you.'

'Good idea,' he replied. 'We can go to my room. No one will disturb us there.'

'Don't you have a room-mate anymore?' Anne asked.

'Well, I did after Stephen, but he got killed first night out.'

Anne dropped her head. 'God, Matt. I am sorry. When is this all going to end?'

They walked outside the hangar. It was bitterly cold again, but the stars were twinkling above them.

'Anne, I don't think it is going to end anytime soon, but we are getting to the end of our tour. We just have to keep going.'

He put his arm around her as they went along the path to his hut. It was very quiet, and everyone seemed to be at the dance. They got into Matt's room. It was freezing in the room, and there was little heat coming from the radiator. They kissed deeply, holding one another closely.

'Let's hop into bed, Matt. I need you very much.' She took her coat off and unzipped her dress. She was wearing the turquoise satin camisole that she knew Matt loved, and she slipped under the covers. Matt took off his uniform and pants and jumped into bed beside her, and they lay there for a while. Anne moved to hold Matt, and she felt him flinch as her cold hands touched him. She climbed on top of him and gently lowered herself on to him, and they lay there rocking gently and kissing. Anne gasped as she came and felt Matt following soon after her. They lay still for a while, and then Anne slipped off, holding him in her hand. This time, Matt had not gone to sleep, and he slipped her breast out of her top and started kissing it. They made love slowly and tenderly, Anne wrapping her legs around Matt and squeezing him as they came together.

After a while, Matt started kissing her again. 'God, Anne, that was lovely,' he whispered in her ear. 'But you know what? I think you've done me in.'

They laughed and kissed again as Anne lay alongside Matt. She closed her eyes, listening to his soft breathing, and then dozed herself until she woke up about half an hour later, feeling a delicious wetness between her legs. She would give anything to stay, but it was late and she needed to get the bus so she eased herself out from Matt and got dressed. She was about to put her knickers on and then smiled and tucked them under the pillow for Matt in the morning. He looked so peaceful as she bent down to kiss him. Such a difference from the last time. It just made her realise the dreadful things that these men had to go through and what it did to them. She had a last glance at him and prayed that soon they would have time together.

***

Matt woke up to Barker's tap on the door. 'Come in,' he called.

'Good night, sir?' Barker asked and smiled somewhat knowingly. He could probably still smell Anne's perfume, and as he put Matt's cup down, he said, 'Sounds as if it was a good do? But I'm afraid you're wanted in the flight office, sir. Sounds like there's a bit of a flap on.'

Matt got up and realised he felt better than he had done for days. A good night's sleep and a wonderful evening with the woman he loved had proved very beneficial. He dressed quickly and walked down to the mess for a quick breakfast and then off to the flight office. His heart jumped as he saw the battle order and found M-Mother on the list. The others gradually surfaced, and he noticed that Freddie and Willie, in particular, looked rather the worse for wear. Freddie looked especially bleary eyed, and Charles didn't look too sharp either, so clearly they had all made a good night of it.

'OK, chaps,' Matt began, 'clearly we don't have the luxury of another day's practice, so we will go up this morning and do what we can. It also allows us to check the aircraft and ourselves,' he added, looking at Freddie.

Matt arranged for M-Mother to accompany the two new crews, and he wanted them to plan a cross-country flight towards Sheffield, keeping at 8,000 feet. He got Control to warn Sheffield defences that they would be overhead by ten o'clock. He took Pain to the aircraft so he could check things out and chatted with Chiefy Bryant whilst Pain climbed aboard.

'Christ, Matt. They look younger every day, don't they? At least this chap should be able to find his way round an engine, having had a *proper* training as ground crew.'

'Well, hopefully, he will shape up OK when chunks of metal start flying about. Kite fine to take out for an hour just now?'

'Yes, top line, Matt. We had almost nothing to put right after your last trip for a change!'

Pain climbed out of the rear hatch and walked towards the two friends.

'Everything looks OK, sir,' he said.

'Good,' said Matt. 'This is Warrant Officer Bryant. If you have any troubles with the aircraft, he's the man. Understand?'

'Yes, sir. Thanks.' Pain wandered off as Matt turned himself.

'Bye, Chiefy. See you when we get back.'

All three crews got into the truck to go to dispersal, and Freddie was his usual cheerful self. 'Now who's got the parachute with a hole in it? Those girls always give someone a duff chute. Seems to cheer them up.'

The new crews started checking their parachute bags, and after a while, one of them asked, 'Sarg, how can we tell which one's got the hole?'

Freddie burst out laughing. Sooner or later, there was always one who asked.

'When you're on your way down. Don't half go quick.'

The new crews looked at one another, and Matt thought one of them was about to be sick.

'Don't worry,' he said. 'It's just Sergeant Hughes' twisted sense of humour.'

The crew from M-Mother jumped down first, and the truck moved off to the other two Lancasters.

The plan was for Matt to follow the other two. It was a grey day with a cloud base of about 1,000 feet, although the Met man had implied that they would break out of the cloud at about 5,000 feet. They would route to Sheffield and then down to Leicester and back home.

Matt and Pain worked their way through the checklists, and Matt was impressed. Pain was neat and precise and seemed to know the checklists almost off by heart. They started the engines and ran them up ready for take-off. The wind was from the west, so they had to follow the others and taxi round to the end of runway two-six.

The other aircraft took off in turn and quite quickly disappeared into the cloud. Matt lined up and took off himself. They were in the cloud almost immediately, not a good feeling when you know that there are a couple of inexperienced pilots in front of you. They climbed steadily, but by 5,000 feet were still in cloud. Charles gave him a course of two-nine-five, and he started a climbing turn onto that heading, hoping the others would be doing the same. The darkness around the cockpit started to lighten, and at about 9,000 feet, they broke out into bright sunshine. The whiteness of the cloud surface contrasting with the clear pale-blue winter sky never failed to fill Matt with wonder. To his relief, he saw the other aircraft up ahead of him and was even more pleased to see that they were going in the right direction.

'Gunners, let fly to check that everything is all right. Navigator, how do things look?'

'OK, Skip. All the kit seems to be working. We should be over Sheffield in about thirteen minutes at this speed.'

Matt kept an eye in front of him and saw that the leading aircraft was turning south at about the right estimated time, followed by the second.

The layer of clouds stretched as far as Matt could see, so this was a good test to see what the new boys could do. At least they had not bumped into one another.

It took about another fifteen minutes to get to Leicester, not that anyone could see it, and then turn for home. With this cloud around, it was going to be necessary to fly down to East Kirkby using the localising beam, but Matt had given them very clear instructions that the second aircraft was not to enter the cloud until the first one was down. They did not want a repeat of the earlier disaster.

All went well, and the first two were down as Matt entered the cloud. Pain seemed to be entirely on top of things, but Matt had a trick he wanted to play just to see how alert he was. They followed the beam down, and as Matt picked up the runway at about 1,500 feet, he noticed they were slightly to the left. He spoke to Pain while quickly shutting down the outer starboard engine to see what he would do. Matt prepared to apply a load of right rudder to keep them straight, but almost without hesitation, Pain feathered the propeller and eased the port outer throttle to balance things.

'Very good,' Matt remarked as he lined M-Mother up for touchdown. 'Glad to have you along.'

They taxied to their dispersal and shut everything down.

'That was good, Tom,' Matt repeated kindly and smiled as he saw the boy blush.

'Thank you, sir—Skip.' He grinned back. 'This is what I have always wanted to do.'

They all got out of the aircraft and waited for the truck to take them back. Matt wandered over to the ground crew to thank them and to let them know that all was well—until the next time!

***

The briefing was at midday, which implied this was going to be a long trip. Matt felt in his bones it would be Berlin. A Christmas present for Adolf! The take-off time had originally been planned for late afternoon but had to be delayed because of the possibility of adverse local weather on their return.

He tried to phone Anne, but she was not around. 'Tell her I love her and I will ring tomorrow,' he told the head porter and then rang off. The briefing went as usual, and there were the predictable groans as the station commander said, 'Your target for tonight, gentlemen, is Berlin.'

They had their 'Flying tonight, sir' meal and then kitted up and collected their parachutes, coffee, and sandwiches. Then they waited for the truck to take them out to M-Mother.

Matt asked Tom how he had enjoyed the dance.

'Very good, sir, Skip,' he replied.

'Who was that gorgeous redhead then?' Matt asked.

Tom went bright red. 'She was one of the WAAFs from Scampton. She came over with Mary, Don's girl. We're going to meet up after Christmas.'

Matt smiled. The truck arrived, and they clambered in along with a couple of other crews.

'Is this the number nine bus?' Freddie asked.

'Where you going, love?' asked the WAAF driver.

'Trafalgar Square.'

'Nah, you need the one behind!' The WAAF laughed.

'Blimey,' said Freddie. 'Hang on then so I can get out!'

Everyone on the truck laughed, and Matt thought how good Freddie was at breaking the tension they were all feeling. He was never sure if it was by intent or just the way he was. It didn't really matter. It worked.

They jumped down when they reached M-Mother standing dark and menacing against the night sky, which was clear and full of stars.

Freddie and Willie had a last cigarette and a wee, and all climbed on board and settled at their stations, checking their equipment. One of the ground crew came on board and went to Matt to have Form 700 signed to show that he accepted the aircraft.

Tom and he went through the start-up checks, and at seven o'clock precisely, they started the engines. Tom ran up the engines, checking temperatures and pressures, and gave a thumbs-up to Matt. They were ready to roll.

They lined up, and Matt opened the throttles, keeping his foot on the brake until the engines revs were sufficient and then releasing them. They were heavily loaded with fuel and bombs and needed every inch of the runway. There was the usual collection of WAAFs and ground staff to wave them away as they raced down the runway. M-Mother lifted slowly into darkness. The undercarriage was raised and the flaps brought in.

They were to rendezvous over Lowestoft and then make their way down the Dutch/Belgian border to south of the Ruhr before turning east to just south of Leipzig and then turning north to attack Berlin from the south. It was a generally clear night, and there was a layer of cloud below the bombers. M-Mother was now fitted with apparatus that allowed the navigator to calculate wind strength and direction and then relay that back to Group so that wind information could be continually updated for the all the main force.

The trip out was quiet with apparently little fighter activity on this occasion.

Charles eventually called Matt. 'Skip, we are just south of Leipzig. Time to turn towards the target course zero-three-zero.'

'Thanks,' Matt replied, and eventually he could see the glow in the sky, which was Berlin. When they arrived at the target, it looked as if the marking was all over the place. Don and Charles had calculated where the bombs should be dropped, and almost at the last moment, Don noticed a green target marker over to the right. Matt altered course and called Don to tell him he was in charge.

'Right, Skip,' he answered. 'Right, steady, left a bit, steady. Bombs gone. Wait for the flash.'

The bombs gone, they turned for home, but not long after, Freddie called, 'Corkscrew left,' and Matt threw the aircraft into a diving turn. Freddie and Willie both opened up at the enemy fighter. As Matt put the aircraft into a climbing turn to the right and back onto their course for home, he noticed flames coming from an aircraft falling to earth on their left.

'Looks like you got him,' Matt called. 'Well done but keep your eyes peeled. We are in fighter country. Maybe they have just been waiting for us.'

He suddenly felt nervous and tense and asked Pain to check that everything was OK.

'Navigator, how long to the coast?'

'Well, by my reckoning—'

There was a huge explosion, and Matt was stunned for a minute before he realised that M-Mother was falling out of the sky and the controls had gone slack. 'Bail out! Bail out!' he called, but he knew there was no one to hear him. He looked over to see Pain's terrified face staring at him before he was sucked out of the shattered remains of the cockpit, leaving Matt alone. Thoughts of Anne flashed in front of him as the cockpit tumbled through the air. He struggled to get out of his seat but knew it was hopeless. He felt his bladder and bowels give way, and suddenly, there was blackness.

AUTHOR'S NOTE

The operations described in this novel are largely factually correct and East Kirkby still exists and is home to a working, but not yet flying, Lancaster bomber.

The so-called Battle of Berlin started in August 1943 and continued through until the end of March 1944. Air Chief Marshall Sir Arthur Harris suggested to Winston Churchill and his immediate superior Air Chief Marshall Sir Charles Portal that 'we can wreck Berlin from end to end if the USAAF will come in on it. It will cost between us 400 and 500 aircraft. It will cost Germany the war'. The USAAF did not become involved, and, in fact, the RAF lost 625 aircraft and 2690 aircrew were killed. The campaign was generally considered a failure, and Germany did not capitulate.

Bomber Command lost 55,573 aircrew during the Second World War out of the 125,000 personnel who volunteered. This book is a tribute to these young men.

Printed in the United States
By Bookmasters